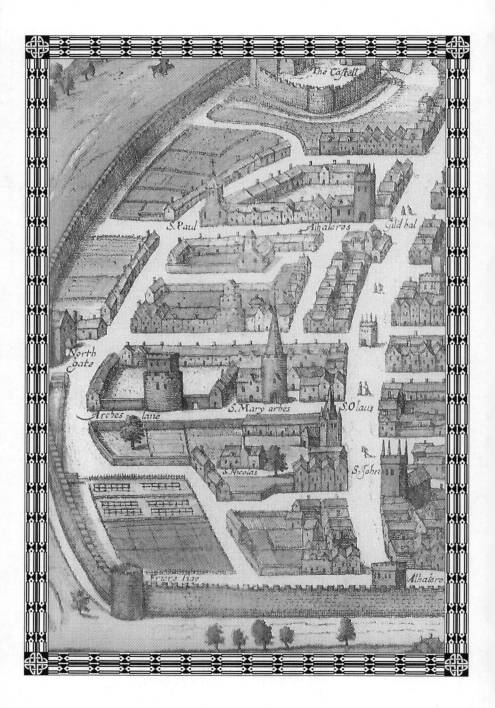

OF FIRE
OF WATER
OF STONE

JOPHILE'S STORY

ZOE KEITHLEY

BALBOA.
PRESS

A DIVISION OF HAY HOUSE

Balboa Press books may be ordered through booksellers or by contacting:

Balboa Press
A Division of Hay House
1663 Liberty Drive
Bloomington, IN 47403
www.balboapress.com
1 (877) 407-4847

Because of the dynamic nature of the Internet, any web addresses or links contained in this book may have changed since publication and may no longer be valid. The views expressed in this work are solely those of the author and do not necessarily reflect the views of the publisher, and the publisher hereby disclaims any responsibility for them.

The author of this book does not dispense medical advice or prescribe the use of any technique as a form of treatment for physical, emotional, or medical problems without the advice of a physician, either directly or indirectly. The intent of the author is only to offer information of a general nature to help you in your quest for emotional and spiritual well-being. In the event you use any of the information in this book for yourself, which is your constitutional right, the author and the publisher assume no responsibility for your actions.

Any people depicted in stock imagery provided by Thinkstock are models, and such images are being used for illustrative purposes only. Certain stock imagery © Thinkstock.

Print information available on the last page.

ISBN: 978-1-5043-6090-6 (sc)
ISBN: 978-1-5043-6092-0 (hc)
ISBN: 978-1-5043-6091-3 (e)

Library of Congress Control Number: 2016912279

Balboa Press rev. date: 03/31/2017

DEDICATION AND ACKNOWLEDGEMENTS

To Elizabeth, Clare and Christopher Keithley.
To Fiona Renton Keithley.
To Steve Hirsch.
To Ian Keithley and Tristan Hirsch.

And with deep thanks for the warm, faithful, generous
undergirding of the family life I enjoy, including
ongoing support for the goals so important to me.

To Jean Hunt, Mary Nolan, and to Gerry Brauneis *in
memorium*: Cohorts all who dedicate their lives to creating
and supporting positive change for workers, students,
families, friends and the communities of our world.

To John Schultz, creator of the brilliant Story Workshop®
approach to writing at Columbia College, Chicago.
Betty Shiflett, an unforgettable and magical teacher.

To Randall Albers, Andrew Allegrehetti, Larry Heineman
who each gave different muscles to my writing legs.

To my own classmates and students at Columbia, for their contributions to me; and now publishing their own works.

My thanks for this story picked up in casual conversation with a man who believed he had lived it so many years ago in England; and now written with his permission. With grateful thanks to Mary Jonaitis and the Michael family for unfailing support during the writing, as well as to Chicago's Newberry Library and the internet for invaluable doors to research.

To Nassiba Cherif, my guide to the Muslim religion, its history, ways and nuances. Without her help and introduction to Salaam Mosque in Sacramento, CA, I would not have experienced the beauty, warmth, strength and contribution of the Muslim religion and deep traditions of community.

To fiction writer Mark Paxson and poet and visual artist Carolyn Kelley Williams for invaluable editorial support and guidance. And to Hilary Bee, Oxford graduate in England, for the understanding of distinctive differences between British and American ways and points of view, then and now.

Eternal thanks to Sara Maitri, Sacramento, for her incredible artistic eye, great heart, generosity and support in producing the book's covers' with perfect page design and type face for story movement.

PROLOGUE

Fall, winter and early spring, the sick come crowding to this small
room the Brothers give me for healings here at St. Bartholomew
Abbey in Exeter, England. Beggars and cotters ("villein" to our
Norman lords) squeeze onto its narrow benches, crowd the floor,
fill the small doorway and spill into the courtyard. Last Fall, as a
mercy against England's cold, the monks cut an opening into the
wall of our healing room to give us heat from the kitchen's hearth.

  Less than fifty years after the death of Jesus, the Romans,
they tell, snatched this village then called Isca from the Saxons.
Time passing, it took' on whatever name suited its next invader
until, in 352 Anno Domini, it became Exeter. And so remains
to this day, with its river, cliffs, woodlands, and us, the poor and
plain, persisting here like burrs.

  I am Jophiel Balerais, an unconsecrated brother here at the

Abbey; and upon this sixteenth day of November, Year of Our Lord 1182, sixty-four years upon God's green earth.

As you know, a time comes when you are overtaken by a fierce longing to tell your sons, daughters, nephews, nieces and grandchildren of who you have been. This for what good it may do them, and as preparation for the claim you will make upon what Eternity you sense may be.

Oh, I have kin would listen and gladly; but to give over to them all I have lived might indeed be a grave strike against charity. And so it must be in you, strangers kindly and curious, that I invest my tale as all I have to leave behind; and pray you may find therein something for your own well-being, and in payment, though modest, for your kindness to me.

And so I begin.

CHAPTER ONE

I am three years old, barefoot, and peering out the door of our hut open a crack into the dark murky air that raises goosebumps on my flesh. Men, long-armed and stoop-shouldered, lurch toward me, their heavy footfalls muffled in the dirt eternally encrusting our paths and hovels. Terrified, I suck in my breath as if to preserve myself.

But no, they pass me by, smelling as always of worn-out flesh, tattered clothes and something salty like hardened tears. And down a foot worn trail they disappear, under a great red-stone arch and into the city I will come to know as Exeter, shire of Devon, in this mighty and miserable kingdom, our England. The year would be 1121 Anno Domini. Oh, but ever after, these men haunt my nights, and when I was younger, their cold miserable forms would wake me screaming.

"But nay, gran'son," Gran'mam Mamoon would soothe,"these be but our own cotters and off to work now. A mite of a lad, they give you such a fright you even see them in your dreams." And I confess those men come yet to me. And there's no running from them. And one time their coming marked the first great turning point in my life.

I was thirteen, then. Parents dead. Brother and sister gone off, and me man-of-the-house for my Gran'mam Mamoon a full year when one night dreaming, the bitter cold of those dark men passed directly into my body and set it to shaking so hard it woke me.

Usually heat from the hearth warmed the loft where I slept, for Gran'mam, lying next it, kept it going the night. Teeth chattering, I reasoned she had been called out, for she was the neighborhood midwife and healer. I chafed my arms and legs; yet the fierce chill prevailed. It was then, and with a great reluctance, I opened my eyes, pushed up onto one elbow and peered down through the slats of the loft, expecting to see Mamoon's covering thrown back and her pallet empty.

But no, there my Gran'mam lay, stretched out full, her head thrown back, dark and silver hair spilling over the pillow.

"Mamoon," I called out. My voice roused her always. Yet on she slept. "Mamo-o-o-n," I tried again, with more force, and with no results. And it was then, all on its own, that my body began to shake while my heart hollowed out as if sucked dry. "Mamoon?" I tried a third time, but more to myself; for all at once it seemed plain enough that during the night the dreaded Angel of Death had come.

I fell back then into a sudden coldness greater than that of any winter; and fled eagerly toward that huge and terrible chill, as if into the great Nothingness at the very edge of Time; and filled with the deepest of loathings ever to enter Time again. And my very body felt dissolved, disappeared; and I gave this no concern. What use had I now for a body?

After seasons, after centuries, and the early light crawling through our shutters, neighbors' voices and rims of carts' wheels cutting punishing pathways across my brain, and altogether against my will, my hands and feet began to reappear. More time, and my feet of their own sought first the ladder rungs, then the dirt floor below I must now cross to her pallet, each step huge and punishing carrying me to what I somehow dreaded to see.

Standing there and looking for her bosom to rise and fall, I reached out for her hand. Oh, hard as wood it was, though it seemed yet to carry some memory of warmth that I felt my Gran'mam had saved for our parting. I settled upon the floor, my knees against her pallet; and wanting one last time to experience its power through my fingers, I took up a swatch of her long hair, dark and silver and always so cool, rich and alive, to pass through my fingers. But no, dry as straw it was. And with that surprise came the dawning that the least part of the Mamoon I knew, of my Gran'mam who daily embraced, laughed with and schooled me, was her body. All the rest, so vast, so deep, warm and wise, I saw now was naught but spirit.

So must it be, then; and with each of us. Well, and the wonder of that learning sank into my deep heart and my soul, and then never again could I see people in quite the same way.

Oh, and I took my time; for when I sent for Uncle Anthony, my father's brother, Gran'mam would no longer be my Mamoon, but belong to the Church and to the earth; for by law, she must be in the ground before sundown. But never again to see her open her eyes nor draw a breath: That indeed was bitter to my soul!

I smoothed the skirt of that gown I knew so well, and drew from its coarse-woven cloth all of what had been our days together. Then there came, so sudden and unexpected, a sense real and deep that my Mamoon was with me still, and would protect and never leave me. And so as I had trusted her who had guarded me all my young years from the brutality of my family, I trusted her now even in death; and then felt her love penetrate me. And a new strength as of a warrior spirit was breathed into me. And it was at that moment I felt myself to become a man.

Then my eye was drawn to her apron folded upon the stool. From its pocket I took her kerchief, scented with herbs. I did not need to close her eyes; but as her mouth lay open in an awkward way, I pulled the chin strap of her cap tighter so that she bore a comely air. Then I knew that all was right; and I went for my uncle.

That night in a dream real as life, Mamoon pulled me onto her big lap and against her bosom. And I smelled that fragrance of woods and hearth she always carried, and rested against the firmness of her body while she rocked and rocked me until we two were blended; and in this way she joined with me in my life for whatever I must endure. And after that, whenever I had very difficult times to absorb, she would come to me that same way, even after I was a grown man and very experienced in the world, and thought that I had no need of such a thing anymore.

CHAPTER TWO

In the early days, Mamoon apprenticed me in remedies and healing.

Together, and always led by butterflies, we'd descend the hillock behind Rougemont Castle to the long brook announced by the calls of Blue Tit, fluting Thrush and the chirping voices of the creek waters. Then up, again, until below us thatched roofs hung like animal fur above the alleys within the arches of Exeter's gates. And I would spot the ashwaddler dragging his box through the narrows of the streets and calling, "Ashes? Take yer ashes t'day?"

We'd cross the wide brook on stones, then climb again, lifting our eyes past the riot of trees to those swelling hills cradling ponds with swan and kestrel; then on to the red cliffs beyond, ancient lords of earth and sky!

Mamoon always wore a vert about her neck, a wooden

license with the owners' insignia of permission to enter the
forest of our betters where she regularly gathered herbs for noble
households, and so was free to mount the stile for our needs as
well, and without worry of the Warden.

I remember her hands like butterflies touching the green
growing things. I tell you I believed then and do to this day that
the plants and rocks spoke with her, and she with them. And
I remember she would school me then about the "Old Ways"
of Nature spirits, of elves and fairies that unbelievers could no
longer see.

And settling upon a log, she would pat a place for me
beside her.

"When folk stopped taking their food from the wild and
made farms, Jophiel, they cut the very threads weave us into
life. And 'twas then that we humans gave up our footprint as just
bein' there and equal with all the others, a wrongful thing and a
sorrow canna be helped now." Her voice would come ancient as an
oracle's; and listening, I would tremble inside fearing that I could
neither grasp nor hold the great words she spoke; yet knew I dared
not lose them. Mamoon would peer to see I was listening, then go
on, her eyes solemn, her voice all shadows.

"This is how we lost the way of our own knowing," she
would pat over her heart, "and our seeing of Nature's spirits right
here amongst us, and with us yet, Jophiel, do you know? For they
are tuned to us as a lute to its player. So if a man be in a black
humor, they will take on that part and act it upon the fields; and the
fields will bring forth poorly then. And so the man will blame the
earth, though truly for all he has brought upon it and hisself. Us it
is," she would jab her finger at the log, "disturbs the earth, Jophiel,
and no other. We turn dark, and so bring storms and plagues upon
our own selves." And she would give a deep nod, and with a little
grunting sound climbing to her feet, point out wild parsley or
violets to pull.

Mamoon told me there was no Heaven like they preach
in church. "And Hell, why 'tis right here, lad. And 'tis us and

nobody else makes it. And a waste they tell us to wait 'til we die for Heaven, when Heaven be here now and we in it, right in Nature's own bosom. So, 'tis our part to be happy as we can while we be here, Gran'son; or how will we know happiness after?" Then she would pause to eye me, fondly. "I give you the good I know, Gran'son, that it may help you one day." And she'd nod deep.

Our cotter's hut, like many others outside Rougemont Castle, was mostly poverty and violence. My father tormented my mother; my sister and brother tormented me; and with no person but Mamoon to protect me. So small myself those days, Mamoon was to me big hips, big breasts, big bottom, big lap--oh, and everything to be trusted and to stand upon.

But even she had ways I could not grasp.

By the time I was fourteen, everything at home had changed: Father dead in a sword fight outside a tavern, my mother Iheld perished from some street disease, my sister married, brother a teamster in Crediton; and myself living then with my Uncle Anthony who had brought me to a place far different from what I had known.

Mathilde, his wife, big-boned, but with brown tresses and a particular softness about her face, had laughing blue eyes and a steady manner very comforting to me. With four children, the house was already full, so a sleeping space was made for me upon a doorless cupboard where Aunt stored foodstuffs and herbs she wanted kept dry next the hearth. My pallet being short, I must sleep knees drawn up while the crackling wood below brought upon its rising warmth wonderful odors from the spices and foodstuffs stored below.

Oh, and I felt I had the best bed in the house!

Aunt, from way up north, was part Scottish, and very interesting with her accent and special ways. Day and night, little ones and cats rustled in and out of her skirts as she moved about cooking, cleaning, or at her sewing. Very spare of discipline with her brood, she would sing to one and all, and to the very day itself in a big lilting voice I loved. And for Aunt, gardening was neither magical nor mystical, but simply the tending of growing things for the family. I can tell you she was very clear about what she wanted done in that garden, for she kept it healthy as you would any child; and so week after week it filled our bellies, and cured our illnesses small and large.

My Uncle Anthony was held to be extremely bright and was under the political protection of Lord Cornwall, and later of Lord Galton. And when a blacksmith in a neighboring village died, Uncle would buy up his shop and take on more apprentices. So after a time, he became a kind of overseer, managing smithies and customers in two or three villages besides Exeter where his own shop near South Gate was by far the biggest and busiest of all.

And it was because of his business judgment that he was set aside from being owned by a lord or the king, but my uncle was a free man. Well, he got along with those above him and with such an enviable repute for honesty he was called to the Moot Hall, our common court, as a primary witness or judge to resolve trade conflicts. And because of all this, he would gain a place for me in the school of our betters.

But before that, I was eight and in my second year in the Common School in the old stable on Catherine Street, and learning to read, figure numbers, to write, sing psalms, and speak simple French. It was then Uncle opened to me the world of his blacksmith shop where he paid me for fetching and sweeping so that I had money to take home to Mamoon. I believe he felt badly about how Teewaye, my father and his older brother, treated my mother Ihelde and us three children. And so Uncle Anthony became the person in the world after Gran'mam I could trust.

Extravagant-looking, and with a ruddy face, Uncle Anthony commanded attention wherever he went. His hair, a blondish red, very bristly and wild, was all over his body. And he looked for all God's kingdom, except for size, like one of those wood elves Mamoon and the old women tell stories about.

Another thing was his hands, very big, pink and red. And fleshy. When I was small and the comfort of his presence made me bold with him, I would call him "Sausage Hands" to make him laugh. And with such hams, I could not grasp how he created such finely wrought work, and out of the heaviest of metals! Gruff of speech and manner, yet he labored to catch himself in the midst of any curtness and turn it to something humorous or harmless. And I had no experience of someone managing himself so artfully, for when my father was gruff, well you just had better get away, that was all! And while both came from the same rough home, my Uncle Anthony found ways to rise above it.

So, not at my lessons or helping Mamoon, I would come down High Street to turn toward South Gate and the blacksmith shop where it stood there just at South Gate.

I liked the noise, the clatter, the testing, the raw display of human strength. I loved the fire turning the workspace into leaping light and shadow, and washing everything with red and gold. And how all the workmen there appeared to live in Hell, their bodies steaming from the flames and the heavy lifting, and the anvil ringing like some great eerie Keeper of Time. I loved all that, and took on a taste for the smell of metal cold, red-hot or cooling in the water barrel.

One day sweeping out a stall, a scream froze the very air in my lungs. A small chip of white-hot metal had exploded into a man's face as he bent over a bolt he heated. He had fainted dead away, his eye, a mass of blackened pulp, slipped down his face on a sleeve of blood. They rushed him outside. I leaned against a wall to vomit. Sweeping up my mess, I realized I had one hand pressed against the same eye as the man lost. And all anyone could do for him was find a surgeon. Some will return to a smithy with one eye. This man did not.

In those days I had a head full of butterflies, trees and jumping brooks. In my first school, the cleric, fists dug into his tunic and eyebrows bunched up, would stand over me. "Well, I see our Jophiel has left us again." He'd tap my empty slate for everyone to laugh. And more than once at the smithy I would wake from daydreams to searing burns. I learned about ash-paste and leaves of plantain for soothing and healing. And I finally saw the need to harness my mind.

As I was the logical person to spare for errands, Uncle would send me a mile and a half down London Road past the Alms House for mead I'd carry back across my shoulders in two foaming buckets swinging, slopping and dribbling into the dirt, never mind how carefully I walked. And the men at the smithy would keep a sharp eye out. As I staggered onto Magdalene Road, their great cheer would go up to fill me like a good meal!

So young, I got the jobs others didn't want. An animal might relieve itself in the midst of a shoeing; and "Jophiel, darlin' boy," the men with their big sweating chests would saunter over, "here's a pretty just fer you. Fetch the shovel afore it goes stale." And indeed I must come running! But as I grew, I would learn the forge, the bellows, the tongs and hammer, the anvil, the water barrel. And one day I would see a boy younger than me on the shovel; and there I would be trimming the curled hooves of cattle, sheep, goats--and horses, of course.

Now shoeing can be dangerous if a horse doesn't trust you or isn't treated well. More than one blacksmith has been killed by the sudden shifting of a flank or strike of a hoof. But Uncle Anthony used to say he could accomplish twice as much when I worked with him because he didn't have to fight the animals. I would speak to them in soft sweet words, and they would calm down--and get a better-fitting shoe as well. And they knew it. I could trade thoughts with any animal, really, would let me near it, for I loved their company; and often could share my thoughts with no one else. And if an animal must die, I wanted it quick and clean.

CHAPTER THREE

One lucky fact raised me to heights no villein should ever reach: I was bright. And so my uncle could take up my case with Lord Cornwall that I be educated. And because Lord Cornwall thought so highly of my uncle, I became a student at St. Bartholomew Abbey along with the likes of Lord Cornwall's own son. Fifteen of us studied at lessons in the rectory of St. Anselm's chapel there. A second group of boys, slightly older, kept to a different room, although we came together for Latin and religious exercises.

Our learning room had a floor not the rammed dirt of our cottages and other buildings, but of carefully cut stone tiles. And this felt to me to be a floor for those with command in the world. The shine of those stones fit together so logically, the shush or ring of a foot upon them, told me this was a floor for the quiet, the orderly, the well-mannered. And to have access to such a place of discernment of the mind, gave me stature within myself.

I can tell you that first day and ever after, I felt the qualities of that room rise up within me whenever I entered it; and knew somehow that I was to become different from my parents, even from Mamoon; that I would transcend my background and move in larger spheres than any of my family would ever know. In this way I felt carried by fate, sensing some destiny that held in a protected way the very path of my life.

You would see us on stools, or four or five to a bench, and studying quite a lot of Latin. While I had found Common School studies hard to absorb, the classes now at St. Bartholomew were longer and more tedious. Also, the taking in of all this information and the giving it back again was entirely opposite the highly physical life I knew. So at first I would nod off any number of times, only to feel a little rap on the back of my neck from the master. And by the end of the day, I was thrilled to go home to feed the animals, chop wood, dig in Aunt's garden, or muck horses at Uncle's shop.

School wasn't all learning Latin; sometimes it was French; and sometimes we spoke in a refined English, unknown in my daily life. Born a good son of Dev'n, I naturally dropped my front "h", replaced "v" with "f", "z" with "s" and would tell my teacher, "G'wan awm drekly fer elpin me Ont, Sir." And Dev'n ways and raw expressions learned from Uncle's blacksmiths sent the students into riots of merriment at my expense. I heard one whisper behind his hand, "Why is the beggar here? To become a lord, I suppose?" The other grinned. "If he isn't hung first."

But if you had met our schoolmaster Father Stephan, a slender young priest with dark tonsured hair, very straight, and a finely sculptured nose, you would have found him kindly about my difficulties, his blue eyes holding good-humored understanding, even as he reprimanded me. So while I got from him the signal not to use a particular expression or to speak in a certain way, I knew he did not think ill of me. And under the cloak of his kindness,

I could keep some humor about myself, come from such a lowly place to this high estate. At home, I practiced my fs and vs on Uncle Anthony, and still remember in his face the mixed feelings that his nephew spoke to him in the tongue of his betters. "You do us proud, lad," he'd clap me on the back. "Would your Gran'mam could've 'eard you."

Of the many other things that separated me from my schoolmates, food was a gully. The first day I undid the wrappings on a cooked baby rabbit the size of a bird, and the others at the table curled their lips or laughed aloud.

"Struck by a wagon, was it?" a thin-lipped lad pointed with his chin.

"Nay, I think his father clubbed it," another boy with horse-like teeth came right back; "but only stunned it, so had to boil it to death."

My neck grew very hot; my hands began to shake. To kill and cook your own food meant that, like a wild animal, you must eat what you can catch. And this made both you and your food uncouth and lowly. It seemed the very walls leaned away while these boys beamed in glee, seeing me stripped and defenseless. It mattered not that they also ate rabbit, for they did not catch nor cook it themselves. I wrapped my meal up fast, and swore never again to bring victuals from home.

Then a bowl and piece of bread was set before the boy next to me. Since at home all ate together from the cook pot, I reached in with my spoon. "Heigh there, villein, keep your filthy spoon out," the lad shouted, bringing down a great clamoring of others upon me. Just then more bowls and bread appeared along with the supervising cleric wiping at something at the corners of his mouth.

But in that fracas against me, I saw something important: That poor as we villeins were, we had largesse about food the rich lacked. There were other natural acts, too, such as wiping at a sniffle on my sleeve, these lads found equally shameful. Day after day my face would burn at being found so unpleasing, and knowing this high learning "stolen from my betters" would cost me a good deal more of the same before I was finished.

To soothe myself at my study bench, I often resorted to the sounds of the horses in the stable out back. Like the sight of the great tree outside the school for villeins on Martin Street, hearing animals large and small call to one another made me at home in myself and the world. Truly, there was many-a-time when the whinny of horses saved me for a day.

A few weeks after the rabbit incident, we'd finished eating and were about to take our bowls out to be washed when the cleric in charge of meals held up his hand.

"Never mind, lads; Jophiel will take care of these for us."

He kept his face, one that folded sallow upon itself, turned from me as he spoke; still I saw the dark satisfaction, and felt the pleasure that rippled through my classmates at this demeaning; for custom was each boy washed his own bowl. I had worked hard to become more correct; but to those youths, my efforts were dust. They tolerated me because they had no choice; and let me know my new chore felt satisfying to them. Still, some carried their bowls and spoons out anyway; but most left their mess behind for me.

But such incidents strengthened me, finally; for I developed a habit at such times of calling vividly to mind the hard-pounded earth of our hut behind East Gate; and by contrast, the polished stones shining now beneath my feet. And forcing myself to see the lesser and greater side by side was a practice that saved me.

And the cooks saved me.

And Brother Frederick saved me.

Outside in back was a well and a great cauldron that hung over a small fire. It was there with a brush I would wash the wooden bowls and spoons and leave them to dry. And in the colder times of year, how I relished my hands in that hot water! For though I wore a tunic and leggings with boots, and with sleeves pulled over my arms and a long vest of hide, still I was always cold. And while large as the hearth was at our lessons, little of its heat reached us. Nevertheless, we were grateful to be indoors.

At my new task, the cooks came to like me because I was so unsure of myself and willing to help. In due course, I showed them some of Mamoon's ways of cooking; later they shared how to make a kind of oat cake between a biscuit and cracker, and very nicely brittle. I liked those cakes and taught the making of them to Aunt Mathilde.

Also, it turned out that the cleric who sent me to do that menial labor did me a great favor; for it was at that fire that I met the teacher who would shape my mind.

It was scrubbing bowls I took note of Brother Frederick hauling wood or bent over the cauldron, his large face dripping. This was a bear of a man with sunken eyes of piercing blue tucked under a bulging forehead and peering over a large nose; a man with a hunch from stooping in that way of very tall people, yet still wearing the kindliest expression, nevertheless. And there seemed no unwelcome task others didn't feel free to assign to Brother Frederick who, like ancient Greeks I would learn of, held everything up with his back.

Brother Frederick always saw me as of equal value in the kitchen, as well as bright and belonging in the school. Because of his way of holding silence, my classmates thought him stupid; but I came to know a most dignified intelligence and kindly heart. When he became my teacher of long-standing, it dawned upon me that for both of us our outsides looked different from our insides; and that we both suffered from loneliness. Over the years I liked to think I gave some solace to my teacher, as he did to me. And it was also Brother Frederick who saved me.

At the school, there was no end to the scorn and merriment of fellow students over my shabby tunic and leggings, my shoes caked with mud from the cauldron or winter streets. Their leader, Peter Anjou, enjoyed muttering to everyone that all villeins were thieves, and that I had surely stolen my garments, for none fit properly. Still, the boys could not make me feel ashamed for long:

For I was in this same room with them and studying Latin; and no one could take that from me!

Our Father Stephan had an innate sense of justice; and even though he did not shirk his duties in keeping any one of us in order, it was ever done with a heart full of patience and humor.

I began imitating him with the younger boys, helping with studies, with getting along one to another. I had a knack there, as I did with my young cousins, and became someone they could talk to. And in this way I began to carve a new Jophiel from the sad, closed boy who came out of darkness to the marvel of this school.

One afternoon, after we'd put trestles back, set stools and benches straight, I went to the wall with hanging pegs to fetch the sack in which each day I brought a few things from home. Given a short rest in early afternoon, we could take care of our needs, talk, or walk outside if the weather was good. I liked to collect stones, and had found three on the way that morning that I wanted to take into the sun for study.

I picked my sack off the peg and noticed it felt more full than before. Just then Roger Ainsworth, heavyset with a thick neck and red face, bumped into me so hard I dropped the sack which he kicked spinning toward the center of the room.

Out rolled the star bread.

This was a loaf specially made for the clerics who taught us. Late each morning, the bread was brought for our noon meal. The baker's assistant came balancing the willow baskets dangerously upon his head, the bottom of his habit jumping out from his feet as he walked. For the students, there were small loaves of common corn; each got one. And though they required long chewing, we were quit of them soon enough, and always wishing for more, for the wafting fragrance of baking bread had set our stomachs to complaining long before we could eat. Teachers were brought more delicate breads, sweeter, by the smell of them, and of flour more finely milled; and sometimes slashed on top as the loaves baked so that the edges curled out to make a star or other design that showed a whiter flour with finer texture.

And you can imagine I stared in astonishment with everyone else!

I bent to rescue the loaf, picking it up carefully, dusting it. This was the bread of our teachers, the food of Father Stephan who treated me like the others and laughed with his eyes to show where I came from was not all there was to be noted about me. I looked around for a basket for the bread.

"I told Father he was a thief," Peter Anjou rasped out, then. Peter had a pale French-looking face with scattered eyebrows and a wide mouth.

"Thief," some of his cohorts began, pointing. "Jophiel is a thief."

"Yes. What else have you stolen?" Eyes closed to slits, nostrils quivering, Peter raised his chin against me. His father was a cousin of Baldwin D'Revrs who lived in Rougemont Castle. "Edward," he called to a boy without moving his eyes, as if I might try to escape, "did you ever find that knife your father gave you? Where is Edward's knife, Jophiel? Have you sold it already?" From the pale pink cave of his mouth came the venomous words. His narrow tongue flicked.

The light of mid-afternoon dropped through the windows to make crossbars of shadow upon the floor. It was early April and a low fire in the hearth crackled and cried.

I felt the darkness of my past laying hands upon me. These boys wanted me a thief, wanted me lost forever to dirt and dumb labor; they wanted one day to meet at the gallows to say they knew I could only come to a bad end, then to see me hang. I felt the hatred of the poor bred by their relatives alive in them while everything in me wanted to run.

But how could they see me as so without moral feeling that I could step into this room of learning and throw away all that it held as if it were a night's waste? My baffled mind ground to a halt.

"You stay right where you are," Peter dug fists into his waist and twisted about as if surveying troops.

Well, you can be sure my effort had always been to stay out of Peter's way! Today he wore a tunic with expensive leather scallops overlaying the shoulders.

"Get Father Stephan. And someone hold the thief," he barked about. "The same as slaves, they are. Why don't we just call them slaves?" He liked saying that; he looked at me, his eyes glittering.

A long time, these boys, Peter at their head, had been hunting me. I might as well already be in the stocks. And if I made any move, they would take it as a guilty thrust for freedom.

"I don't know how it got into my--" I started, looking for those who might believe me. Young Terrance and his cousin George, whom I had helped with their studies, stared back and forth between Peter and me. Terrance ran for the door.

"I didn't take any--" I went on.

Striking my shoulder with the heel of his hand and forcing me against the wall, Roger, out of his costly clothes and overfed body brought out his pitiful stammer.

"G-g-g-e-t over th-th-ere, t-t-turd, ni-ni-nithing."

The loaf I still held fell to the floor and rolled away. Roger jammed me against the wall, gritting pointed teeth and breathing heavily, though I put up no struggle.

Father Stephan hurried through the door, cassock billowing. Young Terrance had found him.

The boys made way like earth under a plow.

"Here, here, what is this?" Father Stephan demanded, brow stitched upward and eyes skipping from face to face. "Let Jophiel go, Roger."

The room whistled with excitement. The boys crowded close as they dared.

"He stole that bread, Father." Peter Anjou, pale and angular, pointed a long finger at the loaf I had dropped. "If Roger hadn't bumped into him, the dog would have carried it home to eat or sell; and none of us the wiser. Everyone had better check his own things to see what else he's taken."

A wave of murmuring rose up.

Father Stephan clapped his hands. Silence descended.

"Now," he crossed his arms upon his chest, "who saw what happened here?"

Someone heard Roger's feet pounding. Someone saw Roger and me collide. Someone had turned to look just as the sack spun across the floor. Someone saw the bread spill out.

No, no one saw me take the bread.

We were sent to our slates to conjugate Latin verbs. Father Stephan called for old Father Greensward who hobbled in to oversee. Then Father Stephan stepped just beyond the door and crooked a finger at me.

Heart pounding, drowning in confusion and fear, I stammered out all that I could remember. I might easily be dismissed for this, and shame my uncle who stood up for me to Lord Cornwall. And lose my dream of a different life. Then Father Stephan dismissed me for Roger who leered as he passed by to take his turn. Next Father Stephan left us all for what seemed like quite a long time.

Father Greensward, leaning upon his walking stick, directed us to put away our slates and begin Latin recitation. He muttered out of the purses of his cheeks that a noble was known by the refinement of his tongue, not by the size of his estate. I dug icy fists into my lap and struggled to push the Latin words from my mouth with the others who looked at me out of the corners of their eyes. Oh, and how I felt buried under their judgments!

That first day in late summer when I came to the school, the students had gaped at my clothing, my rough hands, the clumsy way I held my body. "This is Jophiel Balerais. He will join in your lessons," the rector told Father Stephan. The boys, their curiosity spiked, had looked on with curled lips as Father Stephan strode across the floor to meet me. Now he stood stock still at that same door, sternly signaling me to come with him. And we left in our wake the up-and-down chanting of the Latin future tense of the verb "to eat", amid a great craning of necks.

Father Stephan and I walked the path to a branch of the Exe that was hardly more than a creek and flowed nearby.

He sat upon a log, myself upon another.

The water was churning brown from the rains of March and these first days of April; and you could taste in the air. A bird called high and behind me. Tee-wit, tee-wit. Another, farther away, answered. Purple and pink crocus broke the sod, releasing a held smell of winter mixed with something warm.

And I felt a great wrenching then for Mamoon, helpless as I was upon the rack of my fears. A beetle, its body the color of bark, waddled over the toe of my boot. My heart pounding, I shook with cold, waiting for Father Stephan to scour me, to dismiss me from the school, waiting to discover that, as I had sometimes feared, his even-handed fairness was but a mask for judgments he privately held. But no, he only leaned his arms upon his knees and twirled a twig between his fingers, his eyes caught upon the water boiling by. And for many moments he said nothing.

"Sometimes it's like this river." His eyes finally came to rest mildly upon my face. He tossed the twig aloft.

I watched the thunderous water suck it down, away.

"A great wrong has been done you, Jophiel. That's the truth. But that wrong is as this twig," he said and pitched the bit into the boiling water. I saw it jump from wave tip to wave tip, then disappear in the greedy waves.

"I have been watching those boys, seen their nasty treatment, heard them plotting against you, sniggering amongst themselves. You had nothing to do with that bread. I know you would never steal, nor do any such thing. I know you are a good young man, and that you have a good heart."

A mercy of breath plunged into my lungs dissolving the blocks jammed together in my throat while water rushed in under my eyelids. I blotted my cheeks with the back of my hand. Father Stephan continued.

"You and I are twigs, Jophiel; and the nobles a raging river. These lads, their fathers are very powerful, friends of Lord Cornwall, of D'Revrs, of the king." He spread his hands. "I cannot accuse them of treachery without proof. They might very well withdraw their sons from the school, and with them the money upon which we depend to stay open."

That he would share such things, that he recognized my nature and knew I would never thieve nor disrespect this place of my learning; that he would praise me so forthrightly--. Why that meant more to me than anything that could come from those boys! Let them accuse me. No one except Mamoon had ever given me such a compliment, named aloud my qualities as a person. And she had had no such refined words as this priest.

"Never mind." Father Stephan slapped his knees and stood. "We will beat them at their own game. Now," he brushed his cassock clean, "Father Albert told me I must discipline you." He said this with a twinkle in his eye, and began to look around. "So I must find something with which to lash you." He pulled a dried stalk from under a log. "This corn will do well. Now you must make enough noise that anyone outside the building--and I'm sure any number of them are milling about there right now --will hear you."

He looked at me. "If you can play this game, Jophiel, we will have this little secret between us. And we understand each other, eh?" But they," he jogged his head toward our classroom, "will think they have gotten away with something." He shook a finger. "Never you fear. I will watch them; and one day they will get what they deserve."

Teachers never touched us except in punishment, but Father Stephan rested a hand upon my shoulder. "You have a good heart, Jophiel. I see your kindness toward the younger ones, your charity." He drew across his mouth a small wry smile, then said cheerfully, "So now bend over."

Well, he began beating me across the back with great grunting thrashes, his arm swinging high and down; the dry stalk rattling in the air, then shattering across my tunic to send spent seeds abroad. I hardly felt the blows; but how I howled; and a joy from deep in my belly mixed with my crying-out while the muddy water boiled up and raced on past us.

Finally Father Stephan dropped the corn stub and scuffed it into the current. He laid his finger to his lips and pulled down the corners of his mouth to show I must look serious and repentant as we started back.

And the forest on either side grew jolly with our secret, its shoots of green pushing through the crusty carpet of last year's leaves while small brown birds chittered and hunted for food.

On my pallet that night, I saw again the twig sucked into the river, and pondered that some people, if they knew the story, might think Father Stephan dishonest. But my mind knew him to be a diplomat, clever and prudent in this world of uncertainty and danger. All night I could but revel in the honor of his confidences, and count my shaming as nothing at all.

Eventually, Father Stephan did catch those boys at their little crimes, and they got a severe pummeling from their fathers. For myself, I won in the end, for I saw for the first time that someone not of my family could recognize me for who I was. And Father Stephan became my hero; and, in a way, a father I never had.

Well, and it happened I had a good hand on the slate and managed the soft sharpened stone adroitly. When they showed me a letter or character, I could copy it artfully without any awkward steps. I was told my hand was quite "refined"; but I had to grow before I knew what that meant.

And this talent, a natural outgrowth of drawing for years in the woods, gave me merit among boys who otherwise would laugh at me, for they had to see I could do naturally what they could do only with great effort. After some time, the teacher brought out quills and certain kinds of inks to be ground and mixed. We wrote at first on clay tablets you erase with pumice; but later, on very thick parchment. Oh, you can imagine how I felt, me, the son of a villein, writing on parchment. Parchment! And in a refined hand!

Another thing I liked at school was to sing the psalms. I thought it quite incredible we could sound so beautiful, like hearing angels. And I would swell inside with that singing as I walked home, and through chores, and on my pallet at night to wake with a hungry anticipation of it in the morning. Perhaps I would become a priest, and every day know the ecstasy from making such beautiful sounds.

At this school they served grains new to me; and vegetables like carrots. At home we drank beer; while at school the lighter, sweeter mead. Working hard, I developed a reputation for being worthy of trust; but to be honest, much I accomplished was to gain approval, and usually from Father Stephan.

CHAPTER FOUR

On the way home from the smithy, I might work up a riddle or story to tell while we tidied up together after a noon or evening meal. I especially loved to hear the timid ones break out laughing. I recalled well enough my own childhood where play meant being chased, captured and locked in a pitch-black rotting shed by my brother and sister who would race off in glee and leave me screaming and begging them to release me.

I still had the power to see through children's eyes and did not forget how, when you are very small, the dark can be fearfully peopled; or what an hilarity it is to announce the things animals may think or say to one another; and older yet, how satisfying to watch grown folks make mistakes. By taking time with the young ones, I could give Aunt a rest, though she never asked. Indeed, she made sure I sat after school with the children for a crust before my chores. And soon I would be a workingman, home at night not much before my uncle, for we often must be out delivering finished pieces.

Uncle's house was two-storied, the lower part one large room with an enclosed stable at the front, as most folks had. Above was the sleeping loft on the second story, though you could not stand up fully there. Packed tight as we were, still we had more room than some. We also owned two ponies and a sow I looked after, as well as the goat and cows. And there was the penned yard the animals could be let out to during the day; but not at night or they might be stolen, or dogs or wolves get at them, or who knew what.

Oh, but the sow was my favorite! Pink and white and grey, she was as attached to me and as much a friend as the best dog you could name; and with the sweetest spirit. I swear I could have sat upon her back if I'd a mind. Her hair out of that pink pink skin was very bristly; but most striking were her eyes, for the intelligence that shone in them; and the love. She would give me a nudge under the arm with her snout, or at my backside or into my thigh, to tell me, you know, "I love you."

There were several blacksmith shops in Exeter, but not all featured the same things. Uncle Anthony who did fine shoeing for nobility, was also known for making certain hard-to-get tools, for complex work like locks, and parts for large mechanical functions and structural and ornamental pieces like frames, arches and gates.

When I had finished my schooling, Uncle began teaching me all that must be known about the blacksmith business. He took his time, but also gave me responsibility quickly as possible to help me grow into a man. Oh, but I was still a boy, and too often caused trouble by impulsive acts and my wandering mind.

One day Uncle was showing me steps for making a gear for a mill. The needed parts lay upon the ground around us. Perhaps it was that he called me away from another task, or that there were more pieces than I could absorb, or that it was a day when I was thinking I'd rather be running with the dog or trading philosophy with my pig; perhaps my mind was fixed upon a lass I'd seen, so that I came over to him for instruction with a rod I'd been firing still in my hand.

I listened to him, vaguely feeling some discomfort holding that rod; and without thinking, laid it, still-glowing red, atop a pile of horseshoes there. Now Uncle not only had a quick mind, but a quick eye; and in a smith shop, quick eyes make the difference between well-being and disaster. I turned back and saw him staring downward with horror upon his face as the top layer of horseshoes bonded to the red-hot rod, curling around it. And you can believe my stomach dropped, for a dozen or more costly shoes now were ruined! I raised my eyes to his face turned red as fire, and heard his voice burst past the wedge of his stunned silence.

"By God's blood, are you blind, boy, and all your angels too? Look here what you've done! What do you think that's going to cost us? Get your mind out of your feet, for the love of the Almighty."

Well, I hung my head wishing I were dead, or that the earth would open. After all Uncle Anthony had done for me, this was how I repaid him!

But then, his eyes still glued to the twisted shoes, a rumble began to make its way from his belly to his throat, then exploded in a great laugh. My eyes shot up to see him pointing a finger at the pile, his head thrown back, laughter ringing off the smithy tools hanging from the rafters and bringing the other men crowding around.

"Look at that now, will you? And how pretty it is, too. Fit for a lady! But nobody under heaven knows what it could be used for!"

He roared this at the ceiling, at the gaping men, his eyes streaming.

Hooting, the others joined in 'til you could hear them down the street.

But in shame I stepped away, a most disconsolate look upon my face, I'm sure. And Uncle's eyes followed me.

"That's it, now," he cut the laughter off all at once. "This lad has plenty of work here. Let him get to it."

And that was the end of it; and I would not hear any more of it, chip, chip, chipping the damaged shoes from the rod; and one by one remaking them. It was two days' work. And Uncle knew the right and profitable way to let me redeem my costly mistake, for when I'd finished, I knew everything there was to know about making horseshoes.

Another time, drifting through the shop with the broom and my thoughts who-knows-where, my arm collided with a glowing poker someone just took from the fire. I felt a stab first like ice, then like lightning move arm to stomach; then heard a scream as if from someone else. Just before I fainted, the sickening sweet odor of my own flesh cooking filled my nose.

They carried me to a corner, set me upon the straw there; and in due course my mind staggered from a black hole to dream faces that stretched and shrank around me. Then fumes flamed up my nostrils and liquid scalded my mouth and throat on its way to my stomach. I watched metal objects from the ceiling swim in and out of shadows while they fed me the whiskey, feeling my arm slowly cool in the swaddling of plantain leaves and my pulse slowly grow steady, arm to brain.

And so I grew and learned. And soon enough, I was opening Uncle's business for the day.

Stablemen of the wealthy come early, so I must be there at four-thirty or five to raise the heat.

First remove the "damper", a cover with sliding windows you set over the hearth to drop the fire at night but let air keep embers alive. Next, pull down the big bellows on the rope above and wake the coals to a flame you must coax along with tinder. Then clean all the tools and set them out on the benches and tables. Oh, and fill the water barrel.

Uncle had three other smiths, and sometimes up to five apprentices; but soon enough I became the one who every morning got the place going for him.

Uncle would arrive at six or six-thirty. People didn't always pay when they picked something up the night before because the bill might need to go to the master of the house. So Uncle often figured accounts in the morning. Because he couldn't write, he made marks on parchment for customers and costs. With me there, I could draw the customer's coat of arms and write the name next to it. He knew the coats of arms, so that way he learned to read the names. And as I got more experience, I'd finish off accounts for him; and talk to customers first, if he was busy.

Around nine, he'd send me for pails of ale, and some bread. That was breakfast. Around ten and again one, when there would be a lull, he'd give me a bit of training, then have me take the job over. "And we need twenty more like that," he'd say. Sometimes I'd spend a day just making nails. Nails of all kinds were a big part of his business. And when anyone found an easier way of doing something, there'd be high spirits and a bucket of mead. Then the new idea went out to the other blacksmith shops around about.

Most people ate at sunset or just before; but Uncle Anthony kept torches lit so customers could come late to pick up. At home, dinner was never served until Uncle set foot in the house. If the children were hungry, there would be bread to chew. Winter, it would be about seven o'clock we came home; but summer it could be eight or later.

I had a lamp in my charge for use in the barn mornings; and after supper I was given enough fuel to read, and would find a quiet little spot in the barn or outside. Sometimes outside, I'd draw plants. Doing that made me feel close to Mamoon. And over the years, that way, I came to know plants deeply.

As my growth into manhood came on, my dreams at night would be of women taking liberties with me and setting my organ afire. Mornings, my bedding and tunic would be soaked. The men at the smithy had prepared me for such changes with stories and raw high spirits over what nature puts upon us. Because of this, I took what was happening to be natural. This way they helped me pass to manhood; and I came to feel at one with them in a way I never had before. This new power in me went well beyond the crying out of the body; but held a new sense of vitality and strength, as if I had burst across an abyss to great promise, and so was filled with an unnamed joy and hope.

One day, heating an ornament for a gate in the fire, I heard Uncle Anthony greet a man he called Nicholas. "How long has it been? And is all this yours?" the voice boomed. I turned to see a short heavy man going grey, wearing a cape of good fabric and fine boots. His eyes opened wide when they fell upon me. He took a step forward.

"Teewaye?" he extended his hand.

I backed off, looked at my uncle. The man had called me by my father's name!

"No, no," Uncle Anthony waved the idea off, laughing. "This is his son Jophiel. He's learning the trade and keeping me out of trouble."

"Well," Nicholas stared, "but of course Teewaye would be even an older pile of horseshoes than you, my friend." He clapped my uncle's shoulder with a cloudy laugh; shook his head. "The lad is his double, then."

As they stepped away, he peered at me again, then looped his finger in a salute. "Good luck to you then, lad."

I nodded, tried to smile; but turned back to work disturbed. The man had mistook me for Teewaye!

Plunged into a darkness, I ordered myself to my work, but by evening had but four pieces where I ought have made eight.

"I'll come in earlier tomorrow," I told Uncle Anthony, cleaning my hands on a rag. It was unlike me not to finish. He nodded, putting bills of sale together for the day. "Run into trouble with those fleur-de-lis?"

"The customer wants the join so narrow just where it must fan out at the top. Still, I ought have finished." I took a vigorous broom to the floor. Uncle watched, bills of sale forgotten in his hand.

"What is it, Jophiel?"

"Your friend--"

"Nicholas Croft? One of my first customers. Now he is miller for several lords in Kent. You saw how he dressed."

"But he thought I was Teewaye!" I could not control my voice.

Uncle Anthony looked long at me. A cart rattled past the open window.

"You almost mirror him, Jophiel." He said it softly, then shrugged. "As a boy grows into his man's body, it's natural enough to take on his father's looks."

In the water barrel when I took a dipper, at the pond where I played my poor-man's flute or drew or read, and with Aunt's prized hand mirror amusing the children, I had seen the lengthening of my face into high cheekbones, arched brows over deeply lashed green eyes, the broad mouth and long narrow chin beneath, all framed by chestnut hair in waves to the shoulders. Oh, more and more, I had seen my father there; but had denied it. Now I was filled with terror that, as I became like Teewaye on the outside, I would become like him on the inside. After Uncle Anthony took me into his family, I began to outgrow the shame of my beginnings; and saw that, as in the forest where the stunted could yet grow straight and full, a man could also create beautiful things of himself. Now that bright hope sputtered. I turned away.

Uncle read my face. "You do look like your father, yes. But your aunt has a saying that day by day the heart crafts the body. As your heart grows different from Teewaye's, so the look of you grows different from him." It was then I recalled how nearly all that I had identified as Mamoon had been spirit really. And with this remembrance, the darkness fled; and, to Uncle Anthony's relief, I began to laugh, though I don't know why.

Uncle ruffled my hair then, told me to hurry that sweeping or we wouldn't get a tankard before supper. Then he said, "Oh, forget the sweeping."

Like so many men, we would venture out for a drink of ale

or mead before we went home. I glanced at him striding along, and gratitude washed through me for this man who gave me a secure place in which to grow up. The smell of Exeter's wild grasses filled the evening air. We nodded to those sitting on benches against the pink fronts of their houses, on tree stumps or rocks, and sharing evening talk.

"What made Ihelde crazy?" I knew someday I would ask.

Uncle looked away, then raised his hand toward a sign like a drinking cup. "Shall we put a little coin in Master Inn-keep's purse?" He clapped me on the back.

The narrow door opened to a shallow room, the dark overcome by light flickering from the hearth and wall torches. The owner, Samuel, round like his drinking cups, had always had a kind word for me since I was nine and fetched the mead for Uncle's men.

"Taken over that place yet?" he clapped me on the back.

"Not so long as he rules." I jabbed a thumb at Uncle, "but I watch him close."

Uncle Anthony laughed, pulled Samuel aside, no doubt to ask for the trestle against the wall near the hearth, where we would not be disturbed.

I sat while Uncle got our cups, my eyes drifting to the tavern's open door as a cart rattled past. Six or eight years ago, though it seemed like many more, Teewaye had been killed in a sword fight just outside a place like this.

Through air smoky from wall torches and the fat of chickens dripping at the hearth, I studied the establishment's license above the door, a large disk of blackened brass with raised letters all around, its age and dignity giving me a strange comfort. Uncle brought our mead. He clapped me on the back.

"A man must be the keeper of his own history." He settled himself squarely. "And you are right to ask about yours. My brother never had gentleness nor virtue in him; I don't know why. I remember in one of his rages, I saw him kick to death a dog trying to protect a child from his raised fist." Uncle's face folded darkly.

"He left the child crying in the street, the dog on the ground next to him, and walked off like he felt better. That dog most likely saved the child's life."

I shivered. The splintering of a barrel. My mother begging for mercy while from the lidless woodbox into whose deep corner I had shrunk, I heard my father dragging Ihelde about by the hair.

"Long as I can recall, Teewaye cared for nothing but drink. You've seen men at my shop I've let go for far less than what your father got to. I kept him long on as I dared."

And every day even now, is the baffling mystery of men staggering down the streets, lying with pigs or hauled off the public way by neighbors trying to get on with their business.

"The drunker your father got, the more raging his fire." Uncle sighed. "And a man like that shows up for work maybe twice in a month, and creates more work than he does. And soon his story has gone around town, and other places know better than to hire him."

The gnawing hunger at home. In the forest, in the garden, trapping quick with my hands or bringing in the baby birds. Then Mamoon naming the night's meal after me in her poor French for 'oiseau de Jophiel', like a dish for lords.

"When my brother discovered I'd given Mamoon money, he tore into my cottage one morning roaring at my wife I'd turned his family into beggars. Scared her near to death, and she big with our first; then came on like a storm to the smithy to get at my neck. But my men lined up at the front with red-hot pokers. And after that," he shook his head, the regret still fresh, "I had to be careful how I did things for your family."

"Was it Teewaye made Ihelde crazy?" I saw her again then, distracted, howling, tearing at her hair; then the periods of calm, of quiet and playing sweetly with me, the sweetness erratic as her mad grief. And I never knew what I could trust.

Uncle Anthony held up two fingers for my lord Inn Keep. "Ihelde was not," he searched for a word, "sturdy, but more a wild flower, delicate, beautiful, easily trampled. Oh, I feared for her, a bird caught in a trap marrying my brother. How her father let go of her to Teewaye--." He shook his head. "Probably one less mouth--." He shook his head again, and my heart wrung for my mother.

Across the room, men roared out their own stories. Smoke hung thick. Uncle took another draught, thoughtful, deciding something.

"Mid-morning a year or more after Teewaye had stormed my house, I'm on my way to see a customer and I come upon a crowd in front of the old Widow Nettwyn's place. She's at the door, a face on her like a rooster as she casts a man into the street yelling, 'I warned you afore 'bout yer whores yuh bring in caterwaulin' all the blessed night. Well, my patience is dried up. So good ridd'nce to ye.'

"So the harpy disappears, then plunges back through the door with a young woman pale and fragile as, as a wasted flower; and with the broom sends her sprawling out into the dirt as well. Oh, and how the crowd bawled with pleasure then! Well, I'm peering 'tween necks and see 'tis Ihelde picking herself up, gown torn and slipping down her shoulder, hair undone, feet bare, face all dirt and fear. Well, and the crowd breaks into jeers while the reeking pig pulls his chausses up with a dark look, being shamed in front of his neighbors; but then turns on Ihelde trying to rise, kicking her and shouting, 'Spent happier nights with a street dog, I have.' Fumbling into his pouch, he throws some coin into the dirt, so the crowd can see he's paid her. Well, your poor mother scrambles for each coin while that drunkard complains, 'They said you was a cheap night, but a good one.' He stumbles sideways, 'But that was just talk from fools drunker'n me.'

"'No fool drunker than you, sot,' a fat man bawls out, and everyone cheers. I dig past shoulders to throw my cloak about Ihelde and lead her away, my heart so distressed remembering her at her wedding, supple as a young tree, wild daisies and iris, in her hair. And I tell her, beg her that she needn't do such things. 'Let me see to your family if Teewaye won't.' I pull money from my purse.

"'No, no!' she throws her hands up as if I'd put a snake to

her face, 'He'll kill me outright!' she turns to run; but I catch her
by the elbow.

'I have ways. He'll not know', I say. 'And your children--.'

"But, eyes still huge, she taps a nostril, 'Nay, but he smells
it out. Smells it. And he'll beat me. Beat and beat 'til I be dead.'
Then her eyes turn wild, and stripping one set of fingers with the
others, she cries out, 'And I cannot be shriven; though what I do
I must do for my children. So I must burn in Hell for all eternity.
And the Devil, with his fiery eyes, he comes looking for me in the
dark of night or bright of day, even now. Comes looking for me!'
Then she turns and runs away crying, a most piteous thing that
haunts me to this day."

By now the tavern had folded for me to the single point of
Uncle's voice, the live embers of his words. At last with a deep sigh
he sat back and lifted his eyes to the ceiling, silent for a time; then
went on.

"I tried to talk to Teewaye, brought him into the shop; but
he couldn't stand skittish animals; couldn't put up with his younger
brother giving him orders. So, whenever I knew him to be away, I
would watch for Mamoon on High Street or going to the Hay; or
I'd come to your place." He tapped his thumbnail against his cup,
sorrow and regret in his face. "And, a terrible thing to say, a relief it
was when your father died."

I stared into the fire. And the hearth's chickens browned
and dripped while I felt the jagged saw of the past back and forth.
"But Mamoon used to stop my father just by coming into the
room. I remember. And why didn't she keep Ihelde from--?" My
voice came a bit loud; a man across the room looked around in our
direction..

"Spirits of terror took over your mother, Jophiel. Nothing
could stop them," Uncle shook his head quietly.

We drank in silence. A bit of log exploded.

"But how is it you are so different from my father?"

"Oh, you've seen me explode like that log, Uncle drained
his cup. No woman fine as your aunt would carry our young, keep

a home and cook pig's head for Christmas if I hadn't reformed myself, I'll tell you that."

Our first laugh, then. We relaxed as Uncle went on about Aunt, what she put up with; but his words fell behind old scenes I saw of my mother shrinking when she entered the church, clapping hands over her ears at the sermon; and, though baptized, never to my reckoning taking Holy Communion.

"Ihelde used to whisper to me," I interrupted him. "'A devil smells me out. Don't let him get you, wee one o' mine. Keep a candle lit, stay near the hearth, for he can't abide light. Oh,' and she'd tear her hair; 'I belong with them. They wait for me.'" And I'd cry then over my mother, captured by demons and no help for her, for Mamoon believed a demon had got into her."

We sat in silence again. The fire popped. Most of the other men had trooped out with "Fare thee well." Gripped by my thoughts, my voice quavered. "Knowing the Church condemned her to Hell for her doings must be what made her mad."

Uncle's face all but collapsed. "Along with the horror of giving herself to be defiled--and for a few pence." He grit his teeth.

I was angry too, but for a different reason. For sudddenly I understood why Mamoon wept, bathing Ihelde's eyes, that she saw Ihelde had passed beyond her rescue. "And Ihelde lost her sight," I gasped out. "Her pupils turned white. I saw them, like thin slices of bone. She had to feel her way along the walls." I said nothing for a moment: something building in me; then I burst out, "I wish someone would tell me how God could send a woman to Hell for trying to feed her children!"

My uncle's arm tightened about my shoulder. We sat so for some moments, then finished our drinks.

We stepped into the street, and a door to my past closed. In a way I can't explain, this talk, the memories especially of Teewaye, added sinew to my manhood. I had never before seen my father as handsome. Now I realized he was so, but that his temper and the drink had greatly distorted his visage and mind. Oh, but such would not be the case with me. I was clear about that.

We walked home in the summer night, and I pondered that as in nature, there are forces in people no one can control nor explain. And somehow this made the road before me feel more predictable, safe. Also, I had become comfortable man-to-man with my uncle; and in ways took him both for the father I did not have and for an older brother to whom I could go for counsel.

And I found myself freed up in my body; and was helped in the taking on of my manhood by pleased looks sometimes bestowed by women beyond my years.

CHAPTER FIVE

Life now gave me even less time for myself. Still, busy as I was, I never lost my need for the comfort of shadows or an unlit space others might avoid where I could till my thoughts. Often I sought out a certain pond ringed by slender trees that leaned inward like maidens whispering. There I would play my whistle, draw or read; and at times wish for the company of another youth of like mind and humors.

When Uncle was not around the shop, men at the smithy liked to rag me about caring more for solitude than carousing, or trifling with the lasses. Roughhousing, dicing, bawdy talk--no matter how I'd wish to, I could not join in with a heart.

Neither could I reveal myself deeply to these men, grateful as I was for their good will. So they would joke I studied to become a monk; and on a Sunday on High Street, my arms about a folio, they might come upon me heading down to Little Britayn to see Brother Frederick. "Are you praying for us sinners, then, Brother Jophiel?" they'd laugh and slap each other around, in high spirits on the way to an alehouse across from St. Vitalis where the Village Watch would, for a penny, first announce to each customer, "No drinking here Sundays;" before holding open the door.

I had finished my studies at St. Bartholomew the Spring before. But Brother Frederick urged me to come by when I had time, and also kept me stocked with folios to read at home. And this way he became my special teacher.

Often I found him on a stool cleaning roots for the perpetual soup. Both sunlight through the open door and firelight from the hearth cast shadows of the cauldrons, spice barrels and cooking tools; and there would raise up among them his freckled and balding pate like its own moon. On a bright day, you'd discover his body a marvel of red hair curling like fire... not the red of my uncle's coarse hair, but finer; or find him under the great oak in the kitchen's garden whittling a whistle or animal for the street children. And when he and I hunched over a folio page, it seemed we entered into a brotherhood with the writer, no matter how long ago he'd lived. Didn't we also search meanings in these matters of earth and body, sleeping and waking, toiling and loving and suffering and dying? Oh, and my appetite for such learning was keen as for food!

When I would make my entrance and he'd look up with a twinkling eye to say, "Enter, the Thinker," my heart would lift to be so named by one who cut and bound vetch with Plato on his lips and wrestled oxen from a muddy ditch declaiming Heraclites: "We look and look, and have the thing in our hands all the time."

In those days, one folio at a time, I carried his collection back and forth to Uncle's cottage. My young cousins clamored to feel the pages, but I kept everything in my own hands. At night I slept with the work in a wrapping of hide with my arms around it.

Soon Uncle was asking me to read from it to him and Aunt; and we took to sitting at the hearth after the wee mites were tucked in. Aunt and Uncle liked to hear Herodotus' stories of the wild behaviors of ancient peoples. Aunt relished the custom of stealing noblewomen such as Helen of Troy as punishment for a perceived insult. Uncle loved the tale of the foreigner in Arab lands given asylum in a neighboring kingdom; but who, insulted by his rescuer and king for returning from a hunt with no prey, took revenge by dressing as meat for dinner one of the youths over whom he had charge, serving him up, then fleeing for his life in the dark of night. Uncle passed that one around the smithy. After that, when we'd all leave for supper, the men would call to one another, "Don't put it in yer mouth afore you know who it be."

A certain Sunday in June, my head filled with ideas from ancient religions, I found Brother Frederick separating carrots from their tops in the kitchen garden. I began twisting too, tossing the greens onto a pile the farm animals would enjoy. The wind gusted raising a cloud of fine dirt; but we covered ourselves too late. Brother Frederick sputtered, wiping his mouth with the sleeve of his robe. "With that wind, even a heathen can tell wet weather's coming." He liked to say "even a heathen," between us in jest, for as such the priests at St. Bartholomew described the very Ancients we studied.

I followed him into the kitchen where he greeted Brother Cecil at the hearth, chose a trestle for us and began clearing it of clay pots glowing with that special green glaze known over England to be of Exeter. While I helped stack them in a corner, my mind strayed to a year before when Brother Frederick gave me that first folio to take home with me.

One day, Father Stephan had sent me to ask for Brother Frederick's Plato. Surprised, (the only books I knew of were in the library), I trooped to the garden where the sound of a small ax cutting weeds brought me to his dripping face. Brother Frederick cracked a great smile.

"My young friend. How may I serve you?"

"Father Stephan would like to borrow your Plato, Brother," I said.

At this we both laughed, for the students' fathers often criticized Father Stephan to his superiors for wasting their sons' time on the "useless fodder" of Greek and Roman thought.

Down a hall we trooped then to the third wooden door in the wall, and stepped into his cell. Through its slit of a window, I saw apple blossoms and a scrap of green forest. A cloak and tunic hung on the two wood wall pegs.

Unlatching and lifting the lid, the larger of his two chests gave off a must of leather, vellum, ink and mold. It was from over his sloped shoulder that I spied the piles of books, and hadn't yet closed my amazed mouth when he turned to give into my arms the Plato bound between boards covered with leather. On top of that he laid a work of Herodotus.

"Take it home, Scholar."

Well, I had staggered back, shaking my head, eyes big as sovereigns.

"Brother, I've no place to keep it; and only a little time at night and on Sunday to read. Such a big work, it would take long to finish."

"Take it, Scholar." He waved me off. "Keep it long as you like."

Late that afternoon I wrapped the treasure in my cloak and clutched it to my breast all along High Street to Cooks' Row to Magdalene Street.

But now my teacher's voice snatched me back to today's lesson he put before me, pointing to the bench where we sat to mead and half a dozen rinsed strawberries warm from the garden.

"Tell me, Scholar, which would you prefer; a God of the Ancients or the God you have?"

I shook my head, laughed. "My understanding of the God we have is not great, Brother; but I would hazard those of others could not be more different." I dusted my hands, plucked up a strawberry.

The sloping forehead wrinkled. "Some argue all Gods are alike."

"But how, Brother? As I read, the Ancients have many Gods. And none are kind."

"Some might argue we too have many Gods, and none kind."

I laughed again, shook my head. "We have but one God."

He raised three fingers.

"Well--" I stumbled.

Jesus in the chapel nailed to the cross; the dove above him, descending; and above them the Great Father, hands open and pouring out light. Three, yes; but two, then, from this Father Creator, mammoth and stern, of deep eyebrows and a beard rushing out like the sea. Well--.

I hesitated. "The Jews had but one God. In this they differed from the rest of the Ancient World. And," I concluded, well satisfied, "that God of theirs is the same God we have."

"Oh." he nodded. When considering some matter, my teacher had a habit of twisting his right ear.

"But we know more now than the Ancient Jews," I strode on.

"I hope so," Brother Frederick folded his ear; "but then, what 'more' is it?"

Hissing sounds erupted from the hearth. We turned to see Brother Isadore, a cook, slide four chickens down a board into the pot.

"Well, we know this God of theirs and ours is," I shrugged, "really three."

"Three?" He let go his ear, ragged eyebrows climbing high.

"Three--um--parts." It was the best I could do.

"Three parts? Our God is in three parts?"

"Father, Son and Holy Ghost." I could feel the trap closing; I just didn't know which trap.

My teacher chewed thoughtfully, swallowed. "A Creator, a Savior, a Purifier. This is what you tell me?" Another bite. "To my counting, that makes three Gods." His face now all innocence.

I buried my head in my arms. Mead gurgled into my cup.

"Of course, for the Ancient's there are—" my teacher held up three fingers.

I nodded."Zeus, Apollo and Hermes."

"But Zeus had many children; and I don't recall stories of the Holy Ghost making mischief like Hermes. However, Hermes did cause things to happen on earth, though mostly with business and commerce; whereas the Holy Ghost brought forth God the Savior." He slapped his palms down on the trestle. "How can we be out of strawberries? No one can discuss serious things without strawberries!"

Before I could untangle myself, he was through the door and coming back again, the berries glistening from a pass through the water barrel. He arranged the ten in a line upon the trestle.

"So, we have three Gods then, eh?" He plucked three berries aside, then rolled one to me from the other group. "We'll eat their gods first. They have so many."

"Wait, Brother Frederick. I don't know that I say we have three Gods. I have always heard of one God in three parts--or--uh--'Persons.'" I wished for once I had given more attention to the priests in church and at lessons.

"Oh? One God, you say? Which ones aren't God?" He hiked his robe and settled himself as if about to consume a good bowl of stew.

"I say all three are God. Well," I backed off, "that is what is preached."

My teacher nodded, thoughtful. "But are all equally God?"

"How do you say, 'equally'?"

He shrugged. "Each has the same powers as the others. With the Ancients, not all were equal. Far from it." He finished off his mead.

I narrowed my mind. Here was a wrinkle. "The Father comes before the Son and Holy Ghost, because, as I understand it, they come *from* Him; so that would make the Father a bit more equal." Chicken, leeks, basil, carrots and parsley maddeningly teased my nostrils.

Brother Frederick's laugh, almost a woman's laugh, came high and quick, a spasm that seemed to bounce off the air. Then he breathed deep, lowered his voice.

"Well, Thinker, you are now carousing in the public house of heresy; but that will be our secret, eh? So, you say God the Father is the Creator. What is that?"

"The one who makes things."

"Out of what?"

"Out of nothing."

"The nature of God the Father is to make things from nothing." Slow nodding. "Then what is the nature of the Son? "

"The Son is the Savior."

"Oh." Deep nodding again. "Savior of what?"

"Of us."

"God the Son is savior of the work of God the Father?" Fingers to his ear lobe again. "Then God the Father must be closer to Zeus than we give countenance."

The clang of the Call to Supper parted the air--down-stroke, up-stroke, down-stroke, harsh at first, then feathering over the orchards of St. Bartholomew, the crooked streets of Exeter and the hills of Devon.

"And God number three? Its nature?"

I hesitated. "The Purifier." What could I do?

Brother Frederick nodded solemnly. "Then it appears this God the Father is some kind of apprentice cook needing others to swoop in and fix His mistakes before they show." A lift of his chin in the direction of the door. "Well, your aunt will be looking for you. Take those loose strawberries. We don't want our scholars fainting in the streets. And my thanks for your company of a Sunday afternoon."

I stood as well. What was the nature of the Three Persons? Never before had I asked myself such questions that left me so at sea. But this monk here, and others like him in mind, had sailed, had seen, and had come home again.

He pressed the book we studied upon me. "Fodder for your fire."

I nodded blindly. What was the nature of the Three? And I was half way to the door before I came to my senses I had not even thanked him, nor bade him farewell.

The next week he struck out in a new direction. For it was his way to start me thinking, then leave me to it. He set a pitcher of mead between us and asked, "What of these Stoics, then?"

When I replied that they would do without the Gods of the Ancients, he drew back as if appalled. "No God? Surely then there must be a king to make laws."

"No, Brother. They would have no one but man."

Well, Brother Frederick made out as if I had said an ox should be put in charge of civil order, scoring his head with the heel of his hand and going off to fetch bread.

When he returned with part of a loaf from breakfast, I forged on saying the Stoics believed man to be implanted with a sense of "right reason" by the Spirit of the Universe; and that such knowledge keeps man from impurities. I felt a bit pleased with myself, I must admit. "One Stoic wrote, 'You, O man, are God; and it is within yourself you carry Him.'"

Brother Frederick turned silent as he broke the bread, his mind deep into the Stoics, or some other. The late afternoon light, closed off by the garden door, made the shadowy room feel full of secrets. Brother Isadore cut cabbages into the great cauldron at the hearth. On a far table sat the two loaves left over from breakfast, covered by napkins to keep them clean for dinner. We chewed in silence.

"Who speaks, do you think, when an oracle speaks, Young Scholar?"

My teacher seemed always to ask the most difficult questions just when dinner smells turned my head into meat.

"I don't know, Brother."

He stared away to the open kitchen door, then turned blue eyes upon me. "Who are our oracles then, do you think?"

"The Pope? Bishops?" I proffered empty palms. "But do they speak from the Holy Book or directly from--." I pointed above, hesitant to say the name "God" myself, for I still had many unanswered questions. "Hermits claim to receive words directly from Jesus, or saints or angels; but I do not know if such perceptions come from sound minds."

A great flapping sound, then, and a violent stirring of the air as a large crow sailed through the open kitchen door, swooped low to knock our cups from our trestle and splash mead into our laps. As we stood to shake off the wet, we saw the bird grab from the trestle beyond one loaf of the two awaiting supper, and the cloth with it. Stroking hard, it mounted to the ceiling to fly there in circles while Brother Isadore, his face and scalp a furious red, waddled after it, swiping with a raised broom and bellowing, "Drop our bread, you thieving beggar. God gives you food of your own. Drop ours or by St. Peter I'll--."

We watched the bird's shadow sail the ceiling, then Brother Isadore's, with a raised broom, cross the lower walls. At the open doorway, the two fell into the bodies to which they belonged, then sprang apart again to race into the garden. I heard Brother Isadore's furious rant, "I'll send you where the devils come from, black demon. And God Himself hold me righteous!"

I covered a smile. Brother Frederick let out a little sigh and stood. "We were short on bread to begin with. I'd better lend a hand. I'll pull a few more carrots and cut some rosemary into the soup."

I slipped out just as Brother Isadore staggered back into the kitchen, clutching his heaving chest.

Later in my life, I would come to see that through our conversations, Brother Frederick showed me there is no wall into which a question cannot cut a doorway, then free you to cut more. And I call him "my great teacher" for he opened to me my own mind and set me to using it by taking me down the roads he himself had trod; and so readied me for much that life would demand.

Thus, from about eight to sixteen years, I would go back and forth from Uncle's blacksmith shop to the school of my betters from which, despite its privilege, I must sometimes be absent because of the need for me at the shop. And it was within those walls I found the great teacher who gave me a sanctuary in which to grow my mind.

CHAPTER SIX

Some months later, a young mistress barely older than myself, just sixteen then, came to the smithy with horse and cart. We all knew her from earlier days as one whose body had ripened early and who dressed now in pleasing colors and with ribbons in her hair--a free spirit with an eye on the lads and something not quite proper to say to make them laugh, especially if they were but fourteen or fifteen. And were I outside when she drove by, she would open her full lips and cry out to me "Heigh! Jo-phiel!" as if she were loosing a bird.

She was married early to a slow-witted villein, one easily led, but with a strong body, a scrap of land and small but well-built house. Not more than a few months past the wedding, she began to bring vegetables and eggs to market, and a cart or harnesses to us for repairs. Our men talked amongst themselves that with her lively spirit, she must be missing Exeter; and that living out there so far beyond the wall must be wearisome to her.

This one day, every other man helping to repair a crack in St. Petroc's bell, I was handling orders as they came in. So it was me stepped forward as she pulled up at the front; and with the din and clatter of banging on the bell I could barely hear her.

"Ah, Jophiel," she raised her voice, "I get the handsome one, eh?"

I found her remark forward; still it pleased me a little. But, as a caution, I kept my eyes from her face.

"How can I serve you, Mistress?"

"I fear this harness is about to break," she made her eyes wide and helpless. "And the horse is in an evil temper and could run away with me."

Though married, she wore her hair loose, and a low-cut bodice; and it being a hot day, the skirt of her gown up over her knees to give her legs air. "Also," she twisted and pointed, "I felt the wheel on the left wobble as I came through South Gate. Now, you wouldn't want me losing my control, eh, Jophiel?" She raised an eyebrow and her eyes danced.

The horse started directly toward the back where he knew the stables and hay to be, and where we handled things large as a cart.

I came behind on foot, studying the wheel when I wasn't watching her black hair shaken by the breeze, the sunlight sliding up and down it and breaking into colors. But that wheel of hers, passing then through its everlasting sleeve of brown dust, looked to me to be steady and true. And I said so.

"But you can see yourself from here that wheel is wrong," she stopped the cart in the shade of the huge elm and climbed down.

I came alongside, bent my knees, squinted, then shook my head. "I believe it looks right enough, Mistress."

I could not help but notice a soft scent about her, like

apples and fresh-turned earth. And in the tree's deep shadow, how her skin bloomed white.

"No," she pointed again; "can't you see it's not the same as its mate?"

To satisfy her, I leaned a fraction nearer to study the wheel again; and then she was reaching over as if to grasp me while at the same time I felt myself come ablaze, and a sudden sharp sound directly at my elbow clapping at the air three, four times. My eyes wheeled to the side, and there our smithy's yellow mongrel was bounding back and forth, his gold eyes mad with excitement, his tail thrashing.

Horrified, I pulled back and onto my feet; and, sweat running crown to foot, I escaped to the woods nearby where we men take care of our needs. I quieted myself, combed my fingers through my hair and set my garments in order. I had come face to face with my own appetites and their power to sway me to act against all common sense. It had both stunned and frightened me. And for the first time I understood the merriment at the smithy over such things; and why men and women so fiercely do together what they do.

Walking back, I saw her make a perfectly balanced turn off Magdalene and through South Gate, her raven hair glistening and blowing, both wheel and harness clearly in perfect working order.

One day soon after, in a sweat and lifting the water dipper, I looked up over its rim, and there under the elm sat a young man I had never seen before, and with a small folio in his hands. I remembered a little earlier the wagon of a well-to-do customer pulling up. The horses were to have new shoes, and a hoop on one of the wheels needed repair. It would be half a day's work. Uncle Anthony had taken the order since I was shaping pickets for a customer. I leaned away from the barrel and poured the cool water over my head, then dipped the ladle again.

This youth seemed near my own age, perhaps sixteen years; but taller and more slender-built; and with fine hair the color of walnuts. He dressed in a green tunic with rust-colored stockings and sleeves, all good worsted; and a girdle fitted with a silver buckle. Perhaps he heard the water gurgle, for he looked up, smiled, then bobbed his head.

"I believe your shop must challenge the sun today; and have all of you," he pointed with his chin toward the smithy, "turning on a spit."

I grinned. "Ay, Sir. Could you use some water, yourself?" I had noticed his hairline wet and tunic darkened at the waist.

"Anything to put this smoldering out." He unfolded his legs and stood to join me, the book hanging from his hand. Someone my age who reads! The sight took my breath away. Ah, but beyond matters of business, it was not my place as a tradesman to presume equality with one of wealth. Still, I could not help crooking my neck for the title as he took the dipper, drank deep, put his hand to the barrel to wet his face, neck and hair, then shook out his wet hair like a dog. The water flew everywhere; and when he straightened, he found me blotting my face with the back of my hand.

"Oh! Beg pardon. All I could think of was to be wet."

"Only my pleasure, Sir." I bowed.

We laughed together, then. His frank grey and gold-flecked eyes seemed to conceal nothing; and his manner being so open, I swallowed and dared a question.

"Is it a work of instruction or pleasure then, Master?" I nodded toward the book.

And how his eyes opened further at this; and as if I had by some spell been turned me into a completely different man.

"What, you are a reader then? Why this one is both to me, friend, for it is a work I choose. Can you sit? I'll show you."

"For a moment." I had finished one order and not yet started the next.

He gestured toward the elm tree. I followed, my hunger to share with someone who reads compelling as a meat pie to a starving man. We sprawled where the shade was dense. And how I relished the smell of that parchment as the pages strained against the thick binding thread as he turned them. And from their sound, I slipped into that strange country of safety and peace manuscripts always brought to me.

"French?" I recognized some simple words on the opened page from our lessons at the Common School where, if we made mistakes, the cleric shouted corrections as to the deaf.

"By the way, I am Edward," the young master held out his hand.

This took me aback. To us, the wealthy were at the very least aloof, if not hot-tempered and unpredictable. We hold our tongues before them; and it is usually as if through a stone wall they seem to think they must speak to us. But this Edward, why his face was open, his clasp straightforward as if he saw no difference between us.

"Jophiel, here." I offered in return; and standing at the water barrel, we spoke of the smithy, the weather, of the dizzying tangle of Exeter's thronging streets.

"I come and go to Norman country with my father." Back under the tree, Edward stretched out upon his elbow, "and where he always retires early. So I am free to prowl and see what's going on." He dropped his voice, leaned toward me. "There is a new music and poetry struggling up amongst the young people there; but spoken of and practiced secretly, for the Church and the old ones would be up at arms should they know of it. But I tell you, it has robust life, and soon will be the mode among young men like us, and young women as well. Have you not heard of it yet?"

"Every day my ears ring with the banging of anvils, shouting of oaths and whinny of horses," I grinned, sheepish. "So when I can, I take myself to the woods for quiet.".

"Yes, but you are hearing of it now," he urged. "And so it makes its way mouth to mouth. They call it 'Amore' or 'Fin Amour'." He smiled at my surprise. "Yes, it is about love, a new way to think about love and marriage. And a new music grows from it; and those who compose and sing such songs are called 'troubadours'." And as he spoke it, that word seemed to cling to his tongue as if he could never taste of it enough.

Well, he intended to live by these principles of Amour, he confided, if he should be so blessed as to have need of them. "And how would you judge it if a lad chose a wife by feelings of the heart alone? And a maid choose her own husband? The Church condemns such a thing as license, as I'm sure you know well enough." The delicate and willowy Ihelde given over to Teewaye and his darkness.

Grinning, Edward rolled his sleeves off his arms and propped his back against the elm tree's trunk to practice from a primer the past tense for 'to enter'. The breeze dropped, the heat built up. Above us, magpies screamed and shook the tree's branches. Edward looked up warily and we both laughed. And how was it I could I feel this comfortable with someone above my station and that I had just met?

"When my father was a babe here," Edward gathered his hair and twisted a leather thong about it to give his neck air, "everyone spoke some French. But never mind. Don't we English overcome all others? And we do it not with implements of war, but by swallowing them so slowly they don't notice! And so it is that the Normans as well have lost themselves in us. My father has had a serving woman since he was a boy who speaks French, but," and he gave me a mischievous look, "I'm not sure she knows that to which my songs refer; and" he threw his hands, "t'is surely not my place to school a gran'mam."

"Well," I laughed, "I have heard words on the street from women that made me gape. But you play the lute also?" My own work had now vanished from my mind, for Edward was as a new book; and I could think of nothing but to read.

"I have some experience with the lute." His gaze shifted to a chestnut mare of his father's being shod, but kept dancing away. "That one hates getting shoes. Oh, but when she must walk on stones, why she picks her shod feet up like a princess," he laughed. "But do you play an instrument?"

I shrugged. "The penny whistle. Songs I've heard, a few I make up."

He nodded, paused. "I wrote a thing or two you might have patience to hear some time. Troubadour music is not difficult, except to find the words!" He pulled a scrap of vellum from inside his tunic. "Here are words to something I tried to take down sung in French." He traced along with his finger. "'He went to her chamber fair/ something, something, and something / But ever after on every tongue/ the something, something and something did run/ to Cannes and Rouen, to Paris, to Limoges--.' And that's all I could get." He slapped the book. "If I don't learn French, I'll never find out what or who it was ran to all those places, though I can imagine the reason."

Well, we had a good laugh at that; and our voices must have drawn my uncle for he appeared at the smithy door, took in the two of us, then waved to me.

I climbed to my feet. "More gears," I grinned at Edward, "or something, something and something." How I hated to end our talk.

He stood as well. "My father often uses your services. I come along sometimes and idle about the town. When I learn the words to this song, I'll come by and play it, or bring one of my own; and we'll see if any you have writ will suit this lute."

I colored a little. "I regret work here doesn't always allow me time..."

He waved me off. "When you can. Who knows, with my pate it may not be until Michaelmas next. In any case," he gestured toward the tree, "here is a wonderful place to learn French verbs. And perhaps we can talk again between dippers of water."

I nodded, started away and turned back. "Have you read Herodotus by chance?"

"Lord, yes." Edward rolled his eyes. "What a picture of humans he paints."

I started to laugh. "Sometimes I read from it after dinner to my aunt and uncle. So one day my uncle came to work with the tale about the betrayer who dismembered a serving boy to cook and present as a dinner dish. And all to spite the King. Do you remember?"

"Ay, I do indeed." Edward nodded with vigor.

"Now when we leave for supper, someone will remind the rest to be sure they know who it is before they sit down to eat."

Edward threw back his head and roared. "I'll have to tell that to my father." He wiped his eyes. "The one I like is--"

But Uncle Anthony was at the door again.

"I must go. I am so sorry," I apologized.

We shook hands and I hurried to see what Uncle Anthony needed. I truly hated to leave, I had enjoyed myself so much.

Walking home that night, Uncle Anthony told me he regretted having to pull me away from such lively talk; but that customer who ordered the gate locks had come by. "As you know, he is one must check and check; and wants everything right away."

We trod on in silence in the cooling air, dogs and children underfoot and a fingernail of new moon just rising over the trees.

"Who spoke first?" Uncle Anthony asked me then. I could feel the worry eating him. When I said it was Edward, he relaxed. It was, I knew, most unusual for one who was wealthy to spend time with one below him. Probably it had been for an amusement. Probably I would never see Edward again. And I felt then, keen as a knife cut, my great hunger for a youth of an age and mind akin to my own. And then the old melancholy of so many doors locked against so many flooded in yet another time.

A fortnight later, Old Guill, Barrel and myself were pounding clench nails for a shipbuilder at Exmouth as if the devil himself were after us--one at the fire and the water barrel, one pounding on the anvil, one filing off rough spots--and all rotating like gears in near perfect time when I heard a wagon crunch along to the back, and hoped it was not an order for shoeing.

After a bit, Uncle Anthony had young Thomas set his broom aside to go down London Road for ale, a signal my uncle felt we had things in hand; so we began to work more relaxed and to let the softer sounds of the world came back piece by piece. As the ale arrived, a new sound, one like pebbles dropped in water, threaded through the open doorway. Uncle handed me two tankards and pointed with his chin of red and grey hair toward the back. "Master Edward asks after you." He glanced at the pile of horseshoes. "You're most of the way, now. Let Guill and Barrel finish up."

Edward sat cross-legged under the tree; and I thought I had never seen anything so beautiful as the lute that filled his lap, its long narrow neck bent at the top to a right angle and fitted with wooden tuning pegs, its body the shape of half of a pear; and where on the front the fruit's seeds would cluster, a circle was cut out and embellished with tiny strips of wood delicately wrought to look like the open face of a flower.

Edward looked up and smiled, his long fingers so alive as they arched and sprang along the neck or slid up or down the strings to set the very air aquiver. Rapt, I placed the tankard near him, then sat upon the ground. And Uncle leaned at the doorframe to listen as Edward finished with a flurry, striking across the strings, then pulling his wrist high, palm and fingers a bird flung into the air. The beauty of the gesture made me gasp. Would that I had hands to do such a thing! And I burst into applause. But Edward made a staying gesture. "My teacher points out every day how little I know, my friend." He squinted one eye, as though figuring sums. "Perhaps in a year I may be ready to approach the gentler sex with a simple offering."

And how I wanted to ask if he had someone in mind, but held back out of customary courtesy.

"If you still are willing, and though I am yet no troubadour, last time we met I threatened a song I am guilty of, about a young man moved by the Springtime."

I spread out eager palms; and the slow notes of introduction came; and then his voice, high and sweet.

"I kiss your lips a long, long time.
They are cherries in the snow.
And I would grasp your plentiousness,
and other gifts would know, would know;
and other gifts would know.

Keep not yourself away from me
when time is right withal.
The full-blown fruit does heavy hang
and from the tree does fall, does fall;
and from the tree does fall.

Oh, Springtime is a time for love,
when all God's creatures woo.
'Tis by His law, sweet maiden bright,
your treasures I pursue, pursue;
your treasures I pursue.

So come to me and willingly.
We shall our worship make.
And say, "Amen" and start again
and all our pleasure take, oh take;
and all our pleasure take."

Well, you can imagine that I could but turn to him with
the broadest of smiles, for never before had I heard such desires so
forthrightly tied both to the Maker of our bodies and to this earth
from which we come. Here was praise for the very appetite, so
desired and so dangerous. And God Himself its cause. This was a
song of truth. I burst into "Huzzah!"

"Here," Edward, looking very pleased, suddenly held out
the lute. "Try it yourself."

But I shook my head. "Nay, these are anvils here, Sir," I
showed him my hands scarred from blacksmithing. "Your lute is

too fine-crafted a thing for such rough paws as mine that surely would break it."

"Oh, I think not. And if you can be enough at ease, between us, do call me Edward."

Well, it would be some months before I could come to that; and it was only the eagerness in his face that day gave me courage to take up the lute. The instrument's heft surprised me, though I was terror-struck it might roll off my knees and shatter upon the ground.

"Just pass your fingers over the strings, so." He gave a loose swag with his hand. I tried to imitate it, but purchased so loud a sound I near let go the neck. But no, he would have me try again 'til I could soften the instrument's voice. "Now, to make a harmonic--." He stretched my fingers to press three strings, then; and a beautiful sound, higher but more mournful, spoke from the lute's belly. I went on, but only to drive away the dozing yellow dog and offend my own ears. I handed the instrument back. "With the fingers of a garden fork, I think I'd best listen and not further stress the delicate nature of your instrument."

Edward shook his head. "It but takes practice, Jophiel; and I swear I was your very twin when I began." Suddenly, his eyes lighted. "Have you your flute?" I jerked my head toward the shop. "Entertain me with it, if you will, and have the time." He stretched out his legs and picked a new stem of grass for his teeth while I hurried inside.

As I played "Of A Bright Morn," he took up his lute to pluck low notes, as it were, under my melody. And when he played "Sorrow Flowers," I made my whistle to speak with a high distant voice of longing. And we tried songs of childhood. As you may know, our common women are nursemaids to the children of their betters; and in this way, the songs of the poor become the songs of the rich. So, with Edward's lute and my penny whistle, my new friend and I tested songs we knew or could discover; and so enjoyed ourselves enormously.

After that, when we could meet, if we didn't make music,

we walked Exeter's streets or sat by a brook to argue Plato and
Socrates and other Ancients, poring over a folio page, clapping
one another on the back or pointing to a word or phrase to clench a
case, equals testing in ourselves and each other the life of mind and
spirit. And soon enough, Edward would know my family and pay
them courtesies. And I, his.

Probably you are already familiar with how our cathedral's
massive towers were built by workmen erecting a hill of dirt
to carry to the masons the stones split below. As I passed the
cathedral one day delivering some fancy-worked door hinges, I saw
something in common with that way of building and my own life:
How Mamoon, Uncle Anthony, Father Stephan, Brother Frederick
and now Edward each raised me a step higher than I envisioned
for myself. And there is one other person to whom I must also
give credit for my enrichment. I had since I was a youth of fifteen
years been in love at a distance with a golden-haired maid I would
see from afar at Lammas. Her name was Sarah Dorset; and she
intruded upon my dreams.

CHAPTER SEVEN

August first brings the celebration of First Harvest we call Lammas, a day sacred from pagan times; and one the Church now claims for herself. Mamoon told me First Harvest was practiced when she was a maid; and that in those days no one went to any church for Lammas; and that all those ways she told of came from plain people honoring the earth.

But these days, such customs are preached as sinful; and the practice of The Scattering of the First Loaf, bread baked from the earliest grain of the season, must begin now with a blessing by the priest in church before ordinary people touch it. Plain men and women we are, and know well enough out of our own good sense and for some mite of safety and peace, that we must hold our tongues about what has been taken from us. So we keep our heads bowed for the priest to see, and tolerate what cannot be overcome.

Ah, but the moment we step from the church onto the street, then Lammas since ancient of English days belongs to the people!

The Lord Mayor raises a stuffed white glove fixed to a pole, and two young ones behind him carry the carefully-saved first loaf of the first harvest of the year past. Then down St. Martin's Lane we throng past St. Petroc's, chanting "Follow the glove" and, turning out at North Gate into Hay, big as four pastures and still chanting, "Follow the glove." And there it is that the First Loaf is broken and scattered for the birds. And we feed Nature as she feeds us! And we celebrate!

From among vendors' wagons and stalls, over bursts and trailings of music, you'll hear the racket from feats and contests of lances and shields, wrestling, running races, horse races, jumping tests, stone throwing, javelin hurling, archery as well as cheers and swearing from those who bet on them. Spaces are set aside for rest and pleasant distractions: juggling, tightrope and stilt walking, fire eating, puppet wagons, the singing and the playing of instruments and dancing on the Green by the maids.

And twice a week, smaller markets are held here or other places. To this one, Aunt Mathilde brings her dolls and spiced fruit for sale. When Mamoon was alive, Aunt also sold a special healing honey of my Gran'mam's. I would carry the heavy buckets out, then bring the coins home in a pouch strung under my tunic so Teewaye wouldn't know.

And it was at Lammas I first saw Sarah Dorset. I was just fifteen.

She was the oldest of the brood and came along, the younger ones at her hip or clinging to her skirts, while the mother, big with child, trailed behind, leaning upon her husband's arm. My uncle knew him, a dairyman who supplied the nobles and was also Uncle's customer. Sarah was no older than thirteen then, and with a great braid of golden hair down her back and the promise of womanhood budding in a gown the blue of robin's eggs, the bodice fitted to the waist, and sleeve ends at a point over the backs of her hands. As she walked, I remember, I watched her skirt tumble like wild grasses in the wind. I can see it to this day.

And I noticed her gentleness in drawing the hair off her sister's face, guiding a younger brother with a finger to his shoulder, patting the baby's fat legs as they went along. I found something quiet and joyful in her step, and her face soft, but open, too, as a good day. A rope of fairy gold bound with rose-colored ribbons of nearly the same hue as her cheek hung down her back. A boy about eight led the way with a girl about six. Another boy about three dandled Sarah's braid as she went along, her eyes blue as a summer sky. A fair, fair maid.

Those eyes first discovered me with Uncle and his friends booming by in the other direction, myself a bit ahead and hurrying to a stall of leathers. As she came along, I felt stopped in my tracks. It was as if she were a meadow I'd stumbled into and couldn't leave. When we passed, she raised her eyes to mine already fixed upon her; and in the space of a breath we silently bespoke ourselves of something not yet understood; then both looked away, confused.

I staggered up to the leathers stall and turned for a last glimpse of her, and saw her father stop to talk with my uncle. And how my heart leapt, then fell; for I was too far along to go back with no reason! All I could do was to pass the leather pieces through my hands, breathe the tanning fumes and miss my chance to meet her.

That was a Sunday. Next midday, at work I sat next to Uncle and going over accounts. The day fair and hot, a fine breeze blew through the shop. "I wonder about the man you spoke with at Lammas." Very casual, I held out bread for us to share.

"What man?" Eyebrows pinched, he ripped the small loaf in half. "Oh, Master Dorset, the dairyman?" He chewed and swallowed. "What about him?"

I pushed my lower lip out, shrugged indifference, my face heating. I said I had noticed his bearing was all. Uncle's eyes puzzled over me. I saw rightly, he told me then, for the family had served nobility with dairy goods for four or five generations. Next to Master Dorset, my uncle declared he was but a babe learning to walk, though his smithy was the busiest in Exeter and beyond.

"We do work he likes. Those three wheels there wanting rims are his." I had seen them against the wall, but now they lit with magic. I said it couldn't hurt to have a customer with kin who might also become customers. Bog, so-named for his continual sweating, was fussing nearby with a broken latch and had an ear for our talk.

"Especially that fairest one," he said in a high pinched voice and fluttering his lashes; "Her being the one most worthy of knowing."

Laughter broke out everywhere, the rest waiting to see my face flame. I felt a spike of anger at having my feelings so easily uncovered, but had to laugh a little with them. Bog's eyes softened. "I believe my sister's friend works at that dairy. What would you care to discover about the young mistress?"

Of course I felt the fool all over again, neck and face on fire; and could think only that I wanted to know her, to speak with her about--I heaved my shoulders in a shrug--I couldn't think what.

"Aw," Bog tipped his head and turned to the rest. "Here now, help me get this pitiful flaming wretch to the water barrel afore nothing's left 'a him." This got a resounding laugh, and Uncle saved me by ordering everyone back to their work. So the ringing of anvils took up, then; and I spent the afternoon smoothing nail heads.

But next fair was a search for her, though I told myself, Listen, who needs an excuse to go to a fair? And how could I possibly come to know her, being of a different estate in work and family; and still too young for the things I would not allow myself to daydream? And indeed, I did see her at that fair, but at a distance and with no excuse to draw near. And what chance is there she might ever have an eye for me who must appear a cur of a youth keeping company with a cohort of blacksmiths; and with a family history so easily uncovered as full of violence?

But at Autumn Equinox, luck and my uncle were with

me. Our family and hers passed by, and the two men stopped for a word. I hung behind, trying not to stare. Her gown was of saffron; and she had white roses plaited in her hair. My knees turned to water as Uncle reached for my arm. "My nephew, Jophiel," he said. I bowed stiffly, my eyes pinned to the ground. The father in turn passed my name to his wife, to Sarah and the children.

As the two men talked business, the children lost patience, craning their necks after the stilt walker and fiddler. Master Dorset told Sarah to take them to the puppet wagon and buy them a sweet. As she herded the company off in that direction, the little lad of three years scuttled into the crowd. Sarah turned to follow, but her other charges dashed toward the wagon; and though she called after them, they did not stop; and so she must follow them.

I sprinted into the throng after the little devil. Burrowing under a stall curtain, I caught him up about the waist and brought him back on my shoulders. We sat on the ground to watch the puppets while the little runner pulled at my ears. But I had great patience with small children. And for this chance to help Sarah, who held the fat baby in her arms besides tending the older ones, the three year-old vagrant could have unscrewed my nose for drawing animals in the dirt and I would never have complained.

She went for sweets for the children and a wine drink for us while the puppets pounded one another with poles and brooms and the young ones screamed their delight. Back again, I asked for names. Well, the little fugitive was Thad. Then with each name, she reported his or her particular humors and gifts. I followed with the names in my uncle's brood. Then together we dug out puppet shows we had seen as children; and her laughter came as small waves bursting into a fan of white drops. And all too soon, the puppets flopped into their bows.

Back at the tree, her mother cooled herself in the shade while the men still traded business talk. Uncle got up, ready to go when he saw us. Sarah's father pried the little runaway from my back. And so the day ended with no promise of more, save that Master Dorset had ordered some wheel repairs.

The eight wheels were finished ten days after their delivery to the smithy. Oh, and I made sure I secured a place with my uncle on the wagon to take them to the father's dairy farm!

As we rolled toward the house, Sarah, strewing feed for the chickens and ducks, had her back to us; but when she heard horses and the dogs yapping, she came over to greet us and to say in her soft-spoken way, her eyes touching every face but mine, that she would tell her father we had arrived and get some men to help unload.

Master Dorset and my uncle talked while the rest of us began to roll the wheels down a plank and across the yard to where we would attach them to the cart beds. Being quite cumbersome, it took two or three of us to manage each wheel. Sarah lingered near the door in the shade cast by the roof thatch to watch us work. I could feel her eyes upon me. My face turned red, and as I grappled with a wheel, her father called across the yard, "Lad, best you be indoors. From the look of it, you've been too long in the sun."

This set everyone to howling, and I saw Sarah hide her laughter behind her hand. Well, what could I do but plunge even more into the work? Hands still covering her smile, Sarah ran to her brother and sister, as if to attend them at play; but glanced at me over her shoulder with a worried face, as if she feared she might have shamed me. Oh, but I already knew her heart, that it was too pure for any such intent; and that these things could not be helped, shy as we both were: Shy, shy, shy.

It was near the end of winter before I saw her again. We were just closing up when a worker I recognized from the Dorset place came pounding on horseback to the smithy wild-eyed and sliding from the animal before it was fully stopped, and calling for Uncle Anthony. The alarm in his voice cut through the empty building; and Uncle and I, in the back totaling up, left everything undone.

Mistress Agnes, Aunt Mathilde's sister, was needed. "Mistress Dorset is gone into labor; and her own midwife is ill."

His eyes were wild. Aunt Agnes was the next nearest midwife to
the Dorset farm; and Aunt Mathilde often assisted her. Uncle gave
the rider a cup of mead and sent me with the carriage for Aunt
Agnes who lived out West Gate and across the bridge over the Exe
in St. Thomas parish.

It was dark when I reached her cottage. I had only to
say, "Mistress Dorset's time is come," and she pulled her shawl
about her shoulders and lifted the midwife bag she kept ready. At
Uncle's house, Aunt Mathilde climbed in. These sisters were near
a repetition of one another with strong generous bodies, blue eyes,
round pink cheeks, blond hair; and two years apart. But all I could
think was Sarah's worry for her mother. I whistled to the horses,
snapped the reins and turned down London Road to St.Vitalis
Parish and the dairy farm, my heart pounding above the hooves. I
would see Sarah again.

The moon was up when I pulled in. The cottage door
flew open; light spilled out around Master Dorset. I saw his face
so drawn as he hurried the women inside. "--and heavy pain too
early," he was saying. A stable hand came to take the horses; and
there Sarah was, the little ones at her skirts, and holding the door
open for me.

The large front room held a cheerful hearth, windows with
glass, well-made cushioned benches and trestles for both kitchen
work and eating, as well as hinged boxes, linen cupboards, barrels
and shelves for kitchen supplies, pottery and utensils. Sarah took
my cloak to hang up on a wall peg. Two rooms were to the side;
and from under one, whose door fit imperfectly, came the low
anxious voices of Master Dorset and my aunts.

On the trestle by the hearth sat little toy carts, carved
horses and men in armor. A soft rag doll with a tiny wooden
drinking cup next it slept under a blanket. Sarah brought mead
and we sat while the children knelt on the benches or crawled
through our legs acting out stories requiring we become kindly
goblins popping up with gifts and magic rings, and distracting
them from the mother's groaning and crying out that sent shivers

over my arms. Sarah's face would pale and her eyes go dark; but she put herself to the young ones, busying them with play. I gave rides on my hands and knees, now a kindly and now a disobedient horse, especially for little Thad who recalled our game together at Lammas the summer past.

Master Dorset stayed in the room when the women would allow it, and that not often as he liked. When he came out, he tried to explain things to us in simple terms, or went outside to walk around the cottage. Without comment, we would watch him pass the windows. He was a man of goodly stature, taller than Uncle but not so muscled, yet his body had that hardening that comes from work. And there was goodly grey in his hair he kept tied back; and he had large hands and a squared manly face that knew weather; but it was the fear behind his eyes and need to be near his wife that told me the situation was dangerous.

Finally we climbed the ladder to settle the children for sleep. Since the fire on the hearth was kept up for boiling water, their sleeping platform was comfortably warm. Well, and Sarah could have crawled in with them, she looked that tired.

We climbed down again and went to get more mead for us to drink on the bench near the hearth, leaning our backs against the wall. Her mother's cries would come from under the door, and I could only imagine what went through Sarah's mind. Oh and how I wanted to comfort, to protect her. We could hear my aunts' voices as well, steady, encouraging; but the night wore on with only more of the same; and I believe everyone began to fear the worst. Finally, Sarah and I gave up trying to talk and just sat silent, waiting for whatever would be.

And dark still crowded the windows when a sound thin as a thread, the wail of the newborn, climbed the air. And you can imagine we breathed some relief; but the mother was not safe yet, for there was still the birth sack to come. Aunt asked for more rags, her face lined with fatigue and worry.

It must have been the darkest part of night; and I had my head against the wall, my eyes closed for what seemed but a moment when I felt Sarah's head and shoulders topple onto my lap, and her flaxen hair, come loose from its plait, hanging down my legs.

Well, you can imagine that I dared not breathe, but laid my arms out along the bench top where it meets the wall and held still as I could, dazzled by the gift of her. Then, so moved by all her travails, and by what she might yet undergo, I found I was stroking her hair, but then snatched my hand back, such a thing not being honorable without her leave. Later, her father coming again from the bedroom, glanced down at us and saw my predicament, his daughter fallen asleep across me; but spoke no word, only clapped me lightly upon the shoulder and smiled the smallest smile.

Daylight. The birth sack freed itself as the cock crowed. Sarah shuddered, and I saw her eyes open to stare across the room. Then she turned her head and studied my face above her, then sat up in a hurry, embarrassed, smoothing her hair and kirtle. I didn't know what to say or do; but then she ducked her head and started to laugh. And I laughed too. And we stood up, and she got mead and bread from the cupboard for us.

We ate, and Aunt Mathilde came from the room.

"Your mother sleeps," she cocked her head at Sarah, "and you have another sister now to help one day with those boys."

While my aunts packed up, we waited quietly together. I didn't know how I could leave her, and took her hand, wanting to speak of things in my heart, but finding no words. Small and soft her hand felt; and she let it rest in mine. When I foundered, she covered our two hands with her free hand. "Thank you," she gave to me her face so serious and so beautiful, "for your gentleness and your strength, Jophiel."

Then Aunt Agnes bustled out with her bag; and I took it to the wagon while she embraced Sarah. Then I stood speechless; and it was all I could do to drag my eyes from Sarah's face. Finally I must mount the wagon and whistle to the horses. But to leave her there seeing us down the road tore away something in me; and from that time on, I wanted nothing so much as to be at her side. And I was a man completely in love.

The next day, I would too often find myself stopped and staring into space. One time at the anvil, all the smiths and helpers but my uncle gathered 'round, grinning and waiting to see how long 'til I came out of it.

"He can't be fainted, can he, standing with his eyes open?"

"Look! I think he's coming around now."

"Don't get your hopes up. He may go under again."

"Is it something he et, do you think?" This from the boy who sweeps.

I heard the voices, saw the bodies; but it was some long moment before I knew they had aught to do with me.

"Heigh now! Has there been an accident? Else why would you all be standing around, under heaven?"

Every face turned to Uncle at the door striding toward the circle and brooking no jest. "Is something amiss?" He turned to Bog who opened and closed his mouth, to the others. "I left you with orders. Are they ready then?"

And everyone hurried back to his work.

Toward the end of the day, Uncle strolled over. "Help me with the bills when you finish that piece," he said. "And we'll let Bog close up."

Well, I was glad for the work, to keep my mind on business.

We finished the accounts in an hour, then went over to the public house he favored. The night was mild for early spring, the doors left open. The owner brought half a pigeon and some of the day's bread with our mead.

We spoke first of business: A big order for gates. Who should be put on which job, and who keep our regulars serviced? Uncle prided himself on getting everything done and making everyone happy. He was my mentor this way, and you can believe I felt privileged, young as I was, to have a part in the running of his business.

He ordered mead again. "Did I tell you Master Dorset came by while you took those spokes across town?"

My heart knocked against my ribs. I had missed him and the chance he might tell Sarah he had seen me. To a starving man, any crumb is good as a meal. I shook my head, no.

"Ah," he nodded, took a draught. "He came by specially, he told me, to thank me for the help with Mistress Dorset's birthing."

"Is Mistress Dorset well? And the babe?" I would have cared anyway, but they were Sarah's family.

"Fine. And gaining strength. The little one's a lusty howler. He said he wanted me to know what a great support you were, Jophiel, at such a difficult time, especially to Sarah. He says you helped with the young ones and sat up all night, though she finally fell asleep, it was all so hard. But that you stayed awake in case you were needed." The skin around his eyes crinkled. My face burned, but I felt relief, too, and a happiness I didn't dare to touch.

"Master Dorset says Sarah was so tired she fell asleep across your lap."

His eyes danced. My face burned red as the fire; but I laughed too.

"She fell over on me. And I didn't dare move or breathe. That was how I stayed awake."

Uncle Anthony threw back his head and slapped his knee.

The place was filling now with boisterous hardworking men shaking off the day. Uncle and I leaned closer. "Both Aunt and Master Dorset," he went on, "marked the kindness--and closeness--that seems to have grown between you and Sarah. And your aunt notices that the young mistress returns your interest. Master Dorset, when he was here, told me he saw Sarah's trust in you to be deep, and that she finds a rare comfort in you. The closeness of heart he felt he saw between you as he was in and out of the birthing room, he said struck him; and that you are a fine young man, one to be proud of."

Oh, but those words were birdsong: That our families had spoken of feelings I had not yet dared draw near myself, much less voice.

"So then you favor this maiden, the young Mistress Sarah, do you?" Uncle Anthony was all care, then, studying my face.

In my eagerness, I all but stood, bursting to announce Sarah's virtues to him and to the world: To tell of the deep and courageous heart that lay beneath her shyness; to say I wanted but to provide for her, protect and see her happy. Having thus made myself utterly naked, I stopped abruptly and grabbed my mead.

But Uncle Anthony sat silent, looking long into the fire.

"T'is a deep love," he nodded slowly, eyes still upon the logs, his face serene in a way I have seen only on some after they receive the Host. "When one wants to guard the other and provide, but not with any thought for himself; and would rather a minute with the other than a whole day at sport." He brought his eyes to me. "This is love that goes past the wants of the body to what is finer and more lasting." He shook his head. "And such a love does not come to everyone, Jophiel."

Going home, gemstones of stars blazed above our dark streets broken open by light from windows and doorways. And I drew my uncle's words to me, for they had recognized and honored what I held deepest--and started up again that ache of yearning for her. Oh, and I gathered it to me, held it within me as something altogether precious. You know, I never needed fine words from Uncle Anthony, and so it was a great happiness to get them; but in no way could they compare to the bliss of hearing that both Aunt and Master Dorset had seen in Sarah some kind of feeling for me.

CHAPTER EIGHT

Before I knew it, Lammas had come 'round again. And along with the field work of summer being at its height, everyone wanted gates, gears and tools, outdoors and indoors as well--and that along with all of our ordinary tasks. Even so, we would close the smithy.

And Aunt Mathilde took her quarter loaf put by the year past to the front of the cottage to crumble for the birds that flocked with a racket of wings. Then she served breakfast and our favorite drink of Lambs Wool, a spiced cider with apples floating in it and puffing up white.

When we got to the Hay, where we harvest feed, I knew to look for Bernard, little Thad and Marydine already at the wagon where the puppets pounded one another silly. I hung at the edge of the crowd until Bernard came running, his sister behind him, her hair flying. They hailed me and dropped breathless to the ground among the audience to fix their eyes upon the wagon's stage.

I strolled the direction they came from to meet Sarah and take Thad upon my shoulders. As I swung him up, for a moment I felt he might be my own small son; and Sarah laughed as he buried his fingers in my hair and whipped my back until I galloped off. I made a place for her and the fat-legged six month-old Astrel, her tiny pink toes like flower buds in Sarah's lap. And there, amidst this uproar of puppets and children, I sank into the very heart of peace; for always, near Sarah, peace stole upon me. And we saw the play three times through.

Then the bell rang for the Dividing of the Loaf, and we joined the circle where Sarah's parents, Aunt Mathilde, Uncle Anthony and my young cousins held a place for us. Each family brought a new loaf of bread with an unlit candle stuck in it to pass to another family there. I saw Edward on the far side with his younger brother, and we raised to them our loaves we'd exchanged with the Dorsets. Next, the Master of the Fair, walking the inside circle, lit each candle with his own while we sang harvest songs. And looking upon all those smiling faces, the candles burning, I could not help but think of the heavenly bodies above that abided one another in harmony; and now here were all of us below in harmony, too; and all of nature as well. And I prayed the stars to watch over us and to keep us always thus.

You can imagine I was aching to be alone with Sarah; and when the mothers and small children stretched out in the shade to nap while the older ones scampered off to explore the booths of ware, Master Dorset nudged Sarah and me.

"Go on, you two. The day will be over before you know it, eh, Anthony?"

Uncle Anthony drained his cup and gestured, pushing his porky fingers toward the booths. "See if there isn't something in those stalls to please a young mistress, Jophiel. We know all those sellers await you with high hopes."

Into the milling crowd, then.

Sarah was drawn to a wagon with finger lengths of linen and wool, with tasseled girdles of a new fashion that bind a kirtle cunningly to make the waist visible for the pleasure of the eye. I waited, hoping to see her face light over some certain thing.

Next to this wagon, a weathered juggler kept a shoe, washing paddle, knife, small filled piglet's bladder and an egg in the air, stepping back, forth and sideways to meet each on its way down while children and elders held their breath. Sarah and I applauded as he dispensed the egg in time to catch the knife by its handle. I dropped two pence into the cap near his feet. As we moved away, Sarah turned to me.

"You could juggle horseshoes, nails, keys and a wooden bench next Lammas."

"Well, but I think I must also add a gate and a platter of pigeon to better him."

We stopped at a wagon overflowing with toys. Sarah chose bright painted tops for her brothers and a clay doll for her sister.

Then came the stand with hair hanks, coils, fancy plaits and masses of ringlets. It was the mode with some women, if their own hair did not grow long or thick enough to please them, to add such pieces. The seller carried a great veined nose and wore fiery red locks pulled out as if in a storm above her sagging body.

"Come now Mistress, and try a new look for yourself. And see if your young Master here aren't enchanted," she croaked holding out a lavish hairpiece of black ringlets and a mirror. "If I may--."

She pinned them to Sarah's head, arranging the fall of curls so as to cascade near to the end of her own plait where they jumped and shivered in the breeze. Sarah peered into the mirror. Standing behind her and looking, I saw pale, delicate skin abloom, eyebrows and a hairline of spun gold and a swarming of black locks thick as a horse's mane.

She spun to look at me with a teasing smile; but I rested my chin upon my closed fist and held myself thoughtful and formal. "'Tis a great hank of hair indeed, mistress. But then, how

will your father recognize you?" I crumpled my brow. "He will
see a maid in the dress of his Sarah but with black hair flying like
twelve crows at war; and would surely offer such an apparition a
crust of bread for fear of offending some unknown power, and to
send it quickly away. And all the while he must grieve and search
the road for his wonderful Sarah with hair like sunlight."

"Well, sir," Sarah straightened her face and shook her
finger, the black curls bouncing, "you argue a strong point. And so
sent away by him, what place then would I call home; and where
rest my head?"

"At my place," I wanted to shout. "Here is the door. Rest
your head with me." But then, dampened, I remembered I had no
place of my own; and so must look away, thwarted.

"Thank you, but no, Madam," Sarah, turning, unpinned
the hair, "for I see I may invite disaster should I take a fancy to
such hair." She held the ringlets out to the vendor. "But perhaps
someone else will choose it, and so bring you good fortune." And
as we strolled on, she shook a finger at me. "I never did such things
before I met you, Master Jophiel. I had best be on my knees at
St. Vitalis, and lighting candles for my soul, seeing how wild you
make me."

I held up my palms and backed away, "But I have no
business with wigs, Mistress. I believe it is that antic elf I have seen
peer from behind your eyes, looking for games. He has business
with wigs." At which Sarah tossed her head with a smile.

"Perhaps."

We worked our way on through the crowd.

An older man with white whiskers growing from his ears
played the double flute with such a beautiful and mournful voice
that a chill ran up my arms. I left a coin in his cup. And there
were caps and veils and pelisse favored now as cloaks because of
the lightness of the fabric and novel slits for the arms. There were
leather goods of purses, straps, thongs, fine shoes and boots tanned
in that golden-red and mahogany sally made from willows.

While Sarah studied ribbons at another cart, my eye fell

upon a horn comb in the one next it. Oh, and I could just see its
amber flash through the fall of her hair as she drew the comb
down. So I bought the piece, but hid it. She came back to join me
with a rose-colored ribbon, and we found a little place selling cakes
and ale. Sitting under a tree to eat, I pulled the comb from my
pouch.

"Some of us like the gold of your hair just as it is," I held it
out to her.

Oh, and her hands flew up in surprise. And she turned the
comb against her fingers, then reached back to pull the tail of her
plait into her lap to pass the comb through it.

"Very fine it is, Jophiel. I do not have one so fine." She
beamed. "I thank you."

And her pleasure quieted my heart's need to give her
something until we stopped where a craftsman with a bristled chin
sat upon a tree stump whittling so fast his stuck-out thumb spread
into a blur. Sarah picked up a small wooden bird cunningly carved,
and held it so long I was ready to buy it; but she put it back.

"But does it not take your fancy? I want to buy it for you."

"I have a beautiful comb," she said with a face soft and
serious, "and now there is not anything more here to take my
fancy." She turned as if looking about, then back to me and shaking
her head, "No, nothing more here charms." And all the while she
spoke, her eyes like fingertips traced the planes of my face. "But
there is someone here who captures my fancy, and that altogether.
And his name is Jophiel Balerais. And he is one I would choose
above any other."

Well, I might as well have been struck in the face by a
plank, her words delivered such a blow of surprise. And just then a
hollering crowd of young rowdies pounded through the booths and
broke us apart. I searched across the rush of heads until I found
her, her eyes still fixed upon me as she backed away to give the
ruffians wider traverse.

When we came together again, I caught up her hand and
led her behind a stall piled high with willow baskets. Once, in one

of Edward's music folios, I had seen a woodcut of a love-stricken knight fallen onto his knee to his lady. Just so, and overflowing with urgency and terror (and without even knowing I had done it), I fell to my knee.

"My lady," I called her, "there is none in this world I prize greater than you; and none to whom I would more gladly vow my service and the strength of my body, so long as my breath shall last." These were not my words, believe me, for I had none; but Love poured through to speak for me, as Edward had told me is the way with Amour.

The wind teased the wisps of her hair; and she looked long and deep into me. "I thank you for that, Jophiel," she said. And it seemed for a moment she would say more, for she hesitated; but then bent to raise me with that hand of hers I still grasped. "Come," she said, "we'd best get back. Our families will wonder where we are."

When we found our people, the comb was passed around and won approval. A light came into Mistress Dorset's eyes as she explored its cool smooth surface; and remembering some moment, she threw a quick glance at her husband; and they exchanged a smile. We left the comb with them while Sarah and I and her young sister went to join the dance at the Green.

The women take hands in a large circle for a complicated set of steps and movements. And it is by their own voices that they make the music they follow; or sometimes a fiddler or recorder player joins in. And I watched as the circle moved like one body, a live blossom growing and shrinking and floating in that glorious rich liquor of high sweet voices you can never forget.

Back again with our families, then, too soon we packed our things and paused to say our fare-thee-wells. Then, horses and wagons swaying, and dust rising to meet the wheel hubs, I raised my eyes for a last look at Sarah; and found she had turned to look back at me. We gave a wave of departing while more wagons with children crying, dogs barking, wheels and harnesses squeaking and drivers shouting "Heigh. Heigh now!" crowded between us.

Oh fare-thee-well then, love. Fare-thee-well.

A week later Master Dorset appeared at the smithy. He had left an old door built by the great grandfather. After so many decades, a second hinge had finally worn through; and we were to make a fresh one to match. A brutally hot day, the last of summer burning itself into the earth, I was at the water barrel dousing my hair when he pulled up in his wagon.

I took the harness.

"Good to see you, lad. Is your uncle about? I'm looking for the door you've fixed for me. He thought it would be a fortnight."

"Ay, Master Dorset. He'd be around back."

He nodded. "Good. But first I have a favor to ask, if you can be free for an hour or so. I must collect some grains at the mill. I could use a hand."

"Let me check. We seem to be in a lag right now."

I was back before he could turn his head. He wheeled his horse about and we jolted along toward the river where the mill sits like a huge grey gnome, and pondering its grinding stone.

I asked after his business, though it was other information I sought. He told me of a new cheese made of mixed cow and goat milk and flavored with peppercorns. "The first batch made everyone's noses run. I gave a finger-full to the dog and he buried his head in the water barrel."

We laughed, then fell into a silence while the wagon and landscape rocked in rhythm to the horse's plodding. Wild summer flowers thronged in the fields and we would spy that slip of blue water appearing and disappearing until it grew into the river Exe. Birds dropped from the trees to explore the wagon's bed, and an occasional dog bounded from a cottage to rave at our wheels until, as we crossed some invisible line, it would trot away satisfied, and lie down at its cottage door again.

Master Dorset cleared his throat. He wore no hat and the tops of his ears were bright pink from the sun. Without turning his head, he wondered aloud was there a subject I would like to broach but did not know how to begin.

Since my tongue had clearly frozen, he went on then, that after Lammas last, Sarah had told her mother she and I had come into agreement and would like to marry.

Unprepared for such news, my face flamed and heart, trapped between joy and fear, stopped altogether. I swallowed.

"Ay, Sir, we have bespoke our feelings."

"Well then, if there be a question of marriage, some things come up two men need discuss together."

I stammered I would do all I could to protect and provide--.

He waved me off. The care I would give their daughter was plain as day to everyone. "And there is none more welcome into our family than yourself, Jophiel."

Oh but my heart flew up with joy at that, and with a relief tempered by wonder and humility. While Uncle was held to be an important businessman in Exeter, Master Dorset was the latest in a line famous for its dairy that had served the nobility for generations. He whistled to his horses.

"When two marry," he went on, "families marry as well. You would see Sarah's needs met, yes; but how would you manage your work situation, for instance? We would welcome your skill and knowledge at our business; but what about your uncle?"

Since last Lammas, I had sometimes let my thoughts stray this far, but retreated always at the thought of deserting Uncle Anthony.

"I don't know what to say, Sir," I stammered. "It would be a privilege to bring my service to you; but my uncle has given over more and more to me in the running of his shop. He has sons, but they need some years yet before they can do what I do."

"And likely you are not sure what work situation you would want. His is an excellent place, the best smithy in Devon and hereabouts, no doubt of that," Master Dorset nodded deeply, "and Anthony quite a well-respected man."

Oh, and it did my heart good to hear this praise for my uncle.

"He has given me everything, sir. I owe him more than I know how to repay."

Now we could smell the Exe, see its dew upon the grasses. And for some time I had heard a rumble and felt soft trembling through the wheels of the wagon as we approached the mill, a great building of stone set beside the Exe where its huge wooden wheel scooped the wild water at a steady pace, and sent out a spray like fine rain that blew over everything.

We shook hands with the miller, Master Haverstock, who remembered me from two years before when we replaced the holds on the center pin around which the grinding stone turns. People say they heard the stone crack all the way into Exeter. For the repair, we took our smith shop to the river and worked by daylight and by torchlight while a steady procession of farmers stacked grain beside us, and the miller paced like a caged animal.

Master Haverstock had the order ready, along with a bit of business gossip. The three of us loaded sacks until I began to wonder if the weight would drive the wagon's wheels into the earth; and worried we might need an extra horse; but the sturdy animal thrust itself forward in its harness blowing and shaking its head while the wood of the wagon first trembled, cried out and rolled forward.

On the way back, we spoke of trips Master Dorset had taken to France and Italy. "Of course we have a great cathedral of our own, thanks to our Bishop Warelwast, a nephew of the Conquerer, it is said. Why, I remember the stone hauled in from the hills, wagon after wagon. And with my father's leave, I worked on it myself as a youth, a great adventure climbing walls, pulling ropes and hauling things up and into place."

He slapped the reins across the horses' rumps.

"Now cheese--."

Well, he found he couldn't beat the French and Italians in

their flavorings with wines; but came to prefer herbs, himself. Oh, but superb businessmen they were over there!

Since I hadn't traveled more than fifty miles from Exeter, I replied I hoped to see places I had read about with Brother Frederick: Greece, Rome, Jerusalem.

He shook his head. "Jerusalem is no place to go, unless you want the glory of a crusade. I have heard the next one already brews in France and Italy." He shot a look at me. "Of course, a man must go if he is called; and some say it is an honor to serve the Church; but to my mind, honor is to serve the family and those I know. And I am too old for such business, and am not sorry."

"I would like to see the places where folios I've read were scribed, and to know more of the living in those times. But that is far from what is on my mind today."

Sarah's father gave me a knowing smile, and we passed into the city where the street swarmed with carts, wagons and horses, with riders and people on foot, dogs barking, chickens squawking, a tooting pig chased by its owner. Water from slop buckets ran along the center ditch and raised its stink. Flies swarmed thick there; and it was a relief to get to the smithy where the pestilence was less intense. Before I could climb down, Master Dorset laid a hand upon my arm.

"Things work out where all have best interests at heart, Jophiel." His eyes upon me were kind. "And if someone makes an offer and someone accepts," he waved a hand; "the rest unfolds to everyone's contentment. Let nothing be a hindrance to you, lad."

Relief washed through me. Now I needn't any answer but Sarah's.

"Shall we get your door loaded, then?"

He pushed out his lower lip, shook his head, leaned toward me. "It was really this talk between men I was after today. I'll send someone tomorrow."

And with a smile and a clucking sound, he rolled away, his horse flicking flies from one ear, then another, the heavy wagon creaking over the stones. Sarah's father had thrown open a door;

and the breeze through it awakened me from one dream and into the next: my proposal to Sarah.

After dinner I took my penny whistle to Long Brook. Crested kingfishers flashed from tree to tree, and the busy little brown dippers skimmed the water with cries, then plunged to the bottom. And the trees leaned from the banks as if they shared some longtime confidence, while their green leaves fingered the sparkling light all around and under them.

Now Uncle Anthony flooded my mind: How I used to call him "sausage fingers." How he would take me, still a mite, to his shop, give me a broom and then marvel at how clean I'd made the floor, as if nothing were so important to his business as that. And how he came and saw to Mamoon, and helped me gather my things. And now was I to repay him by leaving?

I tucked my whistle into my belt and watched as a beaver scrambled up the opposite bank, dark coat beaded and glowing. And bit by bit, the woodland, like a patient mother, lifted my chin. "Go on," it told me.

Next afternoon I sidled over to Uncle Anthony and leaned as if with interest over drawings of a gate latch he studied; and then in a voice I schooled to sound casual, asked, "When you proposed to Aunt Mathilde, how did you do it?"

He looked up, studied my face, then pushed the drawings aside.

"I suspect you have a reason for your question?"

I swallowed.

"Sarah confided to her mother that she and I desire to marry. Master Dorset told me this yesterday. I needed to think, and did not want to speak of it before she did." I couldn't say the rest, about the working problem; not then.

Well, and a great smile cracked Uncle's face, and he burst from his stool to clap both arms about me.

"Good fortune to you then, lad. You have his blessing, I'm sure of it, and that of his wife. We, all of us, have spoke more

than once of you two as a likely pair. Good fortune then, lad!"
And he sank onto his stool, shining eyes still upon me, great smile
unfazed until, as if suddenly come awake, he pulled down a serious
business-like look.

"Well now, it must be proposal instruction you're wanting;
and here I am staring and grinning like the king's own jester. Sit,
sit. Lord knows I make a poor example, but I can tell you the God's
truth of how my poor fool of a proposal to Mathilde came about."

And he folded his hands and cleared his throat.

"I was walking in early evening from a supper with your
aunt and her Aunt Adela to that aunt's cottage where they both
lived. When we were together, her Aunt would come along, as was
proper, both of us being young. She, a knowing woman, would lag
behind to give us space, yet keep a eye and ear open. Well, after
a year of careful acquaintance, I found it a cheerful thing to be in
Mathilde's company. Yet I was at war with myself, for to give up
bachelorhood seemed a great shame. Still, if I kept at it, I might
lose her to other young bucks I'd seen eyeing her.

"There was a light rain then, and me daydreaming to bring
her to my bachelor hut to sit by the fire, I turned to see if she were
getting too wet and right off caught my boot upon a tree root in the
road and so fell there and then to my knees like a sack of grain.
Well, she turned, you can be sure, at the great sound came out of
me. And so angry was I at this indignity, and drawn even more to
her by the sweet pity upon her face, that I decided I'd be damned if
I'd get on my knees twice. So I clasped my hands and, still fuming,
growled out, 'Mistress, could you marry this lump of a man would
work his God-given back off to provide you comfort and pleasure,
and only to stay in your blessed company?'

"By then Aunt Adela had caught up with us, her face
stretched out in amazement at me down on my knees in the rain
and mud, and with my hands clasped. 'Are you hurt, then, lad?' she
bent to me.

"'Aye, M'am.' I lifted sober eyes. 'Surely I am wounded
to my core by love.' And I said it out loud, and knew that, truly, I

meant it. And at that, Mathilde clapped her hand over her mouth. 'Oh, get up, Anthony,' she begged when she could find a serious face. 'And, the Lord's truth, you are a fulsome comfort and pleasure to me. I not only could, but will, marry you.'

"And she did." Uncle Anthony spread his arms wide, dropped them, then cocked his head. "Now, you're sure to improve on that, Jophiel if you just don't do it in the rain."

And we leaned toward one another with a good laugh then only to hear from the forge old Guill shout 'God bless us now' at the top of his lungs, and then a heavy piece of metal clatter to the ground. 'And thanks indeed, Lord," he bellowed again in a searing tone, "a twisted-up gear is just what I was hopin' for today." And we laughed again, but then Uncle's face grew thoughtful, and he turned toward the window. The light from it fell upon his brow to raise both the fire of his pate and wiry scrub upon his chin.

"When you think what we ask of our women, Jophiel, to have and keep the babes we give them, to put up with us in all our ways and moods, and on top of the work that has no end, any honest man must agree we should be on our knees to them all day." He shook his head, "And you know our tongues turn to stone just at the wrong times; so our bodies must speak for us. And if all I had was my business, good as it is, without Mathilde, I'd be a pauper." He turned back to me. "You've seen weakness in me as a man." I knew he meant times I'd seen him in the hay with a wench. "If I ever thought your aunt knew." He shook his head. "And this infernal temper!" He scowled darkly.

I studied my boots, then looked up. "But you make it behave toward others," I extolled him. And as his face lightened some then, I went on that when he fell to his knees in the mud, right away he put that to good use as well. And we both laughed.

"Around Sarah, my knees become so weak, it's all I can do to make my legs work," I said, and told him, then, of Lammas just past, of my speech behind the basket stall. "Should she accept me, I must master these knees, for I'll need to provide for her."

He roared approval and concluded that this turn of events

required ale at the public house when we closed. There he reached into his memories of the early years of his marriage. I watched his face glow as he spoke of the birth of each of his children, and realized how much I hoped for some of my own.

But in a dream that night, I set out on foot to meet Sarah and her parents for the proposal. And I had to cross the Exe, but the drunken boatman kept poling in circles. Finally I saw the sun go down, and that I had missed my chance. And I woke in a sweat.

CHAPTER NINE

Next morning in a rush I appealed to Aunt to study her Book of Signs for the earliest favorable time to make my plea. She pulled the old scroll from the basket with her midwife supplies and with a finger scouted the drawings.

"Well, a waxing moon is best." She threw her head back and counted into the rafters. "Four days hence. Now," she crossed her arms over her full bosom, her round face serious, words careful, "Saturday or Sunday are lucky days; make it one or t'other. When you step out from our door, step onto your right foot; and when you arrive there, slide from the saddle to the right; and make sure to step out again onto your right foot." And with that she gathered me into her arms to kiss me on both cheeks. "And God go with ye."

Such common wisdom as hers was always spoken in safe

places, for the Church had ideas about what was of God and what of the Devil, while Mamoon and others held there to be mystic things that mix with our lives and bless us at their will. So, I reasoned, at such an important moment, why risk offending any spirit or propriety?

There were the gifts for all of Sarah's family to be gotten or made. Then, the Saturday next, my stomach filled with caterpillars, I packed everything carefully in the early light.

For the parents I had a fine liqueur of Portugal Uncle got from a customer, and that he and Aunt had been saving. Uncle would not hear of me paying for it; but I was allowed to pay for the nails I made at night for Bernard who had confessed to me after the haying that he had an itch to build things for himself.

Aunt made dolls of shrunken apples and cloth for the younger ones, including a laughing old woman with a spindle. Her dolls sold out at fairs soon as she set her basket down. For Thad, she crafted a squinting fisherman with a pouch at the hip; and for the newest child, a small stuffed cat of cloth.

I scoured the weavers' cottages until I found some fine light polished wool, a mix of brown and grey with a blue thread running through. And oh how the piece gave off a radiance like dew-soaked meadows. The old mistress sold to nobility, but when she heard it was for my intended bride (and had looked me over well), she asked with a great smile empty of teeth but a quarter the price; and then folded the wool handsomely.

A sliver of new moon hung over the meadows next day as I made for the Dorset farm. The family waited their morning meal until I arrived; and we shared cheese and bread and ale. Little Thad kept poking my bag until I fetched out his fisherman. Bernard rolled the nails back and forth across his palm, blind to the rest of us. Marydine stretched her neck and I found her doll. She was just learning to spin and went to sit on a bench at the wall to let the old granny doll with her wheel instruct her. For Astrel, toddling upon the floor reeds, there was an apple doll in baby clothes with yarn hair for carrying.

"And with my respects," I gave over the wine into Master Dorset's hands. He and his mistress opened wide delighted eyes and made a fuss. Then I fumbled in the bag, turned to Sarah and laid the wool across her lap. It could have been my heart. Her mouth sprang open and she buried her hands in it, passed it over her cheek and then shook it out and swung it 'round her. And truly it appeared just as I had seen in my mind, glowing across her shoulders and under her flaxen hair.

"You always know what to get for me, Jophile," she turned and turned for the feeling of the wool swinging out about her.

Father and mother shooed us onto the path to the river that would provide a long walk and plenty of privacy. The sun made a halo of Sarah's hair. Hector came along, knocking his tail against our legs, snuffling the dirt; but after a time, he turned back.

I spotted the ancient oak ahead, a landmark you can see reaching into the sky as you come along London Road. Sarah talked of the gifts, how perfect each one was; and the flutter of her fingers braided wildflowers as we walked, her soft face and the feeling of her gentle ease with me swelled in me until I thought the words I had practiced for days would burst forth before I ever got to my knees.

"Let's rest here, Sarah." I gestured toward the old tree with its branches low like rungs of a ladder and spiraling around and up. "Sit here among these leaves, Pretty Bird, and sing me a song."

She laughed and let me put my hands under her arms to lift her onto the thick lower branch; and the perfume of her body and of the earth around made me dizzy. She looked across a far field for a moment, naming aloud songs she might sing. "He came upon his Horse" or "The World's bliss"? She turned back and I had dropped to my knees.

"Mistress Dorset," the words came of their own, "I am but a humble man. Even so, I make bold to ask if we might unite. I would do everything in my power to make life good and fruitful for us; and, whatever may come, I can promise that our life would be one filled full with love and happiness, for you are my heart's treasure and delight. And toward your comfort and ease, I would bend every effort, as there is none other in this world to whom I wish to give allegiance or to serve."

They were not the words I had practiced; but they made their way onto the air from my heart, and as if chiseled into stone.

But Sarah had no reply. Her mouth trembled and tears began to spill down her cheeks. She buried her face in her hands, and my heart sank that I must have misunderstood all along; or that she had changed her mind. Then she took her hands away and shook her head slowly, her eyes lighted through the tears and fixed upon me.

"To be with you is all I have dreamed of since first I saw you, Jophiel," she whispered." And sunshine broke then upon her face, and she held her arms out for me to take her down. "Of course. Of course I will marry you. 'Tis all, all I have longed for."

And we kissed then. And I held her to my heart, my treasure, my betrothed. And not knowing for how long nor caring, we pressed against one another, kissing, each one's breathing moving against the other's body while the day arched over us, tender and verdant. Then finally, reluctantly, we woke to the fact of Sarah's parents awaiting our return.

Her father opened the liqueur I brought. Mistress Dorset carried in cold chicken and late strawberries. Sarah sat close. Myself, I had an appetite like three days at the anvil, but also wanted Sarah's hand in mine; and so must set it down to eat a bite then pick it up again while her parents watched with amusement. Then her father raised his cup. "To the betrothed!"

Three weeks hence, her mother told us, was quick as everything could be set with the church, with relations and friends.

We nodded blindly. The sooner the better.

Though it was very dear, I wanted Sarah's wedding ring to

be of gold. I'm sure you would be of like mind. And of all people, Bog, with his great hams of hands, could fashion gold; and got the raw stuff for me at a very good price from someone who owed him a favor. He shouted my name as he held his finished work aloft, a shining gold circlet perfect in every way, and perched upon his great smoke-stained finger.

"No payment for me, lad," he brushed me off. "'Twas a joy."

I recall seeing then through the open stable door the trees bounce in the afternoon sun, and birds flash branch to branch as I wrapped the ring in a square of red velvet I brought from Aunt, and tucked it into my pouch.

I thought there would be no end to the jokes at the smithy, but Uncle would not allow them. Instead, I suffered the pounds on the back and fist strikes upon my arms. Two nights before the wedding, Uncle took us men to the public house for beer and fare where the usual raucous tales of the marriage night were forbidden by my uncle as not fitting for my feelings. Although Oswith, we called Snail because his hair that grew to a point down his forehead, asked would I like his dog to dig up some mandrake root from behind his cottage as an assurance for "the night."

And the men started into shop tales then, starting with old Guill recalling me at eight years old shoveling stalls and learning to jump clear of the horses when they let down their water.

Next day, Uncle and I came to an agreement that I should take a loan from him for the merchet, the tax for marrying. Since I profited most from the marriage by entry into the Dorset family business, the larger portion of the tax would fall to me.

CHAPTER TEN

Then came the wedding morn, and Vincent, Uncle Anthony's oldest, brought my boots as I dressed before the hearth. He had gotten himself up early and polished them until light broke across their surface; then held them out to me like the gift they were.

"Thanks to you, lad. Now the King of the Hill won't have to be ashamed of his boots at his wedding," I ruffled the wild red of his hair. "And then it will be you, not so long now; and me doing your boots for you."

He scoffed and turned his face, for he was young yet; though lately I had noticed his eye quick and away upon the young lasses.

He sat as I pulled on the boots, taking in my tunic, the color of cream, open at the throat; and with ample sleeves embroidered in cream thread by my aunt, then covered with a long dark brown tunic open at the front and without sleeves. Breeches were a light nut-brown. I tucked their bottoms into my boots after I pulled dark brown stockings over them, and had fastened these under my knees with cranberry garters. All Aunt's ideas. She knew how she wanted me to look.

The night before the wedding, she had Vincent draw water so I could bathe and wash my hair. The children were shooed from the room, but their eyes shone bright upon me from the loft; and I grinned up at them.

I dried off, covering my body, then called to Aunt who wanted to even-up my hair with shears, then comb it dry before the fire. Finished, she held out her hand mirror. I saw chestnut waves filled with white, blue and rose rivers of light falling to my shoulders. I found the strong bones of my father's face, and his green eyes I forget I have. This was a face Sarah could love, could live with. I looked a moment longer, relieved. No, not my father's face but my own, the pleasing face of an eighteen year-old man. I handed the mirror to Aunt with a small smile I could not suppress. She patted my arm, smiling herself. "Sleep well, then. I'll wake you to shave."

Our family arrived early at St. Vitalis, about half an hour by horse out of Exeter. Uncle brought a gift for the priest, a man his own age with a graying tonsure and patient kindly eyes who laid his hand upon my shoulder as if in blessing. Sick with anticipation to see my bride, I could only return a weak smile and a nod while we stood at the church doors where family members and neighbors would join us to affirm there was no impediment to the union; and to hear our vows and see me slide the ring onto Sarah's finger. Aunt went from group to group as the crowd grew, hugging grownups, patting children. I saw Brother Frederick's large frame stride across the church yard; he would assist the priest at the wedding mass.

Edward wore a brocade vest; he had his lute upon his back. He greeted me with thumps, then stood to the side and began to play. The sound of plucked strings soothed my nerves and pleased our gathering guests. After our vows he would follow us into the chapel and play during the mass; and later treat us to a new love song, he said. His presence gave me great comfort, for no man else understood me so well regarding this love.

Then at some signal I could not see, Edward stopped his music and silence fell. The priest stepped out in front of the church doors and I turned, my heart pounding, to see the crowd part. Edward took up again then, in slow rhythmic strokes, with a hymn I recognized to the Virgin. And there Sarah was, an apparition coming through the crowd on her father's arm. And I nearly cried out at the wonder of her!

Her gown was the blue of the summer sky set against the bloom of her skin; and the pale spun flax of her hair was wreathed round with star ivy and lily of the valley and small pink roses. The hair itself was loose at the front, and in back plaited with dark pink clematis and green leaves.

The bodice of her gown, one that had been her mother's, was trimmed at the neckline with a froth of white lace and drawn down by a gather between the breasts so as in a most modest way to show the shadowed mystery of her womanly cleavage. The upper sleeves alternated long strips of blue silk with the same white lace, and tied at the shoulders in bows. The sleeves pointed well down her hand, and with an edging of the same lace that finished the bodice, the fall of the gown and its small train. And she carried bluebells, pansies, violets, small wild roses and ivy from the woods, herself the most beautiful flower of them all.

And I saw not the maiden I had thought her to be, not the pretty bird I lifted to the branch, but one come now into the authority of her womanliness, a queen more beautiful than any statue in church or figure illuminated in a book; and I was flabbergasted and humbled at the blessing that was about to be bestowed upon me. Uncle Anthony nudged me, then stepped away as I moved to join my bride before the priest. She kissed her father, and he gave her over to my keeping. And something about her spirit, as if she rose from the earth to command the fields and the flying of birds, took hold of me too; and whatever I still held to myself of being a youth fell away then; and I stepped out to meet her, to take her hand in mine, a man.

The priest turned to Uncle Anthony, then to Sarah's father and asked if either knew of any reason Sarah and I should not be married. "Nay," they each said. Then he looked out over the crowd and asked the same question; and my heart speeded up, I don't know why. Silence. The priest nodded with satisfaction and proceeded to the marriage instruction, first in Latin then in English: From this moment the wife's body belonged to her husband and he was to treasure it as he would his own; and the husband's belonged to the wife. The love was to be as that of Christ for his Church, for which He laid down his life. And all here this day were witness to the proclamation of our love, but consummation with our bodies was itself the marriage sacrament that made us man and wife. Did we understand this and were we in agreement with this?"

"Yes," we said.

Then at the priest's bidding, I took up Sarah's hand and all grew still. Her fingers met mine soft and eager, and the gold ring captured the flame of the large candle her cousin held to the side; and a brilliant white star sprang 'round the ring as I slipped it onto her third finger, the one people say is joined to the heart. Then I looked deeply into her eyes and repeated the words that established our contract: "I, Jophiel, take thee, Sarah, to be my wife; and bestow upon thee all that I have for as long as we shall live." They were not adequate words for my heart; they did not say that I knew our two souls now to be one soul and one breath of life. Then I bent, though I had not planned to, and kissed that hand that gave itself to me. When I straightened, it was with her fragrance in my nostrils and upon my lips.

Uncle Anthony knocked at my arm and drew me back to earth with the customary small bag of coin to give Sarah for the poor. But as our hands were still joined, and with Sarah about to repeat her marriage vow, I didn't want to take it then as Sarah was turning away to her cousin, then back again to me, and with a gold ring shining upon her open hand!

For the bride to give a ring to her husband was not seen among us, but was something very new and practiced only by those who follow the way of Amour. I had told her of my talks with Edward; and how, with wonder, I saw us to be among those ranks. With the ring, Sarah encircled my finger then; and kissed its very tip before she released my hand. And all those looking on murmured softly at the sight.

So then the church doors were opened, and we followed the priest inside to stand before the altar to suffer the ordeal of the Mass where the smell of beeswax from the candles mixed with the perfume of roses twined about the old silver holders. And Sarah's presence helped me to concentrate. I knew that she was no more religious than me, but whenever I looked over to her, she would have her head bowed and eyes cast down.

The final blessing then, and everyone could smell the pig roasting in the pit. And Sarah and I, our faces flushed and eyes dancing, led our families and guests out from the church where we stood just beyond the door to receive their good wishes. And Uncle nudged me again with the coins for the poor. I laughed and gave them to Sarah; and everyone watched while she moved toward the far edge of the church's yard, thick with beggars waiting for the customary boon. But as she approached, there came that clacking sound required of lepers at their approach. Two of them there were, standing separate, in shrouds and with faces covered.

These unfortunates were known at St. Vitalis, and a murmur ran through the guests as Sarah went to them first with the pence, and lingered for a word with the others waiting and shouting out, "God bless!" and "Happiness to you, Mistress!" And she instructed the servers set the left-over food where the lepers could get it as well as the beggars. There is a law both written and unwritten that when good comes to you, you remember the poor. And my Sarah returned waving the empty alms bag; and applause broke upon the air.

This duty done, we could greet our guests and watch them fill the heavy-laden trestles already set out when I arrived, and covered during the Mass with white cloths, bread, wine and flowers. And there arose from our guests under the trees a great babble of high spirits while Master Dorset's cousin the fiddler and several of his cronies tuned up and began to scatter notes from fiddle, mandola, harp and drum. And I thought this music to be like a happy heart raising up in joy to sing out everywhere.

As we sat back a little from eating our fill, Edward found his way to us with his lute. And while he tuned it, silence came on in small steps. Then from under his arched fingers grew the notes of a troubadour song he knew had touched me deeply, and whose words I had recited to Sarah after we bespoke our feelings, but before I had proposed.

> "So through the eyes love attaineth the heart,
> for the eyes are the scouts of the heart
> and go reconnoitering for what
> it would please the heart to possess."

And while he sang in a voice of most tender feeling, Sarah turned and took my hand, for we had often spoke of that first time three years before when, at Lammas Fair, our eyes met as we passed, and Amour was born.

Then, to our surprise, there came from Edward a new song of his own.

> "My arm around you, hear the wind's song,
> the pond so wild, the pond so calm,
> We will go by, go arm in arm
> to the sheltering cove in the green wood down.

Oh lay me down, my love so fair.
Unbuckle my hair, unbuckle my hair.
Hear the cuckoo call in the trees so tall,
and marry me soon. Oh, marry me soon.

Your red lips ripe as fruit in June,
I long to taste and quench my thirst.
Your neck as pale as a silver moon.
It holds my heart. It holds my heart.

Oh lay me down...

The shadows lengthen, the sun sinks down
Our bed of leaves gives us perfume.
My love is wild, my love is calm.
I'll marry you soon, I'll marry you soon.

Oh lay me down, my dear love fair.
I will marry you soon. I will marry you soon.

The final notes hovered a moment above that rapt silence;
then the thunderous approval. Sarah's cheeks flushed with pleasure,
and I had to wipe my eyes for I had told him about the comb and
how I had longed to open the plait of my Sarah's hair. And her
father stood then, his arms out; and the babble fell away.

Master Dorset said Sarah had found a most upright young
man who knew the value of pure gold when he saw it, being
made of it himself; and that he came from a most honorable and
respected family and fine business with which he and his family
were greatly enriched in being linked. Next, Uncle Anthony
told everyone he had gained a beautiful daughter who would be
a blessing to this nephew they all loved so much, and to their
family; that it was an honor to be joined with them as well. Brother
Frederick quoted Ovid on marriage and made everyone roar with
laughter. Old Guill and Bog and others from the smithy crowded

together for a song they composed begging Sarah in ragged and unharmonious voices to help me to keep my mind on my work "for the good of business, lady fair. For the good of us all."

Then the dancing. Sarah and I led a reel, and all of us with our stomping and clapping scattered squirrels and birds and made the air ring to fill the afternoon with such laughter and good times that even the cold grey stone of the church lit with color; and we thought we must surely cause to dance those in the graveyard just beyond, and indeed the very hills of Devon this September day to burst again into Spring.

In late afternoon, with most of the wine and beer drunk, and fruit tarts for fertility and wedding cakes toothsome with honey and hazel nuts devoured to the last crumb, some guests who napped now in soft piles with their children under the trees began to stir, to collect themselves and bid us fare-thee-wells.

And there was a wrench to my heart when Aunt and Uncle and the children came so, for I would be going with Sarah now to a small cottage on the Dorset property. I hugged and kissed them every one, for though I would still work half my time at the smithy and see them often, I felt weighted by the knowledge of all they had given me. Aunt tugged at my cheek, her eyes brimming; and, laughing, told me to keep my hair cut. Uncle clapped me into an embrace, kissed me through his wiry beard and told me in a husky voice I was always their family, and now Sarah too.

The evening star was up as we drove from St. Vitalis. And for our first night of love upon a pallet filled with fresh hay and lavender, we were blessed with a brilliant moon standing watch over us and our small cottage.

CHAPTER ELEVEN

And so we lived our dream of love.

I divided my time between Master Dorset's forge and Uncle's shop. Every day I suffered separation from Sarah, and then the glad healing. It was wonderful to be at the smithy with Uncle and the men; it was wonderful to come home to our little cottage and my wife.

Sarah divided her time between chores at our own place and helping her mother. Often we ate with the family; but it was the meals Sarah made at home with her own hands that were magic to me. And at night upon our pallet above the empty animal stalls, we explored the reaches of our love. Afterward, I would turn my head and, Sarah breathing soft in her sleep beside me, wonder why every man in the world was not married.

It was well past pig slaughtering in early November before

I noticed that for three or four nights now my wife had hardly touched her supper. I came behind her up the ladder to bed.

"Are you not well, Mistress?"

"I am well, Jophiel." She crawled onto the pallet and stretched out to gaze upon me, a small smile upon her lips.

"You hardly ate again." I stripped off my tunic and lay down too, the scent of lavender sown within our pallet rising to fill the air.

"I don't feel like eating just now," her eyes danced and she raised herself upon an elbow; "but soon, my mother tells me, I will have the appetite of three hogs; and you will be running day and night to keep me filled."

It took a long moment, ox that I am, before the question lit my mind, then my face. And she broke into a great sweet smile, nodded and held out her arms to me.

"Yes. We are to have a child."

Well, I gave out a whoop I was told reached her parents' house.

I gathered her into my arms, covering her face with kisses. Then we lay back, and I held her until she fell into a deep and peaceful slumber. I would not think of undressing further for fear of disturbing her, so I lay staring through the window at grey clouds torn apart to reveal the stars; and joy burned like a great candle in my breast. We were to have a child!

Sarah gave the required two months or so to nausea; and then, as her mother predicted, started eating like a man home from the fields as her belly began to push her kirtle out. And at night we laughed at her "little porker nose" she declared would oink at me until I ran down the ladder for something to satisfy it from our stores.

November rains kept clogs and boots covered with mud. Nights, we'd sit at the hearth, Sarah scraping leather or patching clothes while I read to her from Edward's wedding gift, a copy of Herodotus *History*; and we laughed and wondered at the ways of

ancient humans; then told odd stories brought to mind from our
own lives.

We woke mornings to steam rising from the earth as the
early sun heated the frozen ground. St. Nicholas eve came. Sarah
and I, like the children, put our shoes outside our door. During the
night I crept down the ladder with some dried apricots and found
she had already tucked a square of fruit bread into my boot.

Then it was Winter Solstice.

Before the feast, some twenty and more of us walked the
outermost edge of the Dorset property to strew handfuls of dried
flower petals, seeds and oat flour to bless and thank the earth for
her gifts to us. Squeak, the fiddler, and two more Dorset cousins,
one on reed pipes and one striking a bell, marked our stride, and
with old earth songs I knew from Mamoon.

"Mother, oh Mother,
your children do bring
bread from our tables
and flour from the mill."

Our voices rose, white winter blossoms. Sarah trod
before me and I withheld my voice a bit, the better to join hers in
harmonia, as I had learned from Edward and in church. Oh, and
it did my heart good to see Uncle Anthony and Aunt Mathilde,
Vincent and the other children walk with us. And so we caroled
Mother Earth as she slumbered in weak December light.

Early that bitter January, Sarah's younger sister Marydine
was gripped by a fever, and with a terrible chest rattle and labored
breathing. Sarah spent every free minute brewing the mixture of
licorice, cinnamon, hyssop and fennel, all sweetened with honey,
for her to drink. And she pulverized millet toasted on the hot
hearthstone, then mixed it with powdered heart's-tongue fern for
her sister to eat between the drinks with a mouthful of bread. And
she applied plasters of flax and clay to make Marydine sweat by
the fire. And we began to fear for her life; but by St. Valentine's

Day, Marydine regained herself enough to braid a love knot with her sister for our doors. And Sarah made a small love knot for each of us.

On the morning of the feast day, Sarah stole a sleeve of mine to wear; and I pulled one of hers onto my lower arm far as it would go; and where it collected laughs all day. And by now Sarah was showing well, beginning to tilt back a little when she walked, as women do with child. And we were a proud and happy couple, cheerful into the snows of early March, which I preferred to the freezing rain and bottomless sucking mud of April.

Spring sowing. And Sarah grew full with the life she bore. And how I itched to make a cradle! Well, I found the best oak I could get my hands on, smoothed every surface so no chance splinter might get under the little one's skin; and, as I planed or rubbed, I daydreamed taking the baby after it nursed and placing it in the cradle and under the coverings Sarah and her mother had woven. And when I had finished polishing that wood, I tell you it glowed like a jewel!

We set the cradle near the hearth just as summer crops began to sprout. Sarah's mother counted, and thought we would see labor mid- to late July. June was a hot month, and we put Sarah's lassitude down to that and the weight of the babe in her belly. She spent much more time now at tasks that asked only for sitting, and drank freely of the yellow primrose water all women take when they are with child.

One midday meal with the family, Sarah rose to fetch bread from the hearth oven and left behind on the floor several bright drops from beneath her kirtle.

"Nay, but sit down again, Love," I cried out, my voice spiked with fear.

She wheeled, looked where I looked, and saw the blood. And fear sprang into her face, too, for this was not a good sign; and everyone knew it.

Her mother jogged her head at me. "Get Agatha."

Heart pounding, I hitched the wagon and flew.

Bed rest, quiet days. Pennyroyal and althea for the low stubborn fever. "Since it is several weeks yet until her time, most likely everything will settle out," Agatha was cheerful. "This is her first, after all."

We drew a cautious breath.

I brought my pallet down to sleep next to Sarah at the hearth. There would be no more climbing for her!

And the bleeding all but stopped after three or four days, though the fever hung on. In the daytime I threw myself into my work to shrink the hours until I could be with my wife. At night I lay with her, worrying and pouring out my silent love as if that could itself be a remedy.

Finally, Sarah took up easy tasks again. Still I worried and worried; and finally I spoke to her father, who raised his eyebrows and shook his head. "Nay, lad. She'll be fine." He patted my shoulder.

Well, Sarah was his daughter he dearly loved; and he had the experience of six births; so it did not seem fitting to argue the matter, nor step around him to Sarah's mother.

A fortnight or so following, while picking pears, Sarah stretched onto her toes and water gushed between her legs. She clutched her stomach and called to her cousin Meg, picking with her. Meg ran for Master Dorset who sent one of his men on a horse for me at Uncle Albert's to come home and bring Aunt Agatha.

When I returned, Sarah was at her parent's house. Sheets, cloths, bowls, jugs of water hot and cool, herbs, lotions and flower petals were assembled under her mother's direction.

In the separate room her parents kept for their sleeping, Sarah lay against pillows upon a raised pallet. They gave me a moment alone with her. I kissed my Sarah, and thanked her for bringing us our family. And she smiled and stroked my cheek; then we held each other, both knowing there was danger. I told her I would be just outside the door. She nodded, then drew her knees up a bit, turned her head and moaned.

Her mother hustled me from the room, patting my back,

"As soon as you are out of here, we can ease her travail with ointments and rubbing," I nodded, and with the door closing over her, I looked back at my wife. I knew that as labor progressed, they would move her to a corner of the room where two of the women would hold her under her armpits while she squatted over clean cloths to make it easier for the baby to travel down and out. A third woman would help soon as the little head appeared.

Waiting, I realized I was sitting on the same bench Sarah and I had used to see whether her mother and baby sister would pull through; and I jumped up as if stung, then, and moved across the room. The trestle had bowls of almonds and dried fruits set out, the custom for a lying-in. Sarah's father, brothers and sisters came and went to the food. I paced.

Toward dinner, Aunt Mathilde had us open all the windows and cupboard doors: and sent the children to untie knots wherever they found them. This was the sign of a difficult labor. We undid our belts, boot ties, the cords that bound our hair. I knew they had already freed Sarah's hair and removed any pins from it. Sarah's father left and came back with jasper and the dried right foot of a crane. He knocked softly upon the bedroom door and handed these through. Evening deepened toward night. A woman cousin, Ann, came with bread, pickled vegetables and chicken; she fed the children and put them to bed. Master Dorset left most of the food on his trencher.

But none of our pacing and worrying did any good in the end. The thin thread of a wail I listened so intently for never came. Near dawn, the baby, a boy, was born dead. They opened the door to me, and silently with a nod bid me come in. It was Aunt Mathilde who put the swaddled bundle in my arms. Oh, and he didn't weigh anything with his sealed eyes and mouth, his little wrinkled face tinged with blue and crinkled-up like a flower. A cry of grief escaped me; and I kissed the little forehead, took in his face one more time and gave him away to the women.

With all my might I pushed aside the flood of grief that wanted to come. Well, what use was it? And how must Sarah feel?

I tiptoed over to her, so small and limp upon the pallet. I knelt and kissed her hand and her face covered with sweat and so deathly pale. She laced her fingers through mine and gave a little squeeze; then her eyelids fluttered shut and her head lolled to the side.

"We'll call you," Aunt Agatha pushed me out the door, her face a mass of worry. "Get something to eat--or try to sleep." Before the door closed I heard the trickle of water in a dish and "I baptize thee in the name of the Father and of the Son and of the Holy Ghost." Sarah's mother. And those words in her voice comforted me for, though he was nameless, our son had been welcomed into the family.

Hours passed. Aunt Agatha brought fresh sheets and carried away bloody ones. I badgered until she finally told me there was trouble with the afterbirth, and with bleeding. My heart clenched; and I had to remind myself sternly it had turned out all right with Sarah's mother. Here were very experienced women who would get the bleeding to stop. So I followed the walls one to the next; or found myself asleep against one and only dreaming that I paced. And I was afraid to step outside for fear Sarah might call. Surely I could help my wife by being with her, I would whisper to Aunt. I wouldn't mind what I must see. Please, couldn't I be with her? The women were very strict about such things, but Aunt Agatha relented and twice let me in to kiss my wife and speak words of encouragement; and then return to my vigil. But the night brought no improvement. Aunt Agatha would come out for a breath of air, a bite of food; then go back, her face set with the full strength of her will.

Next morning very early, Master Dorset brought another midwife at Agatha's urging, an old woman, a Mistress Winkle, with a lean and leathery look, and a great bag of juniper and other dried things she cooked at the hearth after she'd seen Sarah. And there was no idle chatter with her. She made a tea and an ointment and filled the cottage with pungent and bitter smells that replaced the air and clung to everything. Oh, and I heard Sarah cry out after the old woman went in to treat her; and my skin crawled at the sound of her pain. Mistress Winkle left at sundown, satisfied her tonics would turn the tide; and I was allowed to see my wife again.

The women had pulled a covering over her lower body, for the old midwife had packed her womb with clean rags soaked in juniper tea. All night again they had labored, soothing my wife's belly with hands coated with ointment, coaxing it to shrink back, and softly chanting words to the Great Mother that the priest would strongly forbid.

Oh, and I could smell Sarah's blood in the air. Please. Please don't take her, I prayed to whatever God there is.

Early morning next, Aunt Agatha came out, leaned against the wall and began to cry. And my stomach turned deathly cold: She had run out of hope. Oh, and I wanted to escape in all directions, then; but there was nowhere to go, no help to be found; and I couldn't leave my Sarah. I couldn't leave her. I squatted with my arms hung upon my head, staring at the pale green spears of rushes indifferent upon the floor, trying to stop thinking, for my heart had already felt a terrible weight crush it. And now it couldn't bear to lose Sarah too; it purely could not bear it.

And then it was like March and trying to climb a path to the woods, slippery and deep with mud; and I kept plunging into despair. But no, I must keep myself clear and strong for Sarah. I told Aunt Agatha I wanted to be at Sarah's side for whatever she must go through. I couldn't abide her to be denied my presence, not even for a moment if she desired it.

Aunt Agatha opened the door and stood aside.

Sarah was wan, so wan and weak. But she recognized me, and managed a smile, as I did too. They were repacking her womb with the juniper remedy every few hours, and she was worn out from the labor, the birthing, all the handling and days of bleeding. I sat upon the floor next to her pallet and pillowed her head with my arm. I laid my free hand over her hand and lowered my head until it rested against hers and she could feel my breath upon her cheek. This way I held her in my arms as best I could. "I won't leave you,"

I whispered, "I won't leave you, Sarah." And her eyes turned to me from so far away, then; and she tried to smile.

I stayed with her all that day and night. After a while I couldn't feel my arm. I watched her chest rise and fall in the flickering of the taper. Just before dawn she moved her fingers under my hand in a kind of stroking motion. Then she let out a sigh; and her chest dropped and stilled.

I waited for the next breath, panic rising in me. Her mother, on her knees along with my aunts, looked up. "Oh my wee one," she uttered; and covered her face with her arm. Aunt Agatha leaned over and held a finger beneath Sarah's nose; then she placed her fingers on Sarah's wrist and neck. She shook her head, no.

I was ordered from the room. Aunt Mathilde put her arms around me and helped me to stand; but soon as I was on my feet, I fought her. I couldn't leave, couldn't bear to lose the sight of my Sarah. How was I to live without the sight of her?

And Aunt had to call for the men; and then I was striking out at them. Finally, it took three to overpower me. I heard their voices, their words, trying to calm me; but I could see Sarah's stilled body, and feel the terrible blackness filling everything.

Once they got me outside, Master Dorset's overseer barred the door. Then I didn't know where to go. Dizzy, I staggered against a tree to vomit, though I'd eaten nothing for a day; then it seemed the retching would never stop. My head pounding, I stumbled to our cottage, stepped inside and there, in the path of light from the door, sat the damned cradle to eat me alive. My impulse was to hack it to pieces, but I couldn't move. It was our son's.

Sarah's father came in a moment behind, saw me fixed upon it, jerked the cradle from the floor and carried it out while I shrank onto my haunches at the hearth, sobbing in my throat, my knuckles jammed against my teeth. Then, from outside, I heard the splintering, the chips flying; and then, presently, crackling and the smell of wood burning. And Sarah's father did me a generosity that day; for myself, I never could have destroyed that cradle. But then a terrible energy started up within me; and I couldn't think what to do or where to go. I paced around and around our cottage until I heard Sarah's father hammering, making her coffin; for a body cannot be left out long at the end of summer; and Sarah must be buried before nightfall, after her Mass for the Dead. That was the law.

I staggered into the dairy workshop and asked for wood to make a coffin for my son. Sarah's mother had wanted him buried with his mother, but the Church said no, that he must have a grave of his own.

Master Dorset already had the two sides of Sarah's coffin dovetailed, his face grey, sagging, his eyes like holes burned out by a poker. I asked for wood; but he shook his head no and waved toward the back. Then it was I heard the second hammer, turned, and in a corner saw Uncle Anthony, his face stained with tears, pounding boards together for my son. And this was worse than seeing the cradle, for each pound of the hammer split me in two. Uncle got off his knees and took a step toward me, but my throat was closed to speech and I backed away; for to utter even a word of what had happened would mean to relive it; and I didn't know how to do that without going mad. "Let him go, Anthony," I heard Sarah's father say; "no one can help him now."

And I staggered into the open.

Blindly I trod the road toward Exeter; and then was in the small village a quarter-hour from St. Vitalis; and then inside the church to which Sarah's body soon would come.

I found myself gaping at the rough-hewn stones of the church walls with their smell of water and dug earth, at the narrow arched windows with light pouring through them that would never again hold Sarah nor feel my son wade in it. And I watched my feet tread heedlessly upon the grave marker of the first rector there, buried near eighty years before.

"Bury!"

The word erupted from me to strike the walls and bound

back again: Yes. Bury this thing that had happened; and the Jophiel who had lived it. Yes. That was what I must do!

Then wooden shoes rang from the stone floor behind the altar. A woman I remembered a little from our wedding day came forward with downcast eyes, a black drape for the altar overflowing her arms. And a cold dew from the walls seeped into my bones.

The ground where they would put Sarah and my son would be chill like that. And it came to me that I must be the one to dig graves for Sarah and me and for our son; and then join her there, bury with her Jophiel, the husband and father, though the Church demand I remain here a living corpse myself, to eat, sleep and work 'til my bones and flesh finally give way.

I headed back to the farm, then, to hone the lip of the shovel to a fine edge would cut cleanly. And, alone in the Dorset smith shop, 'twas all I could do not to draw that edge across my wrists.

In the church cemetery off the Dorset property, Sarah had once pointed out the family marking stones going back generations. So, shovel in hand, I found again where the three-dozen or so Dorsets were laid to rest.

Sarah and I used to banter, joking and tender, about how, deep in the earth, we would hold each other and tell stories for our own amusement until the Last Judgment when, the Church said, we would all rise in new bodies. Well, I stood there a long time, not wanting to give my wife and son into their keeping, you can understand; and my arm thrown up against the bright sun, wishing to God the birds would stop their damned twitter-twitter so I could think.

Then it was that I heard wagon wheels and horseshoes biting the earth. Then a cloud of dust hung at the church door. Watching from behind a tree, I had to turn from the sight of the coffins and the sound of feet slow-walking to the trill of a recorder, the pluck of a lute and sad tap-tap of drum pacing, for all, all of

it chewed into my very bones, and dragged me back into the raw,
unforgiving moment when Sarah's breath came no more.

I marked a new spot among the Dorsets, hefted my foot
to force the metal lip into the earth, then glanced up to see Sarah's
uncle and brother coming with their own shovels; but when they
saw me and what I was about, they turned back to the church.

Then my shovel bit deep; and the smell of fresh dirt
bleeding out nauseated me so that I had to stop and lean upon its
handle to breathe. Just then the church bell took up, cracking the
air cruelly over the fields far as Exeter and into the deep hills of
Devon for all to hear, to ask, "Who is it for? Who is it for now?"

For Sarah. It is for my Sarah. It is for my new-born son.

The shuffling of feet. Dig. Dig. The closing of the church
doors. Dig. Dig. Silence. Dig. The organ. Dig. The singing, like
ghost music seeping from the windows, from under the door. And
the merciless sun, the sizzling of turned earth until at last I stepped
into the hole for Sarah where my spirit fought me, then, trying
to escape from my body. But I worked on, grim as a man with a
scythe, the music and raised voices fragile mounting the air and
passing into me still digging, pouring sweat and never recalling any
earth so heavy as this.

I knew from years of standing at Mass how long I had
until they flung the doors open again. But also, there would be the
churching for Sarah, with Aunt Agatha as midwife acting for her
and standing at the door holding a candle while the priest sprinkled
her with holy water, reciting the special prayer; then into the nave
to receive God's blessing on her motherhood. And all the while
my Sarah dead in her coffin, our son dead in his. Still, to have her
motherhood honored, to have my son honored; for that something
within me was thankful.

The second hole, being small, did not take long; and
I smoothed the sides and bottoms of both to be comely for the
lowering. Then I laid the shovel down, and thought how when
they put the dirt back into these pits, all of me in this life of love
with Sarah would be sealed in there with her and with our son. I

imagined how, through the wooden boards and the packed earth, we would reach out to our infant boy to draw him to us; for we could not have it that he should lie there alone.

I slid the wedding ring from my finger and watched it tumble into Sarah's grave. The trees around, turning with the onset of Autumn, released a few leaves to drift down and cover it. And I looked up toward the hills of Devon as if to a mother; but they were turned inward to their own thoughts. And in my mind I had already fled like a man with clothes on fire, his hands over his ears to shut out the ravaged voices telling the story, our story, over and over again.

And when the music came to a halt, I turned to flee before they carried my Sarah out. Over my shoulder I saw Bernard, Marydine and their mother stumble from the dark mouth of the church and into the glare of daylight wiping their eyes.

CHAPTER TWELVE

I knew not where to go but to the woods; and felt curiously light as I ran. I imagined that, like Sarah, I had become spirit and must too have lost my body, for I seemed to float, like I'd heard ghosts do. I plunged deep into the living green. At the foot of an ancient tree near a creek, I found a mossy place and threw myself down. Then I slept and slept. And in a dream, my Mamoon came to hold me against her great safe bosom, to rock me, sing low to me lullabies in the old language; and safe in her great lap, thought I could smell upon her trees, plants, running brooks that drew me to peace.

Who knows how many hours later I woke, formless and drifting, feeling myself to be of the same weave of spider webs, and listening to the creek lisp unnamed secrets already within me. I buzzed with the insects, discovered in my throat the chitter of birds and bark of foxes; the snort of wild pigs came from my chest.

And all around and within was a great still pond showing its own life to itself, peering into itself and out at itself. And light! How it shimmered in everything so that I walked as if on tiptoe lest the smallest mistake shatter this safe and sacred vessel holding me, and in which I now would live.

Eventually would come the snap of twigs, the breaking of branches and human voices calling from that clearing just into the woods, "Jophiel! Jophiel!" I would picture my family: The weeping, the baskets of food, their tongues turned to shovels come to dig me up out of my place of refuge. And I would scramble fast as a rabbit through the trees until those voices were no more and the torn silence had healed itself.

I don't remember if I ate or what I ate. I only remember I slept, drank cool water, lay among the dried fallen greenery and threw my head back to let the sun and the sky breathe me in and out. Animals crept close to peer or sniff; and the leaves around and above whispered, "Hush, hush." Days, the sun passed over, and the calling of my name would come dreamlike as that of someone I had buried. Nights, the stars summoned me from their high place, naming me son or brother. And my soul was comforted. But finally, I must build a burrow against the bite of September nights. Mornings now, I crawled out to meet winking of frost.

Lying one afternoon along a small creek and in a doze, the soft sound of animal padding threaded through my mind. Then a wet nose nuzzled my ear; and the old yellow dog Scraps from the smithy dropped down next to me, his long tongue dripping, gold eyes wise and calm upon my face. And he stayed from then on. Soon I would find my hand upon his broad head, or my fingers in the silk of his ears. Bit by bit, like waking from a faint, the heave of his body brought back to me the sense of animal life, though I resisted it; for my freed spirit greatly feared any memories locked within my own flesh.

And Scraps would wander off, then return with a basket my family had left; and set it at my feet until I pushed his head towards it to eat. I did not speak words to him in terror of the avalanche the sound of my own voice might loose; and I could not risk the feeling of life food might bring me. More and more I would remember the trips to the woods with Mamoon, and my hand would discover among the plants that which would sustain me.

And then no voices called my name. And it appeared that at last that I had convinced my relatives and friends I would not return. Oh, and I tell you, I felt relief; but also wept fresh grief that now I had won my own burial.

Some next day after that, I woke just past sunrise, and leaned over the creek to cup some water to my mouth; and Scraps' ears flew up over a small animal I could not see. My stomach clamored, but I lay back down. The leaves above made a netting of green and gold through which I could watch clouds, brilliant white and moving on a sea of blue; and their slow dignified progress lulled me back into a half-sleep.

I don't know how long it was, lying there, arm thrown over my eyes, and I became aware that my dark and buried heart had begun quietly to stir. My eyes flickered open, took in the bushes, the creek winding past, saw nothing new and closed again; but the loosening and lifting within me continued of its own. Since I had known only the most constant and terrible pain, pain that made me want to leave my body, I let myself float in this blessed relief long as I could.

The sun had moved to near its high point before I grasped that I was hearing music, the notes circling as fish might inside of me. And I watched as my spirit followed them, turning and lifting, and rising ever closer to a surface that seemed placid and clear as a pond. Scraps, beside me, rolled onto his back and yodeled a great yawn. And it was then, as my hand felt for his head, that I realized the music was outside of me, where Scraps was.

But abruptly then, the playing stopped; and so my heart plunged into a new grief. I sat up. Where had the music gone? Where had it come from? An old wanderer had once told me if you stay alone long enough in the woods, you could hear the trees breathe. So was it the living things of the forest making a music I had learned to hear?

But then four or five notes plucked out round and sweet started up again; and I recognized the sound as one I sometime had heard before; but now not nearby. And afraid to lose it, I rose to follow wherever the next notes, like luminous string, drew me along.

I must have walked some good while, for the sun was past its high point. The notes, growing ever stronger, twined through my heart like tendrils and continued to pull me forward. And as I trod the forest floor, the special way of the notes coming together, their lift and drop, gave me a comfort familiar as home; and presenting ever closer and clearer, until finally I leaned carefully to peer through the foliage and into a clearing to locate their source.

Through the overgrowth, I saw Edward's long fingers arched with the plectrum, his head bent to his work. Sunlight dappled his hair, the purple of his tunic and tawny leggings where he leaned against a great grey rock to play. And the sight of him, the sound of his music pulled me through the last of the trees until I crept forth softly to sit against that rock upon which he leaned.

Edward did not look up; he went on with the chanson. I laid my head back and closed my eyes. I don't know how long he played while the notes rose and drifted into me with gentle wordless voices in a soothing discourse as if among spirits.

Then, and after what seemed a very long time, I realized I was hearing the music both inside and outside of me; and that I was both in my body and beyond it. Slowly, slowly then, it came that I might tolerate staying in my body and mind if, at the same time, I could somehow also rise above them. I meditated on this possibility, testing it as Edward moved from one song to the next. Finally, like a butterfly ever liable to flee, and on the most tentative and provisional of legs, I crossed over note by note on the bridge made by the music, and raised my eyes to him. Somehow I knew he had felt the look.

But he finished the song, then set his lute carefully against the rock and came to sit next to me, my face wet with tears. Tears shone upon his cheeks as well, and he dug bread and cheese from his wallet. I chewed small bites, felt the life of the food course in me. And because it was Edward, the Edward who knew my mind and heart deeply as I knew them myself, I could risk to let life flow within me again; and even risk my own voice.

"I can't go back." I shook my head before he could speak, look up. "I have no desire to live. It is all I can do to keep from taking my life, lest I never see her and the babe in Heaven. But I have a chance here in the woods. An animal might--." I dropped my head, silent, struggling; then looked up. "How can I live without her, Edward? And without my son I held but once?" I tore at my hair. "I bow to God's and Nature's will; but how can I survive them?"

We sat in silence then a good while. Edward took up his lute again to play softly. The sun had moved a little south, so now more tree shadows provided shade. When I think back on it, his speech to me then was gentle as practiced hands upon a terrified animal.

Did I remember Courtly Love and its creed? Sarah and I were true lovers. Our promise to one another did not end in death, but o'er-leaped it. Again I saw my gleaming wedding ring tumble into the grave. "It could have been you," he leaned toward me, his voice urgent "struck down the day after your wedding, by lightning, by a wagon. And your Sarah would have known that death could not end your love."

It was true. Sarah had said as much before and after we married. I thought of how, married, I would lie with her and draw my fingertips along her cheek or rest my head upon her breast, and some deep vault within me outpoured great and silent rapture, relief and gratitude to whoever God is for the miracle of such unspeakable beauty, and for the merciful boon of this love to me, one of so little value. And this memory dealt out a terrible tearing inside me, then; and I shook my head wildly.

"Oh, but I want to die too; and dare not."

Edward rested his lute in his lap; his face all compassion and worry. "Your own torn spirit is proof your love is beyond the body, Jophiel, for it drives your body yet." He rested a hand upon my shoulder. I could feel his desperation for me. "Don't you see, some Holy Will is operating here, that such a love as yours is fore-ordained and surely lives on? There are mysteries we humans cannot unlock. Music is one. Love is one. And only One has the key."

A chipmunk and its mate peered from beneath dried leaves, each frozen, sniffing the air, a front paw lifted. Edward pushed a crust of bread toward them and we held quiet while they dashed to take it.

Edward's confidence calmed me, though I was yet far from his conclusions. Departing sunlight glowed between tree trunks and washed its red-gold over the wild greenery about us.

"Come back with me," he grasped my hands. "You'll be safe. And it would greatly ease my heart. We are all so afraid you will perish here with Winter coming on soon."

It was true. Every night was a bit colder. I held my head. "I can't face anybody, Edward; not even the kindest person. And I fear that to come among them would make me go mad, for I hold my mind to me by a thread as it is, and as you can see."

All the small creatures except those hunting by night by now had begun nesting while the oncoming night breeze swirled fallen leaves. My arms prickled with the cold.

Edward got slowly to his feet to pack his lute at his horse, the animal so patient all this time, nibbling what it could reach with its tether. And I felt my heart breaking to see my friend ready himself, then; and felt loneliness again fill the space I had opened to him. An owl hooted, then raked along the brush so close the draft from is wings stirred my hair.

"At least take the baskets your family leaves," Edward pleaded, then turned away. Elbows working, he opened the covering for his instrument. I heard the desolate cry of a wolf far off; Edward paused to look at me over his shoulder. Then he turned. "What about the monastery?" His eyes searched my face. "You would have help there against that action you do not want to take. And Brother Frederick is there."

Brother Frederick. My teacher. My heart stirred. And if that didn't work, I could always come back and move deeper into the forest.

I raised my chin as a nod. Edward's face relaxed into cautious relief, for I knew he saw I might still bolt before we reached the gates of Exeter. He handed me his instrument. "Could you?"

It was heaven to touch the smooth coolness of the lute, to smell its fragrance. I slid it into its sewn leather case and tightened the ties while Edward went into the trees and came back with a second horse, a bay twirling a sprig of green into its mouth.

On the road, he told me they had known to come to the woods to look for me because Sarah's brother Bernard had seen me heading there from the graves; and that later Uncle Anthony had come up with the idea of the lute from hearing one played through an open door on his way home from work. Well, nothing else had worked. Edward's face grew soft. "I don't know how it is I didn't think of it myself, well as I know you." He shrugged his shoulders in sad bewilderment; and I caught a little of the loss and sorrow everyone had suffered on my account.

"I heard the notes you played," I told him; "So when they stopped, I started walking, to try to find them. They were the same as food to me."

Edward said nothing. The horses rocked along.

"What was it that made the notes stop?" I asked. Edward brought his head up.

"That's when I was crying."

A young monk, his head pushed forward beneath a taper held against the darkness, answered our knocks at the door. Brother Timothy.

"This man seeks refuge," Edward announced, as much for me as anyone. Brother Timothy glanced at me, then kept his eyes carefully on the floor as he showed me to a cell.

This was the only place among men I could have come, where each tends to himself, his prayers and work, and leaves the rest to Providence. The yellow dog, come with us from the woods, barked twice sharply as Edward and I embraced our goodbye, thumped his tail loudly, then bounded away toward Magdalene Road and my uncle's smithy.

CHAPTER THIRTEEN

In the visitor's cell, I sat upon my thin bedding with a candle to eat the thin soup of barley and onions the brother brought. Then I lay down, and the damp chill of clay and stone rose to my nostrils and brought on a panic I must wrestle the rest of that night until Mamoon soothed me in a dream.

The next few weeks I was with Brother Frederick when I was with anyone. He began to rouse me before dawn for meditation, found a shawl for me to bundle myself and follow him, silent as a shadow, into the chapel where one candle sent pieces yellow light like brilliant and erratic leaves over the altar with its sacred objects and the bent shoulders and bowed heads where we sat with others upon the cold stone floor.

Then slowly, painfully, one day to the next, I learned to travel the thorny thickets, bottomless bogs and treacherous cliffs of my mind, searching for the place of safety and peace I always found in the woods. And at times I would feel my teacher leading me, though he sat silent next to me with eyes closed. Afternoons we spent hoeing and clipping in the kitchen garden, myself just this side of being mad.

And perhaps you will not be surprised to hear that at rest periods and on Sundays, my old teacher would bring out his books to rekindle our fellowship with ancient minds. We would sit in the shadows of the kitchen, or under the great tree beyond as it shed its golden leaves. "Let us ask Plato or Aristotle (or Plotinus or a Stoic) what he has to say today," he would nod, his mouth under his great nose straight and serious; and then press a cup of mead into my hand and set upon the ground a cloth of small rosy apples and a few walnuts. Then he would open the book and point to a passage for me to read aloud.

And always I would find something vital and healing hearing my voice speak such high and powerful words about the soul and man and the world; or about how something is formed, maintains itself, and what it can do then. This way we kept company with the Ancients; and so, by Brother Frederick's deft hand, I was led safely to a deeper part of my mind.

"Why would God have us suffer?" I asked one day of October rain while we sat at a trestle in the corner of the kitchen and Brother Isadore, grown yet more grey and round, stoked his hearth and hacked plucked chickens apart. Without apology, he had set beside us an empty basket and a pile of potatoes to rub off the eyes as we talked, for Brother Frederick, after all, forever had kitchen duties.

"What explanation among our teachers do you find for suffering?" Brother Frederick dropped a potato into the basket.

I replied I couldn't really find anything I liked in the Ancients' ideas of suffering. "Hatred, anger, jealousy, revenge." I shrugged. "All those things we are taught are sins; but we do them anyway. The Ancients claim these things come from the gods themselves. Our priests claim they come from the Devil."

I shrugged and shook my head. "I shall never be free of pain. Suffering changes you inside. It is crucifixion."

Brother Frederick raised his eyebrows and wagged his head, rubbing at a potato eye with his bit of stone. But then he stopped, sent a swift cautious glance at Brother Isadore, busy at the hearth, and leaned close.

"There is a certain religion, one more ancient than ours," he kept his voice low, "I have read of and heard about from travelers. Its founder was born long before the Lord Jesus. His name was Siddhartha Gautama, said to be born, like Jesus, immaculate but also human, and from a lotus blossom in the country of India, in the East, a place taken over by Muslims now for a hundred years. But Siddhartha's teachings have spread. Here, of course, they are heresy. Siddhartha freed himself from suffering, and tried to teach others to reach this high state the same way he had.

To be free of suffering. I shook my head. I had never heard that to be possible.

"He taught that we make suffering through mind and desire; and can release ourselves by training the mind. He teaches that meditation is a spiritual practice for accomplishing this."

To be freed of the thoughts and feelings that still drove me to want to take my life! I hesitated, for if I must then release all thoughts of my wife and son--. I shook my head.

Brother Frederick held his eyes upon me. "You have made a beginning, Jophiel. It is not an easy path, but the surest one I know for anyone who will give himself to it."

Brother Isadore waddled over to look into our basket, which held eight rubbed potatoes he took without comment to drop into his great simmering pot. And in but a few minutes we smelled them ripe upon the air.

One day, the week following, I was called to the room reserved for visitors. I thought it might be Edward, who had already come twice to see me.

But it was Sarah's mother on the wooden bench there by the window. My insides reeled, seared as if someone had thrown boiling grease upon them. Her face was pale and drawn, and with deep pockets under the eyes. She wore a black veil.

I fell upon my knees before her and began to cry, asking her forgiveness because my act took her daughter from her, and from her family. But she leaned forward and put her arms around me as I let loose great shuddering sobs and laid my head in her lap. She stroked my hair. "No," she said, "'twas not you who took her, Jophiel. You gave her more happiness than any living being ever has. God took her; and for reasons we can't know." She wiped her own eyes then, and drew from her gown a sealed parchment.

"This is for you."

My heart began to thump. I climbed to my feet and took it to the window to break the seal. I could not keep my hands from shaking, for I was sure it was from Sarah's father.

In his fine educated hand he asked me to come back to live with them. "You are as truly my son as any I have. You are one of my family;" he wrote; "and whatever you decide, I will always love you. And if you can't come now, come when you can."

Oh, but the Dorset farm was the last place on all the earth I could go, the very last place.

And that night in my cell, Sarah came to me in my dreams for the first time, her hair a soft cloud of light. And she took me in her arms and loved me with her body. And I loved her back. And we rested together as of old.

Some few days later, after the reading of the scripture at Sunday Mass, the Abbot, a short man of middle years with a high forehead and cheeks like a boy, stood to read a pronouncement from the Bishop concerning a call to fill the ranks for a Crusade to deliver Jerusalem from the infidel Arabs. Each parish in England was under obligation to supply foot soldiers, and to fill the ranks within a month.

Crusade! Oh, how the word glittered for me as an easy way to death without going to Hell--as a way to join Sarah and our son!

But the monasteries were only asked to pray for the filling of the ranks. Foot soldiers must come from a lord; and if there weren't enough of these, then from the merchant class. In every parish in England that day, this Holy War was preached; and that we English, together with troops from France and Germany primarily, must dedicate ourselves to reclaiming Jerusalem, the city of Our Lord's death and resurrection.

These were lands, I knew, where mathematics, architecture, the study of the heavens began, the very ones I had spoken of with Brother Frederick, mused about a thousand times with Edward or while shoeing horses, hoeing vegetables, chopping wood for Aunt's hearth. At night I dreamed of walking streets with tongue-twisting names. Some, most men, I reasoned, would not want to leave despite having no choice. And to have choice you must have money and the favor of the king; while to refuse the call brought damnation from excommunication upon your soul. Oh, the Pope, the bishops talked compassion, forgiveness and peace; but when anything, any trouble or opportunity, presented, why they could raise an army overnight.

Well, I had no reason to stay behind; quite the opposite. It took less than a day to make up my mind. Brother Frederick steered me into the garden, to the far wall where we could be private. This was the first time we had clashed over anything I wanted to do.

"Your service is here at St. Bartholomew. You read and write; are a young scholar, a thinker, and just as great a help to the Church as tramping the trail of the First Crusade and wasting yourself on the same failure."

"But the Pope, the bishops, the Abbot name this a 'just cause,'" I countered with the authority of Rome. At this, Brother Frederick turned his back toward the kitchen door, then bent to speak in a low voice.

"I am privy to certain facts. And things were not so fine

as made out to be in the First Crusade; and not so fine, easy nor uplifting as celebrated in this proclamation now. And people here are under strict ecclesiastical censure to be mute about how dangerous, full of horror and suffering, these adventures are. They have told me of the many hapless men suffering mutilations, losing limbs and dying the most hellish of deaths from such adventures."

"So," I hurried in, "I could spare one family the loss of a loved one. Since no one depends upon me, what matter if I die?"

My teacher's chest caved ever so little.

"Well," he flapped his arms then, "I admit I had hopes you might join us here." He gestured about the garden. He looked away a moment, then earnestly back at me. "Think first, I beg of you, Jophiel. Think well."

I said I would, but my mind was set. Two days later he asked if it still felt right for me. I said it did, but I didn't know how I could get the required equipment since I had no money and was not attached to any nobility. He stared at the garden wall where the ivy, now turned red, crawled in all directions, and shed leaves toward the sleep of Winter. He heaved a sigh.

"Well, I see you have already left, Jophiel." He looked away some moments, shook something off, then nodded and turned to me. "I can help you. I have relatives."

I drew a breath of wonder, then; and felt more gratitude than I could ever name to this man who, every time I tried to take a step forward, supplied me extra legs and his arm about my shoulders.

And oh how my heart quickened, for on the crusade, with any luck, I could shorten my time until I could be with Sarah and our son. And meanwhile, I could ascribe some value to being alive.

Two or three days, and Brother Frederick motioned me aside at supper. "You are to report five days hence at St. Olave." His eyes searched my face. Was I still sure? I swallowed and nodded.

"Have you seen your family?"

"Not yet."

Next day, as I approached South Gate and Uncle's cottage, I felt I could hear the neighborhood whisper of my arrival. And while some small part of me stepped forward, eager to meet the old familiar places, much backed away, too wounded, still; and afraid of what might be ripped loose by old sounds or smells; or wounded afresh unintended by loving eyes.

The day before leaving, I walked the familiar route to my uncle's place and South Gate. A young cousin at the rain barrel called out, "Jophiel! Jophiel is here!" Aunt rushed out, all flushed, big arms open and bosom heaving. Tears ran down my face as well. I wiped them with my sleeve, and she sat me near the hearth where a kettle of vegetables simmered, pressed mead into my hand I had scarce put to my lips before Uncle appeared, the smithy in his hair and on his clothing. He clapped his arms about me.

It was a quiet meal of soup and the end of the day's bread; and with all of us save Vincent together again. I had volunteered for the crusade, I broke the news. Aunt was appalled. Uncle gave me a long look; and I saw he knew this was the only decision I could make.

"God be with ye then, lad." He raised his cup. "You make us proud. And you'll see those faraway lands you've read to us about." He glanced around at his children, so solemn, and hefted his voice. "Before we know it, our Jophiel will be coming along Magdalene leading a donkey laden with great carpets and gold cups and bags of spices, and calling out to us 'Where do you want these?'"

They all laughed then; and a love simmered among us that crept into my pores while the hearth spat sparks and bits of flame, then sank to a red glow that sent the children to bed.

Another hour. Aunt sat with her sewing; Uncle and I stared into the hearth's dying flames. Then I climbed to my spot above the spice cupboard for the night, and felt my life of old stream through me. The heat made my body and eyelids heavy and I slept. Four hours later I climbed down, found my boots and stepped out into the dark.

Three final days. Then I found Brother Frederick
digging potatoes, sweat coursing his large nose to his upper lip. I
remember his eyes then as clear and with no sorrow, but only bright
anticipation.

"So, Thinker," he stuck his digging fork into the earth, then
held up a hand, "don't worry. I'll save every potato eye for you."
A squirrel scampered up to tug at the hem of his habit. "He wants
walnuts." Brother Frederick smiled wide and gave his habit a gentle
shake.

I didn't know what to say, my heart and mind overflowing
so many directions.

He nodded deeply. "I will see you anon, Thinker. 'Tis only
a matter of time." I opened my mouth, but he stopped my words
with a raised hand. "And we will find out then what discourses
arise between us over all you bring back from the far lands, and
what I have ruminated upon meanwhile behind these walls."

Mind blocked of words, I bowed thanks, agreement,
respect to him. I left then, throat and eyes burning; and a last
sight of his hand there upon the handle of his pitchfork, the great
tree looming behind. And as I passed over the fitted stones of the
floor and hallway, the tall windows to the side door and street, I
imprinted upon my mind this figure of him: his great nose and long
sloping forehead, tall body like heavy sacks piled up, and through
which leaked the glory of his mind and bottomless wisdom of his
heart. And I felt certain I would never see him again.

CHAPTER FOURTEEN

We set out for St. Olave's churchyard where I would enlist in Lord Hammon's brigade. It was just after supper, and not much of a walk from St. Bartholomew. Still, both Brother Frederick and the Abbott insisted young Brother Timothy go with me since we were heading into nightfall. I had but few things to carry: a cloak, extra chasses, a tunic, pantaloon and stockings all tied up in a blanket. Armor and weapons would be provided.

Early April. It was cold, wet; and everything a sea of mud.
We followed the long bend of Mint Street with its leaning coinage shops, air tasting of metal, and street so narrow it could barely hold two men abreast. We turned right onto High Street filled with oxen, horses, wagons, carts, street vendors and common life rushing past. Brother Timothy kept his silence while his blond

tonsured head bobbed to his gait, the hem of his habit leaping about his ankles.

A laughing father strode by, a boy about three upon his shoulders who held a squealing piglet; and the thought that he might have been my own son but a few years hence pierced my innards. I never knew from around which innocent-looking corner might come the brutal thrust. Well, and perhaps I would replace that father in this crusade and save the boy and mother the torment of loss that ate me.

We approached St. Olave's. I reflected that when I went to Mass with Mamoon, hearing the priest drone on and on laying damnations upon us meant nothing to me. What moved me were the unearthly sounds of human voices weaving in and out of one another. Oh, and my nostrils wed to the uplift of the incense, I remember; and my eyes drank in that pure light spilling through those narrow windows to bless our heads and shoulders.

We turned right again, and through the open gates of St. Olave, its churchyard, usually serene, now crowded with a dreadful babble of voices. Men clustered at fires, bellowing, drinking, cursing and scrapping in the dirt while dogs barked at the uproar. Greasy smoke filled the air. Strewn upon the ground were swords, bucklers, javelins, helmets, bedding, personal things and remnants of food. A group to our right stopped talking to stare us down.

"Will you look at this now," a burly fellow, cheeks and beard glistening with grease, pointed a chewed rabbit leg, "even the monks come crawling out of their caves to take the bloody Infidel down. Now ain't that a lark?" Banners with Lord Hammon's colors of maroon and gold hung across the front of the church and snapped in a breeze prowling from over the river. This man's companion, dense-looking and with hair grown partway down his forehead, pushed up on an arm. "And they will be taking the Infidel whores to the ground with the rest of us, and parting their legs for some well-earned pleasures, I'll wager. For aren't they men like us? I dare say they'll knock us aside, starved out as they be for some good warm meat." And with a lewd snigger, he dropped onto his back and closed his eyes.

"No," another bellowed, "these foot-lickers get all the baggage they want in their cells, only they call it praying. I get religion myself between a fresh set of hams. Thanks to You Lord, and amen."

Everyone hooted then and clapped. Behind the laughter, I heard crows heading for the trees calling back and forth in the thinning light of day.

They made me remember the crows scattering outside the tower at South Gate during the siege, King Stephen's men polishing their swords and helmets; then our men carried back through North Gate, one with a leg gone at the hip and some kind of wax seal jammed there to stop the blood, his face deathly white. Another had his helmet on and red seeping through a gash in its side. "Mother of Jesus," he was whimpering, tears rolling into his mouth. And I remembered again my gratitude to those had fought for our city.

And Stephen's soldiers, I remembered--after they starved Exeter out, and our wells had gone dry; after we had drunk all the wine anyone could find and it was surrender or die--how they entered our city with trumpets and banners, set fire to our roofs with no thought for those lived beneath, nor for the wind would carry the flames through a city with no water. I remembered the charred gaping hole in the north wall of our new cathedral we were building; and seeing through swirling ashes what was left of the nave while heated lead from the tall windows dripped to the floor with a fat sound like blood. Oh, but Exeter's wall stood. Rougemont Castle stood. Our lives stood. We had been overrun before, many times; but always outlasted our invaders. My uncle liked to say we eat our invaders so slowly they don't even realize they've disappeared into us.

Now I turned to see these men, Englishmen, but of that same cast of spirit our invaders had been, and elbow to elbow over the entire courtyard. Oh, how my heart sank. This was a mistake.

I should go back to the monastery and make Brother Frederick happy.

And see Sarah and my son everywhere I turned?

"Where do I report?" I asked the greasy beard.

Hilarity again. "You?"

He pointed out a building next to the church. I thanked Brother Timothy who hesitated, then bowed me farewell; and as he turned toward the gate, felt my insides wrench as if a bar had slid into place.

I picked up my belongings.

A tasseled banner stood at the door to a hallway of fitted tiles. Inside, and next to an open door with a similar banner, I saw a cleric writing at a trestle. I entered; and though my shadow fell across his work, the man continued on without looking up, but held out his other hand, impatient, as though receiving my letter of introduction was the most irksome task in the world.

This man had a narrow face, long ears and very clean fingernails. When I leaned to hand him the letter, he jerked back as if my smell were an offense; then turned with the parchment toward the window behind to read without so much as a glance at me.

From down the hall came a metallic chime of mail

"I'll leave it with you, then." A man's voice, sharp and hurried; then a scraping clatter as of a shield set down. "But by the Lord Who made us, when I come back it had better be here, or your mother'll eat your backside peeled and boiled."

"It will be, Sire, I promise," a youthful voice wavered. Then mail and spurs chimed toward the door and down the steps.

"Balerais, is it?" the clerk asked, his voice high and arrogant, his eyes passing over me again. "You are not Norman, surely" he decided, for that was clearly above my station. He bent away again, reading, and not requiring any answer. I studied the scrupulous fitting together of the stones that framed the window behind him, and mused that surely most of us were of some Norman blood by now; for how many generations had Norman lords sailed to England only to bed whatever of our women pleased them, then collect rents on properties deeded long ago by their conquering king?

"But you have done some soldiering?" The cleric swung back again, still studying the letter. "I see nothing here of that."

"No, sir. I am a blacksmith."

He threw his head in disgust and leaned away. "Oh, fine!" he complained to the ceiling, "We have a dozen blacksmiths already, and of course someone sends another."

And then he raked me foot to head with eyes that clearly did not want to touch what they took in; and I realized how like a pauper I looked. After Edward brought me from the woods, the brothers found some grey worn-out things, too large for me. Add to this my low weight from the wasting of my appetite; so that in no way could I look either like a stalwart recruit. And I began to fear the man might decide against me.

"Well," finally he pinched his lips together, and with a great sigh turned to his list to add my name, shaking his head and muttering, 'Anything we can get our hands on,' is what they want."

My stomach relaxed.

He added some lines to the bottom of the letter, and looked up as if annoyed to see me still standing there. Sounds passed through the window of men's voices hailing, horses whinnying and hoves striking stones.

"You want Quartermaster Kermit." He waved the letter toward the door. "He makes the assignments."

I asked for the whereabouts of the quartermaster from a pustule-ridden lad squatted on his haunches and trying to dig a stone from his horse's shoe. The animal kept pulling its foot away, so I placed a palm against its neck and soothed it with soft words until the stone chinked to the ground. The lad stood to grunt his thanks. I asked for the quartermaster; he pointed toward a tent under the large oak near the far wall.

Crossing the yard reading the cleric's appraisal, I nearly

collided with a tall muscular man with grey hair and beard. He wore a tunic of a deep red such as I had rarely seen, and stood, arms crossed upon his chest, observing me as I approached. His bearing and the color he wore spoke of authority.

"Are you the Quartermaster, Sir?"

He grunted assent. I bowed and handed over the letter, which he grasped in a gruff way, and with a full hard look into my face; but as he drew his eyes away, I saw a light in them that belied his manner. I waited while his lips moved silently and slowly from word to word.

Finished, he looked me over. "Can you read this?"

I nodded.

"Read it to me, then. What does it say?" He pushed the letter at me.

"Master Jophiel Balerais," I began, "of clean heart and good character, strong and able and a blacksmith and humble servant, wishes to aid the Church in its hour of need in the Holy Crusade. We hold him in highest esteem and give him our blessing. We support him as a candidate, as well, through arrangements with Lord Hammon, including the provision of his battle armor and other necessaries. Our prayers will be with him and with all of God's crusaders in this holy work."

Next I read the cleric's note. "This man claims to be a blacksmith. He does not look strong and has no practice with war. Make what use of him you can. It is likely he will not survive first combat. Your servant in Christ, Charles Viscony."

Quartermaster Kermit took the letter to read it again. He stroked his beard and raised his eyebrows. "This is a most important thing, this reading that you can do. I make note of it. And can you write, as well?"

"Yes, Sir. Would you like to see my hand?"

He disappeared into his tent and returned with a scrap of parchment, a stylus and ink. I sat upon the ground and wrote in two sentences my name, birthplace, schooling and work training. When I handed it back, his eyebrows flew up. And you can imagine I was flooded with gratitude I had learned to write, and had the luck of a good hand!

Well, I should put my things down there, no there; he pointed beside his tent to my spot. And so by fate I was placed in as much safety as anyone could have going into war. And to be recognized as useful gave me strength out of which to begin my new life.

"You receive your orders from me. First, you are to inspect the camp;" he gestured a stern circle with his finger, but with a light in his eye; "--and find yourself some dinner."

Straw and reeds were spread upon the mud of April; still, my foot sank every few steps. From everywhere came sucking sounds of feet, hooves, tools and wheels pulling themselves free. I took bread, cheese and soup from the cook, Boar. The soup was so weak I understood right away all the small fires and the roasting of yard birds and squirrels.

Nightfall, I lay outside Quartermaster Kermit's tent with my cloak wrapped about me, but resisted falling asleep; for then might come dreams of Sarah. I might meet her with my son at the hearth in our cottage and in this way fill my famished heart; but other times I would meet those sheets soaked with her blood, or behold the swaddled body of my boy and peer into his sealed face. Months had passed and these sights not faded.

Waking to that first grey of morning might have overwhelmed me, except Quartermaster was up early with orders for me to work on at once while I drank off a cup of mead and carried my breakfast bread hurrying after him.

The next day, he had me do four reports, put off too long he said because of the burden to him of writing. He kept a small trestle inside his tent, and I worked there. The tent was near the size of a modest room, and I was grateful for the softening of the glare beyond the open flap; and for the luxury of privacy. He looked over my work, raised his grey bearded chin with a grunt of satisfaction, signed and sealed each letter with wax and directed me to report to the cleric, who would see to their delivery.

I set off at once.

"You did this for Quartermaster?"

"I did, sir. He has assigned me his scribe."

I watched the man try to digest this fact, staring at the handwriting of a person he despised and must now every day find before him. And you will understand it was near impossible for me not to relish the bewilderment and disbelief in his face.

When I returned to the tent, I found a buckler for my arm, a helmet, javelin, long wood pole, chain mail and boots all piled at my sleeping space. The buckler was painted on its wood face with a red cross, the insignia of the crusade. The helmet came to a peak and sloped down to cover the ears, and with a nose guard that fell narrowly down the front and fanned out above the mouth. It would fit snugly when I put it on, but I would wait until I was so ordered. Neither would I pick up the javelin with its hammered metal point, nor the long wood pole for man-to-man fighting. Javelin points I had made by the dozens: flat and leaf-shaped, a notched point at the top. And chain mail I had made aplenty, too. I examined the work, found it was not of our shop, but passable. The boots were a little large; I would save wearing them against the day of real fighting, or so-ordered.

Everything in the camp was to be put into written inventory, Quartermaster Kermit told me. In addition, every written message of his would now be my province. And I was to attend the drills and military practices for the field of battle, in order to keep myself safe. Right away, he saw my discomfort with that idea. "But a corpse with a good hand can't write for me, now can it?" His eyes twinkled.

And so it was the inventories that took me around camp and made me known in a higher way than would ever have happened otherwise.

As you probably have guessed, it was obvious to all at field practice I was no soldier. I would come panting behind the others

in the hay outside the wall between North Gate and Snail Tower.
And some who finished first would mock me with whistles and
applause as I struggled along, red-faced and covered with sweat.
"There's a gap in the line," someone would bellow; "Tell Cook to
put some fat on that bloke." And my skills with the javelin and pole
were equally poor, though I improved the four weeks before we
left for Dartmouth. As belittling as all this was to my manhood, I
developed no taste for what we learned.

Taking inventory, I made acquaintance of the cook and
blacksmith, and let them know I would lend a hand whenever
Quartermaster did not need me. I found musicians as well among
the foot soldiers who taught me that each fills out his daily food
needs by hunting small game. "Otherwise it's porridge, bread and
weak soup," a stringy fellow told me. And our rations, provided by
Lord Hammon, were actually more generous than those of some
under other lords who left their troops to meet their own needs,
perhaps figuring the reward for the crusade would come with
permission to plunder.

Before we lay down for the night, the wafting of music,
like the scent of lavender, would smooth away the babble and
clatter of the churchyard and the day. I quickly found those who
played, and brought my whistle to join them. This gave me more
comfort than food; and along with those I was coming to know at
the cook shed and smithy, the musicians helped to braid me into
army life.

I found a friend to eat with, too; a reader named Gilbert, a
bit younger than myself, and with a round face, dark hair, serious
eyes and a chuckle that never quite escaped his throat. He had
reading and writing, but not so much as I did. From the village of
Crediton and still unmarried, he was thoughtful, easy to talk to,
and liked to sit apart to ponder the oddities of life.

Lord Hammon, our commander, came only twice to review
us before we left for Dartmouth, where our ships were docked. A
week after recruitment closed, he rode in on a big chestnut stallion
with gold and jewels worked into its saddle, dismounted and strode,

mail, iron boots and spurs ringing, up the steps of St. Olave's where we had gathered to hear him.

"All fealty to God and His Holy Church; and to all that belongs to Her," he cried, thrusting his sword toward the heavens; and the rubies on its hilt glistened like living drops of blood. Well, I couldn't get any feeling for the man. Tough grey eyebrows, ruddy cheeks and a strong squared-off body, he had a big voice that sounded like he was shouting into the wind and not to real men standing there in front of him. But in return, the men gave out with a roar like a wild animal.

When I worked with the chief cook, Boar, I always heard the gossip. A big man he was, of darkened skin I've heard some Irish have, a stout neck and small eyes set close in a square heavy face. His head sat forward on the neck while short graying bristles sprouted from his ears and nose.

As we helped to prepare supper one afternoon, gossip stood that within the very hilt of Lord Hammon's sword was a splinter of the True Cross, the very one on which Jesus had died; and that it was brought to England after the First Crusade by a Yorkshire chaplain.

"Well, our Stephen," Boar went on, "when an abbot took him to the wall over giving a married Frankish the priory there, said that could that same glassblower sing the Mass, he would have made him Archbishop." Oh, and how Boar howled his joy at this, turning the pieces of baby rabbit at the fire. "M-m-m," he smacked his lips, "those little bones make good sucking. And the first dash goes to the cook." Turning the meat again, he called for water for the pot.

The thin older man ran to draw a pail from the barrel. I went to help haul it up, lug it back and splash it in. Boar stepped back from the hiss of steam, then picked up his long-handled spoon and motioned to me for the cabbages which then floated in the pot pale green and like a fleet in a harbor; and then submerged, one after the other.

"This wood of the True Cross, the Lord Hammon has, it works miracles to this day at Bromholm," Boar lowered his voice. "--miracles even to the raising of the dead." He stopped to see we took this in well. "The very dead!" he repeated. "And the man neither a priest nor monk nor lord, but only a glassblower! But he made Bromholm's windows beautiful as any in Norman land. And our Stephen--," he held up his spoon, "Well, we say 'our Stephen' until we say 'our Maud', eh? Or who knows who!" And he looked around for a laugh. But I stole quietly away, for, whether his telling was true or not, my heart could not risk hearing of anyone brought back, and they not be Sarah and my son.

The day before we were to leave for Dartmouth to meet the ships, Lord Hammon appeared once more to rouse us with his battle array and set our wills firm for the work ahead. We were to set off from there with other men and ships, English, Norman, Flemish, Frisian, Scottish and German. And together, he raised his sword, we would be a mighty force for our Holy Mother Church! "And do you want to wrest from those pagans the land our grandfathers bought back with their own blood?"

A roar from the hungry war animal.

Since my early youth at St. Bartholomew, I often pondered that if my teachers were loyal to the Church, out of respect I must allow the ordeal of the Mass and such things as miracles be possible, despite no evidence. And should such teachings prove true, 'twould not be hard to admit to the limits of my mind and stand on the right side with them; for I had no deep feeling for the beliefs of the Church and the violence that could come from them. But when I saw Nature's violence, which Mamoon taught me was a response to and a reflection of our own violence, or was brought on by needs of its own, then that violence seemed logical. But the free-wheeling violence of man--and especially man against man--to me, not so.

"And you can buy salvation for those you love," Lord Hammon went on. "For should it be God's will to take you in your duty, they also will go straight to His bosom, every sin forgiven."

The boon of an early death. The man next to me cried out a mix of grief and gratitude that I knew too. A few nights prior, I heard him tell he had joined up to free his wife from Hell, for she had hanged herself and so could not receive the proper burial to open Heaven.

"And I'll be at your side," Lord Hammon's voice rose again. "And when we march through those lands of our Savior, even now I grant you every soldier's just reward."

A long roar of lust.

"We join Louis VII of France and Conrad III of Germany and others in fealty to Holy Father Eugenius III who sent the blessed Bernard of Clairvaux to preach the righteousness of this endeavor. Some of the noblest lords of England come to lead the fleet: Henry Glanville, Simon of Dover, and Andrew of London. Tomorrow we march to Dartmouth to join the others. Let us go then, and sharpen our teeth on the bones of the Infidel Arab. And we count one hundred sixty-four ships turning sail East to put God's awful dread into the heathen heart!"

And as the beast roared again, I wondered if others also stood, like me, staring at their boots.

Later, Gilbert shook his head. I turned the soup cup in my hand and watched the barley grains follow the movement. "We are men," I pondered aloud, "the Infidels are men. Why should they be worse than us? Perhaps they are better, for their lineage is of philosophers and scientists and mathematicians."

Nodding, Gilbert finished his bread, and as if that idea solved something for him. For me, my other reason for joining the crusade was to see with my own eyes the places from which had come the thought and greatness of feeling that were the very foundations upon which we now so proudly stood.

And so the day of our departure was preached in all the churches. Those from Exeter were allowed until next morning for goodbyes. I helped the cooks scour pots, assemble supplies and pack them for travel. I had said my goodbyes.

We gathered on North Hay at dawn to march across Exeter

to South Hay where the Bishop would bless our endeavors. Lord Hammon sat powerful upon his great horse, and his burnished mail gave off about him a kind of halo. The common folk cried out and threw flowers as he rode past with his clattering retinue. And acrobats, jugglers, troubadours and musicians cavorted as if this were a feast day. One man on stilts, ribbons streaming from his elbows, held high the city seal taking his enormous steps among the cheering crowd. And our men threw back their shoulders to be a part of glory. Their heroism would be repaid with material treasure they would bring home to amaze their relatives and neighbors. The sky hung pure and blue, and with the scent of spring flowers everywhere.

On South Hay next day, nearly one hundred of us waited patiently until old Bishop Waelwerst, grey and worn, arrived from Plympton Priory, propped by cushions and helped to the platform where he stood steadied by a younger priest. Arrayed in golden vestments, he held his miter like St. Peter, and read some Latin over us. Then, at a signal, we sank to our knees, and he gave absolution of all our sins past, present and future, and to those of our families as well "in nomine patris et filius et spiritu sanctus."

Short on belief, yet I felt the great silent lifting, unspoken groan of relief and moment of unspeakable peace while the bishop wafted incense sweet and decaying north, south, east and west, into the morning breeze. Townspeople at the edge of the Hay bowed their heads; and the sight of them, callused hands folded, fired me up with a fierce desire to protect for them the world to which they belonged. And that moment I forgot both my hatred of violence and hopelessness as a soldier.

As the bishop gave his interminable closing words, my eye strayed over the crowd. Bog, his wife and son stood out suddenly; and from behind his shoulder, the flame of Uncle Anthony's hair. Oh, and I turned cold as ice. It had never entered my mind anyone would come to see me off; and I felt invaded, my feelings so threatened I dared not look further, terrified I might see Sarah's family. My heart pounding, I stared instead at the hair of the man in front of me, tracing the plaits and knot of his leather hair thong, and wishing to God Waelwerst would finish this thing off.

Finally, and holding my eyes straight ahead, we stepped out, then made the turn onto the road. The townspeople thronged, waving banners and scarves and shouting huzzah. Oh, I forgot that we would pass the smithy; and it occurred to me suddenly that some of the men might stand out front to cheer me on. And I knew then I would have to look; and did as I came along near the end of the ranks. Old Guill and some of the others were perched upon barrels to get sight of me; and they waved their arms calling out, "Ay, Jophiel! You do us proud, lad! Go get the blackguards!"

I forced a smile and raised my arm to them. And perhaps ten paces beyond, I turned my head to take in one more time the slanting roof of the smithy with its tall spreading oak under which Edward and I made music, and which held the stories of so much that had brought me into manhood.

It was then I saw the women, seven or eight and coming along behind. With birch twigs and brooms, and crying and wiping their eyes, and sweeping away any footprints, any sign we had trod there, so that no dark or evil thing might follow and find us. This was one of a hundred practices from the old ways that Mamoon knew, and that were condemned by the Church with burning or drowning for the sin of witchcraft. But that day no priest nor guard raised a hand in the name of God to stop those women.

CHAPTER FIFTEEN

It was a long day of dust and sweat to reach The Haven, the harbor at Dartmouth. We tramped endless rounded hills of fresh grass and small flowers trembling beneath the dust we raised. "I feel I been climbing nothing but me mam's chest," a short thin man near me threw up his arms. "And 'tis like a bad dream I can't wake from."

Finally we reached the Dart River and followed it to the ocean where the May sun had sunk to threads of red-gold along the horizon, and whose blush clung to the undersides of low clouds reflected upon the waters where the dark shapes of porpoise played.

The harbor, like a bowl with one side out, looked onto schools of the pilchard The Haven was famous for; and that we would catch aplenty to cook on sticks over our fires that night. And from where we ate in the dark, we could hear the ocean breathe,

and the Dart River pushing through its narrow throat to greet it.
And a mighty sound, I can tell you.

　　　The plan was to arrive a day ahead of our ships, get
organized and continue the eternal field practice. Tomorrow would
be the first of seven days for loading supplies before pushing off for
the Holy Land. Quartermaster Kermit ordered me to sleep inside
his tent, for which, you can believe, I was grateful. And before I
knew it, I was blinking my eyes open to him leaning over me in the
grey light before dawn. I climbed to my feet, shivering. He handed
me a heel of bread from his own stock, then threw back the tent
flap. "Everything," he emphasized, "must be inventoried before it
goes on either ship. Everything! This will take all week, so no time
to waste. And now, Jophiel, you will learn what it means to move a
battalion fitted out for war across an ocean. Rouse your men now
and get them going!"

　　　Six young recruits were assigned me when it became clear
no single man could handle all the counting. My men, who could
neither read nor write, were young and alert; and looked as if they
wouldn't be much good at soldiering. So, my orders delivered,
they moved out like spokes from a hub to count and report back.
I too inventoried, there was so much to do, as well as checked
their work, prowling behind them, as I warned I would do. For
Quartermaster had made me see our very lives hung upon the order
and safety of our stores. And I drummed into my men that should I
find any work lacking, that man would be replaced in the blink of
an eye. And since this station was considered "privileged," no one
wanted that! And though I had spoken against it, they continued to
call me "Sir", something you can imagine never felt right since we
were all of the same station in life. Perhaps it felt safer to them to
do so.

　　　The rest of the brigade was up stoking their fires. As I
looked out from the tent, I saw, like a miracle, the masts and spars
of the Boniface and St. Petroc arrived during the night, sails still
up and like reflections of clouds in the harbor's moving water.

And at the sight of their huge double-ended hulls, I felt a leap of excitement.

I studied the ship's castles, fore and aft, the pointed arched windows where Lords Hammon, Andrew and their retinues would pass the journey. I craned my neck to follow into the sky the great masts with the proud purple and gold banners of the owners, as well as those of the crusade. I admired the female bulge of the ships' sides, the carved wooden rudders raised and still glistening from the water.

These were clinker-built ships like ones I had often noticed at Exmouth, bottom and sides of overlapping planks fitted together by a hewer to make a shape that might look, finally, like a great shell of a nut, or the sides of a fish. And I had seen years before what slow work it was, for after a wooden board was in place to be nailed against one already there, the nails along the new plank must be held on the outside by a Helder; while on the inside, the Clencher presses each iron point over and back into the wood; and each nail may not be more than a hand's width apart from the next. And you can just imagine piled up these thousands of nails that hold in place the form of the ship! At the smithy, we were always behind making nails. They would be dumped into big barrels that rode off on wagons while we went on making more. When you see ships like the Petroc and the Boniface floating on the water, held together by nails and fitted pieces of wood and rope, by tar and hair, you must marvel, as you do with a cathedral or castle, at what men with their minds and hands, and working together, can do!

Well, we started by counting small animals crated for slaughter: pigs, chickens, rabbits, Guinea hens; and all stuffed into dozens of wood cages. Next came the salted meat and fish, as well as salted and pickled vegetables, all in dozens of small barrels set out in the sun. Bags and bags of salt, barley, rye and wheat were piled in long rows with the crates of spices, great jars of olive oil and pork grease, and sacks of almonds and filberts for making milk.

And I did not overlook bottles of green glass, very thick

and crude; and wondered if Quartermaster had bought up the work of novice glassblowers at Bromholm or Exeter, for appearance to us would mean nothing so long as the bottles did not leak. And for holding large amounts water, were large earthenware jars of that deep green Exeter glaze you see in every house at home. These, five or ten gallons apiece, stood in a great crowd; and for a moment it felt as if I took inventory of an army of dwarves along with squat and banded ten-gallon barrels of mead and ale that made me recall the cheering would rise up from the smithy as I rounded South Gate, the heavy foaming buckets hanging from the wooden piece across my shoulders.

Moving one place to the next, I found ready for the small blacksmith shop, crates and crates of treenails, iron bolts, chisels, hampers, pincers, saws, sledge hammers, adzes, chains, planks, riggings, rudder fittings, tar, tallow, caulking irons, pitch, mops and bundles of hair, all to keep a ship watertight. And crates holding furlongs of rope, huge wooden pieces, stacks of very long planks roped together; and then more furlongs of rope. All, I was told, were parts of the trebuchet, a new war machine that could launch huge rocks and break open the fortifications of our enemies.

That week I worked furiously, Quartermaster directing me. Oh, and my presence irritated many, for the men had to wait for us to finish our count before they could load. Often things were heaped up in a way I could not address until someone straightened the pile. And only when Quartermaster had approved an inventory were those things sent aboard. The men would leap forward to haul crates, bales and boxes, to roll barrels up the gangplank for stowing on deck or in the hold in a place already marked out for them.

Now, with but two days left before casting off, Quartermaster Kermit shook my shoulder even earlier. Since moving into his tent, I found he often worked by taper into the middle of the night, poring over drawings of our two ships.

"I need to talk with you." He waved me up; then told me to sit and share his breakfast. Such a big active man he was, I could feel the heat from his body through the deep red of his cloak. Above that, in the grey light of morn, his thick white beard, eyebrows and hair stood out.

"Be clear that your duties do not end with loading the ships." He shook his chin for emphasis. "You may be given other work--cooking, cleaning, smithing--should you have free time aboard; but believe me, you will not have much of that. And your duties aboard begin today. I will also have reports for you to write, as we go along, telling of how we fare. We will send them from Oporto, in Portugal, on ships bound for England."

"Yes, Sir."

The chunk of cheese he offered on the point of his knife was white and hard and fragrant. I had to shut my mind against it as I ate it, for it made me think of Sarah's father. The bread, warm from Boar's oven, gave up more easily to my teeth than what we'd got in camp, it being of a finer texture and more like the bread for the teachers at my school.

Quartermaster brushed crumbs from his beard. "We have a voyage long enough in good weather to cause concern about our stores. Supplies must last until we reach port. It is your work to see everything that comes on safely stowed and used; and that your lists match the stowage. And it is good luck for you to be responsible for but one ship, unless you are a very good swimmer."

I laughed, pushed the cheese into the center of the bread with my thumb. "No, sir. I am a pond swimmer, and would be food for the fish three strokes into the water."

Quartermaster threw his head and barked a laugh. "Well, I can't afford to feed fish! I will find someone for the second ship. Have you sailed before?"

I shook my head. He raised his chin he understood, then passed me his flask. "On board, thievery comes with a high price, that of a hand, or even the gallows. As it should. You must make a count of everything each day and report it to me." I nodded, took a swig from the flask and passed it back.

"Remind your men," he went on, "they are accountable if you find their work not right." He took a swig himself, then continued. "On board today, have the sailors show you how they secure things. In bad weather, ropes and knots are what save us. Have them show you the passes until you can make each knot every bit as well as they can. And bring your men with you; for they must learn everything and be tested. Not only must all of you count, but also observe well whether each thing remains stowed as before, or if someone has been into it. If that is the case, you report it to me immediately. Be about these things, then. Here, take more bread and cheese. And wait, take this" He knotted the flask to my belt. "And tell Cook you require more ale." Then he turned again to his maps of the innards of the ships.

That day and next were spent catching up on what had already been stowed, and working out a routine with my men. I made notes about knots, lashings and coverings. We studied them together, then went to the sailors who tied the knots too fast for our eyes. We made them repeat each motion until each of us could do it as well. Afterwards, I told my men what time to report to me each day, and where. I would watch closely to see they could do the work. If they faltered, I would have to replace them. And believe me, I could have used those two days and ten more men to complete everything.

As the sun began to descend toward the horizon that last day, the sight of horse after horse snorting, whinnying and tossing its head and led up the gangplank with a cloth over its eyes is burned into my memory. The animals did not like the sight of the plank nor of the ship--nor, it seemed, the smell of the ocean, for they kept whinnying and blowing and shaking their heads.

I was nervous myself on the plank. It was not so wide, really; and more than once a soldier coming the other way with a big armload failed to see me and forced me aside until I had to fight for my footing.

Now the red of the sun bled across the beautiful shapes of the animals' long noses and through their ears veined like flower petals that, since their eyes were covered, moved to take in what went on around them. The sun bled over the hands and faces of the men leading them, and down their legs to meet the same brilliant rose dancing upon the water.

Days before, I had inventoried dozens of wooden planks set beside furlongs of canvas and rope. Now I saw they were meant to fashion a kind of stable on deck, each with a stall and canvas cradle to pass under the belly of the horse to hold the animal in rough weather.

CHAPTER SIXTEEN

It was May 19th, 1147, Year of Our Lord.

I saw England pull away 'til the tallest of cliffs were but a ragged line riding the top of the water; and then nothing altogether.

May is mild on land, but fierce at sea; and the rolling of the waves brought us to our feet and to the side of the ship for the next four weeks. Even on a mild day, and few there were, the climb and plunge, over and over, did the Devil's work on our bellies.

And we were not lucky with weather. And you can believe the sailors made great fun of us soldiers, staggering about the lurching deck bandy-legged, mast to post, crawling when we had to, their mockery in our ears. After a time, some of us learned sailor's legs and took charge of our stomachs, if only to save face. I never could, but had my position with the Quartermaster to cloak

me from outright scorn. After all, should I find fault with any
sailor's work or stowage, it would be no light matter for him.

Well, and we too must be stowed; and so slept in the hold
on shelves barely wide enough for turning over. That there wasn't
room for us all to eat or sleep at the same time explained men
scrubbing, polishing and sweeping in the dark of night. I would
listen to the wind scream and feel for those on deck holding onto
anything they could, and to one another. And I would hear the
horses in their fear, too; and sometimes creep up to talk to them
and comfort them, despite the soaking I got. And more than once I
hung onto one of their necks to keep from sliding overboard with a
sudden pitch of the ship and the water that followed.

Quartermaster Kermit did not find anyone to his liking to
inventory our sister ship, the Boniface; so every day I must pass
with four aides between ships, hang upon a high watery lip, then
plunge into the open jaws of Death below, and rocking violently
from side to side, the wind screaming, the boat taking on hissing
foam and jumping fish, their gills pumping while the four sailors
knotted over their oars cursed through their teeth and the walnut
shell in which we rode cried out, shuddering and belching water.
White in the face, eyes squeezed shut, we'd clutch the boat's rim,
our knuckles standing up like soldiers. Should water rise above our
ankles, we'd have a wooden bucket knocked against our chests,
lock legs and bail, eyes but slits while fingering for the rim of the
boat to toss the water over. And this was twice a day, ship to ship.
One sailor on the Petroc would peer over the side and call out as
we inched our way up the rope ladder, "Here come the women!"

One day, Quartermaster Kemit, on deck with me while
the ship flailed and bucked, looked around at our fleet stretching
far as the eye could see, tossing and bouncing upon the water. He
grasped a spar to steady himself, hair and red cloak blowing, shook
his head and shouted, "It's blowing up a bad one, Jophiel. This
weather's already cost us a week; and we don't have much margin
in our stores, as you well know."

Almost as he spoke, the clouds above turned a sickly

yellow and the water went black. Screaming from around a corner, and without any warning, came an even more vicious wind. Our vessel, slapped hard by a wave, rose above the gunwales and flopped toward her opposite side. We lost our footing and slid across the deck on our knees and against some lashed barrels.

"Get below," Quartermaster waved his hands wildly. "I can't have you drowned." And he himself looked like Neptune, hair pulled out full length by the wind; and with which came, as he spoke, a great wave from the other direction to force itself under the ship, then draw it high and push us nearly onto our side again. This time water jumped the rail with a crash and sizzled over me. Quartermaster clung with both arms to a lashed barrel while more water boiled me up and into the small boat we used to get from the Boniface to the Petroc. I remember the heartening smell of its flaxen ropes.

And I was not the only one stranded. Up one mast, a sailor used his tunic to tie himself to it, and around which he also wrapped both arms. Below across the deck, the great kettle in the kitchen tore loose and clattered off with a wild hollow voice. I kept my eye out for it because such heavy metal rolling hard could kill a man.

On its part, the storm showed no stopping; and I realized all of us, great estate or low, were at the very mouth of Death. The ship again rose high upon a crest, balanced there, then trembled and plummeted a steep foaming slope, and swayed onto one side. The small boat lashed on board that I was in filled, and I came up gasping, coughing and blowing. And that was when I heard the horses; and a bolt of fear for them shot through my stomach. For I remembered how they had hated the gangplank; and feeling responsible now that they should not be left alone, I became calm and wily. To reach them, I would have to use the pitching of the ship to slide across the deck, grabbing iron rings on my way, or anything that was embedded. From where I was, I could see the water stream glistening down the animals' necks as they stretched to keep their heads above the onrush, their eyes in the gloom huge and white. I heard them thud against their stalls and scream; and in my mind I could see, horribly, their legs breaking.

It seemed an eternity of sliding and grasping until I caught hold of a plank of the nearest stall. Just then, and with terrible loud shaking, again our ship tipped, and nearly onto its side. My feet lifted off the deck and freezing water foamed to my waist. I wound both arms around that stall's plank and buried my face into its rough plane; and for an instant felt my nose pushed against another board in another dark space, and heard the wicked taunts of my brother Michael and sister Leofric as they forced me into the abandoned shed near our hut.

Now, in horror and panic, and my nose pressed against the plank, I watched the horses in their canvas slings, wild-eyed and hanging in the direction of the horizon, each one thrust against the side of its stall, whinnying and thrashing and frantic with fear. All I could do was to call to them in the calmest voice I could find, "It's all right. You're all right. I'm here with you." I could not reach them yet, but they knew my voice; and I reasoned had I been with them in the stalls, what with the bounding and lurching of the ship, one might easily have been flung aside and crushed me to death. So with each pitch, I prayed the water around them support their limbs, though it made them wild with fear. I don't know for how many hours I kept my presence alive to them; and reflected that if I were going to die here, I would rather it be in their company than with anyone else; and then pass over to find my wife and son.

Useless as oars seemed against the storm, whenever the ship was not flat upon her side, anyone who could get to the oars must take a turn at trying to outrun the weather.

And I don't know how many hours it was until finally we managed to round the tip of Iberia. The sky lifted a little then, and I could see our battered fleet scattered across the water. Two days more of hard rowing and we sighted grey and brown and green upon the horizon; and the next day, we saw specks of the towers, steeples and windmills of Portugal; and everyone cheered! We would feel earth beneath our feet again.

Later, remembering being in the very throat of Death, I would meditate upon the wisdom of the design of those female sides of our ship, and how they kept us from capsizing.

And so we sailed into the harbor on the sixteenth day of June, our fleet looking like a flock of chickens a fox had got after.

CHAPTER SEVENTEEN

Oporto!

Had you been with us you would have seen flower gardens reflected in the harbor; and upon the stony hills, brightly-painted buildings in reds, blues, pinks, greens and yellows. All this met us.

Clustered at the docks were small Portuguese vessels of a slender bird shape I heard a seasoned sailor call "barcos rabelos". They hold three men, are of wood with a red color to it, a single mast and long slender oars. An open wood structure at the front can be covered for sun or bad weather; and a flat bed for goods is behind. These slender vessels are used for business on the Douro, a river that crosses both Spain and Portugal, and empties into the sea at Oporto. Wine barrels, I was told, are heavy trade here.

Among our men there was much laughter, swagger, and talk of getting drunk and finding women. "You don't need to speak that Port-o-gesa for them to know what you're after," I heard a young buck laugh as he ruffled a friend's hair and gave him a shove. "And if they don't know what you're asking for, well you don't got all day, now, do you? But be sure you bow afterward and say 'My thanks for your comfort, Mistress.'"

We were given leave to go ashore that week whenever we didn't have work. But work aplenty waited for my men and me: Accounting for and replenishing foodstuffs both present and lost to the storms, and counting supplies for the Holy Land. Well, I was not sorry to be busy, for I would much rather wander Oporto on my own. And when my feet first felt the solidness of earth there, something in me suddenly ached for home, a feeling I could not afford to give over to. But also came the joy at finding myself in a new country with people strange to me, yet so filled with life!

The town called out with its painted buildings, the laughing eyes and quick gestures of its people, the sound of their speech like Alphin Brook in Exeter, cavorting on the surface but running steady beneath. And music and dancing everywhere, and the strange instruments with haunting sounds I wished Edward could hear.

When work was finished, I would search out a small public house where I was unlikely to meet men from the ship. This took time; for the town swarmed now with crusaders determined to bring satisfaction to any appetite manacled at sea.

Outside the eating-places would hang a sign with a painting of a bowl or cup. You drew aside a curtain to enter what was usually a small dark space with oil lamps on the walls, the air thick with spices and the sounds of an instrument playing.

I would sit at a trestle and point to something someone else was eating that looked some way familiar. As for spices, I knew cinnamon, ginger, and a few others; but the new ones woke my nostrils and tongue. Lively and colorful, they made me sweat, and lingered long in my body. One meal I can taste yet was of spiced cheese and turnips cooked in layers in its iron pan and so served. That humble dish leaves me, all these years since, craving it still.

Another of chicken pieces and vegetables baked in bread and covered with a lemon sauce. I remember that too.

The first time I paid for a meal in their money, I felt myself to be really learning the world; and my heart expanded as it had that first day upon the ocean when I turned and saw the huge fleet of ships of which we were but one member.

Once, not yet ready to return to quarters, and wanting quiet and privacy, I slipped into a small church near the public house and sat against a wall. The space was unadorned except for the Virgin, the babe on her arm, and a small ship set upon her open palm. The two candles had been blown out, but the smell of beeswax comforted me.

Then a short heavy older woman dragged a ladder to that niche to mount to one rung from the top. There, using a corner of her cloth and the utmost of tenderness, she cleaned the Virgin's face as if it were that of her own child; then the Holy Infant; then the small ship with its upturned keels and billowing sails. Next she bent and kissed the Virgin's feet. Three times she kissed them, then climbed down, her face a mirror of peace.

Out onto the street again, soldiers and sailors streamed toward the ship while shopkeepers put up shutters for the night, and lights appeared in family rooms above businesses. I thought of Exeter and realized that yes, these Portuguese were different in many ways from us English; still we both cared for the same things. And in the love of their religion, they surpassed us. More than once I saw a man sink to his knees to kiss a street crucifix, or leave a coin at the feet of the Virgin. I mused that had such actions been common in Exeter, and the Church in England as kind as it seemed here, I might now feel different toward it.

As I boarded our ship that last night ashore, I passed the forecastle lit with many tapers; and two or three high men of the Portuguese Church (I guessed from their dress and cast of skin) sat tight about a trestle with our Lord Hammon, Andrew of London, and Simon of Dover. One was a bishop, for he bore his gold miter.

I saw him once before, trumpets sounding, and coming aboard to speak with Lord Andrew.

"It is said King Alfonso is already upon the road," this bishop bent to them with a secretive voice, but that carried to me. "And we will certainly capture Lisbon, for the Moors will be taken by surprise."

I saw Lord Hammon frown and shake his head at this, while Lord Andrew, a fair young man of narrow face and pointed flaxen beard, nodded in vigorous agreement. The bishop half-stood then to press his point. "It will be even quicker and more certain with your numbers and war machine. They have nothing so powerful here in Lisbon. And then you will be on your way, having served both God and Pope." But Lord Hammon disagreed. "With all respect, Excellency, we are expected in the Holy Land within two months. And should weather turn against us at sea--."

Keeping my face carefully forward as I passed, I made my way down to the hold and my narrow pallet, wondering mildly what could gather those powerful men late at night to talk in low voices, and with such energy.

It was three or four days Oporto to Lisbon. We stayed close to the shore, passed peasants toiling along the road with oxen, carts, and raising dust. There were shepherds, their dogs yipping in and out of matted flocks, thatched huts and at least two large castles with stonework much like our own. But compared to green England, the land here looked dry to me, stony and dry.

On deck and checking the work of my men, I overheard one sailor complain to another that we stayed too close to shore to pick up speed. "That captain's asleep or drunk," a second looped his finger; but then they noticed me and closed their mouths. That was when I became aware of many sailors restless and muttering one to another. I imagined they wanted to get into open sea, for they were seamen. Myself, I was happy for less lurching.

Later that day, I saw men climb the rigging to fold down two sails. Then came several lads moving about with bells and

calling, "All men on deck." I looked about. The Petroc had folded
her sails as well. And far in front and behind, other ships had
dropped their sails. Then I saw the crew pouring onto the deck of
the Petroc near us.

Lord Hammon and his knights assembled in brilliant dress
outside our forecastle above. I saw Quartermaster Kermit in his
deep red robe. The sky was high and blue; gulls called and crossed
overhead. Lord Hammon stepped forward.

"Thanks be to God we have arrived safe, thus-far. When
we leave Lisbon, we will be a fleet of over two hundred ships, for
others also bent for the Holy Land will join us there."

A great cheer at this, and gulls on the mast and riggings
flew up with a rattling of wings. Lord Hammon smiled broadly,
raised his arms for silence.

"Our Holy Mother Church has called us to a great and
courageous work, the freeing of Christian places from the hands
of the heathens. And now the Bishops of Oporto and Lisbon, and
the Portuguese king, Dom Alfonso Henriques, with the blessing of
Holy Father Eugenius III, have asked for our aid before we go on to
the Holy Land. Lisbon, the jewel of Portugal, a jewel in the crown
of the Holy Church, has alas too long been in the grasp of those
same Moorish Infidels we are sent to conquer."

We shifted foot to foot while Lord Hammon went on like
a priest; and I remembered how we youths used to move that way
at Sunday Mass, a bit of roof over the altar, no windows yet in our
cathedral with its square towers, low arched doors and old stone
crosses kept from the ancient Saxon church Mamoon recalled
from when she was a wee one; and where I remembered, a wee
one myself, peeking out from under my Gran'mam's skirts at the
young maids standing behind us; and how their eyes danced with
merriment at the sight of me.

On and on Lord Hammon ranted: that Holy Father had
granted Alfonso VII of Castile and all crusaders who follow
him "crusade indulgences." That the fight for the Church was
as necessary in Portugal today as that in the Holy Land. All

commanders of this fleet including Arnold III of Aerschot, Christian of Ghistelles, Henry of Glanville, Simon of Dover, Saher of Archelle and Andrew of London (under whose banner we march) had met with Bishop Peter of Oporto last evening and offered him our humble service.

The stunned silence. The whistle of the wind. The creaking of our vessel. The waves slapping, slapping, slapping us.

The men looked at one another as if they couldn't have heard aright. Then the slow low jumble of voices: But weren't they bound for Edessa? And didn't the monk Bernard preach saving Edessa, and Eugenius III bless our crusade to recover the places lost from the First Crusade? And what about the bishops at home who blessed this crusade to the Holy Land and saving the Holy Land, the very thing they'd left their families for? Oh, they didn't like this, they told each other with their eyes, with the stiffening of their bodies. No. Not at all.

"Silence!" A burly man to Lord Hammon's left fired off a flaming arrow. We backed away to give it space; and where it fell on deck, we stomped it out.

"Holy Father Eugenius III has asked that before we proceed to the Holy Land, we help our brothers here in Portugal," Lord Hammon held up his arms again.

Under the leadership of King Alfonso VII of Leon and Castile, we would wrest Lisbon from Moorish hands for the Church of Rome. We were granted all rights to hold for ourselves the despoiling both of prisoners for ransom and anything else found of value. And the same indulgences given those who go directly to the Holy Land were now given here; and to our families, as promised. "So you are twice blessed, on earth and in heaven. We dock at Lisbon tomorrow. Soldiers of God, are you with us?"

Well, and as if we had any choice, here on the ocean and hundreds of miles from home!

I thought of the woman in the church in Oporto. Those in Lisbon would be like her, wouldn't they? For such people, I could raise my fist; but not my voice, as I heard those around me doing, finally. When theirs died away, Lord Hammon sheathed his sword, turned on his heel and disappeared into the forecastle; and his retinue followed in a great swirl of cloth and color. And as we began to disperse, there came the shouts of the men across the water from the Petroc: "To Lisbon. For God. For the Church."

Oh, and distrust ate at us yet. Portugal was not the crusade; and Lisbon not the city we had dreamed of routing for God! And what of the remission of sins promised us, our families? And what if, at the Gates of Heaven, forgiveness for anything and everything turned out false?

That night my sleep was troubled by the old dreaded dream of those dark hulking men lurching past my door; myself so small shivering there while the chill of the yet unborn day crept into my very bones.

CHAPTER EIGHTEEN

We could see Lisbon even before our ships found the place the ocean first narrows into the Tagus River, and then goes on to feed the harbor. It was June 30, the vigil of St. Peter. On deck I was checking bundles of hauberks as we rounded the lower Iberian point, then onward toward the harbor, a pocket of water and small beach where we would anchor our ships.

Straight away, a young soldier asked for a hauberk, our chain mail, feeling the need in a foreign place. A sailor, older and rheumy-eyed, shook his head. "Think we'll leave them in ashes in a thrice, do you?" A toothless grin. "Well, have a look at thar defenses." He jogged his head upward.

"'Twill be easier, like Our Lord said, to pass a camel through the eye of a needle than to get through them gates to Lisbon."

We studied the small mountain crowding upwards, lip of the harbor to the topmost cliff, and making the whole of the great city to be guarded by a stout wall the height of ten men standing upon each other's shoulders. I sucked air sharply through my teeth.

"Them lower and middle walls ya see marks towns cut inta the rock,"the old sailor pointed,"yuh hafta break yer way through one after t'other; and each with towers, battlements 'n army. And there's five of 'em. Lisbon, she sits up at the very top; and through them towns is the only way to 'er." He shook his head, tied up his mouth with distaste. "And they tell that this here Lisbon's a nest of vipers: Muslims, Latins, Jews even." He lowered his voice. "And I heard tales about Christians disappeared into Lisbon just like Odysseus into that Siren's place and never come out again."

The young soldiers shrugged, laughed. An old man. What did he know? And I watched our soldiers bobbing over the waves in small boats to secure the beach.

Well, we had barely set foot on land when Moors, shouting praises to Allah, and with slings whipping the air, let loose from the rooftops a hail of jagged stones so thick they turned the sky black. Our men raised shields, staggered beneath this unforgiving din while these Moors poured from their refuge to engage. And looking on from the Petroc, it all seemed like some terrible dance, lance to lance, pole to pole; the men in deadly embrace, thrusting apart, then together so tightly they might fit inside one another; and the air thick with the ragged cries that carried out over the water. Hours and hours of this. But finally we drove them back through their gate.

And to speak truly, theirs was the smaller force, and with but few weapons beyond slings and stones, shields, poles and hand axes. We boasted horses, archers, knights, foot soldiers, swords, poles, lances and shields. And as their stones came at us in waves, so too their forces did, as certain numbers of their fighters would fall back to their gates to hand off helmets, shields and weapons to ones fresher for the fight.

I noted this to Quartermaster who joined me at the rail."Few weapons," he nodded. "But fierce fighters. And smart."

And so we gained a foothold. But afterwards, coming ashore to assist recovery and the setting up of camp while trumpets sounded and banners snapped, I heard no jubilation. The back-break of struggle, the heartbreak of comrades dead and dying upon that bloody beach had sobered everyone.

Saher of Archelle and Henry of Glanville ordered tents pitched at the very tops of hills overlooking the towns we must conquer, for our leaders did not want to appear to give any ground after the first encounter. And with the enemy close enough to heave a pig over his wall to land at our feet, as one man put it, withdrawal gave us but little respite.

That night we raised only two great tents. And while some thirty soldiers kept watch in hauberks and helmets, the rest returned to the ships to fall like dead men onto their pallets. And while I slept, the dark men of my childhood dream again came lurching out of the freezing mists, one beckoning me with a crooked finger so that I woke in a sweat, my heart pounding.

Those first days, my men and I were on the run to keep up with inventory while crates and supplies were rushed to the beach for the day's use. We got to the tally quick as we could; but everyone itching for the fight fumed at having to wait 'til we finished.

As I walked about my duties, I'd look up to see, hill to hill, the tents of our nobles rich with banners; the kitchen and small blacksmith shop sending up threads of smoke, men woven together like human ropes passing crates and boxes hand-to-hand, and out of which grew our camps with officers' headquarters, armories, soldiers' campfires and sleeping places, animal pens, slaughtering places, and storage for foodstuffs and supplies. Soon enough there would be hospitals on each hill, and two small churches. Already we had a burial ground.

"Men cannot fight and hunt at the same time, eh?" Quartermaster Kermit next morning laid a knobby knuckle alongside his nose. "One night I will tell you stories of brilliant armies eaten alive by starvation. There's no way to bring enough of everything with us; so we must go out and get the rest." And while he spoke, his eyes shot everywhere, "Here," he shouted at a soldier staggering under a barrel, "watch there before you lose our mead for the day!" Pivoting, he spied an older prisoner strolling toward a stack of crates, "And you, Apple-john, help that poor devil there with the barrel; and be quick about it."

Quartermaster Kermit never missed a detail; and that's why he was quartermaster. He pivoted back to me, eyes snapping. "By the time we get these loggerheads trained, we'll be home again." He pointed with his raised chin, "Introduce yourself to any Catholics out there in the vales might be happy to see us. Test what their goodwill could produce; there's money to be had; and we're businessmen. And put your name on oxen, donkeys, wagons, whatever you need now, so you know you have them."

Busy as I was, I wondered about the lull in the demand upon the men now the first clash was over and camp situated. Oh, there was field practice and the building of the war machine, the trebuchet they call it, a huge kind of sling shot built to launch great stones over long distances; and set up by us right on the beach near where our boats were anchored. I felt the tension as I walked past campfires, saw strain in the solemn faces, the sprawling bodies; could hear unease, the readiness to argue in the low tight voices.

And where was Lord Andrew or his spokesmen, everyone grumbled. And what was to happen next? And the grudge against changes that began onboard now grew roots; for these were foot soldiers, for hire many of them; and like myself, come aboard for their own reasons, knowing that to their betters they were but chaff in hauberks of leather and carrying a pole or lance, not a sword, and a small shield that leaves the neck and arms bare. So to get away from danger, you run on whatever legs you have, and while your betters gallop past, their horses' fittings sounding and gleaming. Yet still and all, the white light of the crusade persists. For you are part of a great body on a great and holy mission

promising great rewards. You are a crusader. You want to get on
with it!

In St. Olave's churchyard, around campfires I had heard
the First Crusade praised to the skies. Heads would bend to the
storyteller's voice paying out heroes taking on the impossible; then,
at the victorious ending, all standing to join in the raising cups or
bursting into a crusader's song. But sometimes, when some don't
be coming home, when bodies are lost forever into the lands of
the heathen, there is only silence. I heard such tales too on board;
but always followed by an upswing of how, in revenge, they would
roast the Infidel, spit up his arse, and have him for breakfast; or
drink his brains or innards from their helmets, take his women and
gold, sleep on his bed of silk, ravish his stores; and all due payment
for a hero of the Church! Why, to kill an Infidel was not murder,
but a holy act of God's will.

Well, the first encounter outside Lisbon changed all that
talk. Now I heard voices with an edge, and empty of bragging. And
as I walked through the camps, I could feel fear like hair risen on
an animal's back. I said something to Gilbert as we carried our
supper bowls to sit and eat.

His grey eyes searched over the campfires. "I've heard
these soldiers say it is bad luck to change leaders during a war, like
we have now to this King Alfonso. They say we have been sold to
Spain like so many furlongs of rope." He stirred the hot broth with
a forefinger and quick timing, then cursed, "Oh, for Christ's blood,
No meat! Again! Not even a scrap!"

I found a bit the size of a chicken's under-feather and
flipped it into his bowl. Gilbert had lost weight on the voyage.
Myself, I had no appetite.

My friend hunched his shoulders as if to look about for
someone listening in. He lowered his voice. "There's a chaos just
barely below the surface. Can you feel it? As if everything could
fly apart any minute. A flock of crows came and sat in the trees
over there," he pointed toward the edge of camp with his chin, "and
got everybody in an uproar, slinging stones and shooting arrows.

No soldier wants a black bird to show up in camp. The men think our nobles have been tricked by this Portuguese bishop's preaching, or were bought by this King here; or that nobody knows what they're doing!" He picked up a pebble and threw it. "It seems a bad way to go into war. But then," he shrugged, "I know nothing of war."

As it turned out, our nobles had met at King Alfonso's request to arrive at agreements regarding our part in the victory we expected. Then their representatives met with the Muslim leaders to explain we had come with a large and powerful force to take back what belonged to the Catholic Church; and that it was our duty to God to do so. The Muslims, in turn, having been in Lisbon nearly five hundred years, considered it their duty to hold Lisbon for Allah. Thus both sides agreed to war. And, if you can believe it, this conversation took up to a week, while our men's nerves slowly unraveled.

The search for food among neighboring farmers and hamlets was a godsend for me. We got away from the preparations for battle and building of the trebuchet, took three carts, two oxen, a donkey and set out over the hills. And to come upon a single farm with its thatched roof and simple walls, animal smells and sounds of toil, was like entering a heavenly glade.

It turned out we would make many trips while the siege took hold and wore itself out; and always brought along this certain man who had made us an offer of language. And being Catholic, he knew others of his faith.

The Muslims in Lisbon, he told us, did not persecute Catholics. They simply boarded up most of the churches and encouraged everyone to come to the mosque. Still, people were allowed occasional Mass, their crucifixes, statues and small shrines. And Catholic Portugese held no great animosity toward the Muslims in power for so many generations now; and who, it seems, treated everyone decently. But since the Moors long ago had taken Lisbon from the Church, these people were more than willing to help us get it back as long as it did not bring trouble upon them. And of course our money was always welcome.

Sometimes we would be gone two or three days, sleeping at night in fields or woods, or on the property of the farmer helping us; then bargaining in the daytime. Over the four months of the siege, I made real friendships with some of the farmers, and with one blacksmith in particular. It gave me great comfort to be around him in his work, and sometimes to pound out a rod of iron for him or finish a few horseshoes in the fire and on the anvil while my men loaded the carts or rested under a tree.

While it helped that we had money, in most cases it was their loyalty to the Church that brought these peasants to share what they had. Luckily it had been a generous harvest that year, though the quality was sometimes indifferent; and some batches of grain had weevils the size of a fingernail.

Well, and my men needed the rest. The camp was unnerving, especially now the battles had started. We were told the Muslims picked up the gauntlet by leaning over their balustrades with the vilest of insults: The Christian soldiers should not worry, their wives were not missing them; even now they were giving birth to many babies while their husbands were but poor fools, coming across the sea to take another's belongings because they felt their own too poor to be of value. Neither did they hesitate to utter terrible blasphemies against Jesus and the Holy Virgin at the tops of their voices, asserting the most vulgar possibilities there; and to hold high a crucifix, then spit upon it. And one pulled down his chausses, grunted, wiped his backside with the crucifix, held it up for all to see, then threw it over the wall at the crusaders. Stunned at such desecration, finally one soldier gathered it into a cloth for the priest.

And then there was that horror that you didn't know who would never come back to camp, or come back mutilated or dead.

One lad told his story. "Well, there's no way to see 'em come attcha, them so--so thick; an' me knowin' I was just waitin' fer death. So finally, I give out a loud cry as if struck, an' fell ta the

ground an' lie like a corpse atop my shield and pole so I won't lose
'em. An' bit by bit then, I burrow sideways an' 'neath a crusader
dead; an' lyin' still as poss'ble in somethun wet 'n sticky; 'n
breathin' but mites uv air fer I dunno how long. Then, near sunset,
ar trumpets signal vict'ry. Still I wait, not movin'. Then, open an
eye but a slit, an' seein' are own men gatherin' up the corpses, I
crawl inta the open, me face slimy with blood of the man I been
hidin' under." He took a drink from his flask, then spat it out again,
for no matter what he did, it seemed he couldn't stop tasting blood.
"An' all that practicin' in the fields, 'tis nothing to what yah meet.
What they shud teach ya is ta dig a hole deep 'n fast as ya can;
climb in 'an lay yer shield over the top."

The dead and wounded were carried to the hills at the
end of the day. Our trebuchet hurled huge rocks to soften the
Muslims' walls; but we lost, I think, more men from it than from
the Muslims, for our men were not skilled handling it, and the
enormous hurled stones would fall short and onto our own soldiers.
And too, there would be sword, knife and javelin wounds and
crushed bones, all on our side. Some kept count of the victims
on their shields, and made noisy wagers amongst themselves. But
many, after a siege, sat apart pale, vomiting, or propped up by a
tree.

I would help the physicians by holding down a screaming
man, jam a rag soaked in an herbal wine between his teeth while
the limb that could not be saved was sawed away and the stump
burnt to stop the blood, then wrapped. I would lay my palm over
the soldier's forehead and talk to him so he would know he was not
alone. Some days I would make trip after trip with buckets of blood
and hacked limbs to a special plot blessed by the priest, for they
were held to be extensions of the baptized soul, and bucket bearers
like myself would take part in a short prayer ceremony before
everything went into a pit.

Our trebuchet finally broke through the walls of the first
town. But taking one town did not make taking the next easier. I'd
hear men come back cursing the narrow streets you could hardly

pull a cart through. While at times we lured Infidels from behind their parapets, Gilbert, sent out to fight every day, told me the enemy could be stubborn, wily and courageous beyond belief. It was over three months before the second and third towns fell. That night, after we celebrated and a largely drunken sleep crept over the camp, a group of Infidels stole out to our trebuchet, painted it with something and set it afire. Our lookouts woke too late.

Attending to our supplies and helping with the wounded was all my focus, so while I noticed the second lull in the war, I didn't think much of it. Our men needed rest. But after a day or two, discontent and speculation started among the troops from gossip overheard by a guard or server. Again, confidence in our leaders faltered. Our men wanted to be in Edessa with the French and Germans when it was taken. This was their right, what they had signed up for. And tarrying here, they would miss all the glory!

As we fought our way through the next towns, Quartermaster told me with tight lips that the lords were in conference about whose forces should be first to enter the gates of Lisbon, for it was thought a great honor each force coveted. I looked at him more closely, took in the wear about his eyes and mouth. Suddenly he stepped past me to bark at two men lazing toward the armory. "You jack-daws, put some life in those legs before I take a strap to 'em. And get down there and clean up that rubble at the tents. Are we to live in filth all our days here?"

Then he turned back to me and said in a low voice laced with scorn, one I had never thought to hear him use, that as we stood here talking, our five noble leaders were assembled on the far field to fight each other for the glory of entering Lisbon first. He held aloft his open hand, a big hand shaped by physical work, his eyes fierce with disgust, and hissed, "--and while our men lie about, broken and half beaten now, those ones strut for each other like roosters. Real leaders remember their cause. And real men rouse the spirits that need it, if only for their own safety. But not these cock-jays." He spat the words at the ground. A light wind had turned toward us that day, and the dry irritating smell of char and ashes filled the air. And the sky was grey and low, so between breezes the air was stifling.

Quartermaster dug a handful of coins from his pouch, hesitated, dug a second time. "Here," he held out the money, "go find something good to eat for these men that will make their blood move. And they need it in their bellies before nightfall." He waved, "Go into one of these towns, if you must. But pay for whatever you find." He turned from me to gaze at Lisbon where, looming upon the crest of its hill, it sat hunched like a bird of prey.

And so, as our forces readied themselves for the next assault, I scoured the countryside for anything for which we could bargain.

When I returned, a new story travelled among the men. Before any siege could proceed, and while we were on Portuguese soil, our army, leaders to foot soldiers, were to swear fealty to King Alfonso. Believe me, the men balked mightily at swearing fealty to any other but their own King Stephan and own lord. Also it was agreed that English, Norman, Flemish and German leaders each choose one hundred sixty men to enter the city first, and there take deliverance of it according to arrangements for surrender proposed by the Moors the day before.

Gilbert was in the ranks of first entry. He asked if he might bring a trophy for me; but I did not want blood goods. I learned later from him that when the men reached the gates of Lisbon, the leaders of the Germans and Flemish had cried out that for the sake of their honor they must be allowed to enter first; and somehow they secured this agreement. But that talk about the needs of their honor was all a ruse, for they secretly packed their ranks with more than two hundred added men and pushed through the gates and broken places in the walls to despoil the city. Meanwhile, the rest of our forces, honoring the given word of their leaders, stood aside.

We sat at a fire later roasting on a stick a bird I'd caught. To protect our supplies, we had the men out foraging for their own fires when they could. Gilbert looked like an old man, propping himself on one arm while we talked, and kept snapping his head to look behind, as if some horror might overtake him unawares.

"Our forces came in the gates behind the Archbishop and bishops who carried the Holy Cross raised high, together with King Alfonso and our leaders. It was a great sight as that cross of the Holy Redeemer was fixed to the highest tower for all to see. We sang Te Deum, Laudamus and Asperges Me, and followed that with prayers of praise and thanksgiving to Our Lord and the Holy Virgin for victory over the Infidel."

Fat dripped from the bird roasting. The hilltop was crowded with fires like ours, shaped from branches into small steeples, flames leaping up the center. Talk was low. The air smelled of smoke and the coming of night.

"Then our troops dispersed to ransack for spoils." Gilbert looked away; I saw him swallow hard. "Passing through the city to take what we wanted, we saw those first in had already ravaged everything. The women raped, and houses and mosques and other buildings set afire after they'd been stripped. One group of our soldiers came upon the body of the old Catholic Bishop there, his throat cut. And you remember the Infidel forces within the city were to be released unharmed, by agreement of the surrender?" His mouth twisted. "We found those wretched souls, every one of them, in the big mosque. Murdered--" now he was shouting--" killed outright. Two hundred men. Their holy men, too. And eight hundred wounded. And the sick as well. And by OUR crusaders! And the stench of death in the air so that--"

Well, he couldn't finish, but only stagger to his feet and away for privacy. I couldn't eat, either, and so searched out Quartermaster to see what I could do for him. I had to keep busy.

From the despoiling of Lisbon, we brought out some eight thousand seams of wheat and barley, and some twelve thousand pints of oil. And our share of all that must be recorded, and everything stowed. As I made my notes, I turned it over in my mind that if miracles were worked, as reported, to ensure our success, then how would our plundering and murder now stand before God?

Quartermaster went into Lisbon himself to see that Norman and English got fair share of what was left. I went along with others who did not fight, to a hillside half a day from our camps to prepare graves. Our vantage point there let us view the gates of Lisbon and the line of oxen pulling wagons piled with the dead. In some, bodies were laid out respectfully; in others, just piled in a jumble. The wagons rocked along foot trails over grass and stones toward where we had dug pits deep against wild animals. But we were not quite ready when the dead arrived, and had to put something over our noses and mouths against the stench and taste of death. Flies covered the waiting bodies, and I wondered why the wagons had not at least been covered.

A complaining of vultures began as we started on the graves, the birds circling and waiting for the wagons too, the shadow of their wings upon us as we worked. And I remembered the black crosses over the fallen that first day on the beach below Lisbon; and finally, the great pits ready, crusader and Infidel alike must be buried now against the spread of illness.

You and your partner grasp the ankles, or under the arms and heave. And how it tore at me not to be more respectful, enemy or not. And those left in Lisbon, hiding or starving after our ravaging and brutality, how would they ever come to embrace Rome or to believe in the love and compassion of Jesus, the Savior Rome preaches?

Next day, Quartermaster sent me and my men into Lisbon to bring back anything might have been passed over, for we would be at least a month on the water, and it was his responsibility to see that we had what we needed. I had heard tales of all that went on in Lisbon, had seen the dead; but had yet to see the city myself.

We found no men save the very old sitting listless in doorways of ravaged buildings in that silence like held breath that haunts the air after violence. Otherwise, only the most desperate were on the street, begging. I sent my men in five directions with

their carts. "Protect yourselves, but harm no one; and take only
what we came to get. Those left behind here have been pillaged
more than enough to satisfy the terms of surrender."

And you can imagine that I could not get the massacred
Infidel soldiers from my mind, nor keep from putting myself in
their place of expecting to meet the loved ones we'd fought to
protect, only to have the gates thrown open and Death storm in.
Onto the littered and bloodstained streets, we had come with huge
feet and terrible mindless hands tearing everything apart to satisfy
our wastrel appetites. And in this, weren't we surely friend of the
Devil himself?

Then I noticed sitting in the great shadow my wagon and
oxen cast upon a wall, a woman in the doorway of the small house
behind her. I was searching for grain or whatever I could find. She
held a child of about a year against her breast and covered all of
him but his face with her veil. For a terrible instant I saw Sarah and
our son. Usually I kept them from my mind during my work, for I
could not bear to have the filth in which I lived touch them. Then
this woman raised an open palm, and said something to me in her
tongue.

So devastated must she be, so beyond hope and fear, I
marveled, to sit in plain view risking rape or death to beg food for
her child! I stepped closer, saw she had her thumb in the babe's
mouth. In Exeter, I had seen mothers, their milk dried up from too
little to eat, do this very thing to stop the little ones from crying.
Again I felt overwhelmed with disgust and shame at what we
crusaders had done. And now must we take every last living scrap
from the very poorest who had no part in the conflict and can
neither protect themselves nor escape?

The woman reached out again. I laid my finger to my lips,
then turned back to the wagon, my eyes shooting every direction
to be sure we were not watched. I lifted down a sack of grain of
a size she could carry and set it at her feet. And her great dark
eyes turned upon me filled with amazement. Then she dropped
to her knees, the babe clutched to her breast, to touch the ground

with her forehead and chant a short prayer to Allah; and then rose
again. And I made fast running movements with my fingers: Get
away quickly!!! And as she grappled with the sack, I laid my finger
hard at my lips once more, that she tell no one, NO ONE. For any
person desperate enough for food might kill for it.

As she rounded a corner, I became aware of other eyes.
Five or six little ones covered with street dirt stared from a
doorway behind me, looking from me to my wagon, to my oxen,
back again to me. I listened hard for the sound of my men's voices,
for the wheels of their heavy carts. Finally I heard faint laughter;
but far enough away.

Around the doorway then, where the woman had sat, I
piled small sacks and jars just out of sight. The children watched.
I could feel the longing in their bodies, and the hope that I would
finish quickly and leave. At last I put my hand to the harness of the
oxen. The animals had picked up my uneasiness, and the whites of
their eyes shone like crescent moons as they stomped at flies and
snorted into the dirt around their nose rings. I clucked to them,
and saw the children duck out of sight again. I waited, and one
small face brought big brown eyes carefully around the doorjamb.
I held my finger to my lips and shook my head slowly: Don't tell. I
repeated this silent language again. He stared at me long, then put a
finger to his own lips and nodded gravely.

My much unburdened cart rolled more easily now. I must
find another neighborhood where I could fill it up; or else say this
was all I could get. No one would challenge me. And we crusaders
could manage with a little less so that some of those we had ruined
might live on.

It would be over a month to the Holy Land for those who
chose to go. Nearly two-thirds of our men stayed on. With land,
homes and animals as booty, and all their and their family's sins
forgiven, and their gullets already overloaded by the sea, who need
go further? My friend Dominic planned to work his way back

to England. And I boarded the Boniface to a rumor Gilbert of Hastings of our forces was to be the new bishop of Lisbon.

And it disturbed me so many stayed behind. Despite the Portuguese and Spanish who had joined to fight with us, and whose ships added to our fleet, we were now a considerably smaller force: three hundred-thirty and some. I leaned upon the railing and watched the sails fill with wind. I should have felt peaceful at an easier trip once we rounded the Gate of Horn, as Quartermaster Kermit promised; but despite the blue of the sea deep as any reminiscence, a dark foreboding stained my mind.

CHAPTER NINETEEN

It was August of 1148, Year of Our Lord, and our ships a full month at sea after the bloody year in Portugal. Our victory cost us one hundred fifty men on hills, beaches and streets, not to speak of the many more who chose to stay behind. We approached the Holy Land under grey skies. I saw from the deck the apron of sand upon which we would make landfall, the rocks ascending from it toward the summit of a plateau.

There nothing grew but small beaten-looking green plants and rare clumps of flowers rather like our own lilies bending under the low wind. Despite the calls of great-winged brown pelicans and small grey birds with curved needlelike beaks scavenging the sand and noise of waves thrust out and dragged back, it all felt too still. I couldn't get "ambush"out of my head.

Our last supper on board the night before had been a mix

of barley, pork scraps and pickled vegetables, along with a festive dessert of frumenty pudding Cook made from wheat, almond milk and our scarce stores of honey and nutmeg. Ale we had, too, from the captain, to prop up our spirits. And a young fiddler rose to play "I Know A Maid Bold," but a weathered crusader waved him off. "Put that thing away. Now's not the time, lad."

He spoke for most of us.

We were to dock between the bishoprics of Acre and Berytus. This was convenient since our first destination was Damascus, somewhat to the north and east. From the deck we had seen nothing save a hamlet or two of stooped huts, flapping tents and the greasy smoke of cooking fires. As usual, Quartermaster Kermit wanted an exact inventory of foodstuffs, supplies, repair materials, armor and weapons, horses, pack animals and their condition--in other words, everything on both ships before and after unloading. And I now had under my command just five men, for Slander had stayed in Oporto.

Working on deck, I took notice of the young lad of about twelve who came along with his father. I introduced myself one day. His replied his name was Khalil. Dark hair and eyes, light olive skin, he daily amused himself defying the bucking of the ship by walking toe to heel, arms out like wings, around the tops of the huge coils of rope stored on deck.

"If you tire of that," I joked to him one day, "the crew would welcome another hand scrubbing down the deck. I could arrange it for you."

"I came to get out of scrubbing," he laughed. "I'm here to learn from my father the skills of a fighting man; and to force those heathens to give back what is not theirs."

I admired his spirit. "But perhaps it's lonely at times," I suggested, "without your friends and the rest of your family?"

"'Everything costs you,' my grandfather says," he shrugged. "I wanted to come."

One day, close to the end of our sea journey, I was doing inventory of blacksmith supplies when, tilting with the pitch of the ship, my man Jerrod staggered toward me with his numbers from below deck. As I took them, his eyes swept the shore. "I think this to be a land for ghosts, and that's the truth. Good Holy God, but where's the trees?" He looked around again and spat. "Well, at least there's no bloody walls with bloody Infidels dropping bloody rocks on yer bloody skull."

"There's that blessing," I nodded dryly, then glanced up from his numbers to take in the land skinned and tanned by a murderous sun. And my heart sickened.

The horror of Lisbon had left me fighting an urge to cast myself into the sea rather than go on; and I had to ask myself how I could have been so blind to what this crusade would be. Ah, but I had needed to get away too badly to ask the right questions or to listen to my teacher. In Exeter, there were beheadings, burnings, drawing-and-quarterings on the Southern Hay often enough. And those held up as holiday sport. Once I was old enough to understand what was happening, I was terrified not only by the violence of a government and its citizens against a single person, but the relish in the public display of it, as if it were a thing to celebrate. And when I knew there was to be such a "holiday," I would go to the woods so as not to hear the ghastly screaming, nor see the blackened flakes of the victim float through our windows and doors. And where my feelings could be healed from such controlled murder.

Our own viciousness in Lisbon not only went unchecked, but was encouraged and celebrated as right and our due. No limit was put upon appetites of any kind. And it was only loyalty to Quartermaster Kermit and, like them or not, our own men and their claim upon me, (now become nearly as strong as that of my family), that kept me from death at my own hand--along with the fear that the Hell preached by the Church might be real; and going there, I would never see Sarah and our son again.

We were a full week working upon that beach somewhat south of Acre, unloading the ships, standing guard and sleeping in our bunks. Finally we started inland, most of us on foot behind our nobles on horseback. But at once the heavy wheels of our carts sank into the sand; and whipping the oxen, their feet sinking like ours, improved nothing. We had to put our backs to the wagons and push until we could reach something solid. And how the sweat ran!

"If I drown in me own water, when you get home, carry me pantaloons to me m'am at St. Mary's Steppes for me young brother," a man with a thumb missing called to his friend, whose tunic too was soaked. And this only the first hours of the first day of our march.

We were told we would join French and German troops in the desert beyond, as well as men from the north of England, coming over by land. The meeting place would be an outcropping, a low hill of rocks about two days' march this side of Damascus. We would know it by its one end uplifted and squared like a whale's head, and the other that swung upward like flukes. And no one seemed to know how many weeks' or months' march was needed to reach it. So we bent our shoulders to our wagons' backsides as our oxen stumbled up the first stony rise that wore on my boots and made my calves cry out. Finally, we gained the plateau to find naught but a pale sparse grass with which to refresh our animals; and, not often enough, a scrawny tree to throw its shade.

Into the silence again, then, with the squeak of wheels and clatter of armor and implements of war. The plan was to march eight hours, then camp. Our army depleted, supplies were still strong; and we would soon get further support from the French and Germans, we were told; and undergo but minor skirmishes with local Arabs.

A single drum kept the beat. Since Lisbon, we'd lost our taste for heraldry and banners; time enough when we joined the others. Edessa, to the north and east was the first Christian kingdom established by the First Crusade. Its loss now to the Arabs caused the call from Pope Eugenius III to take it and Jerusalem back for the Church.

Well, and there is no way to prepare for the heat of the

desert; nor its beauty that knocks your heart apart, God knows, with the flowing, folding and billowing of sands like waves of the sea far as your eyes can reach. And both wearing queenly raiment, and having that peculiar humor of nobility that rises without warning to smack you down, blind you, sear the very flesh from your body, then gather you in to smack you down again.

We had furlongs walking this bone-colored silk that holds no print in memory. And soon enough a heated spike took to pounding into my head with each stride; and something like raw horsemeat bubbled and spoiled in my stomach. Too soon these changes grew familiar; so that when I looked about me, I saw on every other face and body signs of the same struggle. Oh, and it would become worse, much worse for, as a "barrel of strength", we were as yet but moderately drained.

In sand hills broken by outcroppings or low mountains, I saw a second Devon or Cornwall; but ghostly, bone-bare and glittering. Hills shifted, and plateaus with them until we didn't know which way we had come from or in which direction to move ahead; nor whether we were traveling in circles for days, as turned out to be the case more than once. And the sun? It took passage fare, pounding our heads until spots danced before our eyes, swelling our tongues to fill our mouths, wringing the water from our bodies. And this but introduction.

Then, like a miracle, there would appear the green of a small oasis where we and our animals could slake our thirst at a spring or rock well sunk into the sand, and rest our throbbing legs and heads.

It was not many days into our march when I became seriously worried about heat damage to our foodstuffs. I turned my oxen over to a young helper to have a word with the cook, Boar; and walking toward him where he lumbered at the rear of the wagons, and with my back to the march, suddenly there was no mistaking the muffled thud of hooves; and the terror I saw upon Boar's face made me whirl around.

In a cloud of sand, fifteen or twenty men in turbans or

helmets, their skin the color of tanning bark, and with raised swords, daggers or bows and arrows, bore down upon us. I remember how the brilliant colors of their billowing robes cut at my eyes.

"Infidels!" an English voice bellowed hoarsely, but too late.

Raging through us like fire through dry grass, the enemy came, grinning around their brilliant teeth, their eyes lit by what seemed a fierce joy. And many of our archers never mounted an arrow before they were sliced down. The smell of fresh blood turned my stomach. I saw one Infidel take a knight's head off with a shout of "Fa inn Allah!" to which the other Arabs joined, throwing the words after him to the sky, "Fa inn Allah!"

It all came on too fast for fear. There was time only to grab your wits and act. Boar, eyes huge, jammed the hilt of a sword into my hand, yelling, "The bastards'll be after our grub."

We pulled in one soldier after another until we'd built a barricade about the supply wagons. Then, swift and silent as they'd come, our attackers vanished. I saw the rumps of their horses shrink while the heads of some of our fallen swung by the hair from their fists. And they left behind but few dead tribesmen of their own.

"What way is this to wage war?" I turned to Cook who had dropped his sword and was now leaning against a food wagon and mopping his red face with the back of his hand.

"They come on like that," he huffed. "I've heard so from old crusaders. Come out of nowhere, like the very Devil hisself."

Customs of war in England require that only when both sides are drawn up and ready is the battle signaled to begin. It is a matter of honor. But these Arabs sprang from nowhere, dealt their blows and vanished.

The silence fallen upon us was broken only by the cries of the wounded. We lost sixty or seventy men--dead, or too badly maimed to walk. This attack had brought our numbers to one hundred-sixty now. No supplies taken. Our oxen spared.

That was when I noticed the lad Khalil who had boarded at Lisbon, weeping now over his father's corpse, the man's life pooled beneath it. The boy, I was told by Quartermaster, was of Norman and Arab blood; and spoke four or five tongues. The last of our troops ran past, fearful of another attack and looking over their shoulders. And we must hurry on behind them with our wagons.

"Come," I reached for his hand. "Your father is beyond all suffering now. He is in Heaven." I dealt the words out gently as I could, though I needed him to make haste, for none of us could afford to be left behind. But he jerked his hand away and lay his cheek down upon his father's chest again to let his grief gush forth the more. And I gave him all the time I dared, then grabbed him into my arms and ran after the others while he soaked my chest with his woe. I vowed then to keep him under my wing; and, God willing, deliver him safe at the end of this horror to his mother.

We leapt over limbs, trunks, heads. I saw a priest raise his hand to bless as many bodies or parts as he could, kicking sand over them for burial as he hurried to catch up.

And so we ran the more, having trespassed what kingdom we knew not, nor how wide it might be. Our lords kept us going for the sake of our very lives while our minds blanched under the terror of another attack at any moment; and for which we could not prepare. All night and the next day we ran, slowing to a walk only after dark to save our energy, or hightailing a short distance away to let water and take care of our other needs.

Five days of this. Seven. We would climb a plateau of pale green only to exchange it again for more desert; and always hoping we were gaining distance from our attackers, though we never knew from which direction they might come flying out, shouting, and their swords glittering cruelly in the desert air.

Boar, our aides and I brought up the rear.

"The very Devil hisself, that's what they are," Boar burst out one day when we were allowed to slow to a walk; "the very brats of Satan, like our Bishop told us." He fixed his eyes upon the horizon. "And it's Hell itself that comes with them. They mean to swallow down into their filthy stomachs the very holy places of Jesus, of Our Lord." He raised a clenched fist. "But we will take His places back for Him, or die in the trying; and with God Himself helping us."

Well, I held my peace. I did not have his feeling for what we were defending. I couldn't believe that Jesus or any holy man would want us to kill one another over the places he'd lived, or ground he'd walked. Still, it touched me to see men like Boar, come from so hard a life, have such feeling for the stones upon which his Savior may have set his foot.

Late an afternoon some days later, Boar and I and Khalil were bringing up the wagons at the end, and getting ready to ask Quartermaster for instructions about making camp when, over a dune, a single figure in Arab garb pounded toward us astride a great white Arabian horse. Because he was alone, I took him for an ally, perhaps from a Christian kingdom; or someone lost or needing help.

He caught up with the end of our line and reined his horse, dancing, to the side as if he would speak with Boar. I continued counting recovered bows as I had been when Boar bellowed out, "Look sharp, Jophiel; he means to shoot you!"

Without a thought and in one seamless movement, I grabbed up a bow and set the arrow. Whirling, I pulled the string just as the rider released his own bowstring. I felt the arrow feathers pass by my neck and saw him topple sideways to the ground. My shot had lodged in his chest near his heart. His horse leaped aside with a wild whinny, shook itself free of him and galloped for the dunes.

Heart still racing, I approached watchfully where my enemy lay upon his side, hand still gripping the bow. Boar, right behind me, pushed at him with his foot, and he rolled onto his back. It was then I saw he had no face hair, and could not have been more than twelve years old. And it purely sickened me to see one young as Khalil or my nephew dead now, and at my hand; and before he'd even had a chance to live.

Boar held out to me as my property the youth's bow and quiver. I shook my head. Instead I placed them carefully upon the youth's bosom, that his people, when they came for him, might honor his hard-won manhood. I squatted, hoping beyond reason to see his eyelids flicker or chest rise and fall. Finally, I pulled his robe to cover his face, and tucked it under his head.

CHAPTER TWENTY

Near every day now there came an ambush; and it was a week or ten days before we could risk putting up camp again. When we did, I made a place for Khalil next to me, and through the night kept my arms around him for shelter and to soften his grief. Daytime, I put him in training doing inventory with one of my men; or would send him to help Boar's slave with the cooking or to go out with his sling, for he was an excellent shot and soon became famous for the birds and small animals he downed for our pot.

These Seljuk Turks, whose kingdom this was, I learned, still came at us from nowhere and anywhere. And before it was all over, I would have to kill more than one man to keep from being done in myself. Slowly I began to understand their strategy: Always on horseback; strike, then disappear before we could organize

ourselves. And they knew the desert, a place that daily blinded us
and left us helpless with confusion.

Turks were not our only enemy. The sun killed us outright.
Men staggered as they ran, then dropped. My training with herbs
gave me a quick eye for the sick. I noticed that those who first grew
pale and cold to the touch were the ones in the greatest danger,
although there were also those who turned bright red, and, despite
sweat pouring from them, grew hotter still. Both were bad signs.
Dizziness and vomiting. Terrible pains in the head and eyes. Chills.
Complaints of the bowels. And there was nothing for it but to suffer
the sights and smells of one another. If I was ill, when I could I
would go behind a bush or outcropping to squat and take care of
myself.

Well, and we became crazed. Once a young foot soldier,
exhausted by the heat and an ambush that had that left his mates
dead or dying around him, leapt upon a Turk that had lost an arm
and already bled to death. Crying, he pounded the corpse with his
shield, as if to mash him to a pulp. Several of us pulled him off to
tie him to the top of a supply cart until he could come to himself
again.

And there were those who just walked off, pointing and
calling to the Virgin or Archangel Michael or Jesus himself.
Quartermaster Kermit restrained us from going after them. "When
they see visions, they are already at Heaven's door," he told us. "It
will be opened for them."

And the first time it happened to me, I was suddenly seven
again, in Exeter and looking through holly bushes opposite our
hut, my blood turning cold from hearing my sister Leofric split
the air with terrified screams of "Mamoon! Mamoon!" Then I see
her fly past the church down the road, knees reaching high, head
thrown back, long red hair blazing like a banner, and gasping for
air while a man near twice her size, one hand reaching for the back
of her kirtle and with the other pushing his chausses down gets
closer and closer. But then from behind the greenery at our hut,
Mamoon steps out with a pitchfork squarely between Leofric and

her pursuer. The man skids to a stop while Gran'mam, half his size, shoves the pitchfork straight at his parts.

"If you don't want to lose that bag of filth between your legs," I hear her say, cold as winter, "you'll turn around right where you stand and run the other way as fast as ever your legs can carry you."

And I see his face go white, watch him gasp, then heave around and away; but then it is just the ragged soldier in front of me lurching forward trying to manage the sand.

Well, what was happening to other men was happening to me. And that's when it came clear that the sun with its unforgiving heat had come to claim my mind and my senses. And this was the first but not the last incident that taught me how truly fragile for all of us is our grasp upon our minds and life. And lashing ourselves to one another had become necessary now, and for more reasons than the wind. Once a man is sick, he cannot keep up. So we simply must step over him; and if he is dead, we spread sand if we have the strength; then go on. We also reasoned correctly that once a man is sick, he cannot keep up and, as you can understand, we cannot wait for him.

We had to ration our water; but cheered ourselves we were gaining ground to meet the Germans and French who would have plenty.

By some miracle, raiding bands never broke through to our supplies; but finally the wagons slowed us down too much. At least when we butchered the oxen, we could salt the meat; and we were happy now the Muslims had burned our siege machine to the ground. Well, French and Germans forces would have siege machines.

When we first saw Muslim turbans in Oporto and Lisbon, they had looked awkward and strange; but in these grim desert lands, we understood their value, took them from the fallen Infidels to protect our own heads, eyes and necks; stripped them bloodied, when we had to, and felt the warmth of the life just taken linger in the cloth against own temples and foreheads. We discovered the turban's crown lets sweat escape; discovered the genius of the long tail of cloth left free to protect the nose and mouth.

We took their clothing and weapons, all of ingenious design and more beautifully wrought and suitable for this land than anything we carried proud from England and threatening now to drive us by its weight to our necks in the sand. And in these turbans, billowing robes and goatskin boots, we were transformed from foot soldiers to a corps of ghosts in the dress of the dead, and running for our lives in tatters with reddened eyes, scourged skin and lips blistered and blackened by the blowing sand that stunted even the rare twisted trees we would pass by.

Quartermaster was always up early to organize the day. As his aides, my men and I slept nights with the supplies, for we must protect them from our own soldiers as well as the Infidels. I don't remember how many weeks into our trek, when, early one morning in the dim light of his tent, I found Quartermaster laid out upon his pallet. I heard the ragged breathing and my heart faltered. He had been pale awhile now; but so were many of us under our sun-scorched skin; and losing hair and body bulk like he did. Now he laid a hand softly upon my arm and searched my face.

"I will not be going on with you today, Jophiel; and I am sorry to my bones, or to what's left of 'em. This body makes me a deserter. For that, I beg pardon of you, and of all the men. Please tell them that never of my own accord would I have left them until we returned safe home to England and victorious."

My throat filled. "Nay, Sir. A deserter is the last thing you would ever be." I put an arm under his head and gave him a drink from my flask. He let out a gasp as I laid him down again, then turned his face from me. I settled upon the floor next to him. I had thought nothing could touch this man. After a few moments, he turned back with that particular wave of his hand I knew so well.

"Get out there and see to our supplies. They are the only weapons we possess against this place. And, as you know, camp must be broken and everyone on the move by dark." Lately we had taken to traveling at night to save lives from the sun and for secrecy. With great effort he raised upon an elbow to set fierce eyes upon me.

"You have been my good right arm, Jophiel. Now you must take my place. I assign you Quartermaster. Our men's lives are at stake, crusade or no crusade; and they are now in your hands."

And with those words, he transferred the weight of that awesome trust to me who staggered beneath it. He saw this, and his voice grew stern. "You haven't been at my elbow all these months for naught, Jophiel Balerais. You know what to do. At all costs, protect our supplies." Then his eyes softened a moment before, with a groan, he dropped back onto his pallet.

I found my feet quickly. "Yes, Sir. I'll see to it. Do you need--?"

He waved again. "Get to the--."

I had not wanted these last weeks to admit to myself how sunken his body had become. Not only had the sun brought him down, but also that sickness of the bowels so common among us now; and there was his labored breathing. To be honest, every morning fewer men got up. Our numbers, given raids, sun and increasing disease, were now perhaps eighty; and less than one-third still had command of their health.

"Quartermaster Kermit will not be going on," I told my men. Their eyes opened at this; then acceptance came. They too had seen he was sick. And I read another look; the same one that at the sounds of splintering wood had leapt to the faces of sailors during the storm off Iberia. So I bulked up my voice, threw my head. "Come, come. Quartermaster Kermit has trained us well. And we are yet his good arms and legs."

I sent one man to count our armaments, one to take Khalil and count food and healing supplies, one to count instruments for repairs and one to report on our few horses. I went back to attend Quartermaster.

"It was a lucky day for me when you walked across the yard at St. Olave's, reading the insults that enlistment cleric leveled at you." He managed a laugh. I laughed too. Then he steadied his eyes upon me. "I want you to know it was because of you that I could hold my part of this mess together. Otherwise--." He shook his head.

I dropped my eyes, so touched, but also saddened, and trying to think of words to return my thanks to him, for he was not a man to accept praise, no matter how justified. But before I could find words, he had turned his face away from me again. And he was gone by nightfall. We wrapped his body in his tent and buried it deep as we had time to dig before the rising moon pulled us into our march. And I could only hold him in my heavy heart, and speak plainly to him as I tramped along of all he had meant to me.

We battled snakes, bats and desert rats, sand spiders, scorpions, fleas, flies and bugs we had never seen before, suffered bites and droppings that brought on swelling, running infections and raging fevers. We battled sandstorms I thought would tear the robes from our backs and the skin from our faces. One terrible day I saw three of our men blown out of ranks, crying out as the wind tumbled them beyond our reach. And we would use every chain, rope and strap we could find to secure our weapons and provisions. Men would lie down across our grain baskets to keep the wind from tearing open the sacks.

And I am seven again, my stomach hurting from hunger; and hurrying to our hut with a load of wood before Teewaye starts looking for me, his big hand raised to knock me into the wall. Then I am in boots Mamoon got from a neighbor, so big and heavy I can barely lift my feet to walk; but must flap the boot toes ahead of me instead down High Street while the other children skip behind chanting, "Quack, quack, Jophiel's a duck." Or my older brother Michael drags me out behind our hut, teeth clenched, thick fingers into my neck and I cry out in the pain, "Michael, I can't breathe."

Then I am in sand again, and walking with tattered men ahead and behind, lost, lost, lost far from England, burnt reeds all of us, struggling for our lives. And every day now, someone runs off laughing, raving, crying or calling out toward something or someone until they are swallowed forever from our view; and this with our animals, too.

CHAPTER TWENTY-ONE

Boar disappeared with his slave three nights after Quartermaster died. Next morning no breakfast ready, and a large portion of our food was gone. I knew Boar to be less than trustworthy: I often would find him wiping a full mouth or sucking honey from his fingers. Such things meant nothing until we made landfall and food became scarce. Still, Quartermaster had told me to look the other way. Boar wouldn't eat that much, he said; and four men together could not do what Boar could do.

Overseeing meals now became part of my duties; and since I had worked with Boar, I could train his two remaining helpers to be cooks, and add some raw men to assist them. I told my man Jerrod to count food supplies four times each day, though there were not so many now to feed. Truth be told, if it were not for those who died, I don't know how many of the rest of us would have lasted this long. We hunted lizards and snakes to roast upon sticks; and even meat with a bitter and hateful taste made our eyes tear with gratitude because it was fresh. We pushed on, holding to the vision of the overland crusaders we were to join. Then one day, as if we had turned a corner, the meeting place rose up in the distance with its peculiar rock formation; and a soldier called out, "Yonder! Look! There it stands! The whale!"

Our eyes picked up the outcropping with one end raised like flukes. But the hurrah stuck in our throats, for as far as any eye could see was naught but silence, the eternal sand, and no sign of any living soul having ever set foot upon it.

We had counted on the supply wagons and a hospital tent we carried in our minds like a last precious mouthful of water; and on fellow crusaders running to greet us with meat and drink and a clap upon the back, showing us to a piece of shade to lie down; and ourselves, later, unwinding our stories for them, and them for us.

"This cursed wind erases everything," my man Hervey hissed at my ear. "Maybe they were here and left, thinking we wasn't coming." I saw the fear in his eyes. "Maybe one of our knights on a good horse could find 'em still."

"We've got no horses left," I reminded him. And a deadly weariness crept over me then, as if my body were filled with stones. Our knights had been plucked like apples from a tree; and near all the rest slipped away with their horses in the dark. Now we had two left, one with six knights, one with four. Since Lisbon, I had seen so little of Lord Acton, to whom we owed allegiance, that I hardly ever thought of him. My men had friends among his foot soldiers, and it was Hervey who told me one morning with big eyes as he handed over his list of stores, that Lord Acton had left in the darkness. "His knights are gone with him."

"What was taken?"

"The horses, swords, shields, food. And the wind took their tracks out." His voice dropped lower. "Who will be our lord now?" I could feel the faltering, like a man caught in torn rigging and looking about for anything that can hold.

"Why, Henry of Glanville is with us. He has big wings."
I gave him a clap upon the back, took his list and looked it over.
"Check your numbers again, eh? Everything we've got is precious
now." And he turned away strengthened, a man with a task to
accomplish. In my heart I walked with him, for I don't know how
many times I might have let the sun take me, but for my duty to
help get these men out of this Hell.

Right of the outcropping was a small cluster of trees
where our company could take turns in and out of the shade. Lord
Glanville told us to set up camp and wait for those would join us
for the siege of Edessa; and hope flared again that by some means
he knew of, other crusaders were still on the way, or coming back.
So we cleaned weapons and shields, practiced with bows and
arrows and dug out a ragged banner.

A week went by. Another. A third. After a month,
Glanville and his six knights mounted for Damascus to hear word
of those we were to meet. He vowed to return in a fortnight. My
eyes fixed upon the cloud of sand raised by the hooves of his
entourage and growing smaller and smaller like water escaping
down a hole. And the man upon the stony flukes was now required
to keep watch for Glanville as well.

So we waited, but like men had lost their bones and could
not stand nor take hold for themselves with all our lords and
knights gone now, and no one in charge. As Quartermaster, I had
some standing, but when it came to the desert and soldiering, I
had but poor means to offer. Our one remaining captain, a sinewy
older man called Titus, with leathered skin and a beard the color of
stone, swore we were still an army and set times for drill. But with
no lord to back him up, he got but lame effort from the men, no
matter his swearing at them.

I directed the strongest men to hunt, treated the mildly
sick with what few herbs we had, and made the desperately ill
comfortable as I could while they died quietly in the heat and
were buried quickly as possible. Food stores allowed for two small
meals a day. We had little water. Mead was low as well. And so we

drifted in a terrible dream, and scanning the sand hills for Lord Glanville to come back and save us.

A month passed and the men stopped trying to care for themselves in the simplest of ways. Perhaps Glanville and his knights were attacked before they reached Damascus, or on their way back; or got lost in a sand storm, we would argue the case to one another. We did not want to think we were deserted. Then, near sunset of the last day of the fourth week, with the Lady Star rising above the rim of the highest stony fluke, the red crusader banner of our watch unfurled into the evening breeze. Someone approached! Old Titus barked us into our hauberks and into ranks.

But it was not Lord Glanville, we soon discovered, as the tiny rider and horse grew larger. Coming from the West, the horse held to a steady loping pace meant to conserve its strength. A small cohort of us buckled shields onto our arms, picked up our swords and stepped thirty paces or so out to meet him.

Nearer, I saw the walnut coloring of an Arab, the quick chestnut eyes, the hair and skin of a man forty or so.

"Crusaders of Pope Eugenius III," we hailed him, our hands near our weapons.

"Abdil of Edessa. A son of the Church. God save you."

"God save you," I rejoined, my spirits lifting.

I assisted him as he dismounted. "But how is it you speak English, Sir? You look to be from these parts."

"Yes. Born here in Edessa; but raised in England, near York. My father was a trader of fine cloth to France, Italy and Spain."

As we walked back to camp, he answered the other questions that sat in our faces. The family became Christians in Edessa, and after they moved, kept a hand on their land here through a swarm of relatives. But finally, his mother missed her people too much and they all moved back except for one brother. "For a long time, it was very good living here; Edessa was a Christian kingdom. But three years ago, the Turks took it. This made the entire Kingdom of Jerusalem and toward Mesopotamia prey to the Turks. We are badly in need of help, and had hoped your crusade might reverse things." He glanced over us.

Our own situation was clear enough, and we kept our story simple. We offered him a small bird we had dug beneath the fire to bake. We sat.

He was returning home from a meeting at Acre, near where we made landfall what now seemed so long ago. Conrad III, of the Germans, and Louis VII, of the French, and bishops and nobles of our crusade were in attendance. No, he had not seen any Lord Glanville, nor heard of him.

"I came to Acre bearing a letter of introduction from Queen Melissande of Tripoli, who did not wish to be present but wanted to be kept informed. Her family holds land near ours, so she has grave concerns about these Turks as well."

"What do you hear of the fate of the German and French crusaders?" My need for tidings of them burned a hole right through me.

"I'm happy to tell what I know," Abdil wiped his mouth and settled back upon his elbows.

"Those armies were whittled down to good as nothing. And all by bad choices, sickness, and bloodletting by the Seljuks near Constantinople; but mostly, to my view, by bad choices. The Germans, mark this, decided to take two separate routes. The Seljuks ate one group nearly whole at Doryaleum," he used his turbaned head to point north, "where the First Crusaders won fame. Meanwhile, the second Seljuk force showed itself, pretended to retreat, then turned on the crusaders like vultures and picked them clean." He shrugged, "Scraps left, is what I heard. And those scuttled away."

And with this I saw the dream of rescue disappear from our soldiers' eyes. Our visitor seemed to hear their soundless groan and sat up to peer from one face to the next.

"These Seljuks are not Muslim. Do you understand this? They don't follow a God or Law such as we know, but some ancient ways of the lusts for blood and claiming of all rights for itself. They wanted Edessa; they took it." He shrugged. "We here had great hope for this crusade, but we found," he tapped his temple, "empty heads steer it. From what I saw of that Conrad, once he's set his mind to a thing, he's open to naught else. And that black humor of his masters him every time. Then no man can tell him anything."

"And this French King Louis?"

I reached to pour him ale. We had found some drink partway buried under rocks when we cleaned up Lord Glanville's camp. I saw thirsty eyes follow the flask while he tilted it and swallowed. Desperate for tidings, for anything that might help us, I poured again, trying to warm him to more talk while the cold night leaned upon our shoulders.

He wiped his mouth. "Louis VII is called The Pious because he has no law, no thought right nor left but of his vow to this crusade. For that he prays night and day, and," he snorted, "leaves the action to the Holy Spirit." He snorted again. "I can tell you it was a great disappointment to us here to see who these nobles and bishops really are." And with this last, he got nods around from those of us whose fealty to any and all lords had long ago worn through.

"You must know," he went on, "that the First Crusade would never have been successful if not for help from friendly kingdoms here. My mother's father was with the crusaders who took Edessa." His face grew dark. "He told me those armies raped and pillaged even those friendly to them. That was the thanks they returned." He slapped his knee again. "By the Rood, you don't attack those have helped you. And the memory of that lives long. So now when Louis the Pious' men rape and pillage like their forebears, Louis finds no friends here offering bread, nor any place to sleep."

For some moments then, Abdil grew silent, gazing into the fire, bent on other thoughts, perhaps of the old crusade, or this one.

"I came down to Acre," he went on, "to see what your leaders thought they could do to help our Christians here, though everyone knows your forces are already near spent; and

that Conrad has been sick, and now seems taken over by these
Hospitalers for a trophy, if you want my mind on it. Meanwhile,
Louis sails between Antioch and Acre, dogged by confusion,
religious fervor and that wife of his, Eleanor, who is stronger than
he is, word has it. And he wears his troops on foot to rags following
his ship back and forth along the coast."

Eleanor of Aquitaine!

I am on my stool in our school in the old stable in Martin
Street. Suddenly we have a visitor. I can tell our cleric has had no
warning, for when the door is thrust open, his eyes grow to the
size of trenchers, as if it is the Virgin Mary herself crossing the
threshold. Her skin is the color of nutmeg and glows against the
white rabbit fur lining her hood. Of slender build, and extravagantly
dressed, the skirt of her gown under her tunic is a deep berry color
and richly embroidered. From under her hood, I see a small aigret
of peacock plumes; and the heavy braid of her dark hair upon her
breast from over her shoulder. Oh and her brown eyes shine with a
warm and lively light that makes me feel happy suddenly, and safe.

"Bonjour," she nods to the cleric. "Et bonjour, mes
enfants," her voice peals out. Then, eyes still twinkling, she lifts
them to gaze at the crumbling walls, the ceiling with its sagging
rafters and gaps, then across the room to discover our ragged
tunics, handed-down shoes, red necks and noses; and then she
brings them to rest, finally and kindly, upon our faces.

"Une chanson, Madame, de ces enfants, en votre honneur,
s'il vous plaît?" the cleric offers at last.

She bows again, looks for a place to sit while we sing
our song in her honor. An aide rushes out a stool to see her safely
upon it.

Then our cleric sounds the familiar starting note and,
giving out the old French song with all our might, we obediently
fill the gaping rafters with the thin watery warble of our voices.
Finished then, we wait in silence while her eyes pass over us like a
Spring breeze; then rest upon us one at a time, like a mother's hand
one at a time.

"Mais, c'est bon!" she stands, bows to us; "Trés jolie! Enchantant!" She shines a radiant smile, and the whole room swells! Oh, and I fall in love with her; we all do! As she leaves, passing amongst us, touching one, then another; and with fingers light and quick, she ruffles my hair and I feel her magic!

The door closes, and our cleric tells us we have just seen Queen Eleanor of Aquitaine. And for some long time after that, every night I fall asleep feeling safe because of her. And right this moment, she is out there on that very ship among those kings and lords!

"Mind you," our visitor has gone on, "no one here wants Seljuk Turks for a master. I had hopes we might at least put up a wall against them; but I saw from the meeting at Acre all Germany will offer is a stiff neck; and all France will offer is a prayer book. And they could well have saved themselves the trip for what it's been worth to anyone."

A young soldier, his nose broken and scarred from Lisbon, leapt to his feet then, fist in the air and shouting, "So we must to Edessa. To Edessa, to take it back!"

And Abdil turned to him mildly, then away to stretch his legs and groan--and think how to respond to this outburst, was my guess.

"Well, that is why I went to Acre, my friend," he turned back,"to see if the crusaders could keep their promises." He paused again. "With our forces together, something might be possible. But these kings told us they were making a change in plans, that they would not go to Edessa after all; instead they would take Damascus."

We waited, stunned. Damascus?

"Do you know Damascus?" He swung his head around like a teacher never tarrying for an answer. "Why Damascus is the only friend--mark, I say ONLY friend--Christians have among Muslim cities in all this huge Seljuk Kingdom." And Titus, next to me, gave me a dig in the ribs that the man was right. "These crusader Kings of such power and high mind," our visitor went on, "plan to make a gift of Damascus to the Pope; and in that way

be quit of their duty. Conrad easily talked Louis into this action
for the reason that Louis wants nothing but to complete his vow
and go home. So they decide to take Damascus, our--YOUR--only
friend here!" He shook his head at such profound stupidity. "Well,
we here want no part of such insanity. And none of us came to
that meeting, not from Acre nor Tripoli nor Antioch nor any other
Christian kingdom here. If Damascus were such a boon, wouldn't
we be mounting--?"

"To Damascus then!" That same soldier was on his feet
again, his face shining. And others joined in, bellowing to enter the
fight they came for.

I couldn't understand it. Had they forgotten Lisbon, the
attacks in the desert?

Abdil shook his head. "I tell you, if you value your lives,
turn around and go home! The Emir of Damascus will call for help
from the Turks soon as he sees your crosses approach. He hates
Seljuks with all his heart, but he will take Seljuks any day over a
siege from foreigners in hauberks! And I say the lot of you will
not be enough to lay hold of that city. There is nothing to gain, and
your very lives to lose!"

By this time, the dark of night had closed 'round. We sat in
silence.

Later, Abdil agreed that on his way home he would lead
those who wished it to within sight of Damascus; a two-day march.
He would ride slowly, for all were on foot, and tie a scarlet cloth to
his saddle so they would not lose him in desert haze or a storm.

And those forty-five, three of them my own aides, packed
and left at sunrise.

Then old Titus, the only experienced soldier among us,
took charge of what remained of able men. He had the idea of
buying a guide to get us past dangerous places and to the sea, for
anywhere on the desert we would be targets for Turks and those
whose territories we might blunder across. So he sent off three men
in three directions with money. Khalil, wanting to play a man's
part, begged to go since he spoke several kinds of Arabic; but I

refused. It was too dangerous; and besides, I didn't trust any of the men we sent.

Awaiting their return, I occupied Khalil and my remaining aides with inventory, repairing what equipment we had, hunting and cooking. I tried to keep life orderly against a rising panic I felt within myself and saw in the faces around me. After two weeks, one of the three returned with the money and a further collapse of our hope: Our food was nearly gone now, water low, and all of us weak and sunsick.

That night we roasted lizards, so little was there now between us and starvation. And we ate them with gratitude. I kept Khalil close; and since he liked Titus, we sat next to him for our meal. I passed once around to each group the last small barrels of pickled vegetables and a flask of Lord Granville's ale, each man taking a mouthful to finish it off.

Well, the men got into telling stories of terrible situations and hair-raising escapes they'd heard of from the First Crusade and other wars. And to this day I can see that battle-eaten old friend of Titus who had never said three words to anybody, his eyes a-shine with a tale about his Gran'fer, like us, lost in a desert and starving. He and his soldiers decided to creep into a village at night and steal the local dress for protection. Thus garbed, they got work on a caravan, crossed the desert to the sea and worked ships back to England. "So they come home with no booty but their own lives; and their own lives they had then," he finished with a sharp satisfied nod.

A hush fell over us. We envied anyone had escaped and lived to tell of it. Titus shook his head and drank; but then looked around at us, one face to the next, there in our head wraps, the firelight a-dance upon our faces.

"Well now," he fingered a grisly beard, and a smile began to spread, "I believe that there's the best bloody plan any one of us could come up with yet!" He raised the flask. "And I drink to it!" And as he drank, the light slowly dawned upon us too, the fire leaping and lighting a wild horse of hope, throwing in our lots together. Yes! Dressed for it we already were; all we needed now was a caravan!

We would leave as the sun sank. Some, too weakened or dispirited, stayed to trust they would be found by crusaders returning from Damascus, or would regain enough strength to strike out later on their own. We left them with the last of our foodstuffs, except for a little bread and mead and our weapons, for whatever good they might do us. Some among them I had come to know, and so bid them good-bye with a weighty heart. Thirty-five we were then, wrapped up like Arabs, unwashed, unshaven, hollow-cheeked, the poorest of the poor. A few carried a crusader cross open or covered upon their shields. Each concealed a dagger.

And we continued our trek across the sand.

Skirting the first village cost us two days and our bread. I figured we would at least catch lizards or snakes to eat; I hadn't realized we were too weakened now to hunt, and barely able to stagger forward as it was.

And too soon there grew the feeling of something tugging, pulling and squeezing mercilessly at my organs, and never letting go. And I am on the ground behind our hut in the clutches of my brother. His knee digs hard into my stomach until I think it will press through to my back. Then I am staggering in the sand again with the others; and that blind pounding in my head never stops. My throat feels narrow, hot, and pulled toward my mouth like a fish on a line. And I experience a vast unredeemable weakness. I want to crumple onto my side and pull my knees into the empty pit below my ribs. But I must stay on my feet, skating and sinking, pulling one foot at a time up and out. And I tell you, I don't know how I do it.

Oh, and would not have made it long as I did except that, huddled together at night to sleep against the piercing cold of the desert, Sarah would come with food. And I would dream we made love in a meadow, or picked apples in the orchard, or harvested greens from our garden. And as my Sarah didn't abandon me in Portugal; so she didn't abandon me in that desert.

CHAPTER TWENTY-TWO

Late the morning of the fifth day, the sun high over us, I spied a herd of camels watering at the edge of a settlement, one marked upon our map as friendly.

We kept out of sight amongst a clump of trees. Titus gave Khalil money and told him to inquire for the caravan master in order to plead our case. "Don't make up any story. Say who we are and what we are and what we need. And if anyone from the village stops you and says he don't like us here, say we'll move on."

I wanted to go with him, to keep an eye on him; but when I saw what an air of manliness came over him rising to this task, I thought the better of it. No one would hurt an unarmed lad, I told myself. He spoke their language. And he had a dagger.

We waited, restless, sitting close. The sight from afar of those tents had kept us walking; now we would see what they could bring. Abdil claimed these were a mix of desert peoples, and of no special religion. The sun crawled across the sky. Dogs trotted up to smell us while we froze, then mildly trotted off. Shadows shrank only to grow once more until we heard mothers call their children for the evening meal; and the wafting aromas of fresh bread, meat and vegetables nearly drove us mad. We pulled our knees tight against our stomachs and wrapped our arms around them. I would take a sip from my flask, hold the mead in my mouth long as I could, then swallow drop by drop.

The setting sun was throwing red, purple and gold over everything as Khalil trudged back. He had had to wait all day for the caravan master to return; and only to be told no new camel tenders were needed.

My heart fell.

"But there will be another coming through."

"When?"

Two village dogs raced around Khalil, nipping at one another.

"He said three weeks."

Three weeks and no food or drink. Well, we would all be dead!

We slumped together like sails had lost their wind.

Just then a man's voice called out, and we looked up. Several caravan drivers with robes flying were coming toward us across the sand. Out of habit, our hands sought our daggers as we scrambled to our feet and drew close together.

It was then we saw they carried a pan-shaped bread, two large bowls and two-handled jars upon their shoulders. They must have read from our widened eyes how unexpected was this act of mercy, how it threw us back upon our heels. Shame covered me, reflecting on what savage enemies we English had been to Arab peoples; and how, were we in full numbers, well equipped and either glorying in our strength or humiliated by defeat, some of us would have destroyed the camel train and this village and everyone in it for the pure enjoyment of it.

The men bowed as they gave us their gifts of food and water. And many of us bowed in return, along with "Thank ye kindly" and "God bless ye." And there were some who could not grasp these Arabs' intentions, or know what to do or to say. And they looked down at their feet, or stood and stared, tense and with daggers at the ready.

For myself, as I saw them striding toward us, sand swirling about their feet, desert wind whipping their garments, head wraps low against the sun and sand, food and water in their arms or upon their heads and shoulders, I saw they had come to rescue us! And something in my chest, invisible until that moment and like an opening of the eye of the mind, cleared my heart. Here were the same men as our own outside of war. Here was need met with compassion and kindness. The rest, as my teacher would say, is not worthy of man who daily reaches to that Great Spirit, whatever Its name, and to which we are all joined by the breath of life. Then tears flooded my eyes. Happiness and regret. And a knot I never knew I had within me until that moment untied itself.

They left us to eat in silence and with tears upon our faces, we were so famished. We knew to suck very small amounts from our fingertips, else our swollen bellies would not keep the food down. And no one had to tell us to save the flats of bread. We passed the bowls around and around, for hours it seemed, mostly in silence and until our polishing had made them shine. I can still smell that red sauce pungent with cardamom, nutmeg and anise; and feel it melt across my tongue. One soldier near me sighed, "Oh, 'tis like the perfume of a fair beauty." All the men laughed.

And it had been days since we'd had aught to drink but mead, and but little of that. So the first mouthful from that water jar was the sweetest I'd ever tasted, sweeter even than water from my forest creek in Exeter.

The sounds of the village dwindled. We let our small fire reduce to embers, then set a guard. When you have been hunted for months, your mind starts to change; and the more fearful you become the more dangerous you are to yourself and everyone else.

Therefore we set a watch that no man steal another's dagger or bread, and to protect ourselves while we slept.

In my dream, my Sarah pulled a covering over me with a gentle hand. Partly waking once, I thought I smelled the lavender she liked to braid into her hair; but I met only darkness, desert insects singing, and the wound that smell of her had left in me.

After that it was the people of this village who fed us.

It seemed families took turns sending their children with dishes of whatever they'd cooked for themselves. These were young boys of eight to fourteen years with liquid brown eyes who came eagerly, curiosity and enthusiasm sitting open in their faces as they studied our weathered skin, dirty knotted hair and beards, and scrawny, boney bodies, reached to touch our shields, drank in the strangeness of our speech and hovered over our games when some of us dug dice from beneath our robes.

With quick eyes they took in the play and soon were sitting with us cross-legged upon the ground, shaking the small cubes carved from oxen bone and letting them fly. When they won--and we saw to it they did often--we would give them something we had managed to hang onto from Portugal or from home in England, or that we had picked up in the desert: a coin, a bead, a fragment of crockery, most of us grateful to be able to thank them for the generosity of their spirits that began to give back to us the lost humanity of our minds.

It was three weeks before we saw a long line of camels strung along the horizon. The young boys who played at bones with us spotted the caravan first and ran to report it. A bell began to toll and people poured out to welcome tenders and animals burdened with spices, cloth, rugs, crockery, grain and other things for purchase or barter.

Titus sent Khalil to use his Arabic on this next caravan master. We waited. Word was the man had purchased thirty-two extra camels for a large shipment of goods to be delivered down south.

Khalil came running back.

"He wants to see us."

Oh, and I shrank inside, dirty and frail-looking as we were.

He was a small man, older but wiry. He motioned first to one, then another. Thankfully, he took Khalil as well, for I could not have left without him.

CHAPTER TWENTY-THREE

The allim, our teacher named Ibram, stood before us, bandy-legged and under a huge purple and white amama wound to spread over his ears and rest upon his heavy black eyebrows that sprouted wild on his brown furrowed face. He looked us over as we waited near the camel pens, thirty-five crusaders, strangers to jamal, the camel. Our allim opened his mouth.

"Jamal ask, 'Who see to my food, my water? Who protect me?' So this way, Jamal is close cousin to man." Low laughter from us at this. Behind our allim, the striped tents of Berbers flapped in a wind so noisy we must strain after his voice, for our very lives depended upon pleasing this man. And the sun's heat caused us to feel thin and ghostly while sand threw itself at our faces and our stomachs raved after the fat rich smell of roasting goat rising from huts nearby.

"Jamal is herd animal," Ibram went on; "but your jamal not keep his eyes on jamal at front. No. He watch you! YOU his lead jamal, his winch. And you tell jamal with voice, hands, body you know always what to do! Then jamal go anywhere for you."

From his robe then, our teacher drew forth a whip of slender handle and long narrow lash that flew out quick as a snake when he snapped his wrist. We jumped back. "You never use whip on camel," he said. "Use tip where lash hang."

I happened to be standing at the front of the group. The allim motioned to me to step forward.

"This man be jamal. You want jamal step back, tap on jamal chest, say, 'Step back.' Trained jamal move right away." I felt the tap, light as a finger, and jumped back. The allim approved. "Ah, this one I not sell. Is quick learner. I keep for me." He raised his hand to our laughter. "You want jamal kneel? Tap knees." At his tap, I dropped to my knees; at another, rolled to my side, then lay down to a burst of approval from the men.

"What make caravan costly?" Allim Ibram raised his voice. "Feed, clean, teach jamal. And handler. No teach jamal--", he held up four fingers, "no trade, no job, no owner money, no worker money. Come," he waved us toward the pens then where the camels, who reminded me of our bishops at home, gathered at the rails to look us over. Our allim reached up to one that had pressed near and grasped its beard in a familiar way and continued talking as we scanned the pens, hoping our camel wouldn't be the one with a leaking eye or slobbering or crying out every three steps.

"Jamal foot spread out, ride on sand. Hump store fat, food for months; and eyelash lock out sand and flies, eh? Jamal carry heavy heavy load for days in heat can kill and not fall down. Many times check halter and jamal nose and feet. Sick or hurt jamal slow caravan, cost owner. Owner make less, you make less. So be humble to jamal. Respect. Be soft. Evil temper only come in jamal hurt by man. Many times a day, check halter, jamal nose and foot."

And the camels, looking us over well, flapped their ears, opening and closing their nostrils and flicking their tails. And as our allim talked on, we shifted from foot to foot, wishing, like the camels, for something to eat. Most handlers had a single camel; but I was given Bibka and her calf, Mishabibka. All legs, brown and grey fuzz, and great-lashed eyes like a doe, the baby would gambol beside her mam, sucking at a tit best as she could as we traveled, and with great earnestness when we stopped. I was warned to watch for marauding wolves, hyenas and cats that might snatch a baby, especially at night. So long undefended and in starvation myself, I had grown something of the mind of a wild animal now, and so watched by habit for anything with teeth. Also, the caravan carried bows and arrows, and some swords. The first week we were attacked by bandits. We lost but two jars of spice, and no lives.

Bibka was docile so long as her baby was safe; and she called to her calf sharply if she strayed. Mishabibka almost never obeyed me. When she did, I gave her a sweet and ruffled the fur under her chin. All this pleased her dam who then would put her nose down for me to stroke; and I would speak softly, making the sound uh-uh, which I learned comforts camels. These animals have large sensitive lips, as horses do; and after a time, Bibka would use hers to ruffle my hair or nibble at the rims of my ears, as she would with her calf.

The wind on the desert howls strong and wickedly as at sea. Camels know to lie down in such a wind while we handlers tuck ourselves into their haunches. I have seen a camel save a man by grabbing his robe in its teeth and at the same time leaping away from quicksand opening under its feet. Some say camels can smell hyenas, wolves, cats and quicksand. In time of danger, I would always grab Mishabibka and keep her close to Bibka's head for her to smell her baby.

Bringing caravans through sandstorms, saving handlers or riders, and leading heroic charges in battle; such were the camel stories around the night fires. And I can tell you a galloping camel is both more fluid and faster than a horse, and an amazement to the eye. Our longer market stops included camel races we put on for the local people, with wagering everyone loved. Camels talk by grunts, barks, calling, burbling, bawling and groaning. Patiently, Bibka taught me camel. I remember she once started up a loud complaint that spread to the whole pen, and that sounded like an hundred women keening into hands clapped over their mouths.

Like the people of Amitab, those who hired us showed no interest in our past and treated us with respect, though we were largely a gang of thieves, bandits, deserters and murderers ourselves. But this was Muslim law toward strangers, I was told.

Despite different tongues, gaming brought the men together after animals were bedded down; and its language belongs to every man. So we became a small hamlet where singing would arise around the fires; and foreign instruments, mournful and tender, made me long for Edward, his lute and the great tree behind the smithy, and for the sight of my uncle's red hair coming and going past the open windows.

Hassan, an older and more experienced camel handler, was a big square man with a commanding posture, not unlike my uncle's; but with skin the shade of oak bark, and light ginger-colored eyes. My first day on the line, he came striding past with his camel, Zarif; but slowed to watch as I tried to get Bibka onto her feet.

Goods are fixed upon the camel's body with riggings of leather straps, ropes, cords and hardware. And Bibka knelt well enough to take the load, but then would not get up. Others passed by, but no one had time to stop over a new man clumsy at his work. As I tugged at her harness and talked to her, this man came over, spreading thick fingers, wagging upright hands and shaking his head.

"Bibka know before she take ten steps, everything come apart. And she too proud to be undressed, eh? He fixed his eyes upon me, "And you waste goods, you pay." He rubbed his thumb and forefinger together. "Eh?"

I nodded, drew a breath. I did not want to lose my job and the only safe way out of this desert; but I, who had mastered every knot on land and sea, could not master the setting and loading of camel riggings.

Hassan undid my mess and started over. I shadowed his every move, burning it into my memory. He instructed me with his hands, a scattering of English and a rush of Arabic. To this day now, I could teach you where everything goes on your camel: either side of the hump, before the hind legs, before and between the front legs and hung from the hump. And this wizard had me safely in the line well before the rear approached; and so my errors brought no notice.

"Shukran!!" Thank you! I shouted as he walked away, his gold robe billowing beneath his blue turban. He raised a hand, but did not turn around. I watched his shadow and that of his camel ripple over the sand. I gave Bibka and Mishabibka a sweet; for by refusing to move, Bibka had saved my place as a camel handler.

Our caravan would stop at small clusters of six or eight huts as well as tent dwellings we in Devon would call hamlets. Our camels with bells and bulging baggage raised a fever of excitement, and people flocked to see us arrive. I saw the eagerness of children in the weathered faces of the men as they dug for coin, or held up hides or handiwork for barter. Business would take about half a day. And if the weather turned bad, we would stay put, for our Overseer would never risk us in a storm.

On our route, we found the quara--villages of thirty or forty or a hundred or more--to be far fewer than hamlets of twenty families or less. And when we stopped at these quara, we often found other caravans unloading wares there too.

At Tel Bashar, about an hour north of Edessa, a souk or market was under way in the commons. It was a high market like we might hold on Bedford or South Hay at home. We were directed to camel pens nearby. Across from them was a stable with empty stalls, but fresh straw; and it was a great luxury for us handlers to sleep there, drowning in the sweetness of new cut grasses. We took turns guarding and caring for our animals; and had a good bit of free time as well.

I was just finishing my half-day when Hassan came around to take me on an inspection of the village. He had kept a friendly eye on me after my disaster the first morning on the caravan.

Like any desert place we stopped overnight, Tel Bashar was built upon an oasis; and its trees, flowers and small parks were a feast to the eye. Awnings in cunning weaves and patterns billowed above overflowing stalls far as you could see. And in its narrow streets crowded with small dwellings, Tel Bashar looked like a giant spider's web.

Moving out from its center were the clustered dwellings of the poor, most swags of cloth just strung upon tree branches. Fewer still set sloping boards covered with fabric against the village wall. And each dwelling kept its own small fire. Groups of tents shared an oven.

Hassan explained there were more tents than usual because the Berbers were in Tel Bashar. In Exeter, we were taught the nomad Berbers were the sons of Cain and damned by God to wander forever without a home.

You will know a Berber because the skin is very light, nearly white; and most have blue eyes and refined features. They are a loud, colorful people--drum-beaters, singers and dancers--as well as excellent craftsmen: Whatever they weave wears forever. And you will experience how the sounds from their drums go before you and follow after you to stir your blood and argue with your heart.

Hassan knew every hamlet and village on our route like the palm of his hand; and had learned bits of several other languages on his trade routes. Old men, soldiers from the First Crusade, gave him his English. Exploring crowded streets, we took our time, found an eating-place. I listened to the cadences of tongues, studied the dark glistening eyes of the men heavy with lashes, noses often with an unexpected hump or wide flare of nostrils, took in the toughened undersides of brown feet greyed by the sand, and the quick hand gestures slicing the air in time to voices.

We ate roast chicken and parsley spiced with something like cinnamon, warm flat bread and mint tea. And I recalled that bubbling pan of turnips and browned cheese in Oporto, and reflected that by some miracle I had lived to be in this place with Hassan, a storyteller and given to detail wild and generous. Now we sat over a fig-glazed bun you pull apart.

When we finished, Hassan slapped the table. "Come. I show mosque here."

From the east side of the great commons it rose, and facing East toward Mecca, its walls covered with a gold Arabic script whose letters both hug the earth and fly upward toward the shining dome rounded like a woman's breast and finished with a gold minaret. And the sight of it raised a surprise of tenderness in me, and an unexpected kind of joy. Mosques did not seem to fight their way to Heaven like the cathedrals of Christendom; but instead breathed in and out the beauty of earth, womanly, adorned, adoring, and shimmering under the sun.

Hassan told me Tel Bashar harbored any number of Muslim sects, as well as those of other religions. He threw his broad leathered palms toward the sky. "And nobody fight in Tel Bashar. Show respect, mind own business, give help. What a miracle, no?"

Still, I had to wonder whether Islam was not, like the Catholic Church, a stern parent, jealous of the loyalty of its children and slow to forget wrongdoing. Muslims could be fierce and unrelenting; I had seen that; but some had saved our lives.

At the arches to the front porch, my friend laid a hand upon my arm. "They say anybody may go into mosque; no law forbids." He notched his head to the side, shrugged ever so slightly. "Still," he kept his voice even, "you, right now, might make problem."

His words were a drenching that brought me to my senses as to who and what I was here. The corpses in the mosque in Lisbon, the boy with my glistening arrow shaft in his chest, heads flying with eyes sprung open, the ring of swords and battle axes, the ungodly screams, the taste in the air of fresh blood. Every time I pulled the drawstring on my bow, I felt myself a living part of an engine of Death; and wished again I had fled back to St. Olave's that first night.

We walked along. The clamor in Tel Bashar with its overflowing stalls, babble of voices and sounds of instruments called back the great market days in Exeter. Here were small drums called ouds but sounding like our lutes, something else like our recorder, wood pieces clacked together in rhythm, small objects that jingle as you strike them; and even something that sounded like a bagpipe. And all this left me filled with wonder, and made me drunk with life.

While the mosque was of stone, common buildings here were one story of baked mud mixed with grass and pebbles or larger stones, finished smoothly, then painted in bright colors with exotic designs of birds, leaves, flowers or Arab script. People with their camels, horses and other domestic animals, wagons or carts crossed the commons in front of one another; and you could hardly be heard for the din.

"Five caravans here now!" Hassan shouted to me, his face flushed as if such a thing were a triumph.

I purchased a tooled purse of Berber leather. Hassan signaled me he wanted to cross to see two Arabian horses, penned-up for sale.

As we stepped forward, a woman all in green and balancing upon her head a large flat basket piled high with loaves of bread while also grasping a small boy by the hand, crossed into our path. Though we jolted back for her, she, at the same time, stumbled and the basket slipped sideways and onto the street. And the bread was all over then, and underfoot as well.

Feeling for her loss, I bent to rescue what I could; but when I stood, she had backed away as if somehow horrified by me. Fearing she meant to leave without her purchase, I took a step forward, holding the basket out.

"Mistress," I cried, "here is your bread! Don't forget your bread!"

The deep brown eyes were all of her that I could see for, as you may know, in public, Muslim women cover all but the eyes with a veil or a garment called a hijab drawn over the nose and mouth. Holding out the basket, I took a few more steps toward her; and how her eyes sparked with rage then! And she turned with her little one and began to run away.

But Hassan hurried after, calling out in her tongue. Then the two stood facing a few paces from me, Hassan waving his hands, the woman, eyes above her face veil, her hijab, downcast, while the crowd jostled past. I kept my own eyes downcast too, confused and embarrassed, my face and neck hot. Somehow I, or something, had given offense. But what or how? When Hassan's voice halted, I looked up and saw the little boy, his face among the folds of his mother's robe, and peeking out at me.

At first the woman just stood, as if deciding something; then finally she nodded. And Hassan waved me over with the bread.

"It is Harâm, forbidden by Muslim law, for you, a man, to look upon a woman, or to help her," he explained. "And she wants to know why you are making trouble and disrespecting her when she is only buying bread for her family. I told her, "'mafi Darar, no harm is meant; for this man saw the bread fall and wanted to help you. In his country, the men are permitted to help the women. He meant no violation of you.'"

First petting the boy's hair, then she raised her eyes to me, oh so briefly. Now neither fear nor anger clouded them; but instead they smiled as the eyes smile, warm with human connection, knowing and gratefulness; and with the opening of the heart. And it struck me that a person can truly meet with someone through nothing but the eyes, and without ever seeing the whole face.

And just that quickly, then, she closeted her eyes again, took the basket upon her head, felt amongst the folds of her robe for the little hand and turned, first to cross the commons, then to enter a street so pressed upon by people and small, squat buildings that the most experienced wagon driver could hardly squeeze down it. There she dissolved into pitched shadows, her green robe with its silver threads flickering for a moment, then gone.

Well, I had to drag my eyes away. And as we turned the other direction, the thought crossed my mind that she was someone I would never see again.

CHAPTER TWENTY-FOUR

$\mathbf{H}$assan and I found the horses he wanted to see, glittering, pawing, arching their necks. He slapped his forehead. "So beautiful; but for rich man."

Then we wandered the spokes of the wheel of the town, then had another meal. Since joining the caravan, my appetite had come back; and now I was always hungry. Twilight descended. Prayers passed. We were deciding to return to our camels when we came upon a crowd of men in the street looking up at the roof of an eating-place. There, four drunkards, passing a small keg back and forth, cavorted wildly, loose and awkward, laughing and falling to their knees, then climbing aright again to hurl more lewd comments at one another and their onlookers below.

Two were our crusaders who had decided not to follow our campfire visitor but to come with us in the hope of a caravan.

Hassan commented the other two were not Muslim either, as believers don't drink; and the crowd was mostly from other caravans, for no Muslim would be out at this hour, nor entertained by drunkards.

Notes rose from a flute; and then a small drum started up clapping from the crowd in a beat that stoked dancing upon the roof.

The crusader with the dark Welsh look wrestled the keg away for himself, planted his feet, tilted his head until his black beard pointed toward Heaven, then drank and drank to clapping from onlookers coming on now like giant footsteps. Then suddenly all four men were off the roof in a jumble of legs and elbows and flying hair, and yelling out their fear as the street of stones rushed up to meet them and the crowd jumped back, laughing, hooting and clapping.

Some of us pushed right through to the pile of the injured. The two on top got up to untangle arms and feet and stagger away. But our two men lay beneath, unconscious.

Local men lifted the lanky one, probably from Cornwall with his pink farmer's face, quite white and bloodied at the mouth now. The dark Welshman beneath I thought might be dead, his neck, thick as it was, broken, being first to hit the street, then hammered down by the others. Face ashen, blood poured from the back of his skull. As two men lifted him, a flap of scalp with its matted dark curly hair hung loose. His head must have struck a stone or piece of pottery.

The men began to move off with the victims. The crowd parted with a murmur.

"Go to Healer," Hassan elbowed me, "over there." He indicated a white curving wall some hundred steps away.

We all stopped at a high gate of carved peacocks painted with fan-like tails of purple, blue and gold in a cunning design. It seemed Tel Bashar had a special umma within its walls, like a town inside a town, that I guessed to be family or tribal where people kept life more to the ways they preferred.

Two older boys opened the gate to the bell, eyes big at the sight of the injured men and the blood; then ran toward the neat dwellings beyond overhung with flowering vines and edging a courtyard.

"Healer here," Hassan nodded. "Maybe these men not die." And his worry for the two drunken crusaders touched me.

The shadowed courtyard carried a marvelous calm. Twilight deepened over the stable and animal pens while night birds tried first notes. Family dogs lay panting. Children peered around mothers or older sisters. A woman in a dark robe, pinning her hijab into place hurried from a dwelling. Two youths followed with mats she gestured be set upon the ground near the porch.

Hassan jabbed me with his elbow. "Is woman with bread you insult." He raised his chin toward the porch. "Man here tell me is her uncle's house." Hassan, talking back and forth with anyone and everyone near, gobbles information like a hen does bugs. "-- live here with her children. Is Healer."

Other women, veiled and with robes flying, rushed out jars, casks, winding cloths, boxes of herbs, soaking bowls and simple surgical tools. We stepped back. Hassan went on that this woman from earlier was named Aysha. He jabbed me again. "Like red-haired third wife of Muhammad. Prophet tell followers once, 'Ask her your question; she know more than me.'" A grin split his face.

As the Healer bent to her work, most of the crowd departed. But Hassan and I moved closer, recognizing the men as from our camel train.

Aysha directed one woman to wash each man, both still unconscious. And as she inspected the wounds, children were soon on the run to pick fresh herbs; and an older man left in a hurry to buy a tincture for head wounds from a shop behind the mosque. Oh, and I remembered Mamoon bent upon wresting someone from the Reaper. This Healer with hands that moved light as butterflies seemed practiced as Mamoon, and with the same will.

Young boys fed the fires for the cooking of remedies.

Someone brought those of us who'd stayed on some food while the umma quietly withdrew to supper, clean-up, then children and animals to bed.

The Healer studied the men's faces, the rise and fall of their chests. She put a drop of their sweat to the tip of her tongue, rolled another drop between forefinger and thumb while overseeing the mixing of remedies and brewing of special teas.

And oh, but she had an expert touch; except when she tried to part the Welshman's hair to examine the wound still bleeding heavily, his eyes flew open and he roared and reared up as if to choke her. She cried out something to Hassan, he and I being close; and we forced the man down flat again.

"She want you speak him English; hold him still," Hassan translated the Healer's sudden hurried language.

So I sat behind the crusader, then; and pulled him up between my legs and held him firm, my arms over his, and legs over his shins. And I crooned low into his ear that everything was all right, that he was with friends. I stroked his arm and hummed a lullaby Mamoon used with sick children, studied his sweat-beaded face, and remembered that he was the one on the Boniface who gave me trouble about the casks of pickled fish.

All through twilight until dark, the woman and I worked to slow the bleeding, to urge the flap of the wound to begin to knit; and this with naught but gestures, as if we'd done this many times together before. And I felt somehow I could sense what she was thinking; and before she asked for something, I was doing it.

Finally, with the man from Cornwall well asleep and looking better, and the Welshman in and out of his deep faint, the moon rose, huge above us. Hassan, stirring healing teas, worried aloud that for either of these men to come awake suddenly to a strange place--he shook his head--somebody would get hurt.

"And this Healer need sleep. So you stay, English," he slapped me on the shoulder; "you speak language and have muscles." With that he rose and left, his shadow, long and black, striding before him.

Well, and luck was with me, for neither man woke,
although the one with the flap shouted out a name once or twice in
his sleep; and because I could speak his language I could soothe
him and keep him from waking.

Next morning, Healer Aysha brought out tea and bread.
And the Cornwall man was sitting up; the Welshman, still bereft
of his senses, had a warmer feel to his skin. And so the small son
Aysha called Farhaan led me back around the wagon wheel of the
town, and to our camel pens.

But that afternoon, I was searching Bibka's ears and nose
for sores when I heard small feet and felt a yank at my sleeve.
Little Farhaan, wordless, but with eyes huge and urgent, tugged me
straight off in the direction of the umma.

The Welshman was raving again, bloodshot eyes seeing
boiling oil rushing toward him, a flaming arrow in the man at his
side, a severed arm looping through the air, then the sand opening
at his feet. And often enough, flaring out of nowhere, I had seen
such things too. Deserters and heroes, our bodies and minds
carried these horrors like so many galls grown into a tree. And we
know this about one another.

Well, no man at the umma would come near a mad stricken
crusader. Aysha, the Healer, too, stood well back, preparations at
hand and eyes following him as he staggered about the courtyard.

I drew near to him, and as I would to a frenzied horse,
calling in a low voice and getting close enough to lay a gentle hand
upon his forearm while I put the other about his shoulder and held
him that way. First he quivered violently, and then became soft as a
child and let me take him to the mat. But when Aysha brought a tea
to help him sleep, he flew into a fit at the sight of the cup; and I had
to force my knees into his chest and force his mouth open digging
fingers into his jaw hinge 'til the remedy got into him.

I stayed the rest of that day. When the tonic wore off, we
gave it to him again; and, with me on his chest and arms, Aysha
could treat his head further. Gradually his black humor lessened;

and by the time mothers called their children for the evening meal, he had fallen into a deep sleep. Aysha studied his breathing, tasted a drop of his sweat, considered him, then looked at me and nodded. He had passed through the crisis. I pointed down with my finger: Stay? She shook her head, no.

While I would rather see her through a tranquil night, I crossed to the gate. I had not reached it when I felt a tug at my sleeve and looked into little Farhaan's upturned face. He pointed to where his mother stood. When he saw my eyes had found her, he dropped to his knees in the Muslim way, looked up at me, then bent to touch his forehead to the ground at my feet. He remained there a long moment, then straightened, stood and gestured again toward his mother. Having delivered me her thanks, he ran back; and she put her arm out and drew him to her. I bowed in return to both, then staggered out the gate, moved by such largesse to one who had been of their enemy. And a crusader myself! I should have been on MY knees!

Now I owed time to those who had kept watch on our camels. Still, my mind could not pry itself from a tilting of her head, her shoulder claiming or giving up space, and each and every movement causing wonder and joy to fill me until I thought I must burst.

That midday, Khalil strolled over with a flask of tea, bread and cheese to sit with me in the spindle of shade cast by a palm tree. I took the food and chewed dumbly with no sense of him next to me.

"Is anything troubling you?" Casual, he passed the flask.

"Why?" A little annoyed, I straightened, searched his face.

He shrugged. "When we eat, we usually solve the problems of life. Today you don't talk."

"You haven't spoken either." I brushed sand from my crossed legs.

"Because I took you to be talking with yourself."

My face grew hot; a sharp retort crowded my throat; but his brown eyes were filled with naught but care for me.

"Forgive me, Khalil. Something makes me poor company."

"Never poor," he shook his head. "Talking or not, I just want to be sure you're all right."

He fetched up a twig to twirl between his fingers. He seemed every day to grow more from a youth into the man he was to be. His face had lengthened. The scar along one cheekbone from an arrow scrape had healed to a silvery line that gave him a manly look. And he had these days about him a serious air that was very pleasing. Also, he filled in expertly for different handlers, and had high standing amongst all of us because of his gift with language. It was nearly two years since I took him under my wing. These days he liked to talk man to man.

"I thought you might be suffering feelings for someone."

"Why would you think that, Translator?" I held my eyebrows high.

He lifted his chin, spoke as if to the sky, "For one thing, I heard from Hassan how she looked at you when you brought the men through the gate."

I shook my head. "She looked at the bleeding soldiers."

Sitting close to the pens, you smell baking dung, sharp and heavy and oddly comforting. Behind us, I heard grunts of pleasure and turned. It was a young male camel rubbing the matted hair of its neck against a corner post to rid himself of sand lice.

"Hassan said she asked for you to assist her," Khalil persisted

"Oh, she needed some English." I waved the idea away: Youths like Khalil saw love everywhere; but my heart had leapt at his words.

He hesitated. "She is widowed, her husband killed by crusaders. Her people are a special something, maybe something called Sufis, though that word means 'wool'; and what would wool have to do with religion?"

But I had stopped listening, trying to grasp that this woman could see any crusader as other than the murderer of her husband, of her people; and I scoured my eyes with my fists, so moved was I. Khalil just waited. I don't know how long it was before I turned to him.

"I need to sort some things in my mind. Could you--?" I asked, gesturing toward the camels milling around empty feedbags. "An hour or two?"

"Just make sure you come back," he called after me. "They look mean today."

A brief walk from the pens took me to a quiet area with a few small trees and clutches of flowers; but otherwise deserted except for two white-haired men talking under a tree. I found a white flowering shrub to sit behind and suddenly realized how often I had seen small struggling plants with flowers like this one in the desert reaching up from a clutch of rocks, or standing brazen in the sand under a blistering sun and blessing the landscape and all those who passed with their intelligent fragile bodies, long reaching heroic stems and green leaves puffed with water and springtime blossoms, delicate or brazen, of pink, blue, deep red or brilliant yellow. And I could have spent longer in this reflection with the sudden gratitude it brought; but inside, I was a fish thrashing in a net. Thrashing.

And finally I buried my head in my arms and reached out in my mind to Mamoon. "I believe I loved this woman from that first look, Mamoon, when she took her bread from me; and felt I have always known her; and we somehow are the same. My caravan moves on soon. I don't want to leave her and lose this opening of the heart between us. And I don't want to give up the chance of having what it could become."

The sun started its descent. The old men stood. Even if, by some miracle, I, a crusader, could be permitted to be with her, would she be willing? Or, by being with me, might she become an outcast to her people?

"Help me, Mamoon," I begged, "to understand what I am meant to do or not to do."

Exercising my animals the next two days allowed me to pass by the peacock gate, but yielded no sight of her. And time was draining away. Our caravan would not be here much longer. And so I must take action, mustn't I? But who could guide me?

Khalil came behind leading Mishabibka, now half the size of her mother. As we passed the mosque, my eye was drawn to two white-bearded elders, their heads bent in conversation. We held our camels back to let the men by, and a new idea broke through: An imam--an elder--of Aysha's people would know what was right, and might be possible!

CHAPTER TWENTY-FIVE

Khalil somehow managed an appointment for late the next day with an elder of Aysha's umma, a man whose work included speaking with foreigners. "I found the best, too," he swaggered. "Elder Yusif is a scholar of Islam. Everyone makes way for him." Then a sudden hunger for Brother Frederick dug through me. Oh, and to study again! Could I be so lucky?

Midday well past, we made our way to the gate of peacocks where a youth showed us to a small building, its inside hung with a fabric of yellow and white roses. Large scripted tiles embellished the walls, gleaming as if made wet by the light of the sandalwood candles on the low table.

Almost immediately, an older man, surprisingly tall and

with eyebrows like birds in flight, and wearing a robe of very deep red, bent through the curtains with a rustling sound.

Kahlil and I stood.

He bowed.

He had a long face the light brown of English oak, and a thin beard, grey and white, that straggled to his waist from beneath a narrow sculpted nose and over barely visible rose-colored lips.

He sat.

We sat.

Khalil spoke in Arabic the words we had composed at the camel pen.

"Honored Sir, my friend Jophiel Balerais, a man from England and a crusader, wishes to express his gratitude for your kindness in meeting with him. There is a matter weighing upon his heart that involves a woman of your umma."

The older man kept a penetrating and unwavering gaze upon me as Khalil told of the bread spilled in the street, of the drunken crusaders and my assistance with the fallen men at the request of the umma's Healer. The room, softened by shadows and the scent of sandalwood from the flickering candles, helped to calm me.

Elder Yusif nodded, raised open palms. "How can I help?"

"My friend finds himself unsure about how to fulfill a great sense of care and responsibility he has come to feel towards this widow; and wishes to know what acceptable action, however humble, toward her well-being he might take. He has deep respect for your culture and ways, and would not want to distress her or any of your people."

A small smile broke from the Elder at this, and his eyes upon me deepened with kindness. Then he furrowed his brow and stared into the turning thumbs of his clasped hands, while from behind a curtain to our right came the chink of pottery. The Elder's thumbs stopped. He spoke, and Khalil turned to me.

"Have you the thought to marry the widow, he wonders."

Marry her. My eyes widened.

If I had dared think of that, I surely had kept it a secret from myself. I swallowed. "But I must present myself truthful, honored Sir. I am taken quite by surprise at the effect upon me of this woman, and come to you in confusion and in ignorance of what is possible or not, right or not, for myself as well for her."

The older man waited for my translator to finish. Chanting from the street. The candles sputtering. A fly buzzing at my ear. The curtain moving aside; a woman with a tray. Peppermint tea to open my breathing. The chink of the Elder's cup upon the table.

"Your request is unusual. And I do not have an answer for you, but will think on it. This much I can tell you: Should she accept you, and for her to be secure among her people, you most likely would have to marry her, and in a way that her people can understand and accept," Khalil translated.

"And what way might that be?" Perhaps I had already guessed.

"Englishman, it is both simple and not simple: For to marry her, you would have to marry her umma; and to marry her umma, you would have to marry her religion. You can see that it could not be otherwise; for what attracts you to her is the umma flowering in her." He gestured a wide circle. "What else has formed her? Her parents. Her tribe. And what has formed them? You cannot separate her from her umma any more than you could separate color from a leaf." He eyed me keenly, then. "And you cannot marry her umma unless you marry her religion, for her umma is the fruit of her religion; and she the fruit of her umma." He dropped his hands, his eyes at rest upon me, kind and serious." I tell you these things now."

A cart rattling outside. A spider spinning thread in the window.

I had thought only to serve her in some way, to support, to protect; and to be near her, if possible. I had to admit I had not thought to marry her. Marry her! And this new idea gave me unexpected joy. But to marry her umma as well, to marry her religion? I spent some long moments tracing the nail beds of my fingers with my eyes. Finally I lifted my head.

"It is in their living that people make a difference to me, not in their country or religion. In England I have found good men and bad, in Portugal good men and bad, in Arabia good men and bad. What I have seen and know of your religion and of your umma draws my respect. I have felt peace in your umma; found kindness and mercy there. So it makes sense that if I am drawn to this woman, I could also be drawn to her umma and religion. I do not know. But I could try, and see what happens."

Elder Yusif gazed into hands now filled with his long thin beard, his breath steady as the tides. And in light of what I had just said, I felt anxious to be certain he knew I was not yet clear within myself. So when he looked up again, I repeated this, adding, "You have given me much with which to search my mind and my heart, Sir. I will do so."

The Elder nodded. He sighed and rose. "And I will seek opinions from other elders about what might be possible. If I learn something useful, I will contact you."

He bowed. I bowed.

Then Khalil and I were outside and shouldering through street traffic.

And after that, each day when I exercised Bibka and Mishabibka walking through Tel Bashar, I scoured it for signs of Aysha, while at the same time ready to duck my head, afraid to see her. Likely she was having a good laugh over me, or angry that a crusader dared to seek her. By the third night, I was sure Elder Yusif had decided to speak to no one about his crazy visitor. And in this way my mind wore me out raiding me with doubt, with hope, with fear.

So I sat with my warring thoughts, leaning against Bibka, studying the stars, so big and close. And how I wished to climb among them. I pulled my cloak high to meet my head wrap and tucked myself into that place where Bibka's stomach curves against the sand, for her body heat made it possible for me to sleep. And Bibka blew air and gave out a grunt of satisfaction.

Late next afternoon, bending to scoop grain for her feed sack, I saw through the beads of sweat stinging my eyes two gnarled sandaled feet; and above them the hem of a robe of a deep red. The Elder! Since Arabs hold it wrong to interrupt someone at their work, my visitor sat himself in the shade of a small cypress while I fed my camels hastily, then called to Khalil, feeding his camels as well.

Then, heart in my mouth, we joined the Elder climbing to his feet. "I have spoken to Aysha's uncle; and he told me, 'If she is interested in this man, and as long as he becomes her husband within her faith, such a thing would be possible.' And if you now wish to go further, one of the elder women will speak of your interest to Aysha." He paused a long moment, his old eyes keen upon my face; then spread palms.

"Do you wish to go on with this?"

Why, I had not thought of marriage; only of what decision the elders might make. But as he offered the possibility of a life with her now, every other path fell away.

"I wish to go further." I bowed. "And I thank you, Sir, for your kindness." As Khalil translated, small grey birds with yellow markings and sitting upon a roof beyond us rose up as of one body, and with a wild chittering, turned once, twice in the heat, then shimmered away.

"So. The matter will be brought to her then," the Elder nodded. "An Elder Woman will contact you directly if Aysha is interested."

Then he was gone, red robe billowing and snapping; and the sand leaping about his feet in delicate twisting ropes.

I turned and ruffled Khalil's hair. He looked at me, eyes big at what I had just got myself into. I grinned, threw my shoulders high, let my arms slap at my sides. Then Bibka, complaining in her long broken speech, brought me back to the wind, the heat, the sand and my camel's appetite.

Well, the fourth day passed, and still no word. Oh, and you can imagine I gave it all up then, my insides a clay vessel filled with spiders. Why, I must have been crazy to think that she or her elders would accept me! But then, bent over and stirring a sweet into Bibka's afternoon grain, I saw the small brown feet three or four steps from me.

Little Farhaan tugged at my sleeve. I held a finger in the air. And while I watered my animals, he drew in the sand with his great toe. But soon as I set down the water vessel, he grabbed my hand while I looked about desperately for Khalil, my translator. But oh no, he was on an errand!

The little tyke guided me along the crowded streets to the gate of peacocks, and we crossed into the courtyard. Young maids sat upon a porch cleaning vegetables and glancing at one another as we passed, clapping their hands over their mouths, their eyes adance. Sure that I was now held to be nothing but a fool by Aysha's whole umma, my face flamed. And I had to rein myself in or run off.

That same room at the front of the dwellings, and Farhaan pointed me toward a cushion, then was out the door. And a terrible heaviness suddenly filled my heart that they had brought me to refuse me. Of course, the courteous Elder would insist everything be done with respect. And perhaps he pitied me.

A veiled young woman brought with downcast eyes artful slices of fruit bread and seed cakes. I bowed my thanks, and didn't know how I could eat. I watched shadows cast upon the walls by the candles in their slow erratic dance. Voices of children. Hammering. Wheel rims biting the earth. All passed and left me wrenched with longing suddenly for my uncle and his family. Twice more the young woman appeared. Somehow I forced down more food.

Then Farhaan came with Khalil by the sleeve, pointed him to the gold cushion next to mine and disappeared, leaving upon the air his small boy's scent of hot sun. Khalil raised questioning eyebrows. I shrugged, shook my head with a sickly look. More tea and cakes. Khalil ravished the tray for us.

Then the curtain was pulled aside.

An Old Mother on a walking stick attended by the young woman who served us came in. We stood, eyes to the floor, sweat trickling from my armpits. She sat. We sat. The candles, burning low now, carved deep shadows everywhere. And realizing with a jolt that I was looking upon this elder woman, I hurried to drop my eyes while her words spilling like grain onto a winnowing sheet were thick, clipped, sharp and so unrelenting my scalp flicked. And as Khalil gave them to me in English, she turned upon me her fierce and blazing eyes. Having once again forgotten the dictum against a man looking upon a woman, I slammed my lids down in terror while she locked together her fingers with nails the color of ancient wax.

"She asks that I tell you," Khalil spoke carefully, "the Elder Women have conferred and agreed that she should carry the message of your interest to Aysha. She did so this morning. And she says to tell you--" I steadied myself--"that Aysha accepts you."

Well, you can imagine a jolt of joy split my chest; and my eyes flew in gratitude to the Elder Woman who stared back fiercely and with a cold light of enmity, as if to say that in putting forth my feelings for Aysha I had committed an unspeakable and filthy act; and the fact that I just now had raised my eyes to hers showed clearly I had no respect for the simple and most basic rule against looking upon a woman. Aysha may have accepted me; but she, the Elder, certainly had not.

And my heart sank. How would I ever learn to behave so as to satisfy such a person?

"May I see her?" I dared the question finally without looking up. And Khalil made his voice humble as I made mine.

"You may NOT see her!" Her words exploded like stones in a fire. "You will go to the Elder. You will learn the Five Pillars. You will study the Qur'an. You will study the Hadith and Sharía. You will learn to recite by heart the words of the Messenger (Upon

him be all blessings!)--words that raise a man from the nature of
a beast and keep him from the lust of his loins, the violence of his
mind and the greed of his heart. You will fast for Ramadan. You
will learn to pray each day the Duhr, the Asr, the Maghrib, Isha
and Fajr. Before you pray, you will three times perform wudu to
purify with water your head, nose, mouth, forearms, hands and
feet. You will learn all that is required, all that is forbidden and
all that is allowed as if you were already Muslim. You will live a
blameless life."

She paused, and from behind her veil drew upon her lips
with a long sucking sound. "It means nothing that Aysha accepts
you. It is we," she thumped her breast with a knotted hand, "the
Elders of this umma, who must accept you." She raised her chin
and pushed a sharp burst of air through her nostrils so that her
hijab rose like a tunnel, and I caught sight of the bony neck,
weathered and roped like an old tree trunk. Then with a jolt, I
remembered my eyes. She slapped the table. The candle flames
jumped.

"You will study and do as you are told until we are
satisfied you are ready, should that day ever come. And I doubt
it will. Our Holy Book says: 'God does not guide unbelieving
people.'" Again the sucking sound. "The Holy Book says, 'Whether
you manifest what is in your mind or hide it, Allah will call you
to an accounting according to it.' You are to meet Elder Yusif at
the gate tomorrow evening, and every evening without fail. You
must prove yourself worthy of a Muslim woman of good family, a
jewel among jewels. We do not throw our women like bones to any
dog that slobbers after them." She raised her arms and at the same
moment a great bird with huge black wings overtook the wall. "We
are the gate behind which she lives," she cried out in triumph; "and
we are the sure lock upon that gate!"

Under her barrage, my happiness staggered. Still, nothing
could destroy it. I had the impulse to say I thought of Aysha
only with the highest respect and would do all I could--but the
Old Woman was closed up tight as a fist. Never mind. Aysha

had accepted me, a crusader, a Christian, a camel driver without prospects who could not so much as speak her tongue. Surely she too must have felt the same power I did drawing us to each other.

The old mother was given her cane. Khalil and I leapt to our feet. The young woman drew the curtain aside. The Elder, no bow to us, hobbled from the room.

I shrugged as we walked to the gate. "Why should she trust crusaders, Khalil? We don't even trust them."

The street teemed with commerce, droppings and dust, while overhead the sun cooked everything without mercy. And I noticed none of it. Happily, and I tell you not without quite a little fear, I set my foot upon this new path; and like the quartermaster I had become, began to inventory my resources.

CHAPTER TWENTY-SIX

Elder Yusif met us just after Maghrib, evening prayers. Though I had heard only the imam's voice chanting, it was as if in his voice all voices were lifted up, flung far, then gathered back over streets and rooftops and the humble things of man and nature. I was to learn that the Salat was the obligatory prayers said five times each day.

This form already felt familiar because of Canonical Hours chanted in the monasteries at home and learned as a student in the school of my betters, and came to mind after awhile lost in the woods. So Adan felt familiar; and the idea of the practice was welcoming.

The Call To Prayer is given by a mu'addin from a platform fixed to the minaret of the mosque from which his voice rises musically as an instrument of praise:

God is Great
I testify there is none worthy of worship except God
I testify Muhammad is the messenger of God
Come to prayer!
Come to success!
God is Great
There is none worthy of worship except God.
And each chant repeats.

As Islam has no priests, prayer is led by an imam, one
held in the umma as most learned in the Qur'an and other books.
To hear the rustle and sigh of those rising and bowing low, and
the "Ameen" breathed out as if sealing a secret--all this stirred
me. For such cries of the soul felt more to me than all the prayers
of the Church with its rules for holding off God's wrath. I have
seen in Exeter and on this crusade, both bishops and lords bend
rules and easily to meet their own ends; and at the cost of the most
defenseless of us. So while the ways of the Church were those of
my people, all that high preaching was turned to ashes by what we
must do and see; and it lit a fire in me against those had left us to
wander the desert while they saved their own hides, though I never
felt hatred before, not even for Teewaye.

That first evening, the Elder led us across the courtyard
while the young maids forever cleaning vegetables crumpled
together in merriment at the crusader with his blushing face and
young translator, both ducking heads and keeping a respectful
distance behind their teacher. The room had its usual low table and
suffa, a new word I had now along with ka'k (cake), tabaq (dish),
and al-jubun (cheese). And beeswax candles held at bay the dark
that would steal upon the day before we finished.
The Elder offered his full name: Yusif al-Musurani, a
name tall like him and that flowed like his robe. Khalil translated;
and I thought I had repeated it exactly, but before I drew a breath,
the Elder put me right with an uplift of fingertips.

"Yoosif. Oo. Oo. Yusif al-Moos-uhr-ani."

"YOOsuff al-Moos-uhr-ani," I tried again. "Thank you for teaching me." I bowed. I had no trouble honoring one who might hold the key to my happiness.

He bowed in return; then gestured. "Please to be seated."

I let my eyes drift toward a wooden chest against the far wall, and saw again Brother Frederick in his cell lifting the lid to hand out the Herodotus History. Beloved Brother Frederick it was who opened my eyes to all to be gleaned from the Arabs in science, mathematics, astronomy, healing, art, bookmaking, and the building and crafting of all manner of useful things including hand weapons of such excellent design a soldier pocketed one if he could get it, not only to put it to use immediately, but to show off when he returned home. Oh, and it purely baffled me that we were sent to destroy the very people upon whose shoulders we had clambered to create our own betterment.

"Now," my teacher held up a finger, "we start with the first of the Five Pillars of Islam: îmân or Faith."

He closed his eyes then and repeated aloud the Shahadah, the Muslim Declaration of Faith:

There is none worthy of worship except God,
and Muhammad is the messenger of God.

And I felt the very weight of it in him even before Khalil translated the words. The Elder opened his eyes then and spoke with a grave sincerity.

"Upon the Shahadah rests all our belief. From it man can divine the purpose of life: To obey and serve Allah (Blessed be His holy name!) and His words through the Prophet (Peace be upon Him!) writ in the holy books and telling us what we must know."

"The Qur'an, the Hadith, (stories of those who had heard the Prophet, like our gospels and epistles), and Sharía (the book of Islamic law)," I repeated after Khalil, and with a nod for each one.

Well, I was to begin by learning the Five Pillars, as well

as to recite the Salat, (obligatory daily prayers) taken from the ayat (verses), in surah (chapters of the Qur'an).

So many words I needed so desperately to know; and coming so fast they set me to sweating!

"And all that the woman Elder told, you must also learn. And more." Elder Yusif rested a thumb against his chin to study me, then let out a sigh. "And there will be tests."

I dropped my head, hesitated. "Is it permitted to ask a question?"

His lips curled into a small smile, then. "Ask what moves your heart. Your questions are a gift of which Allah has made you messenger to us."

While his fierce eyebrows looked as if they could leap out and peck something to death, my teacher rested upon me a calm warm gaze which made something clenched-up in my chest relax. Then he stood. We stood.

"Shukran, (thank you). I will work hard," Khalil translated for me. I bowed.

He bowed in return. "Tomorrow we begin."

Finding our way to the camel pens, Khalil wore a look of foreboding. "It will be a dangerous thing, Jophiel. Muslims see you as an idolator they have permission to kill. And do you really think you could live in this village as a Muslim?"

I held my peace. The sky was near dark. Cooling of the day's heat left beads upon rocks, tent posts and animal pens. Khalil picked up a supple stick to swat the air as we walked along. "But truly, could you live in this village and be Muslim?"

"I can't say, truthfully. What this Elder may teach, I have interest in it. And that path that could bring me to Aysha's door. So I must try."

"But can you learn all that?" He searched my face. He had the beautiful dark-lashed eyes of so many Arab men, the gift of his mother.

"To be Christian I had to learn much." I picked up a small flat rock to skim the air in front of us. "You learn what you need.

I knew nothing of being a Quartermaster until I needed it. And perhaps the Old Mother will lose her fierce interest in me."

Khalil barked a laugh, then sobered. "But you speak no Arabic. How will you get along?"

"I listen to you. As-salaamu'alaykun. And peace upon you."

"Wa 'alaykum as-salaam. And upon your peace," he returned. "Well, and you know a few words from the men in the caravan." He grinned, then turned serious. "But what about England? Isn't that why we are on this caravan, to get home?" There was a pleading in his voice now, in his eyes.

"But first of all, my friend, we have to stay alive."

With a low howl, a wind pushing treetops, awnings, and sand thrust at us. A brass pot clattered across our path, and a thin man, knees low, bent after it, one hand reaching out, the other in a death grip upon his amama.

I pointed toward a small eating-place.

It was narrow and dark, except for a hazy shield of sun across the open front; and candles upon four small trestles. Neither of us spoke until we had devoured lamb pies and vegetables.

"And I don't know if I can pass their tests." Back to our subject with a sip of tea. "And I don't know if her people will accept me; or if they do, I don't know how I will see things then."

"But how can you get into something so--and not even know her?"

Oh, but I knew her that first day--only how to say this? Then I saw in his face the poorly covered anguish, and understood at once his worry about losing me, his family now since his father died in that bloody attack near Acre.

The wind had softened. On the street a young woman, hijab billowing and dying about her legs, passed by, a rolled rug long as she was tall upon her head and balanced by a slender hand. The setting sun struck the thin gold bracelet on her wrist and sprang from it as a white needle directly into my eye. I blinked and pulled my head away.

"Listen, little brother, you have most of your life yet to live. There will be changes you choose, and changes that will come upon you. This woman appears now upon my path. How can I know what I am to do except by what is put in my way? And how can I know if it is good or not except by where it leads me?"

"But what about England, your family?"

"I joined the crusade to escape England. There was too much sorrow there for me." I fingered coins onto the table. "What about you? Does Lisbon call?"

"My mother." Khalil kneaded his scalp. And I could feel in his body her waiting for him. "I swore to return." He dropped his head, then raised it. "She was afraid I would stay here; she knows I love the language. Still, she was an obedient wife. Now her husband will not come back to her." He fell silent. "But someone must."

"I swore nothing to anyone. Nothing." But these words I spoke in my mind. I turned back to him. "Khalil, if I were God creating the world, you would always be where I could see and talk with you. But we may some day take separate paths. One day you will hear a call you must heed. That is life." I shrugged. Khalil let his body relax, and I knew some good had come to him from my words. "And how would we beaten soldiers ever have saved our lives except for a brave lad with a magic tongue?"

He replied by looking up at me cross-eyed, his lips slackened into an idiot's droop. I laughed, and knew he was all right for now. But one day he would have more questions.

That night, a terrible dream came upon me. Opening the camel pen for Bibka, crusaders storm up. One hooks his arm around my neck to cut off my wind. Then out of the corner of my eye I see they have Khalil by the hair, a knife at his throat.

I woke leaping to my feet, sweat pouring, my breath coming fast and hard while my young translator slept sweetly alongside me. Well, but I must be on my guard every second. For myself, I didn't care; but Khalil had a mother waiting.

Next night, Elder Yusif brought forth a great rolled manuscript embellished with Arabic tiles. Lettering like long-necked birds in gold, black, green, red and silver crossed the cream-colored pages. Chanting, he carried the Holy Qur'an to the table. The fragrance of its vellum drew up gratitude in me like groundwater: I would be a student again! Under my crusader's skin still lived that never-sated hunger for learning. And the anger of the Old Mother, by her unflinching demands, would see it fed.

Through Khalil, Elder Yusif explained that it was by chanting the text that we come to know all that Allah says about how man must live to be healthy and happy.

"The Holy Qur'an is the final gathering through the Prophet (Peace to Him forever!) of the last revelations of Allah (Blessed be His Name!). You know Ibrahim was first to receive commands from Allah; so he fathers Jews, Muslims and Christians." He watched amazement rise in my face at this; his eyes twinkling. "Muhammad (The blessings of God upon Him!) is His last Messenger." Again, at St. Petroc's, the painting of Isaac upon the altar, the knife held high, the shining angel's hand raised against Abraham's sacrifice.

"First chapter is Al Fatiha, a short prayer to Allah," Khalil translated. "Allah the Beneficent, the Merciful, Lord of the Worlds, Master of the Day of Judgment, keep us on the right path."

All Muslims recite the Qur'an. And I must too, though I was forgiven certain sections in the beginning. "And he who finds difficulty reciting the Qur'an will obtain a double reward." The Elder raised his eyebrows to me, eyes twinkling, and patted the vellum, his long thin hands roped with veins.

I was to recite faithfully each day the ayat, verses of the Qur'an for that day. "Do so and you will receive into your body and mind the highest prize, the peace of God," he told me, his eyes flashing a solemn fire.

But what manner of peace is it that God knows? I pondered.

And so it was that this elder taught me as he would a small

child, using the twenty-eight letters of the Arabic alphabet, (the first of which is written like our "t": Alif) and a word beginning with that. "Akl, food. Allah puts akl for our bodies in the earth He made, in our minds by the word He speaks; and in our hearts by love He places there for His creatures and Himself."

Since my teacher wanted me to chew upon what he taught, we would have a taste, then taste again while from beneath the flight of his eyebrows, and with eyes so alive, he would study me.

Like Brother Frederick, my teacher demanded I ponder, determine what I understood and in what way, then write these thoughts down to bring to our next meeting, along with the first sentence of whatever we had read, but written in Arabic. And like Brother Frederick, he wanted examples from my own life to show my grasp both of the teaching and how I would use it in living. Oh, and Khalil was excited by such a teacher, and so was happy to come those days of my early efforts which boiled up many a good laugh between us afterwards at my own confusion and fumbling.

Before my caravan must take me into the desert again, Elder Yusif insisted I know the Five Pillars of Islam: Salat, Prayer; Zakat, Alms; Ramadan, Fasting; and Hajj, Pilgrimage to Mecca. Oh, also Wudu, "ablution," the ritual of washing five times each day hands, nose, mouth, face, lower arms, hair, ears and feet.

For the nose and mouth, you take in water, then expel it. And I remembered how Mamoon demanded we leave our shoes outside our hut because of the filth of our neighborhood. Oh, I couldn't help but think then, how my Gran'mam would have admired these Muslim ways!

My teacher also instructed me in the prayer movements:

To pray, stand with the palms of your hands forward and near the ears. Drop to your knees to prostrate with forehead, nose, chin, chest against the ground, toes tucked under. Now raise up onto the knees, then prostrate fully again.

I knew standing, kneeling and prostration from Mass at St. Vitalis and schooling at St. Bartholomew. With Christian prostration, I felt flattened before an awesome Power; but in the Muslim way, more curled like a child.

And these were to be my practices on caravan. "Each man has for a priest no one but himself." Elder Yusif told me, then closed his eyes. "Allah waits for our voice. We wait for Allah's voice. There is silence, there is speaking." He opened his eyes. "Treat your enemy better than your friends. Care for all lives as your own."

As Khalil and I stood at the door, he gave me an Hadith for my journey: "Coarse talk comes not into anything without disgracing it. Modesty comes not into anything without adorning it."

I liked that, the elegance of it. Delicacy and balance seemed a silent force in Muslim life.

Finally, the Elder gave me five more words from the first letter of the alphabet to write about during the trip. I was also to review our lessons and write upon each. And each day I was to translate the first sentence of my writings into Arabic.

I had not yet seen Aysha, for according to the Qur'an, I was an Idolator. And you can imagine it would be hard to be away from Tel Bashar and the comfort of the wall behind which Aysha lived; and away from Elder Yusif who led me toward a life with this woman.

Nights, Mamoon came in my sleep to feed me strength. And Sarah came. Smiling. Happy for me.

CHAPTER TWENTY-SEVEN

Leave I must.

I brushed Bibka down, checked her teeth, hooves, the bags of grain, boxes of spices, beads, great rolled rugs. Packing a camel is like packing a ship. I reached to hoist a net of boxes, felt a tug at my pantalones and looked into the upturned face of Aysha's little messenger who pushed into my hand a small leather bag. I bowed my thanks. He bowed, flashed a smile, turned upon his heel and was gone.

That night I hung at the fire until the others had crawled off to sleep, then untied the cord with clumsy fingers and probed to find three small parcels wrapped in silk. The first revealed an opal, like looking deep into clouds. Next, another opal the pink of cherry blossoms. The third was a green as young and alive as budding leaves. That Aysha would send me any gift told my hungry heart she had accepted my suit, that I could trust her love. I held the stones close and sent to her through them a longing so fierce the press of it threatened to shatter my chest.

After our morning bread, I showed them to Khalil.

"Opals are for protection; and the pink one also for love." He gazed at me with mixed pleasure and pain. "Green stones like this are costly gems; they declare love with no conditions. Very rare and costly," he swallowed, handed them back.

Not since Sarah had I felt heir to earth and its happiness. And how I wanted to give a gift of such meaning to Aysha; but had no money for anything so beautiful. Days on the camel train I racked my brain how to remain in Tel Bashar. Nights I studied the Qur'an. And so the month on the camel train dragged along. Finally we returned, other caravans jamming the streets along with ours.

First thing, I searched out a smithy I'd seen off the Commons. There two sweating men hefted a large piece onto the forge. The one I guessed to be owner was tall as me, thick, and full of quick energy, sweat rolling through the black hair of his chest I bowed, gave my name and pointed around, then at myself to show I also was a smith. He bowed with a smile. It did not seem to mean anything to him that I was not Arab.

He pointed to the bench. Sitting beneath the tools hung from the ceiling, seeing the mounds of nails, feeling the blast of the forge, hearing the hammer against the anvil, the hiss from the water barrel, taking in the smell; and taste of metal in boxes and barrels was heaven!

As the older man seemed suddenly to falter, I jumped up. With a grateful look and grunting his thanks, he gave me his place. Then back and forth with the other, the owner I thought, we hefted the end of the rod into the flame, began the shaping of it into three leaves, then to the water barrel again, then to the flame and back to the anvil. And oh, it swelled my heart to feel these movements my muscles had known since my very early years, and restored me to a rightful place upon the earth.

The owner's name name was Zaba. I liked his shop, his demand upon himself, and pride when a customer was pleased. Oh, he would brush the praise off; but when he turned to put the money into his pouch, I saw satisfaction flush his brown bearded face.

The other smith, an older man, rambled as if lost in prayer one task to the next. Both Uncle and Quartermaster would have sent him to the stables with a rake. When I began to worry I had stretched my welcome. I dusted my hands, nodded and gestured about the shop, said "Shukran, Zaba," and stepped through the door.

"Shukran li musaa'adatuki." Zaba bowed. I stepped away. "Thank for help," he called after me and flashed a smile like dawn breaking on a mountain.

Well, you can imagine how I turned in wonder. Zaba spoke English!

I grinned and waved. He watched me go, fists dug in at the waist of his blacksmith's apron, head glistening in the sun.

Next day I was back with Khalil to repay Zaba's hospitality with some tricks I learned from Uncle and from smiths in the crusade; and ways with metals I discovered myself. I noticed orders piled up for grills for coverings for windows or doors, a necessity here. Through Khalil, I told him that in England we used grills, and many different grills, on churches, public buildings and homes of nobility.

Zaba replied with a sweeping gesture that the shop was mine.

I took up a piece of grillwork, laid an edge on the forge, pumped the bellows until the edge grew red-hot, then heaved it onto the anvil and with quick downward strokes rolled the edge under section by section until all edges were agreeably rounded. Back and forth, water barrel to forge to anvil, Zaba, at my elbow now, holding the piece with me, his eyes lighted. This trick I'd developed at my uncle's shop. It made grills both tight and comely; and came to be in demand in and around Exeter.

Next, I showed him my way of making a woven grill.

"Instead of building in sections," Khalil translated for me, "I thread sidewise slats through the uprights already fixed to the frame; and then hammer all the joins so nothing sags after cooling; and the piece stands erect."

While I worked and talked and Khalil translated, Zaba stayed on the bellows following every move until I held up the finished piece.

Light streamed through the open spaces and threw the grill's weave giant upon the wall. Zaba was jubilant.

"You come more," he stabbed a finger at me. "You do good." He patted the grill.

"Shukran li mus'aa adatuki." I thanked him, bowed; and we grinned at one another as I left, two blacksmiths happy at their work.

Hurrying toward the camel pens, Khalil's eyes were big. "Do you think he'll offer you work? Did he want help? Could he pay?"

I shrugged.

We jostled through the crowd, needing to tend our camels, eat and get to the Elder before the call for Adan, as it was now not acceptable to me to walk while others prayed. We passed a cart selling cooked goat. "We'll get some pies," I offered. "You worked all day too."

Then we sat with them near our camels, my teeth breaking into the pastry. The food was heaven.

Next day I went by again with Khalil. Zaba offered me a job.

He would pay what he paid his assistant. But I told him I would work for him my free hours while the caravan was in Tel Bashar, and he could see how he liked me.

After a few days it was clear I could do everything and also broaden his services. He was a warm man and with enough English that we could talk. He had traveled with caravans himself, and on the sea: so he spoke a little of a handful of tongues. His mind was quick, and he was great-hearted. Then he began to take me along for tea, to introduce me to his friends in a big voice as the new man in his shop from England who does these and these special things. His listeners would raise an eyebrow, give me a long look, then relax: Well, if Zaba has taken him on--. That's how respected he was.

And because of Zaba, I began to find it easy to adopt the Muslim way. I already liked the freedom of the full trousers, the robe that flowed when you walked and gave a sense of privacy in public. And I learned long before this that an amama on my head could save my eyesight.

One day Zaba crooked a finger. Look, here was a small room behind the shop I could clear out for sleeping. Here was a rug to cover the door. Why didn't I just come and work all the time? And no charge for the room. If I was here, he could give me projects. And I would be paid more.

So in the end, he was paying more than my work with the caravan.

But Allim, my caravan teacher, poked his grey-bearded chin out at me. "I teach," he shook a crooked brown finger; "You learn good. Now run off." He sighed and dug into his purse for my pay.

I bowed. "Thank you. Alssulâmi. Salam. Peace."

He bowed too, his yellow robe breathing and falling. Then he was gone, an old man the size of a lad of twelve, wily and stern, a most valuable teacher. My heart sank with regret. Then I cringed to think of leaving Bibka and Mishabibka. Oh, and there would be Khalil.

You can imagine, it was not what Khalil wanted. He sat braiding fresh leather into Bibka's harness.

"The only change will be my job," I reasoned to him, a

weak thrust. "And how else will I know Bibka and her calf are safe unless it is you who watches over them?"

"Come yourself then, if you want to know they are safe," his eyes slid over me to the ground.

"The days you cannot come with me to Elder Yusif, I will have to limp along; but I will remember for you all that he teaches." And I kept on as if I had not heard him nor let the sorrow behind his anger pass into my bones. "And you will be here for weeks at a time. We will make the most of them." I reached out to ruffle his hair; but he drew back.

"Then come work for Zaba, Khalil; and we can be blacksmiths together!" I was desperate.

"Fah!" he hissed. "And never see my own country again?"

I dropped my hand. "I feel shameless to have traded so upon your love for me, Khalil. I pray Heaven soon will let me repay you. And when you are not here, I will miss you, truly miss you."

He threw the finished harness at me and strode away. As I watched him, my heart a stone of sorrow, I prayed he find a way to forgive me.

With the help of Khalil and now Zaba, I started to read Arabic. And Elder Yusif had already said he liked my writings. While the months passed, my body at the smithy regained much of its old form. And though I still had not seen Aysha, I felt focused and peaceful.

One evening, my teacher paid me a compliment on the sincerity of my thought grappling with the Muslim faith. He raised a finger. "So says, Allah in the Hadith, 'If anyone draws the length of a span near Me, I shall draw the length of a cubit near him; and if anyone draws the length of a cubit near Me, I shall draw the length of a fathom near him. If anyone comes to Me walking, I shall come to him at a run, and if anyone meets Me with sins the size of the earth but has not associated anything with Me, I shall meet him a similar amount of forgiveness.'"

He gazed upon me some moments, his eyes steady and soft, then said, "Well, until tomorrow." And stood.

Walking back with Khalil, who had somehow found a way to pardon me, I reflected aloud that I owed so much of my progress here to Brother Frederick who trained me not to flinch from barbed issues, but to keep on until I was clear and had answers that satisfied me. "I do not have answers yet," I told my young friend, "but the forge and anvil give me a place to turn and turn the questions."

And Khalil traded with me through his eyes then a lively interest, and questions of his own.

It must have been near Ramadan, for I remember it being Fall when Elder Yusif told me that because I had studied the Qur'an, had written each night, and had shown ability, he and the Woman Elder would make a test to see what I had learned. Khalil was in town, and offered to come shore up my limping language.

Well, you can imagine the terrible dryness of my mouth; and the room feeling crowded by the four of us; and with the Old Mother from over her hooked nose and deep-set and watery eyes, training upon me, intense and cold, her clear distaste.

Each Elder had ten questions about the Qur'an, and Muslim prayers and practice. Back and forth: my teacher, the Elder Woman, Khalil's voice, my voice; outside, the grind of cart wheels, murmurings of people passing, and, like bird tracks upon the air, the laughter of children.

It was the Old Mother's turn. How would I prepare certain dishes she named? Muslim law, like Jewish law and that of the Church of the West, covers everything down to the smallest detail of living. But this question of hers was a trick.

I gave the proper preparation for three of the four dishes. "But I would never prepare that last dish, honorable Elder," I bowed, "because it contains pork, a meat that is haram, unclean and unlawful, according to the holy Qur'an."

And I could feel chagrin stitching her insides, and dropped

my eyes so as not to provoke her further, allowing myself to look up only with my teacher's next question, and there to see the sparkle yet in his eyes.

I finished the test; the two Elders excused themselves. Khalil and I drank tea. By the time they returned bearing my fate, my heart had sharpened its beat at the base of my throat. My teacher spoke first.

"While you have by far not yet completed everything, you have worked hard and taken a clear and strong step forward. Therefore--"

"--But no more than a step!" the Old Woman croaked in, and opened withered fingertips as if to release smoke. "One slip, Idolator, and everything falls." She scattered the air with her hands and ran her eyes over me. "An animal in hunger is not to be trusted. A mind that slips into evil easily disguises itself. But Allah is never fooled. Allah sees every wickedness sewn into the human heart. And Allah will answer."

I could feel the dark satisfaction as she rose and, with the slightest of nods hobbled from the room.

We waited in silence. My teacher gestured to me to sit.

"Ha-ha," he burst out then, smacking his knees, "this time The Hawk goes hungry." He leaned toward me, beaming. "For myself, I never need fear tricks from one whose heart is clean from the very start."

And it was then I saw that Elder Yusif, from our first talk, had recognized my intentions as pure, found in my plea a cause worthy to champion, and had been doing all he could to help me. I wiped my eyes.

Next evening, he came in, near-bursting with news, fluttered his hands for Khalil and me to sit, and looking back and forth between us, fixed upon me. "M'allim Jophiel," he started in, and I blushed to be addressed with that title of respect, "because you have shown sincerity, faithfulness and openness in your study--," he wet his lips, "Aysha's family invites you to their table for the holy feast of Ramadan." He paused, clapped once and broke out a short high laugh. "The Hawk has approved you as Aysha's suitor!" He howled this with glee. "She must have or you would never have gotten so far."

And my heart all but burst through my robe, shouting, "At last I will see her." I sat beaming, but quickly remembered myself, stood and gave a deep bow of gratitude first to my teacher, then to my translator.

We left, and I felt Khalil withdrawn and aswarm with questions. No, a shake of his head, he could not stop to eat for he had two camels to tend and it would be dark soon.

"I'll help. You always help me. I'll get food to take with us."

I bought curried lamb, flat bread and dried figs from a stall. With excitement in the air approaching the great feast of Ramadan, the seller gave us extra bread.

We sat at the fire near the pens and ate quickly in silence under the weight of camels bawling for feed. Khalil got up to fill their bags. I put a brush on each hand and went to work on one side of Bibka. Khalil took her other side. We were the only two left grooming; sand scuttled about our ankles. The air was pitted by the sound of camels grinding feed.

A few long brush strokes; Khalil spoke up.

"If you go on, it will not be long before you are Muslim."

"You sound angry, Khalil. But you know I was never a crusader; I came along for my own reasons. The Christian religion is how we live in our countries, the Muslim religion how they live here." I rolled hair from the brush into a ball with my fingers. "And what am I to do? Wherever I go I find a religion I somehow must live with. That is life." I opened my fingers to let the breeze take the ball where it would.

Khalil sighed. "Yes, it is everywhere." And he turned toward the far mountains. "You know more than me of this world, Jophiel. To embrace the religion of your own people is one thing; but to take on one so different, one that everyone you know hates--." He held me with troubled eyes, as though I, as near a brother as any he had, were slipping away down some dark hole. He swallowed. "Our own men--."

I said I knew some had never cared for me being over them, and might still enjoy revenge. I retold a terrible dream I'd had more than once in which he and I are dragged behind a rock by men of our company pulling out knifes and hissing "Infidels, traitors." Then I grabbed him by the shoulders.

"I could not bear that a hair of your head be harmed because of me, Khalil." I choked on the words. "I could not bear it!"

In the silence that followed, I heard bats whistle through the dark closing in. Khalil looked up, his eyes clearer, more alive.

"No, you are an enemy to Muslims and Christians; but I am a friend to both for I have Arabic blood and a magic tongue. And anyway nobody pays any mind to anything I--"

"Please. Listen to me!," I grasped his arm. "When I saw this woman, I was swallowed by something at home we call 'the meeting of the eyes' or the French word Amour, for a new kind of love. And I was lost to resolve anything of that except with your help. And I did not think about how dangerous it could be. I have been careless of you, taking you with me to the Muslim compound. Please forgive me, Khalil; thoughtless and careless. You must stop going now."

He stared at me in silence, then puffed himself out, arms folded across his chest. "What, and give up the chance of a teacher like him? Now I can know as much as you--or more!" And then he grinned that special grin of the young in triumph over their elders.

But I argued on, afraid for his safety until finally, he wore me down; and I asked myself finally how I could deny him the flame of his own spirit?

I forced the brush under Bibka's chin where the sand fleas love to bite. "To learn a new religion is a mountain to climb. But at St. Nicholas, with Brother Frederick's help, and myself no more than a cotter, I read the great ancient writers. And that was a mountain I climbed." I let the brush swing from my fingers, "Elder

Yusif told me Aysha is in some way made of her religion. If I want to know her, I must know it too. And because of you, Khalil, I have a teacher to help me."

He looked down at this; kicked at the sand. "Sometimes I wish I'd never found him," he growled and began brushing again, his elbow following his wrist back and forth. "And who knows what you will discover about this woman," he reached the ruff on Bibka's neck; "but have you found anything in the Muslim religion that lifts you more than in the other?"

"They seem much the same, to tell it true, except Muslims have no priests." I gave a wry smile. "So I must save my own self from Hell's fire and get my own self to God." I spoke lightly, but out of an unexpected relief come over me the weeks I had been digesting the idea that every man is his own gateway, redeemer and priest.

"But I think the imam is just another kind of priest." Khalil pulled at Bibka's ear to brush it; "and I think religion takes too long." Bibka pulled her ear free and gave him a swat in the face with it. Khalil wiped his cheek. "And so then must you lift your own spirit? And there's nothing in the religion to help?"

I shrugged, "Well, there are the holy writings that seem much like the writings of the Church." We lapsed into silence. I went after Bibka's other ear. Then something broke upon my mind. "But, the chanting lifts my spirit, like a kind of music. The standing, kneeling and bowing are a kind of solemn dance. Singing was the only thing that reached me at St. Vitalis. This singing here feels more powerful; perhaps because the voices are of ordinary men like myself. They touch me in the same way as my friend Edward's lute did. I told you how he drew me out of madness with it."

Khalil nodded. He knew the story.

Then I fell silent, puzzled that out of the great Muslim religion that had built civilizations and commanded so much of the world, it was such a small thing I had fixed upon. We squatted to brush legs. "Early in my lessons, the Elder told me I needed to learn Arabic so I could chant the ayat properly. He said if I didn't have the language right, the chanting would be helpless to do its work for me."

"What work?"

"I don't know."

"Well, your soul looks good enough to me," he muttered, then lifted Bibka's front foot to pick for stones while I combed matted hair on the ankles of her other legs.

"I have lived in the midst of religion all my life and confess I never understood what it was for. From Christianity, good works come; but the suffering that comes as well to the helpless and innocent have turned my stomach until I have wanted to strike down those who hurt them."

We began to brush then, each to a side, on Mishabibka. Khalil told me about his Gran'fer, his mother's father in Lisbon, with whom he went both to church and mosque because it was expected. One day he declared to his Gran'fer that if he were king, he would free all people, and especially young lads, from the burdens of religion. The Gran'fer raised his eyebrows and gave him a long mild look and said, "Well, that might be a big mistake."

"Why?" young Khalil had asked. "What good is religion to anybody, anyway?"

"Well, my walad," Gran'fer replied, "religion gives people dignified patterns to follow day by day that keep their thinking higher, more noble, and offering more kindness, each to the other. In this way it purchases more prosperity, less cruelty and fewer wars."

I tossed my brush aside; ran my hand over Bibka's coat, gathering loose hairs. I saw again the face of a woman at home as she was burned for witchery. At Lisbon, the buckets of blood and body parts, the little ones abandoned in doorways, the upper room piled with corpses. And it seemed to me still that without religion, we'd most likely have more kindness and fewer wars.

"Your Gran'fer was a thoughtful man," I acknowledged, not wishing to disrespect his elder; "yet it appears that when teachings, no matter the religion, are laws of the land, misery and violence replace much that was good to begin with." I shrugged. "I never thought I could kill, but when that youth aimed his arrow at me, I shot before I could think."

Mishabibka nosed deep into my armpit, which she liked to smell; I scratched under her chin. "That Muslims can kill in the name of Allah, of God, we know well. Also that some ummas may be different from others. Here they treat you evenly no matter what you believe; and I feel a generosity I never did in England. I don't know if it is their religion or what they eat."

Khalil laughed that it must be the goat pies.

Then we led the camels to the pens. I closed the creaking gates, tied the leather thongs. "What I will come to believe I don't know, Khalil; nor whether what sometimes moves in me during prayers, faint as a breath upon the back of the hand, will be a sign great enough for them to accept me."

With his foot, Khalil smoothed a place in the sand for us to sleep. "But if it is that faint," his voice came low and late, "then maybe what you feel is but a wish."

I sighed. Oh, I had that thought every day.

We settled on the ground, and Khalil seemed to drift off. My own mind strayed to Ramadan coming. What if her family didn't accept me? My stomach turned. Well, I would stay in Tel Bashar. At least I would know I was where she was. And what was there to go to now in England but low weeping skies and the notched blade of memory?

"But which God do you think is the real one?" Khalil's voice separated the air. Flat upon his back, face turned toward me, I saw little more in the darkness than the rumple of his hair and whites of his eyes.

"I don't know." I rolled onto an elbow.

"But don't you have to know sometime?"

"Do you think your Gran'fer knew?"

No answer.

"Well, Khalil, what if God wears different dress for

different people? I think the dress doesn't make Him God; He is God because He is--Whoever He is."

Then I turned over and left him to grapple with that until he fell asleep. He would not fight me much longer. I could tell he had begun to feel the pull of his own path. He asked me questions, but was looking for answers for himself.

CHAPTER TWENTY-EIGHT

R amadan with Aysha's family meant proper dress.

By now I knew from Hassan what to buy and where to find it. And Zaba was my ally, my teacher, telling me what to expect from this month of family dinners that broke the daily fast.

Of course I must fast as well, my teacher said.

Oh, but I had already decided that!

The first day of Ramadan, the first Call To Prayer seemed to linger upon the air as Aysha's little messenger came to collect and lead me across the courtyard while, hands clapped over their mouths, once more the young maids collapsed against one another in merriment at the sight of us.

And then I saw her!

Aysha!

Imagine a blossom emerging from the shadow of the

portico and into the light. Oh, the long dark silken hair to her waist. And how her eyes lit at the sight of me; how she broke into a laugh, then, like a song of pure pleasure. I had never heard her laugh before, and you can imagine her voice hung like silver bells in my ears. And well, you know I had never seen her without her hijab, nor seen her smile. But the biggest gift of all was the music of her laughter!

Before, with a man's life hanging by a thread, she had been very serious, very focused. And although I had seen her in the market place that first time, I'd had the feeling of her being taller, perhaps from carrying that bread upon her head, and then from the strength of her will that those crusaders not die. Some have a strong will and are silently controlling; but with Aysha, I could feel she had been through so much suffering that she'd simply learned to hold her own center. She was very strong that way, but at the same time pliable and surrendering at the surface. And these qualities gave forth both an ease and fluidness about her.

But she was not tall! Why, the top of her head came perhaps to the bottom of my neck. Small-boned, she was, too; and delicately made, an exquisite work of nature in womanly form.

All this I took in as she approached; but I went straight to those eyes of hers had held me captive from that day in the market place; and to those eyelids curving in an ancient way from a deep and private place, moving out and over to fall away again into that same secret place. Large those eyes were as well, and deep as a secret woods; how my own could never meet hers without my heart melting completely. And her lips? Pink and alive as ripe fruit, they were; and all this beauty set into a heart-shaped face that lifted now to welcome me. And you can imagine I turned weak as water, for I'd had no way to prepare for how exquisite she would be!

The long tables set up in the courtyard were filling with relatives. She sat me with the family men under the portico, a great honor; and with a smile for me that made my heart leap. Her older brother, across, had the place of honor, of course. The father was dead, and the mother, I had learned from my teacher, not able to get around anymore.

When Aysha introduced me, her elder brother Mahjed looked up, gave a nod, then drew his eyebrows and head down to stare over thick arms at the food set before us. Her uncle was seated next to me, a long thin man with dancing eyes like my teacher, and set in a face half buried in a graying and very curly beard. Elder Yusif, the other side of me, whispered behind his hand that the uncle also spoke of the Elder Woman as The Hawk. And that, his uncle had said, if I had met her demands well enough to sit with the family for the great and holy feast of Ramadan, I must be some kind of magician. And you can imagine, since we all fasted sunup to sundown, this particular mix of the eager physical and the tempering spiritual.

Aysha handled our food--oh--like a priestess, slicing and arranging meats, breads, fruits, vegetables on platters with a tremendous sense, I don't know, of appreciation and respect, her hands like dancers along one platter, then the next. And when our ears stretched over the wall, we took in soft music, a low buzz of neighbors' talk along with the perfumes of lamb and duck and cooked rice and winter fruits on large platters we had before us.

Well, talk flies around me. I recognize some words, but the speech is too quick, too complex. And since I am like a cripple, no one puts demands on me. I am free to sit, to observe, to enjoy the food. The family treats me kindly, except for Mahjed who chews, leans his handsome face toward his relatives and chops the air to make a point. Whenever by accident his eyes strike my face, they leap away like a pebble flung at a wall. I try a little simple talk. "aT-Taqs mumtaaz al-'ahn." I offer that the weather is excellent right now. Mahjed grunts, rolls his head up and away.

At my lesson the next day, Elder Yusif tells me Mahjed is angry that he was not consulted about his sister's interest in me, and what should be done about it.

But things were not to remain so between Mahjed and me. One night as I came in through the gate, he stood looking at his wagon atilt, one wheel off. Walking past, and because I have a good eye for such things, I saw the metal part that had broken at the axle, and understood right away what needed to be made. The next day at the smithy I fashioned the part, took it back and hammered it into place. And that ended Mahjed's bad feeling toward me. Now he was my best friend.

Five months passed, and I was welcome in Aysha's family, though the laws regarding our relationship were strictly observed. And I had no desire that it should be otherwise. To see her was reward enough. And we exchanged simple sentences, when that was allowed. I took my lead from her, from her family and my teacher, happy every day for this miracle I had.

And though I could not yet enter the mosque, five times a day I stood with those around me, knelt and bowed until my forehead touched the ground. And I became eager for Salat, dropping into a pocket of peace while the imam gave out words that entwined us, and to which we would all breathe out, "Ameen!"

By March, I could recite large sections of the Qur'an; and speak, read and write simple Arabic. I observed all religious laws and behaviors; and then was tested a second time, and with close attention from the Old Woman, on Sharia, Islamic law. And while Elder Yusif declared me good as any Muslim, The Hawk, eyes frozen to her hands, did not smile. Finally, and as if they contained a most vile taste, she squeezed the long-awaited words through her tightly pleated lips. "Now we begin the marriage preparations." Then she stood, offered a bow to the room, turned, and left.

Elder Yusif lifted his eyebrows. He nodded.

"Allah knows what He knows. And He brings about what He intends." Then he laughed and stretched out his hand to me.

"Come."

So we stepped together out under the stars and into the sharp clear air of a new night. And together we crossed the courtyard of the umma that was soon to become my home.

CHAPTER TWENTY-NINE

Wedding preparations took a month. I had studied the Qur'an's teachings on marriage, and there found nothing I was not ready to give myself to with all my heart. And you'd think, having climbed such impassable mountains, every detail of the reward would have pressed itself forever into my memory; but nearly all those rich and feeling-filled days spilled past in a blur. The moments still etched in my mind I can give you.

Having completed my training, Elder Yusif set a date for me to perform zeyhara, the practice given children initiates of going door to door to present to their neighbors their knowledge of the Muslim faith. I was to recite sections of the Qur'an and certain prayers as well; then sing a special song that says Allah is all-knowing, all-loving and merciful; and praise be His name.

My teacher kept our rounds to neighbors door to door.

They appeared with a smile, little ones at their knees, to say,
"MarHabanbika", "Welcome", to listen patiently to my part, and
then take up the special song for zeyhara with me. At each dwelling
we were offered food or drink. Aysha's little Farhaan brought along
big eyes and a piping voice, and helped greatly with the eating
and drinking. And to this day I believe that humble ceremony did
more than anything to make me feel accepted as one among them,
and on the merits alone of my efforts to respect their culture and
become a part of it. Also, I was Elder Yusif's student. And you can
imagine that counted for a good deal.

I knew that once The Hawk commanded me to marriage
preparation, Elder Yusif would introduce me to the mosque. He and
Aysha's people were faithful to a mosque but a few steps outside
the gates. I had often given myself neck pain gazing up at the
domes and minarets of mosques. Now, my friend Zaba belonged
to a different sect from the Elder. And once I told him I was to be
taken to the mosque, he wanted nothing but to talk about mosques
and what it took to build one.

And I was interested. After all, we are blacksmiths, and
in our own way are engineers and builders, but not of something
so huge and complex. So that day, while we worked on two three-
part woven iron grills for a huge gate, he hurried to unpack all he
knew about mosques. And by now, as you can imagine, my Arabic
had grown a good deal because of him, and his English bettered
because of me.

"Cathedral take many years to build, no?"

I nodded.

"Mosque also."

He pointed toward the window. Through it you see fig and
olive trees, and then the east wall and dome of a mosque.

"What is first thing you do build mosque?"

I shrugged, shook my head, then grunted as I heaved the
bottom of the grill onto the forge. Zaba pumped the bellows. The
fired metal blazed and threw off a tang that stung my nostrils.

"First thing you build is nothing! Ha!" Grinning, Zaba

clapped his hands at his own wit. "First thing, you find on ground very place point to Mecca, where Muhammad is born. Then you draw line from there go straight through heart of mosque to Mecca. This called Kibla line." He pumped the bellows. I watched the iron turn pink, red, and began to soften. "So first place to look in mosque is for Kibla Wall, stand over Kibla Line. This holy place." He cupped his hands. "Is from here imam lead prayers."

"Oh!" I had known to face Mecca to pray, and had heard about the Kibla Wall; but somehow it had not yet come up with my teacher.

Zaba's customer wanted two grills in four days, so while he worked like a wind shaping sand dunes, at the same time he could spin out the tale of a huge mosque he had seen raised as a youth in Jerusalem. Why, he had worked in a shop that forged the very knots for its walls! And this mosque had included prayer rooms, courtyards, a matbak (kitchen), a hama (bath) with hot, warm and cool rooms, and a medrese (school).

"It take ten hundred men make this mosque." Zaba held up thick fingers. "Shovel, dig, saw wood, make brick, cut marble, make knots and grills, forge lead for dome and minaret. Take father and sons, and son's sons; and more."

I knew. And I remembered then the proud bones of Exeter's cathedral rising only to be set on fire by Stephen's men. Later, all of us, even very young boys, cleared the charred mess, cleaned what still stood and started it upward again.

Zaba moved away from the forge to cool himself.

"Tell me, English, how you think dome so high, and no pillar?"

I set down my hammer, shook my head.

"Dome heavy," he hurried on; "push and push out. So how not push itself to pieces, eh?" His eyes sparkled. "We Arabs, we build and we know secrets." He tapped his temple, then pulled me to the bench. "Now I tell." He held up a finger

"First, make lower part of dome heavy, two, three times heavy." And he shoved a shoulder against my chest to press me against the wall with such force my legs shot out. Then he jumped away, and the bench rocked forward to dump me on the floor. Zaba flashed a brilliant smile, opened his hands wide.

"See? Push, you stay. No push, fall. Push, wall stay. No. Wall fall."

I laughed, dusted myself off. I saw!

He explained the brick domes were covered first with mud, then with felt, then sheets of lead. "Ha! And by Allah, we do great things!" He clapped his hands, then turned and turned. "Now where hammer go?"

It was a few days later that Elder Yusif brought me to the mosque. And oh, my heart lifted like a child's to be among all those others drawn to this special place to bow before the Creator of all things.

Though small and humble, this mosque was filled with light and open space; and every surface gleamed. And though we were inside, the windows and doors were set so that every angle opened somehow to greenery and blue sky, while at the same time, we remained cooled from the fire of the sun, our hearts balanced and at peace.

Well, and the building bespoke order. It bespoke calm, and the quiet joy of forms come together as in nature. I took off my sandals to step through the door with my teacher; and the quiet authority of the marble floor made me recall that first day at St. Bartholomew with its floor of fine wood fitted and polished, and that so uplifted my mind and spirit.

We unrolled our prayer rugs while the imam arranged his robe, and I noticed behind him the smoothed and graceful niche that made that wall the Kibla Wall. Then the imam's voice leapt up suddenly like a bird; and facing Mecca, I thought how strange life is that I bow now in the garments and religion of the foe of my Church while hungering to embrace a daughter of "the enemy" and she to embrace me, a terrible transgressor of her people.

It was the custom that the bride live with her new husband

and his family; but I had neither home nor family here; so her uncle offered us a room in his bayt, his house. I would work for Zaba and also do any smithing needed by the umma. Islamic rules were that widows be cared for in a respectful way. Aysha already had such care in abundance, and shared all that was hers with me. And myself, I wanted but to love and protect her; and to provide for her and her family whatever I could.

The Elder advised me on proper attire. Zaba helped me select material of a delicate green for a tunic and pantalones, to find a tailor; and, on the day of the ceremony, saw me carefully and properly dressed. The little messenger came for me carrying a neck ribbon with a strand of fragrant white jasmine, a gift from Elder Yusif.

We stood under her uncle's portico. It was late morning. The family, dazzling in festive robes, fanned out into the courtyard where lengths of bright colored qazz, raw silk, were hung between the trees for shade. I remember the musicians a respectful distance from us with oud, flute and drum ready to play between the prayers offered by the kâhin.

Elder Yusif, all smiles, gave my shoulder a squeeze.

I waited quietly under the portico. I had expected to feel nervous; but instead was light, and like a sail full-blown above a blue sea, my heart calm and soaring. In my deepest place, I felt everything, no matter how odd the circumstance, right and meant to be. The music started in. At once, those standing waiting in the courtyard parted, and Aysha's sisters, brothers and uncle brought her toward me through that bright corridor of well-wishers.

She wore a long veil over her face that allowed but a suggestion of her features, and then only when light struck it in the right way. She came forward, eyes ghaz basar, downcast, hands clasped within her sleeves, a woman of modesty and respect wrapped in layers upon and within which moved a radiance like the dawn. The fabric showed wild flowers growing from one another and flashing gold or silver as the layers breathed about her. Dumbfounded, as you can imagine, I beheld a goddess, a woman crowned with white trumpets of hibiscus lit by early morning; and she coming to meet me. Oh, if you had only been there, friend!

Partway, the sisters fell back to join the relatives; and her uncle brought Aysha to stand opposite me, but a little way apart; and my eyes became drunk taking in the sight of her. And just before the imam began to speak, she raised first her veil, and then her eyes to meet mine. This simple movement nearly caused my knees to fail, for clear as day in those eyes stood her heart, open and with no reservations. And in this way the immaculate dignity of her soul presented itself to me.

The imam went on in three voices: that of the imam, and through him that of the arees, the groom, and the arûsa, the bride. Back and forth in our presence, and in the voices of relatives and the umma as well, speaking the nature and meaning of our lives and of what we were giving in our sacred promises to one another, repeating and confirming this.

Of the celebration--the eating, music, dancing--really, I can recall for you so little. I remember her hand in mine through dinner, and the deep sense of trust that came from that hand telling me she was entirely comfortable and belonged with me. I remember being stunned by this mercy and miracle, and drinking her in there next to me, and receiving our guests while waiting this last wait until, finally alone in our room, I could look as long and deeply as I wished to into those eyes of heaven she gave to me.

That night, upon our ferash, our bed, with the fall of her dark hair across her breast, Aysha held me with those eyes where I stood taking off my tunic; and, in the sweetest of all voices, sang these words:

> Only Allah could see into my life
> And how I hungered for one such as you.
> Only Allah could make me your wife
> And give me your heart for my home.

And she opened her arms to me. And, my heart both

melting and on fire, I gathered her in. Oh, and just before we slept, and high and bright in the far corner of the window, there sailed the mariner's star!

And then our life together was woven into that of her large family and the umma. Oh how we loved our room with its low table and large sitting cushions, the ferash where we slept raised upon a platform and enclosed by the light thin fabric of the birdây. Sometimes we would have morning tea in this room. Other meals we ate with the family.

Aysha rose early to start the fire for water and cooking, and to feed the children. After we ate, I went to work at Zaba's, came home for the midday meal, and for 'asha, supper. And we had our nights, and a love that needed no voice; although often, when we were alone, it would come overflowing into words.

I spoke Arabic readily by the end of that first year, mixing with the people of the umma for whom I performed services, and with Zaba's customers. I attended mosque and practiced the religion. Aysha's family was warm, and I was comfortable with her sisters and brothers, with her children. She had two brothers and six sisters, two who lived away with their husbands. Besides the little messenger, Farhaan, she had an older son, Abdul, twelve, and a daughter, Jameela, ten years old, and a beauty like her mother. I realized I had missed having a family life since England. Also, the week after the wedding, Khalil left without word or note. That was how he had to do it. And happy as I was, I missed him.

Well, and the older son, Abdul, was wary of me, with good reason. I was a white man and a crusader like one who had killed his father. Aysha seemed relaxed about her children finding their own way to me, and I followed her lead. I noticed Abdul stayed close to his uncle Mahjed. But gradually the boy became warmer; and he and I and Khalil amused ourselves in a popular game where players line up and kick a goat stomach stuffed with hay, passing it player to player. When cousins, uncles and neighbors began to join in, we had to take it to a field.

This way, I traveled effortlessly upon a tranquil sea, working, playing, loving and praying. Always Aysha was there like a green shore to welcome me. And before we knew it, we had been married two years.

Late the first year of our marriage, something began to happen during the daily prayers I set myself to morning and evening, and with the men during the day.

At first it was something like a fragrance drifting in through the nostrils, and that eased the sharp edges of me, and gradually dissolving them bit by bit in the chanting. And oh, I developed a real taste for the prayers, for words that softened things that I didn't know were hardened in me. At first I noticed only that I felt better rising from prayer. Then I began to notice that when Aysha prostrated herself, she dropped every burden like a child does to walk into the arms of its father. How I envied such trust, and so sought it for myself! But it was a long time coming; and when it did, I began to recognize that experience as very like the way I always felt in Exeter walking into a forest.

Five times a day from the muezzin The Call to Prayer went out over the village: "God is great! Muhammad is His messenger. Come to prayer. Come live the good life. Prayer is better than sleep. God is Great!"

And we would repeat those words and others, reciting the Qur'an in our hearts and aloud, joining voices to raise up a sound like grain in a field under a repeating wind, or water over stones in a full creek. And our voices and the words let loose in us a vibration that teased the body open and woke it so that it could feel the soul. Or so it seemed to me. And those words with their feelings came to flow into me, then out of me, swollen with my own feelings they provoked; and I would rise filled with gratitude.

I remembered Elder Yusif saying that I must learn Arabic so the words could do their work. And it was through the words I think, that my hunger for Allah began. And the more I fed it, the deeper I felt it. And in this way, The Call to Prayer came as a respite from the rawness of the day.

The first experience of ecstasy was a surprise. I had heard stories at home in the church and school of such moments of uplift for saints and religious; but had never experienced anything like that in Exeter's churches save during the singing. But one time here, as so many raised their voices, and my own with them, I felt the trembling sound lift me; and I expanded in it until I was lost there, and could find no name to call it but Allah and, saying this name was like throwing myself into the sea, then the sea pulling back into itself and setting me down softly, washed clean upon the beach.

After that, when we prayed aloud, "Allah is faithful," my soul would prostrate in assent. When I told Aysha of this, she grew solemn, her love for me deepening in her eyes. "It is the words," she nodded. "Arabic is the tongue of Allah, the tongue He has made for speaking with us."

And this losing of myself came perhaps once a month, and sometimes praying on my own. And the only other happening like it I could recall was when I was young and in the forests outside the walls of Exeter. Sent by Mamoon to harvest forest greens, I would lose track of time; and some way I would become part of the feeling of all that was growing there, become swallowed by it and lose my own boundaries to it. Half a day could pass before I found myself again. And I believe that when I went mad, this is how the forest saved me, by drawing me like a mother into its belly.

CHAPTER THIRTY

It was at the start of the second year I began to notice when Aysha
came in from outside the umma, she sometimes had been crying.
I didn't bother her about it. Our trust in one another was so deep
I felt if anything were wrong and she needed me to know of it,
she would tell me. And by now my sense of our life together had
convinced me whatever it was that sometimes disturbed her had
naught to do with me.

   Then one morning, waking to her children's voices beyond
our room, I was surprised to find her still asleep beside me. And
I heard the ragged struggle to draw air, and leaned across to look
upon her; then drew in my own breath with sudden dread, for
circles like dark bruises lay beneath her eyes. I had seen such
things traveling with Mamoon hut to hut, and knew dark circles to
be a sign of danger.

My mind raced. She was well when I met her, and all that first year of marriage. The crying started into our second year. Perhaps being with a foreigner had--. But I could not let that thought go further. I climbed carefully over her and went out to start the fire; but her sister Amine already had water heating and had fed the children. I hesitated, hating to alarm Amine, she and Aysha were so close; but then told her Aysha was ill, and what I had seen.

I hurried back with tea to find Aysha awake. I gathered her to me and stroked her hair in silence. After a bit, I asked softly if she had been crying those times she came from the village because she had been to a Healer.

She nodded yes, wound her hair about her hand to pull it off her neck and looked up, so tired, her chest sunken and lips drained. "I hoped Malej could help me. We kept trying different remedies. And I would cry because I was afraid you might feel I had deceived you by withholding this weakness in my body from you before we married."

I began to protest, but she put her fingertips to my lips, shook her head, her dark eyes urgent, earnest. "When I met you, I thought this weakness had gone. And I was so happy because of you, I didn't even think about it." Her eyes deepened. "I would never deceive you, Jophiel, ever."

She unwound her hair from her hand, then, and lay against me silent and worn out by so many words. Her eyes closed. But after a moment, she opened them to tell me the story of this illness.

"When I was born, my parents were told I had a weak heart. But after a few years, it grew stronger until it no longer troubled me. For the most part I forgot it. I grew, married and began to have my children." She ran her tongue across her dry lips. "Then last Lailut ul-Barat," (she meant the Night of Emancipation, two weeks before Ramadan, the time each person's destiny for the year is fixed) "lighting the morning fire, my heart begin to gallop until I thought it would jump through my bosom. When it stopped that, the old death-like weariness fell upon me like a stone, and threw me down so hard I could not even raise myself. It was early morning; no one saw. And I hoped it was something passing, and closed my mind against it, for this was how it was for me when I was young." A breeze stirred the birdây about our bed. She took a sip of tea, then continued.

"It was at the birth of Farhaan, a very difficult one that took all my strength, and really more than I had, that this feeling of weariness, the old draining away, started up again."

She closed her eyes, her chest rising and falling with shallow breaths, then slipped her small hand up under my armpit. I closed my arm over it to hold it. She opened her eyes and went on.

"I was a widow before I gave birth to Farhaan, and wanted my family and the umma troubled by no more of my difficulties. My little Farhaan would come in the mornings and find me unable to rise from bed, or lying beside the fire I wanted to make. He would try to help me sit up. By the time he was four or five and knew his way around, I would send him to the Berber woman near the wall for a little wine. It was the only thing I found that would rouse my strength. I would take a mouthful or two each day, Allah forgiving me."

Aysha reached forward with her chin and I gave her another sip of tea.

"Little by little my trouble came less often; then not at all. So I supposed the problem had started up again from Farhaan's birth, and had taken all this time to right itself. I felt released, hopeful, and put it from my mind. And then, from the day you picked up my basket in the street," she smiled up at me, "my heart was filled with wonder; and all I could think of was you."

I kissed her forehead, then rested my head against hers, taking her words into me.

"I never thought such a one as you would come into my life," she went on, "one so pure, so deep and gentle, and of so open a heart. I never knew a man could be the way you were. I would reflect as I went about my tasks that perhaps the suffering you had endured had formed you into what you are, one I could trust with my life and to whom I could give my love without reserve, and in whom it would be safe. You are the greatest gift Allah ever gave me, Jophiel. Your love crowns my life."

Oh, then I could only take her even more deeply into my arms, to rest my chin upon her head and let my tears fall into her hair, for my heart was breaking with love.

It was a long time until she stirred again, and pulled away to continue.

"When the trouble started up last Lailut ul-Barat, I recognized it as of old, and sought out Malej the healer, and held onto hope as we tried one thing, then another. But I am a healer," she gave a wan smile; "and bit by bit, I knew his remedies had no power for me."

Now daylight crept up outside the window, pink and gold upon the white courtyard wall, lighting its green hem of bushes, climbing its trees.

"It is so unfair to you," her eyes lifted, filled and spilled over, "for me to do this after all you have given up to be here."

I opened an astonished mouth. "But I have given up nothing," I shook my head, took both her hands and kissed them. "And instead I have gained everything, Aysha. Everything! It is to you this is so unfair. And it breaks my heart."

"No." Her voice firm, she touched my cheek where she let her fingers linger. "This comes from Allah. And it can only be given in blessing,"

But I could not respond; I could see no blessing.

I heard the voice of Farhaan lilt from beyond the portico. He would be lying upon his back in the sun-baked dirt under the fig tree, singing to his favorite cat, the black one with amber eyes, stretched above him along a branch. Aysha heard him too, and with a rattling sigh laid her head against my chest.

Later, she called her family around and reminded them about the problem from when she was a child. But she had not let them know, she met their eyes, that after the birth of Farhaan, the condition had returned, then died away again. "I hid my distress," she wiped her eyes; "I did not want the umma burdened by a widow with children, and who also was sick."

Her relatives murmured, shook their heads.

"Now my illness has come on again. And we do not know what more to do but hope; and to wait upon Allah's will. Subhanahoo wa taala. Glorious is He."

And I saw her family shrink then into themselves and into each other to become a single body struck dumb with grief.

Aysha went on, "Each moon that passes Allah gives as a pearl into my hand. He has counted out my portion from the beginning; now it appears to be near complete."

One after another, her family bowed in submission, as I did also, despite the sorrow the words brought us. Oh, but we would not give up hope yet, not one of us!

For the next two months, I watched my beloved wife grow old in a body eaten by its own distress. The family gave her every attention, and didn't leave much for me to do. So I woke each morning with one question. What could I bring her that evening?

Each evening I came like a small boy on tiptoe with a flower, a pebble, a tiny basket from a hawker, a comical doll, a love knot I fashioned on the anvil. All I wanted was to fill her moments with love. And she would smile at my gifts, for my sake trace over them with her fingertips. But nothing I brought was what she really wanted. What she wanted was for me to put my arms around her.

So I finally forgot everything but to hold her. Before the sun rose, at dinner time when it bled heat over the land, in the evening as it gave up its color to the tree trunks and leaves, the roofs and walls of the umma; and when the moon washed over us with its cool white light I held her, hoping. And so that she should not feel alone, I held her. And so that I might have one more day, one more night of closeness with her, I held her. I did not care if I ate or slept, for she might need something. And I could not bear to lose one moment of feeling her against my chest until the dawn when I would look into her face for some little flush of greater life upon which to hang my hungry hope.

Perhaps it was less than two months, I don't remember; but one night, after the Mariner's Star had crossed the sky, I felt her heart stop. It stopped, and yet I held her and could not surrender her out of my arms though her soul be flown. Finally the unwelcome dawn crept across our coverlet; and then the women were up stirring, and I knew I must go out to them. So I laid her back upon the pillow gently as I could, her arms along her sides.

"It is finished," was all I could say to Amine. And her sister went in to her, then, while I waited for the uncle to awaken. Word went around the family and the umma. And a great silence fell.

CHAPTER THIRTY-ONE

Muslim law required Aysha be buried before sundown; but first came the ritual ablution to be performed by a family member of the same sex. Her sisters did this, and wrapped her in a white burial shroud. She lay upon a pallet, body and face toward Mecca where I knew she already lived, for I felt her with me, strong and rising up in love and joy to lessen the agony of my grief.

Her uncle, brothers and I carried her upon our shoulders; and it came to me that Mecca must be an earthly name for Heaven; and that all good souls live in Mecca even before they die. For else how could I feel her in Mecca and within me, the same as when she was here with me before?

As was the custom, people came from their homes to join the chanting of the Shahadah, the Profession of Faith, and to walk a distance with us and her as her pallet passed. Joining my voice to those of others lifted me a little beyond myself and into humanity, and held me until we reached the mosque; and then again to the burial place where she was laid without coffin, her wrapped body lowered into the earth like a beautiful seed.

And so began the year of mourning. Whenever her name was spoken, we must follow it with Rahimaha Allah, "the mercy of God upon her." But I couldn't conceive anything about Aysha that would require the mercy of God, she being pure goodness; and when the worst of the raw grief wore away a bit and I heard Rahimaha Allah or spoke those words, I told myself it must mean that her death was a mercy to her, a gift from Allah I could not fathom.

My first concern was her children; but I saw them taken into the families of her brother and sisters; and as the seasons passed, woven into the larger family, happy and well loved. The boys lived with their uncle Mahjed. Jameela was absorbed into Amine's family. I was still the smith for the umma, and every day also went to my work with Zaba.

The first time Aysha's sons forgot me for their game with the goat stomach, I knew her children had no further need of me; and the will of my spirit to live in the umma and Tel Bashar was gone. I could have made an offer to an unmarried sister, and it would have been gladly received; but I could not be with any other woman.

Then the dreams began. Night after night I was in a forest, always in England. I roamed the woods of my childhood as if I had never left, found myself at Alphin Creek, played my pennywhistle there and paused to listen to the brook in response. But most often I was in the forest behind the church to which I had fled after the deaths of Sarah and my son. The trees in these dreams hung their branches low to cover me, and small animals climbed into my arms, sniffed my fingers and hair and settled, balls of down, into my lap. And when I awoke, everything around me felt awkward and alien; and I knew I didn't fit here anymore.

One night, Aysha came, her face soft with understanding. "You should go on if you need to, Jophiel. Go where it calls you to be." And with a smile unutterably tender, she passed her fingers over my cheek. And when I woke, I could still feel that movement upon my face.

Well, these dreams were a rudder that turned me a different direction; for while I felt solid in my life in the world, the life of my soul, where was that? And except for moments of ecstasy given as a gift, I didn't really know. In some ways I felt hollow, while in others as in a kind of springtime struggle out from under snow. And so I finished the year, when came the memorial celebration for Aysha. Then I felt freed to attend to my own life. I needed more awareness of my soul. And this Allah, how could I draw closer to Him? What kind of life would favor this need? And these questions would not leave me alone.

I had deep feeling for the life here, one more refined and in every way beyond the one I came from; and with a religion whose practices opened my spirit. Yet there were no monasteries in Islam. Those very advanced in practice lived the life of a hermit, and taught those who could find them. Myself, I was but a beginner. Perhaps England, then. Still, I felt unsure.

But one day after an ecstasy, the forests of Devon beckoned me to come, to be knit up from this second rending; and perhaps to tell me who I am, and what this Allah Who so ravishes my heart is to me. But for such understanding, I would have to go back to the green of England, and to things familiar. Brother Frederick would be dead by now; so if not to St. Bartholomew, then to some other place that hopefully would have me. Or the forest itself would make me a home!

I spoke with Zaba before anyone. He had seen me through the year that followed Aysha's death, and knew I no longer thrived, though work with him was satisfying and his company a hearthstone. And I did not want to disrespect Aysha's family which had taken me in with such warmth. I did not know how to tell them of my decision to leave. I'm sure you understand.

"Honor them before you go." Zaba dipped his bread into a spicy sauce. It was late afternoon, and we sat under a small tree with our food. I no longer always went to family meals, but often ate with Zaba.

"How? My thanks for all they have done is the size of a mountain."

"Give feast for family, for umma. Wonderful feast!" He stretched his arms to show the size and splendor. "Kill lamb. Make beautiful food. Have music. Honor family and umma. This is right."

I let out a deep sigh of relief. And I had saved money the past year; I could do that.

"But how you get to England, English?"

A cart rolled by, and its wheels of two different sizes raised a cloud of dust. We covered our bread and closed our eyes. I shook my head, rubbed my wrist across my lips.

"I don't know yet."

Zaba chewed in silence. I watched a woman with a basket upon her head step back quickly to let a teetering cart go by and I felt a terrible wrenching, for she had Aysha's small trim body. I saw again the spilled bread, my rush, clumsy and wrong, to help.

Zaba slapped his knee. "My cousin Sulyman work on docks at Acre. Ships go everywhere. We send letter, book passage- -Crete, Sicily, Sardinia, Corsica. I stop those places on fishing boat to Spain, Portugal." He wagged his head and grinned. "And they take your money, friend." He laughed, rubbed his thumb and forefinger together. "ALL money, if they can! They LOVE money!"

I laughed too. And my heart lightened.

Well, I waited a fortnight to hear if Sulyman was agreeable to book me. Word came back: Yes.

Then I sought out Amine. Since Aysha's death, she was the

one I went to with questions about the children or what was proper in the umma. Aysha once told me that even though such men as her uncle and Elder Yusif seemed to have the greater authority, often the women were consulted first to chew matters over and find a solution.

"My soul is calling me to England," I told Amine.

She looked at me a long moment out of those eyes so like her sister's, eyes that shifted into sadness then. "Well, so you must go," she nodded. "Everyone will understand."

"First I want to honor your family, the umma with a feast."

She looked away, paused, looked back, smiled a little. "Your feast will be in the stories of our family and this umma ever after. And in this way you will never leave us." She looked toward the minaret of the mosque, looked back, her eyes wet now. "We women, we will help you."

Oh, I could only drop to my knees at her feet then, and touch my forehead to the ground.

Next I must speak to Elder Yusif, for he would be the one to tell the men. I found him playing at jumping sticks with the children. We stepped aside into the shade of a tree. He thought a long moment, his head down, then looked me deep in the eyes, nodded, sighed and put a warm arm about my shoulders.

CHAPTER THIRTY-TWO

I bought a young goat to cook two days in a deep covered pit, the fire burning on top. The delicious smell would fill the courtyard bit by bit. I bought the best of whatever was needed of grains, vegetables, fresh and dried fruits and spices for the dishes and drinks. I engaged five musicians to play oud, tabla, qanun, nay and daf (the Persian drum); and one more to sing. I hung coverings over the courtyard to protect everyone from the fierce sun.

The day of the feast, you could smell bread baking and vegetables cooking. Later the children decorated the tables with flowers, leaves and candles. At sundown, after the little ones had their own special feast and the musicians playing for them first, they were put to bed. Then, as the music continued, people poured out across their porches.

Dressed in the pale green of my wedding garb which I had kept carefully folded and wrapped in a chest, I greeted each one. They sat and exclaimed over the flowers, dishes of carved goat, vegetables, bread and condiments set before them. And they leaned against one another to take in the music and singing like wild flowering vines climbing over the walls and into greater Tel Bashar. Flagons of mint tea went around more than once, followed finally by dates rolled in crushed almonds and sugar, and small fig cakes shaped like crescent moons.

It was then I stood and raised my hand. The music ceased, and all those eyes, so familiar now, turned upon me. I looked from one face to the next so as to mark deeply within my mind each one like a page in a folio. And then I don't know how I found my voice.

"My heart is filled with gratitude," I began. "You have been willing to see me not as a white man, nor a crusader, but for the one you found me to be. And with great kindliness, you took me in, put up with my ignorance of your language, ways and religion. You let me walk my path, let me be what I am, a European brought by fortune to Tel Bashar. And you opened to me and enfolded me. And now there is no way I can give proper thanks for the great generosity of your hearts toward me."

And having so unburdened myself, I dropped to my knees and pressed my forehead to the ground. No one spoke or moved. I don't know how long I stayed there. I heard the rustle of cloth, of leaves, and the far off cry of a hawk on its way to the sea.

I had perhaps a week for projects before the caravan left for Acre; and one took me into the streets to buy goatskin parchment of the quality sold to scribes and cut to a size that would fit Farhaan's small hand.

I sewed the pages for a special book with my favorite prayers, and stories I made up about nature: a little grasshopper, a little mouse, a butterfly, a small leaf being brave waiting for rain- -stories that he could draw close to his own experience of life. On those pages, with ink and a thin brush, I drew pictures of different plants he knew. Then I put a cover to it.

I knew Aysha's little messenger would be up and outside chasing something small and scuttling away, being about seven years old then. I sat upon a bench and watched him for a few minutes, then called to him.

"Farhaan. I have something to show you."

He trotted over straight away, his great dark eyes full of curiosity. He rested a small trusting hand upon my knee.

"What is it?"

I handed him the book I had wrapped in fine purple cloth.

He laid his hand upon it, but did not take it. He fingered the wrapping. "Are you going away?" His eyes searched my face.

"I am, yes." I put my arm around his waist and drew him to me.

"Are you going back to England?"

I nodded, my throat filling, struggling again with the decision, seeing so close now what it would cost. I could stay for Farhaan, couldn't I, until he was older? But I knew the answer.

"Do you want to open your gift?"

I helped him with the wrapping, and his eyes grew wide with wonder to see a book. He turned the pages. Birds, dogs, cats, bugs, trees, flowers, weather. Prayers I loved, sayings of the Qur'an, poems and little stories.

"Did you make these drawings?"

"I made them for you. And the writing I made for you."

His body relaxed a little. He climbed onto my lap.

First I read to him, the perfume of the parchment soothing the air. He loved the little leaf waiting for rain, the baby bird wanting to fly but afraid. Then I asked him to read to me, and he did, piping the words and sucking in air between them through his small teeth. When we closed the book the second time, he buried his head in my lap, and I could smell his tears. I laid my head upon his back and stained his robe with my own.

And, as you can imagine, to leave Zaba was very hard.

He punched me in the arm, then boomed, "Watch your money, English; watch their fingers. They LOVE money!" And he kissed both my cheeks hard and stood in the doorway of his shop, fists upon his hips while I walked away as if against a stiff wind, tears burning my throat, so loathe was I to do without him.

"We will meet again, English."

I heard his voice, felt his eyes holding me until I rounded a corner toward the umma and my last night there.

Next morning I bade farewell to Elder Yusif, touching my head to the ground out of thanks from my heart.

He lifted me, and pressed into my hand a small book of prayers. "My old teacher gave me this. May it keep you close to what you have learned and remind you of our time together. You are by far the best student I have ever had, M'allim Jophiel; and I thank Allah (Blessed be his name!) for our time together."

And then I must cross the courtyard to open and close one last time its beautiful gate of peacocks.

CHAPTER THIRTY-THREE

I had no trouble finding work on a caravan heading toward Acre. I had an older camel with no fight left in him, but needing careful tending to stay on his feet. After more than a week, I began to smell water, and excitement stirred in me. At a small village, I gave up my place to another man anxious to join the caravan, hoisted my sack, and pay in my purse, headed for Acre. It would be another ten days on foot and with any rides I could get, as Tel Bashar is far to the north.

Well, and I had no difficulty finding Sulyman, a small lean man with dark hair and a lined forehead. He sat upon a pile of nets, his arm sweeping back and forth, mending. I bowed and greeted him. At first he simply sat and looked at me. People in Tel Bashar grew used to my appearance, so I forgot someone who did not know me might draw back at the light color of my skin, my green eyes and straight features. And all this in Arab dress!

When I told him I was the English traveler his brother had written to him about, he smiled, stood, and with a bow invited me to eat. But I insisted that he be my guest; and we found a place that smelled of fresh-made rice, and of fowl simmering in fruits and spices. There was to be a ship in two days, he said, pulling a chicken leg apart and sucking his fingers. Would Corsica do? It would. I walked him back to the dock. "Come tomorrow," he told me. "We will see what I can find. Or come sleep at my place tonight."

But I shook my head with a smile and bowed. I needed to be outside, and to be alone.

I walked the narrow streets of Acre crowded by shops with thick ancient walls, and bumping arms with travelers like myself-- some I guessed, wandering crusaders--and townspeople with loud voices, braying animals and overloaded carts. The air was heavy with human and animal smells. Everywhere I looked, the fronts of buildings were hung with goods for trade. I pulled my eyes upward and searched until I found the minaret of the Mosque of El Jazzar, its spire to one side of the great dome I had seen near the harbor. I would wait just inside the door with the opening words of the Qur'an ripe upon my tongue, and my ears aching for the voice of the muezzin giving the Call to Prayer.

Afterwards, I slept outdoors next to a wall of the mosque. In the morning, I found Sulyman had arranged passage on a ship leaving the next day. I bought him a meal when he was free, introduced myself to the captain of the ship and helped a little with the lifting and stowing.

At Corsica, I bought new clothes; but only after a great deal of trouble changing money. My strange garb put people off; and they wanted their own kind of money from the green-eyed Arab who was too tall and too light-skinned. Some became my enemies just upon seeing me. So I kept to myself until I got a ship for Portugal. My Arabic was good, and I had enough of other languages to make myself understood.

We put in at Lisbon. I remembered the beach: Picking
up the bodies, its narrow climbing streets, hungry children in
doorways, the young mother begging for her babe's sake. It was a
dark place for me, Lisbon; I did not want to stay long. But I had
no trouble with the money exchange. I bought Portuguese dress,
and after a few days got passage on a fishing boat to Brittany. New
money and new clothes again in Brittany. Another fishing boat; but
this one bound for England.

And at last we put in at Cornwall. My throat filled, though
Exeter was still a week away by friendly oxcarts and on foot.
Hearing the miracle of my native tongue, wondering what I would
do when I got there; and then suddenly, in the far distance, Exeter's
old red walls, the shouting banners of Rougemont Castle and the
cathedral throwing its proud steeples against the blue sky. As the
sight thrust itself upon me, I felt my heart tear with grief while at
the same time also mend with relief.

One night on the ship to Brittany and alone at the rail,
gazing into the black waters churning past, I saw the waves
separate one moment, and in the next be of the whole again; and I
thought of those who, port to port, looked at me strangely, and of
those who made a decision I was enough like them to feel safe. But
not once had I felt like any of them, nor of any nation. And though
I follow the path of the Qur'an and therefore call myself Muslim, I
realized I felt to be of no religion.

In the mosque in Acre, voices around me raising an Ameen
and my own joining in, the great lifting up had happened again,
expanding me until I was lost in Allah while everything else
dissolved along with my name and the name of That in which I was
lost. Not Arab, English, Christian nor Muslim, but a child of that
Greatness that breathes me out and in again; and that I call by the
name Allah, for that is the name that opened the door to me.

I crossed the wooden bridge over the Exe, its water blazing
red in the setting sun; and passed through West Gate, not an
Englishman home from the crusades, but a traveler setting out upon
another journey.

CHAPTER THIRTY-FOUR

Through West Gate, my feet turned of their own onto Little Britayn, then past the orchard just coming into bud, and that I remembered as smaller. Then, the sun sliding past the rim of the earth and long shadows fingering the stone face of St. Bartholomew's monastery, I waited for a brother to answer the bell; and I remembered that dark night so long ago when it was Edward who rang, and Brother Timothy opened to us. But this was a young monk strange to me let me in and secured for me a pilgrim's bed. And I entered; and so left behind forever the world of women.

Before sun-up. I rose to my practice, and felt the sweetness of Aysha (rahim Allah) near me in the dark and in the silence. And as I pressed my head to the floor, my heart opened to let out grateful tears that I would not have to continue on without her.

Then came the call to chapel.

Afterward, we sat over bread and mead. Older monks who remembered me shook their heads it was a miracle I had come back as I did, for Brother Frederick, vastly ill near three weeks now, was in such a deep sleep they had all finally left him in the hands of God; and then, just two days ago, he suddenly awakened. But who knew how much longer he could last?

"Is he in his old cell?"

"Aye."

I remembered the way down the narrow hall, even the door. A young monk waiting upon him rose to give over the room.

My old teacher's face was turned away; and I drew in a sharp breath, shocked at his feet extended beyond the bottom of the blanket, how the bones stuck out; and at how they were matched by those of his hands at rest upon his chest rising and falling so slightly I had to study them to be sure I really saw movement.

I set the stool near his head, then sat in meditation upon him and near the oversized ears he still carried. His hair lay dry, sparse and snowy; and the long bone of his great nose rose above fleshy drape from his cheekbones.

Midmorning, I silently answered the Call to Prayer, "Allahu akba: Praise to Allah, Cherisher and Sustainer of the worlds."

At noon, when the bell tolled the Angelus, in my mind I prostrated: "You do we worship, Your aid do we seek. Show us the straight way."

I did not go to the midday meal, and don't know how long it had been when there came this little dry cough; and Brother Frederick turned his head. And then his eyelids, the thinness now of old parchment, quivered. Then he let out a sigh and I took in the odor of death. Then two slivers of light like skiffs on water or parings of a new moon appeared at the lower edges of his upper lids.

Then how my heart leapt! Perhaps I yet might speak to him!

I waited and waited; and finally had given up hope of anything more when he turned his head as if toward a presence he sensed, and in the direction I sat. And it was then that I beheld the whole ravaged gauntlet of his dear face.

And it was long until he opened his eyes more fully and they came, finally, to rest upon me. I spoke no word, but simply sat. More moments; then his eyebrows rose a little, and a soft breath of peace seemed to wash through him. Then his eyes closed again.

So moved was I, for I felt he had seen me, that I took his bony hand upon my palm; and the faintest sense of warmth rose to meet my flesh. Then another long pause like a held breath, and his lids quivered, trembled upward; and his eyes fell full upon me and rested for what seemed forever. Then he wet his parched lips with the tip of his tongue.

"Jophiel?" he whispered hoarsely, "is it you?"

My throat full, at first I could but nod and hold his hand the more firmly.

"I came last night."

A crooked smile in return.

"I've had a (breath) feeling (breath) of you (breath) for some time; (breath) and thought (breath) I must have (breath) died and was with you (breath) in Heaven."

"No, Brother, we are still here."

He squeezed my hand weakly then, and tears began down his face, as they did mine. And so we sat in communion amidst noises from the kitchen, and from outside with the sounds of birds and carts and dogs; all of them holding his cell in place as he fell asleep again.

Finally I went to find something to eat. When I returned, he had himself propped upon some pillows, and gestured a circle with his hand, meaning: Tell me everything. Clearly, it wore him out to speak; but his eyes were bright; and he would not be denied. Myself, I kept my own eyes downcast.

"I fear to tell you all, Brother Frederick; for then you may

find me an Infidel." And those words must be the hardest I have
ever needed speak to one I loved so much.

But he tapped my hand with his forefinger; then wobbled
the finger back and forth; then laid his long hand upon his
chest. "Good heart ... you have ...," he whispered; "I know
everything ..." and he made a weak circle in the air with his finger,
"you have lived...", a weak circle again, "... is pure gold." And the
old brilliant light flared in his eyes. "Tell...me."

I began with enlisting at St. Olave, and the Quartermaster.
If he had a question or comment, he put it to me with but few words
or with face or hand signs while the muffled life of the monastery
shuffled back and forth outside his cell.

I told of the sea voyage, of our near shipwreck, of the siege
at Lisbon and our wandering in the desert under attack. I told of the
desertion of our nobles. And then I had to let him rest.

The next day we took up again; this time about being saved
by "our enemy" with refuge, food and drink. And the opening of
my heart. I told of the caravan job that took me to Aysha; about my
instruction in her religion and the mystical change its practice had
begun in me; about her death and my decision to return to England,
to the forests where I was so lifted up as a boy by what I didn't
recognize as the Great Being that Muslims and others call Allah
and we call God. And though Brother Frederick was not a priest,
still it was a true confession, for I left nothing out.

When I finished, he lay still, then raised his hand over me
with that sign which before men means "go forth blameless." And
the floodgates of my heart burst open. On my knees I kissed his
hand and wet it with tears I could not stop. "You have been my real
father." The words rushed out. "You gave to me in my need and
steadied my growing with the hand of your wisdom until I could
walk in the world and not lose myself. The last talk we had before
I left for the crusade was about the soul. Surely this was a seed you
planted that came to sprout on foreign soil, and which I now bring
back to England to tend." Then I knelt and bowed before him in

the Muslim way, my forehead touching the floor. "And from the bottom of my heart," I told him, "I thank you."

I continued to stay with him, for there was nowhere else I wanted to be but in that little cell with its old trunk of books against the wall, and light from the single window spilling over the floor and warming Brother Frederick's feet. And the monks in the kitchen told me he was eating a little more now because it was me who brought him his food.

Then he seemed to be resting, but I knew he was thinking; and in that second week he told me in a few words dug out from among the rocks of his body that I must stay on at St. Bartholomew.

I said I had not yet decided, but was thinking of trying to make it on my own in the forest.

He shook a bony finger, pointed twice toward the floor, then folded his hands as if in prayer.

And I understood that I must stay here where I could be safe and yet follow the life my spirit demanded.

He labored onto an elbow. "But ... be ... careful," he whispered hoarsely, eyes intense. "Many ... ears ... here," he wobbled a circle with his finger and shook his head, "cannot-trust-now." He rubbed a thumb and forefinger together. "Spies ... for Church here ... like bugs."

And suddenly I realized that like Mamoon, I was an Infidel now, and in a place where many would be hungry to deliver "a defiler" such as myself to the Church court. "I will be careful." I nodded.

Then a day passed before he spoke again.

He began by tapping his forehead, his eyes, then pointing to his pillows. To have his chest upright made it more possible for him to see, to breathe, and dig the words out.

"Here," he pointed downward, "need herbalist."

There had been an old man before, I remembered. And it seemed Brother Frederick recalled that Healers had surrounded me earlier in my life, Mamoon, Aunt Mathilde, Sarah; later, Aysha.

Now I was the one to raise my eyebrows and tap my forehead. "Ah. And Healers must go into the forest. And often."

A toothless grin cracked his face; he nodded, arched a white eyebrow in the old way and croaked, "And God's…will…be…done." Then he lay back with a deep sigh and closed his eyes.

Talking ravaged him; but that night, before I left for bed, he asked an attending monk, a thin grey older man who wore a displeased mouth and who I recalled from before as a lesser authority who disapproved "my sort" being let into the school of my betters, to ask the Abbot for an audience.

Next morning the Abbot, squat and square, appeared with his secretary, a somewhat taller and younger man with quick darting eyes. Brother Frederick motioned for me to stay; and I helped him up against his pillows; then set the stool for the Abbott to sit upon and lean forward toward my teacher.

"My last days. My final wish." Brother Frederick pushed the words out.

And he told my story, then: that I had offered my life in the service of the Church in the crusade, had suffered greatly and nearly died in the desert, and now needed a place of peace for healing and to be close to God. It was his last wish that I be allowed to live here at St. Bartholomew from now on. I could be useful; I knew plants and healing. And all the while, Brother Frederick never took his eyes from the Abbot's face.

Oh, and I could feel the Abbot's struggle that it was not possible, when no sin was involved, to deny a dying man, and the most elder of their community, his final wish; and this a wish that must be honored perhaps even beyond the Abbot's own time.

Silence.

Silence.

Silence.

Finally the Superior cleared his throat. "It shall be as you desire, Brother." Then he blessed my teacher, and casting a cold look upon me, left the cell, his assistant like a bird's tail, flashing around the door behind him.

Brother Frederick lay back, his withered mouth growing into a smile.

"I know now why I could not leave, Jophiel," he whispered. "I was waiting for you to come." And his eyes shone bright then in the old way.

That was the last time I heard him speak my name, for he slipped again into a deep sleep that night while I kept vigil in his cell.

Spring was fully upon us by then, and one morning some days later as I sat next to his palette, I smelled blossoms from the hazelnut outside the window and turned to study its boughs and the castles of white clouds behind them. Then a blackbird flashed past, and I felt a change within me and around me. Have you ever been with someone when they died? Suddenly you feel everything to be different, to drop away or to be replaced by something else. And I turned back to the cot and saw Brother Frederick had gone; and a great gladness came over me that he could leave so peacefully and perfectly.

And I went to find the Abbot.

CHAPTER THIRTY-FIVE

Well, I made myself useful about the kitchen and smithy; and more than once the Abbot saw me digging and weeding in that garden so sorely overrun. I organized sprouts, made happy neighbors of plants, trained vines to the lattice, and pruned the apple, pear, hazelnut and walnut trees near the wall where Brother Frederick and I used to talk.

For healing, a garden must have rosemary, peppermint, lavender, basil, sage, butterbur, cabbage, chamomile and comfrey It was Aysha I saw use comfrey. And that was but a start. There were still old volunteers; and if they were not vigorous, I would seek fresh ones in the forest. There I also discovered healing plants I had forgotten since my days as a boy when I assisted Mamoon in making remedies. The cook told me Brother Frederick was forever carrying in great handsful of herbs to add to the pot to "bolster our bodies". He dabbed at his eyes.

And gradually, I observed the changes in the monastery Brother Frederick had pointed out. It was as if new sinews of alertness now ran through everything. Before, each man was more or less drawn into himself and the life of his soul, into his private reasons for being here. Now each turned to the study of his fellows as well. And I felt I found some root to this change in the Abbot's preaching about the "purity of the community." We were gatekeepers now, stewards of others' souls as well as our own. And no man was above the Rule, as no man was above the law of the Church.

I reflected as I went about hoeing, digging or firing horseshoes, that in the Muslim religion they let you hang yourself; but here in England, they seemed eager to give you a hand up to the gallows. And things were political now. The Abbot echoed the Bishop who echoed the Archbishop who echoed the Cardinal who echoed the Pope. The Rule of interior life I knew when I left for the crusade now came burdened with new duties. And being a heretic in their midst and practicing an Infidel religion--. Well, I doubted the punishment would be any less than for witchcraft.

So I began prudently to build into my days all of the ways they now approved here. I never missed Mass, nor chant of the hours. I made myself useful, kept my eyes downcast and spoke only if needed. And I sought no fellowship amongst them, which they seemed to see as reasonable, since I had been "broken" by the last crusade.

Then, after three months of watching me, the Abbot appointed me herbalist. He gave me a small room that had been used for storage since old Brother Sylvester died, and that shared a wall with the kitchen. So I began to salvage anything I could: mortars and pestles, small cauldrons, rubbing stones, blades for harvesting and chopping, jars and bottles from mixtures that had burst through the wax and run down the side; and would have paid out an overpowering odor except for the slow crawl of dirt here, here, and here.

And after a bit, I began regular trips into the forest.

So as to exchange their healing force with the one in need, Mamoon taught me to send living plants home with the infirm, strung around the neck or potted. It is a way kind to children and the very old whose bodies cannot bear strong tonics. And from my brothers in the kitchen, I would beg or borrow time at the hearth to dry herbs or cook mixtures, then store them in bags or jars and bottles sealed with wax.

When I began treating the sick, I would call upon Mamoon to guide my hand; and it would be as if we worked together. And every morning, the sick would be on that little bench, or on the floor, or waiting in the doorway, or in a queue outside the little room.

I don't remember how long after it was that I became aware of Sarah and my son's graves appearing in my mind; and that something in me wanted to shut them out; but then, with time, some other thing came to feel comfortable having them there.

So one morn, no sick at my door and a high summer day, I borrowed a mule. The roads, broader now and their surfaces leveled and hardened by time and more travelers, were rich with feeling and memory. My eyes searched the horizon for shapes and buildings I knew all those years ago. Then the spire of St. Vitalis Church, where Sarah and I were married, rose up.

But I did not turn in there; and, puzzled by myself, passed the cemetery a few furlongs away and rode on some half hour more, a green eagerness now coursing my body.

The Dorset farm came into view. Like everything else, it had grown. There were more cottages now. The cheese sheds had doubled. A new barn stood where the old one had been. Larger pens stretched out behind for cows, pigs and sheep.

The smithy I once knew was twice the size as well. Outside it, two men struggled with a stubborn wheel that would not release from its axle. I dismounted and came over and gave the axle a kick with the heel of my boot. The wheel shuddered and we tugged the axle off.

The taller man with a shock of wild honey-colored hair and warm brown eyes slapped his thigh. "Why is it that the last kick always does it?" he laughed, and then brought himself around, remembering his manners. "Our thanks for your good heel, Sir. Are you looking for someone?"

He barely finished his question, his eyes all the while moving over my face, when he fell back and cried out, "Jophiel? Is it you? You lived through it, then?"

"Aye, I did," I laughed, and realized it was the older of Sarah's brothers, whose name I had forgot. We embraced.

"Matthew," he turned to the younger man, shorter and with a face that had also begun to look familiar, a cousin of Sarah's, I thought. "It's Jophiel, Sarah's husband! You remember."

I asked after the rest of the family.

Sadly his father was in the ground five years now from a terrible fire that took the barn; but his mother was just inside there, at her endless task of shelling peas.

I knew the door, and stepping through it into the shadowed room with its padded benches along the walls, I took in again the smells of all those years ago. An old woman in a plain cap sat with a large basket. Light from the window fell across her gnarled fingers plucking the brilliant green balls from their cases and dropping them into a small cauldron at her feet.

And oh, how my heart tore upon itself at the sight of her there absorbed in her work.

I came across the floor to squat at her feet. I reached and fetched out a pod to strip.

Her old eyes were full of dreams. She looked up then, and let them rest mildly upon my hands, then travel to my face, thinking I was one of her sons. There they wavered slowly over my features, my hair. Then her hand began to shake and she dropped the half-stripped pod to the floor, her mouth wide with disbelief. And then the old and terrible memory opened her face and body, and tears started down her withered cheeks. And the same dagger ripped open my chest as well, so that I must slide to my knees and lay my head in her lap while everything so long ago buried came back to life. And we held to each other and cried it forth, the love, the horror, the hope shattered, the terrible destruction, the madness that swallowed my mind and drove me off. We cried and cried it. All that. All of it.

On the way back to the monastery, I stood at the graves of my wife and son, greatly sunken now and become a part of the worn blanket of the burial land. Had he lived, my son would have been nigh the age I was when I first saw Sarah. I thanked them both for all they had given me; and in my mind and heart embraced them. And then I called out their names with the purest thing I could offer: rahmiah Allah.

Nearly two months passed before I found myself at Uncle Anthony and Aunt Mathilde's cottage. Lifting my fist to knock, the door was suddenly flung open by the hand of a little lad perhaps seven, a redheaded boy with freckles across his nose who barreled over the threshold and into my knees. He wriggled away in a panic, backed into the house and shut the door. Well, then I waited a few moments to knock again. This time a young mistress with a babe upon her hip opened. I said I was looking for Anthony and Mathilde. A shadow crossed her eyes. Both dead now. How did I know them?

She invited me in, and sent the redheaded one to get his father.

Oh, but how the old place crowded upon me, like walking into my own skin I wore so long ago! My eyes climbed the ladder to the platform over the herb cabinet where I'd slept, took in the hearth before which I had my wedding bath when Aunt Mathilde nearly scrubbed the scalp from my head, scanned the trestle at which we all had eaten the night before I left for the crusade.

Two more small children peeped around their mam's skirts as I took a seat on a bench outside to wait for my oldest nephew,

Gabriel, who owned this house now, as well as Uncle Anthony's smith shops. His wife, Helen, gave me mead to sip as I watched neighborhood children play at King of the Hill.

Suppertime, my nephew kept pounding me on the arm, praising and celebrating me. I could only smile a little and shake my head no. For never would he be able to grasp what that crusade had been.

He had two additional smith shops now: One near Rougemont Castle, near the old neighborhood of my childhood; and one near St. Vitalis. He had grown into a fine man, and had his father's twinkling blue eyes and wild hair, more brown than red. He told me of his brothers and sisters, all still alive and married except for the youngest, an apprentice at the shop. I smiled and nodded, remembering myself shoveling horse dung and running for buckets of mead, my hands burning for a chance at the anvil.

I asked if he knew anything of my friend Edward. At first he shook his head, but then said he thought Edward had gone traveling and settled somewhere near Aquitaine. It felt right to me that Edward still pursued the purity and trustworthiness of Courtly Love. We two had been after the same thing, really.

And it was perhaps two weeks later that I had visitors.

There in the front room sat Sarah's younger brother and my nephew.

And both seemed barely able to hold down some great excitement. My nephew waited until I brought mead for us; then the words cascaded like a great thrust of water at the mill.

It seemed a shame for me to hide away here in the monastery when I could have a much more exalted life in the world, a life I deserved, they both agreed, because I was a warrior and fought for the Church and for what England holds closest to her heart. Now, come home at last and safe, I should be rewarded. Many did not come home. Surely God meant it as a sign that I was to be fruitful in my later years. And everyone agreed, including several nobles, the chancellor and mayor; and all were anxious to help. This last Sarah's brother put in.

And right there, something in me began to back away. Perhaps it was the fevered look in their eyes or the push of their words, as if everything need be said now or sooner. Perhaps it was the reverence, the fantasy I saw they embraced about who I was, what I had done, what the crusade was and had done. And I remembered again our ranks walking past Uncle Anthony's smithy, the furlongs of us cheered on by families and neighbors, and going to our deaths one way or the other, most of us. I saw the shining lie of it all ending in the rape and pillage of the innocent; and the higher-ups deserting their soldiers when their own necks were in danger.

These young men had no idea that a crusade meant the destruction of a great culture as well, and dealing death to a people who in the first place gave Europe most of what she had. I tried to keep all this from my face, but my stomach turned so that I could scarcely make myself hear the plan they had devised out of the innocence and adventure of their hearts.

Investors would build the ship. I would lead expeditions to the Holy Land along trade routes now opened ever wider. I would be paid handsomely as well for all I bought in the name of their company and delivered back. Why, I had been over and over these routes, knew what was available, desirable; and I had good contacts. I spoke a number of languages, could read and write. I had been a quartermaster, so knew how to care for and keep track of goods. Really, I was most highly qualified for such work, and would have a hand in designing the ship and a percentage in the company.

Well, surely you can see there was no hope, them leaning toward me with their shining faces, of making them understand. And wasn't that just our problem here in England? We didn't understand what we were doing to ourselves and other people; and that the Church had become blind to all in her path, and so became not a savior, but a great dealer of death.

Well, and it was pure truth saved both me and those young men: I was not well enough for such duties and obligations, nor for the rigors of travel. And what I had been through had left me fit for little beyond cooking herbs for the sick, and the simple, quiet life here at St. Bartholomew. And I truly thanked them for honoring me so with their trust.

Well, but if I should change my mind--.

I didn't expect that would happen, but if it should--.

I watched them down the street, hardly older than myself off to the crusade; and felt a stone of anger that their young minds and hearts should be deceived by those who might feel free to call upon their lives, and even to the giving of their lives. And all in the service of ends so tainted.

We waved once again; and as I turned back, the monastery bell began to toll the Angelus. I stopped, bowed my head and silently began the opening. "Praise be to Allah, the Cherisher and Sustainer of the worlds, Master of the Day of Judgment. You do we worship, and Your aid do we seek. Show us the straight way."

CHAPTER THIRTY-SIX

Late one afternoon the following September, near the feast of St. Justin, Brother Aloysius, assistant to the Abbot and curator of the library, came to me for something for headaches.

He was a small energetic man who drove himself endlessly, and whose tonsure was just beginning to grey. I could see fatigue about his eyes and mouth, and in the pallor of his skin. The monastery library was his pride, and he spent many hours attending to its needs. As I gathered herbs from my store, I reflected that Brother Frederick's private books, now he had died, would no doubt further fill the collection; and one day I might have permission to explore them.

I boiled a mixture of dried sweet marjoram, white willow and papaver rhoeas for the Brother's pain, and to help him sleep. While he waited on the bench, his eye strayed to several drawings of plants I'd made with a quill pen in the forest that morning, and had not yet put by. The forest had brought back to me the urge to draw. I used spoiled sheets of vellum one monk saved for me, and who saw to it I had a quill pen, a penknife and small pot of iron gall ink, a newer ink that did not crawl so readily and lasted longer than the lamp black mixed with gum we'd used before. The gall ink went down brown, but quickly turned black upon the vellum.

Brother Aloysius took the drawings to the open door for better light.

"These are yours?" He turned and waved them. I wondered if he might reprimand or report me for drawing when my work in the forest was to harvest; or for taking scraps of used parchment. I nodded, brought a steaming cup to set upon the bench to cool.

He raised his eyebrows, studied them again. "Fine," he murmured, "very fine."

I poured the rest of his remedy into a flask, corked it and set it next to his herbal, still too hot for drinking. "Take a mouthful before you sleep, then again in the morning. The headaches should be better. During the day, try to rest your eyes." It was useless advice for a man like him; still, I felt required.

But he raised his hand, reading the few sentences I had written at the bottom of each drawing, and shook his head. "We have no botanicus in our library."

Outside on the cobblestones, two stray dogs, one yellow and one black, squared off, snarling and circling. I stepped past him and pitched a few small stones at them to bring them back to their right minds and send them off in different directions.

Brother Aloysius looked at me a long minute as I stepped through the doorway again; then, his face enlivened, he shook the drawings at me. "Could you do this, make a botanicus for us?"

"If these are deemed worthy enough, I believe I can, Brother."

"I will speak to the Abbot tonight," he cried and rushed out the door with them. And, medicine for him in each hand, I hurried after, calling for him to wait.

So it came to pass that I was allowed yet more time in the forest, studying and rendering the shapes and folds, textures and reaches of our most harvested of several hundred plants. I could do one at a sitting when the weather was good; and on days it was not, I recorded at the bottom of each page everything I knew about the plant and its uses. Much that I knew came from Mamoon, from Aunt Mathilde, from Sarah, from Aysha. And some was my own.

Through the drawing, I grew into still greater sympathy with plants I had already closely observed. I would see them again, but study them with infinitely more admiration and patience, least I miss the Spirit in them that shapes their living parts. Less and less would I look at my rendering and more and more let contact between my eyes and the herb guide me until one day I found myself on the valerian plant, and walking across a leaf as I drew it. Another time I felt the wild iris pushing on its green scroll to unfurl, perhaps the way a woman might push forth her infant; and felt that from the center of myself in drawing it.

Brother Aloysius would ask to see the drawings from time to time. He digested them with great appetite; and they only seemed to make him crave for more.

This work took well over two years; and when it was finished, was bound in wood covered by tooled leather and set amongst the medical folios; and only a few shelves from Brother Frederick's books where one day I had noticed his copy of Herodotus.

One evening after Compline, the Abbot, Brother Aloysius at his elbow, stopped to talk to me.

"Brother Aloysius showed me the botanica you made, Jophiel." His grey eyes were a surprise of softness, his tone direct and voice very quiet and respectful. "As monks, it is our duty to remind others to welcome all gifts God gives us. The beauty of the natural world is one of those gifts meant for our joy and healing. Your drawings and writings open that gift more deeply to all of us." I bowed to my Superior. "And in making this folio, you give St.

Bartholomew a greater way to answer Our Lord's call to heal the sick. Your botanica will offer guidance and direction to others."

When I felt him begin to move away, I raised my eyes a moment to Brother Aloysius whose own eyes, a-shine with happiness for me, met mine, then quickly dropped as he stepped out to follow the Superior.

The following Sunday, in a talk before Compline, the Abbot used the botanica as an example of dedicating our humble gifts to the glory of God and the benefit of mankind. He never spoke my name, for that would have transgressed humility; but everyone knew who went to the forest and came back with drawings. Afterwards, the Abbot approached me again. "We would like other monasteries in Devon to have copies of your botanica. Will you give us leave to have it copied for them?"

"Of course, as you wish, Father Abbot."

This was an honor almost beyond speaking, for copying was very costly and done only with that held to be of great value. And now, wherever I went in the monastery, an aura of respect hung about me, for now, not only was I an herbalist, but had made a book helpful to others. These merits, along with the deathbed promise to Brother Frederick, made my place at the monastery secure. Still, I never let myself get careless. I understood that the actions the monks expected of me were as much also my spiritual practice as reciting the Qur'an and holy prayers; and that it was strict attention to behavior that made it all possible.

Some months after completing the book, and in the forest collecting herbs, I remember it was a beautiful day in early summer, I spied a single purple stem of lavender I needed for my mixtures. I gave myself a moment to admire the glow of sunlight through its petals and regal feminine posture; then said a prayer of thanksgiving to it and for it, as I do with any plant that gives itself to our needs. As I bent to harvest it, a little nonsense song Mamoon taught me all those years ago filled up my mind and flooded over my lips.

"Oh, there was an old man with a wart on his nose.
'Twas big, 'twas round, 'twas red as a rose.
And oh how the birds lov-ed
to perch there to play.
Heighdee dee, heighdee die,
heighdee doe, heighdee day.
Heighdee dee, heighdee doe, heighdee day."

And it dawned upon me then that here I was, a great full-grown man, and singing away like a small child! And it was then I realized that I must be healed, that the lonely little Jophiel who learned that song, and the young blacksmith who lost his world when his wife and son perished, and the crusader who escaped death in the desert by becoming a camel tender and found a second love and wife as well as his God through the name Allah, and who now was returned to England and to a monastery to leave behind forever the world of women and instead become a Healer, had healed himself!

My brother monks go to chapel, brother Muslims to mosque. But my soul is neither Christian nor Muslim; and goes wherever it is called to worship its Creator, to chapel, to mosque, to the forests of Exeter where, in radiant sunlight and amidst the whispers of shadows from rocks and soil and green growing things, the scuttle of bugs and scurry of foxes, the ruffle of peahens, the glint and caw of crows, jays and starlings, the drifting of clouds and the beading of dew, He comes Who silently soothed my body and mind all those years ago in the forests of my youth and young manhood; and there set His mark deep within me against the time of His claiming.

And every day He shows Himself in whatever my eye meets or ear hears or skin feels as I step among the trees. I see Him bask shining and at leisure from out each thing large or small. And He tells me that I have never been anything but His own, even in my most lost years. And this communion draws me into hal, into ecstasy, where I am my own self naught but His blazing presence, wider and deeper than Heaven.

There is a promise spoken through the Prophet in an Hadith dear to me that often comes at such times. And then I kneel and press my forehead to the earth and recite these words:

And know that God intervenes between a man and his heart;
and that you shall all be gathered back to Him.

And now I rise each day filled with wonder, for this promise is the story of my life. Who are we, creatures, to question the paths of our openings, we who know so little about ourselves to begin with? This is my experience: The path opens from within me and in answer to something calls to my deeps. I do not know what it will be until I encounter it. And when I do, it will claim me. And then I must either answer to it or throw my own happiness away.

And to you my friends who have done me the kindness to sit, gracious and patient, through my story so that it might not be wasted, I thank you with all my heart. For when called finally to my Maker, this tale is all the wealth I will have to bring with me, and all that I have to leave behind. So let us then be at peace, no matter how things show, for the one Great Power holds us each Its favorite; and safe and cherished in Its bosom.

Jophiel Balerais

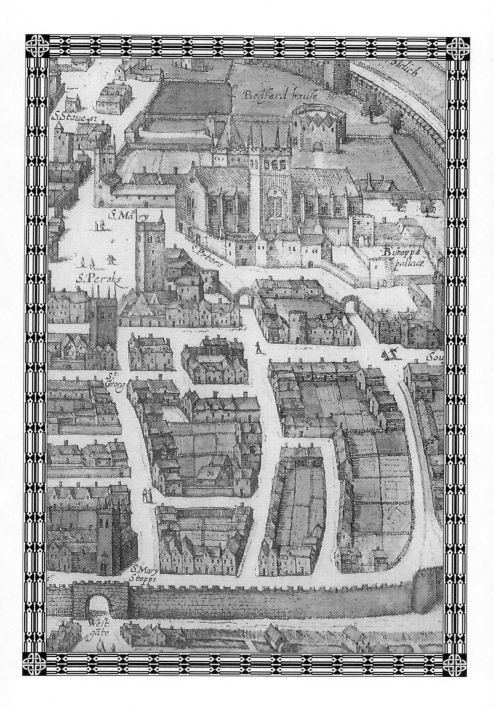

ABOUT THE AUTHOR

Zoe Keithley is the author of The Calling of Mother Adelli, a novel, and Crow Song, a book of poems. She is a native of Chicago, has a Master of Arts in the Teaching of Writing from Columbia College, Chicago, and lives now in Sacramento, CA, where she writes and leads writing workshops.

Printed in the United States
By Bookmasters